The story of Josephine Cox is as extraordinary as anything in her novels. Born in a cotton-mill house in Blackburn, she was one of ten children. Her parents, she says, brought out the worst in each other, and life was full of tragedy and hardship – but not without love and laughter. At the age of sixteen, Josephine met and married 'a caring and wonderful man', and had two sons. When the boys started school, she decided to go to college and eventually gained a place at Cambridge University, though was unable to take this up as it would have meant living away from home. However, she did go into teaching, while at the same time helping to renovate the derelict council house that was their home, coping with the problems caused by her mother's unhappy home life – and writing her first full-length novel. Not surprisingly, she then won the 'Superwoman of Great Britain' Award, for which her family had secretly entered her, and this coincided with the acceptance of her novel for publication.

Josephine gave up teaching in order to write full time. She says, 'I love writing, both recreating scenes and characters from my past, together with new storylines which mingle naturally with the old. I could never imagine a single day without writing, and it's been that way since as far back as I can remember.' Her previous novels of North Country life are all available from Headline and are immensely popular.

'Josephine Cox brings so much freshness to the plot, and the characters . . . Her fans will love this coming-of-age novel. So will many of the devotees of Catherine Cookson, desperate for a replacement' *Birmingham Post*

'Guaranteed to tug at the heartstrings of all hopeless romantics' *Sunday Post*

'Hailed quite rightly as a gifted writer in the tradition of Catherine Cookson . . .' *Manchester Evening News*

By Josephine Cox

THE EMMA GRADY TRILOGY
Outcast
Alley Urchin
Vagabonds

QUEENIE'S STORY
Her Father's Sins
Let Loose the Tigers

Angels Cry Sometimes
Take This Woman
Whistledown Woman
Don't Cry Alone
Jessica's Girl
Nobody's Darling
Born To Serve
More Than Riches
A Little Badness
Living A Lie
The Devil You Know
A Time For Us
Cradle of Thorns
Miss You Forever
Love Me Or Leave Me
Tomorrow The World
The Gilded Cage
Somewhere, Someday
Rainbow Days
Looking Back
Let It Shine
The Woman Who Left
Jinnie
Bad Boy Jack

JOSEPHINE
COX

Looking Back

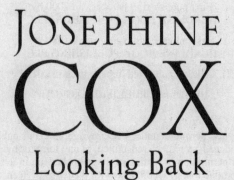

HEADLINE

First published in hardback in 2000 by
HEADLINE BOOK PUBLISHING PLC

First published in paperback in 2001 by
HEADLINE BOOK PUBLISHING PLC

This edition published in paperback in 2017 by

HEADLINE PUBLISHING GROUP

3

Cataloguing in Publication Data is available from the British Library

ISBN 978 1 4722 4579 3

Typeset in Times by Avon DataSet Ltd, Bidford-on-Avon, Warwickshire

Printed and bound in the UK by Clays Ltd, St Ives plc

Headline's policy is to use papers that are natural, renewable and recyclable
products and made from wood grown in well-managed forests and other
controlled sources. The logging and manufacturing processes are expected to
conform to the environmental regulations of the country of origin.

HEADLINE PUBLISHING GROUP
An Hachette UK Company
Carmelite House
50 Victoria Embankment
London EC4Y 0DZ

www.headline.co.uk
www.hachette.co.uk

I have to tell you about my shopping expedition in Woolworth's (Cyprus).

I was in the café, sipping my lime and lemon, minding my business, when all of a sudden this almighty, ear-splitting scream went up. I leapt out of my chair, eyes big and startled, to see a sight I swear I'll never forget!

This middle-aged woman of handsome face and ample proportions was hopping around the floor – skirt up round her nether regions, and dripping from all angles – with her husband in hot pursuit ('hot' being the operative word!).

Apparently, he had spilled his tea all over her, and now we were all being treated to the unforgettable and terrifying sight of huge buttocks all ashiver, and frilly bloomers the like of which I have never seen!

But as she said when all had calmed down, 'I thought me arse were on fire!'

All I can say is, 'Go to it, Mavis. If you've got it, flaunt it, and to hell with the consequences!'

Contents

Part One

SUMMER 1948

FACE FROM THE PAST

Chapter One

'Hello, Amy.' Soaked to the skin, the stranger stood at the door. Beneath the trilby hat his face was oddly familiar to her.

He smiled, but it was a nervous, guilty smile. For almost an hour after the fierce summer downpour he had paced the streets outside, afraid to come in . . . afraid not to.

'It's been a long time,' he said, his steady gaze giving nothing away. 'I'm not sure you'll even remember me.' But he remembered *her*. 'Nineteen years,' he murmured fondly, 'and I'd still know you anywhere.'

At thirty-nine years of age, Amy Tattersall was still a good-looking woman, he thought admiringly, with the same thick, chestnut-coloured hair and pretty brown eyes. There was a time when those eyes had looked at him with love, but now they showed only bewilderment.

'Who are you? What do you want?' She stared at him for what seemed an age, while long-ago pictures spiralled through her mind. She thought she knew him. There was something about his manner; the confident way he stood with his legs astride, his hands in his pockets and his head cocked cheekily to one side. Recognition was slow to unfold, but when it did she gasped in amazement. '*Jack?*' Her voice trembled with emotion.

Taking off his trilby, the man revealed a thick shock of dark hair. 'I've still got my hair and all my own teeth. Not bad for a forty-year-old, eh?' He laughed, a low, musical sound that rolled back the years. 'What's more, I can still cut a fine figure on the dance floor.' He gave a little wink. 'Do you remember how we used to smooch till midnight down at the Palais?'

Still reeling in shock, Amy needed a moment for the truth to sink in. '*Jack Mason!*' The ghost of a smile twitched at her mouth. 'I can't believe it!'

At first she had doubted her own eyes, but there was no doubt now. It was the same Jack the Lad! With the same, wonderful smile that lit his eyes and had taken her heart all those years ago. But what was he doing here? Had he no shame?

'Well, my beauty, are you going to ask me in, or what?' He took a step forward but stopped when she drew the door to, barring his way. 'Ah, don't turn me away, Amy. Not now, when I've come to make amends.'

He tugged at his clothes. 'I've been outside for ages, plucking up the courage to knock on your door. Look! I'm soaked to the skin. Likely to get pneumonia if you don't let me in.'

A kind of longing washed over her, but fear gripped deeper. 'Soaked to the skin or not, you look like you've done all right for yourself.' Her glance swept past his disappointed face to the smart black car parked at the kerbside. 'Yours, is it?'

'Bought and paid for.' A sneak of pride coloured his weathered features.

'Hmh!' His pride touched her deeply. 'Like I said, you've done well.'

He shrugged. 'Well enough.'

She noticed his expensive overcoat and his smart suit. Then she saw the confident gleam in his eye and her fears were heightened. 'All right, Jack – out with it. What do you want with me?'

'Trust me, Amy,' he pleaded. 'It's not like it used to be.' He gave a deep sigh, his gaze downcast for a brief second or two.

'All right, I've made mistakes, but I've learned the hard way. And yes, you're right,' he gestured at the overcoat and at the car, 'I've made a pot of money, but it's not been easy. I've been through the mill, gal. I've changed . . . grown up. Everything I've got was earned through my own sweat and tears.'

Amy felt herself weaken, but she persisted. 'You still haven't told me why you're here.'

'Can't you guess?' Reaching out, he touched her hand, seemingly oblivious to the turmoil he was causing in her emotions. 'I'm here for *you*!' His quiet gaze found hers. 'I'm here to put things right between us, to make up for what I did all those years ago.'

She wanted to believe him, but the old fear was strong. 'Go away, Jack!' she told him. 'I don't want any trouble.'

He shook his head. 'I'm not here to cause trouble.'

She laughed – a hard, accusing sound. 'You were *always* trouble!'

The slight tug on her skirt made Amy look down; it was her two-year-old son, Eddie. 'All right,' she told the infant. 'Go to Lottie now, there's a good lad. Mammy won't be long.'

Looking backwards past Eddie, she saw the other children sitting on the stairs. Beckoning to the oldest one, she asked her to take the little boy into the kitchen. 'I'll not be a minute,' she promised.

Returning her attention to Jack, she told him firmly, 'You'd best go. I've things to do. Besides, Frank will be home any time now. If he finds you here, there's no telling what might happen!'

Jack's expression hardened. 'Still the same old Frank, is he? I'll lay good money you don't love him the way you once loved me.' Guilt showed in his face. 'Believe me, Amy, I deeply regret the past.'

'So do I, but it's all water under the bridge now.' There was so much to regret, and he was only a part of it. Her voice fell to a whisper. 'Go away, Jack. Leave me be. *Please!*'

Jack's gaze went down the passage, to the children. Huddled together, wide-eyed and scruffy, they looked pathetic. 'How many are there?' His quick eyes went to the huge mound beneath her pinafore. 'Not counting that one?'

'Four little 'uns and the two older girls. Six altogether.' She rolled her eyes. 'Might as well be sixty, the way they drive me to despair.'

Horrified, and unable to take his eyes off the army of children, he asked, 'How do you manage?'

'I get by.' She laughed. 'I don't know how Frank will cope though, when this one arrives in a month's time. He doesn't know one from the other as it is!' Her laughter faded. 'He . . . likes a drink of an evening.' Seeing Jack's look of contempt, she was quick to add, 'He's no different from any other man in that way.'

Having done his homework, Jack knew her situation and so chose to ignore the comment. Instead, he brought his attention back to the children. 'Seven in all, eh?' His eyebrows rose in amazement. 'Good God, Amy! You're a glutton for punishment, I'll say that for you.'

A rush of guilt caused her to turn and smile at the children's upturned faces. 'Oh, they're not bad – as kids go.'

He sensed her warming towards him. 'I'm really soaked through, Amy. Summer showers are always the most penetrating, I reckon.' Shivering noisily, he huddled deep into the collar of his coat. 'A minute or two, that's all I'm asking. A hot drink and a warm at your fireside, then I'll be on my way.' The truth was, he just needed to get his foot in the door.

'Why should I?' Forgiveness didn't come easy.

'Aw, come on, Amy. For old times' sake.' When he pleaded like that, she had never been able to refuse him anything. 'Besides,

I've a proposition to make.' It was his sole purpose for being here. That, and a longing for her that had never gone away.

Her interest was aroused. 'What sort of proposition?'

'Let me in and I'll tell you.' He winked. 'I'm not leaving till I say what's on my mind.'

When she hesitated, he reminded her, 'Do you remember how I used to sing when I'd had a pint or two . . . and how you used to try and shut me up? "By! You've a voice to wake the dead", is what you used to say. Well, I can sing when I'm sober, too. If you shut that door on me, I'll sing so loud the neighbours will all come running. Is that what you want?'

Opening his mouth, he prepared to launch into song. Horrified, Amy grabbed him by the shirt collar. 'You do, and I'll throw a bucket of water over you!'

'Let me in then?'

Fearful the neighbours had seen him, Amy glanced nervously up and down Victoria Street. It was a long, cobbled street flanked by tiny terraced houses, filled with ordinary God-fearing folk who had nothing and wanted nothing.

'Did anyone see you knock on my door?' she asked edgily.

'No, but if you don't let me in they will – I'll make sure of that.'

'You always were a rascal!' But the smile in her voice made him take heart.

Amy's busy eyes scoured the street. At the top end, Maggie Lett was arguing with the tiresome old man who lived next door to her. About halfway down, old Jimmy Tuppence was chalking his wonderful cartoons on the drying pavement, watched by a gang of snotty-nosed kids; and only two doors away, a young window-cleaner was scampering up his ladder and whistling to his heart's content.

Amy was relieved. None of them seemed to have noticed her visitor, thank goodness. 'Come in then!' Taking hold of his collar with both hands, she gave an almighty tug, jerking him into the passage and almost choking him in the process.

'Bloody hell, Amy!' Red in the face he quickly undid his shirt. 'There's no need to throttle me.'

'There's *every* need!' Quietly smiling to herself, Amy led the way down the passage to the back parlour. 'Five minutes,' she warned. 'I've got a fire on but, you know what it's like . . . winter or summer, these houses are never warm.' As he came into the parlour she repeated her warning. 'Five minutes, and no more.'

Curious but wary, the children remained on the bottom stairs and peered through the banisters. 'I'm hungry, Mam.' Small and mischievous with vivid blue eyes, Milly was six going on ninety.

'Take the children up to bed, Lottie.' Amy's anxious gaze went to the older girl. Despite her hazel eyes and long fair hair, Lottie's beauty was only skin deep. At fifteen years of age, she already betrayed a sly and greedy nature, together with dangerous ambitions far beyond her station. Her more gentle, loving side was currently submerged by the moodiness of adolescence.

'We're not tired,' she answered sulkily.

'Tired or not, it's half past eight and you've to help Bob Sutton in the fishmongers in the morning.'

'I don't want to go,' Lottie whined. 'It stinks to high heaven there!'

'Stink or not, you'll be there by seven-thirty, same as usual. We need every shilling we can muster and well you know it, my girl!' Wagging a finger, Amy reminded her, 'You'd best do as you're told. Your dad will be in soon, and you know what he's like if you're not in bed by half past eight.'

Lottie was persistent. 'It's Friday. He won't be in till late.' She regarded Jack craftily. 'Anyway, he won't like you having strangers in the house.'

Grabbing the broom from behind the door, Amy swung round to send them all running up the stairs. 'You little sod.

I'll tan yer arse, I will! Into bed the lot of you!' She was in no mood for a confrontation with Lottie, especially not with Jack there to witness it. Even after what he did to her, she still had some pride left.

From the top of the stairs, Lottie had the last word. 'Why can Molly stay out late, that's what *I'd* like to know!' With that she scurried away, bundling the other four into their bedroom. 'You lot had better not start fighting,' she snarled, 'or I'll box your ears good and proper!' Hot air and bully tactics, that was Lottie's style.

Downstairs, Jack grinned ruefully. 'Looks to me like you've got your hands full,' he told Amy.

Sighing, she smiled back. 'Not so's you'd notice.'

'Who's Molly?'

'She's the eldest. Lottie gets a bit jealous of her. I keep telling her, "Molly's eighteen and you're only fifteen, that's why she's allowed to stay out later".'

'Out now, is she?' He had to be certain they were on their own.

'I'm not sure. She might be with Alfie, her boyfriend. He lives a few doors away. Or she could be with her friend Sandra – that's Alfie's twin sister, and a right little devil she is an' all. If she didn't have Molly to steady her, Lord only knows what sort of an end she might come to.'

'Sensible lass, is she then, your Molly?'

Amy smiled fondly. 'They don't come any better,' she revealed.

But what she didn't *reveal was that Molly was his daughter, too.*

When Jack Mason ran off all those years ago, she was already three months' pregnant, but he never knew, and now he never would. Not if she had anything to do with it.

Levelling her gaze on him, she thought he was still handsome.

7

He hadn't lost any of his arrogance, nor did he seem embarrassed to be here in her home. Jack Mason was a law unto himself; he cared for no one and gave nothing away. He was ambitious and ruthless, and up to all sorts of tricks, but somehow all of that only added to his charm.

Suddenly feeling shy and ill at ease, she told him, 'Say what you've come to say and get out.' Bitterness flooded through her as she recalled what he had done, and how her whole life had been turned upside down because of it.

'Do you really want me to go, Amy?' His voice was soft, seductive. Same as always.

For a long moment she kept her gaze averted. She could feel his eyes burning into her. In that moment, in spite of everything, her heart began to skip.

'Amy . . .' His voice hadn't changed; richer maybe, and aching with a kind of loneliness. But it was the same voice, the same Jack, creating the very same mayhem inside her. 'Look at me, lass.' He wouldn't give up. She knew that from old.

Slowly, reluctantly, she lifted her eyes. 'I still can't believe you're really here,' she murmured, 'just an arm's reach away.' She hardly dared to think about it.

There was a long, intimate silence while each regarded the other, their thoughts not so different, their needs surprisingly alike.

Nigh on twenty years ago, Jack had done what he had set out to do. He had made his money and learned from his many mistakes. Now, if only she would have him, he was back to claim her.

'Not a day went by when I didn't miss you,' he said huskily, and took a step closer. 'I'm here to take you away with me.' He glanced towards the door. 'But not the kids,' he told her awkwardly. 'I've never been fond of kids – you know that.'

She gave a wry little smile. How like him, she thought. 'You were never one to take on too much responsibility.' Her voice was hard.

'They'll never want for anything though,' he promised. 'I'll see to that.'

'What you're asking is impossible.'

'*Nothing's* impossible.' Now he had her hands in his, and she was visibly trembling. 'You and me were meant for each other.' His mouth brushed her hair. 'Admit it, Amy,' he urged. 'You still want me. Say it, girl. *Say it!*'

Drawing away, she glanced nervously at the door. 'Lottie was right,' she said. 'If Frank comes home and finds you here, he'll kill you.'

'More likely I'd kill him, for what he's brought you to.' Thrusting his hands in his pockets, Jack gave her a curious look. 'I was surprised to hear you'd married Frank Tattersall, and so soon after my departure.' He shook his head disapprovingly. 'I never thought he was your type. Bit of a waster, as I remember.'

He stared round at the tiny parlour, with its tatty curtains and worn-out chairs. 'From what I can see, he hasn't given you much to be proud of, has he, eh? Except for an army of kids to age you before your time.'

'And what about *you*?' Anger marbled her words. 'At least he never ran out on me!'

'That's why I'm here, I told you. To make amends.'

'It's too late, Jack.' Over the years, Amy had tried to hate him, but it was hard to hate someone when all you really wanted was to be with them again.

He took a step closer. 'Don't turn me away, lass. Not now.'

Drawing herself up to her full height, she told him sternly, 'You'd better go. *Now!* Before Frank gets home.' There would be no explaining with Frank. He was possessive and nasty, especially when he'd had a drink or two.

'Mam!' Lottie's voice rang out from the upper reaches. 'Eddie wants the potty!'

Sighing wearily, Amy rushed to the bottom of the stairs. 'Fetch him down,' she called out. 'And be quick about it. Your dad'll be home any minute!'

Suddenly Jack's hands clamped on to her shoulders and he swung her back into the parlour. 'Get off me, Ja—' Her voice was smothered beneath a long, hard kiss. Afterwards he held her for a brief second, his eyes locked into hers, and his hands like iron fists around her arms.

He was the first to speak. 'I have a house in Bedford, and another by the sea. I've money enough to give you whatever you want.'

'I don't want anything from you!' she cried. But her eyes and heart told a different story.

He smiled. 'Oh yes, you do,' he said huskily. 'You want *me*, every bit as much as I want you.'

The moment was shattered by Lottie's frantic voice. 'Mam!' Already halfway down the stairs, she had the child by the scruff of the neck. 'Eddie's messed himself!'

Ignoring the interruption, Jack said intensely, 'I came here to take you away with me, but if you really don't want to come, it's all right.'

He was playing a game and she knew it well. 'I'll stay a week. That's all the time I can spare, even for you, Amy.' Knowing she wanted him to, he kissed her again. 'I'm staying at the Darwen Hotel in Blackburn,' he confided, 'but I'm out of a night-time, seeing old friends and catching up on the news. Most nights I'm to be found in the Sun public house, top of King Street.' Preparing to leave he reminded her again, 'One week. After that I'll be heading back south and I'm telling you now, Amy: I won't be coming this way again. Ever!'

'Goodbye, Jack.' In spite of the turmoil inside her, Amy decided that least said was soonest mended.

Turning her gently, he fondled her breast. 'Like I said, we

belong together, you and me. But I can't force you, Amy. It's got to be your choice.'

'I *can't*!' Desperately unhappy with the life she had, Amy was torn in two by his offer. 'The children . . . everything! Surely you can see how it is?'

Grabbing her to him, he shook her hard. 'I can see you're a bloody drudge! I can see you're shackled to six kids and another on the way – used by a man who doesn't give a toss about you. *That's* what I can see, Amy. And I want you out of it!'

Eddie's loud cries as Lottie smacked and berated him on the stairs smothered Jack's closing words. 'For God's sake, Amy, leave it all behind,' he urged. 'Trust me – I'll look after you. The kids won't want for anything. I'll make you an allowance so you can send them whatever they need.'

'And what about this one?' Stroking her swollen midriff, she looked him in the eye.

'That's up to you. Give it away – leave it for *him* to look after. I don't care, so long as I never have to clap eyes on it.' When he felt her shrink from him, he reminded her, 'No kids, Amy, that's the deal. I'm no good with kids. I never was.'

Before she could open her mouth, he was gone, down the passage and out of the house.

When the door closed behind him, she stood there for a while, her lips aching from his kiss and her breast tingling from the touch of his fingers. 'You're a heartless sod, Jack Mason,' she whispered. All the same, he had brought her hope, even if there was a price to pay.

For a moment she was back in the past, fancy free with a future and a sweetheart. It had been a long, lonely time since she had felt like that.

Lottie had seen it all, but said nothing. Instead, she brought Eddie down and watched while her mother took off his soiled nightgown. 'There's a clean nightie in the scullery cupboard, and a bar of carbolic under the sink. You'll find a flannel there, too,' Amy told the girl. 'Fetch it for me, will you? Oh, and get the bowl out of the sink, while you're at it.'

While Lottie followed her mother's instructions, Amy brought the kettle from the fender and poured a measure of warm water into the bowl. Dipping her fingers into it, she made sure it wasn't too hot for the toddler's tender skin. 'Just right!' With a warm, wet flannel, and a good rub of carbolic, she soon had him comfortable again.

'There!' Planting a kiss on his mouth, she fastened the top of his clean nightgown. 'He'll sleep now,' she told Lottie, groaning as she climbed up off her knees. 'The bairn's weighing heavy,' she confided. 'It won't be too long now.'

The sooner the better, she thought. It was getting her down, more than the others ever had.

Before she went upstairs, Lottie gave her mother an accusing, quizzical look that unnerved Amy. 'Is there summat on your mind, lass?'

'That man . . .' Lottie saw the fear on her mother's face and was wickedly delighted. 'Who was he?'

Wary, Amy gave a vague answer. 'Somebody I used to know, that's all.'

'What did he want?'

'He was just visiting – why?'

Lottie shrugged. 'Doesn't matter.'

Worried now, Amy couldn't let it go at that. 'If there's summat on your mind, it *does* matter. Out with it!'

A smirk crossed the girl's pretty features. 'He kissed you.'

Amy groaned inwardly; so Lottie *had* seen them after all. 'Sometimes old friends do kiss,' she said casually. 'It doesn't mean anything special.'

'You blushed . . . I saw you!'

Angry now, Amy retorted, 'You're imagining things!'

'No, I weren't. He kissed you and you went red as a beetroot. I saw you!'

'Go to bed, Lottie.' Lifting Eddie into her arms, Amy carried him to the door. 'I want no more of this silly talk.'

'It's a good job Dad weren't here.' Seeing how she had her mam worried, the girl continued relentlessly.

Amy gasped as an unexpected pain seemed to break her back in two. 'There's no need for your dad to know he was ever here,' she said, taking a deep breath. 'I don't want you telling tales, causing trouble when there's no need.'

Lottie saw the pain in her mother's face and was afraid. 'Is the baby coming?'

Amy shook her head. 'No. Now go to bed, there's a good girl.'

Momentarily shaken, Lottie assured her, 'I won't tell about the man. Not if you don't want me to.'

'Listen to me!' Amy resisted the pains that swept through her. 'He was just an old friend, come to say hello. Tomorrow he'll be gone, and that'll be the end of that.' More's the pity, she thought sadly.

There was an awkward moment while Lottie quietly regarded her mother – the flushed face and that faraway look in her eyes. So tomorrow he'd be gone, eh? And that'd be the end of that. She suspected there was more to it.

'Will you be sorry when he's gone?' she asked.

At the end of her tether now, Amy rounded on her daughter. 'It'll be you who's sorry if you don't get yourself off to bed, my girl!' Thrusting the infant into Lottie's arms, she muttered, 'He won't be back, that's all you need to know. Now, for the last time, get off up them stairs afore your dad comes in.'

'Were you sweethearts?'

'That's enough!' Amy felt a warm blush running up her neck and over her face. 'I'll give you one minute . . . afore I run you up them stairs at the end of my foot!'

With a sly little grin, Lottie backed off. 'All right, all right, I'm going.'

Grateful, Amy's mood softened. 'Goodnight, lass.'

'Goodnight, Mam.' Lottie's smile was deceivingly innocent.

Eddie offered his face for a kiss; not Lottie though. She wasn't that kind of child.

Amy closed the parlour door after them and leaned against it for a time, eyes closed. The encounter with Jack had set her pulse racing and her mind working. Then there had been the inquisition from Lottie. She had a pain in her lower back that was taking her breath, and the idea of Frank coming home, probably drunk and raring for a fight, was putting her on edge.

What with one thing and another, it was all too much. If only Lottie could manage to keep her mouth shut, things might work out all right. But Amy had a bad feeling about it all. She shook her head. 'That lass has a spiteful streak in her a mile wide. If only she was more like Molly.' Her eldest girl was a different matter altogether. Loyal and loving, she was a real treasure. 'Lottie takes after Frank,' Amy sighed. 'The Lord only knows who our Molly takes after.'

She chuckled wryly. 'One thing's certain: she doesn't take after *her* father. Jack was never loyal. He was loving though – too bloody loving!' There was no denying they had had some good times together.

Amy settled her considerable bulk into a chair. 'If Lottie does open her mouth and tells her father,' she whispered tremulously, 'it'll be God help us all, an' no mistake!'

Chapter Two

'Will ye look at that? It brings a smile to your heart, so it does.'
Digging her old daddy in the ribs, Rosie Craig winked. 'Sure they
can't keep their hands off each other!' Laughing her loud raucous
laugh, she threw the dishcloth at the young sweethearts. 'Hey!
That's enough o' that,' she teased. 'You'll put me off me tea, so
ye will, and besides, isn't it time young Molly went home to her
mam? The little ones will want putting to bed, and I don't expect
yer father will be home till the pubs close.'

Her own father, Michael Noonan, sat by the cheery fire
smoking his pipe, his weathered face crinkling with a cheeky
grin. 'Aw, come on now, Rosie,' he gently chided. 'Leave the
young 'uns alone, why don't ye?'

A lovable, mischievous man, Michael had come over from
Ireland many years before. He had seen life in the raw and worked
until his back was near broken, but he had loved and laughed, and
been satisfied with his lot until six years ago, when his beloved
wife had died before him, and he was left all alone.

When his only child, Rosie, persuaded him to come and live
with her, he was plagued with doubts. 'Are ye sure I won't be
in the way?' he asked. 'Will it be all right with the twins? Alfie
and Sandra are eighteen now. They'll want to be bringing home
their sweethearts.'

Old though he was, Michael had not forgotten what it was like to be young and in love. 'They'll not want an old codger like me in the way,' he protested.

As it turned out, Alfie and Sandra were of the same mind as their mam. 'It will be good to have you here with us, Grandad,' they said. And Michael was persuaded.

Now, after four years of contentment, he was rooted to this little house and as close to his grandson as any man could be. 'Away with ye, Rosie. Leave 'em to kiss and cuddle,' he urged her now. 'Thank yer lucky stars the lad's found a lovely lass like young Molly.'

Rosie gave him a hug. 'You're an old romantic, that's what ye are.'

In the glow of the fire, with his eye on the young sweethearts, the old man grew dreamy. 'Ah, sure, I can recall me and yer mam being in love the very same way.' Taking Rosie's hand, he gave it a fond squeeze. 'You and Bill an' all,' he said. 'You had a good fella there, so ye did.'

'Ah, don't I know it?' she sighed. 'There's not a minute of the day when I don't miss him.'

There was a moment of quiet contemplation before, in his inimitable way, the old fella plucked a battered mouth organ out of his waistcoat pocket. 'This was yer mam's favourite,' he told Rosie, and began to blow a merry tune, his feet tapping and fingers drumming on the instrument.

Rosie cried with delight. 'Yes, Da – I remember that as if it were yesterday!' Leaping off the arm of his chair, she kicked out her feet and danced round to Molly, who was promptly plucked from Alfie's arms and made to dance alongside her. 'It's an old folk song,' Rosie shouted above the music, 'and me mammy loved it! As soon as the tune got started, she'd be off like the pixies . . . dancing the night away.'

She hummed and whirled round the room. 'Come on, Alfie,

me boy,' she commanded. 'Get yer arse outta that chair and dance with your fiancée, why don't ye?'

Alfie was embarrassed. 'You two do the dancing,' he said. 'I'll do the watching.'

Rosie gave a little chuckle. 'Will ye look at that?' she told Molly. 'He'll fight the world and have a thousand people cheering him on, but he's too shy to dance with his own folk, so he is.'

Molly gave him a reassuring wink. If Alfie didn't want to dance that was all right by her; so long as they danced cheek to cheek the next time he took her to the Roxy.

For the next few minutes all was forgotten as Michael filled the room with music of a kind that came from the heart. The two women danced with all their hearts, Alfie cheered them on, and when the tune was done, everyone laughed and clapped and it was time for supper.

Breathless, Rosie reached up to the mantelpiece for her husband's photograph; he had posed for it in his naval uniform only weeks before she had received news that he was lost at sea. 'Bill was shy, too, where dancing was concerned,' she told the others. '"Don't force me, Rosie," he used to say. "You know I've got two left feet."'

When the tears threatened, she looked at Molly with a bright smile. 'You know about our Alfie, don't you?' she asked. 'How he didn't come home from school one day. He was over two hours late and I'd no idea where he might be. I was almost out of me mind so I was! The naval recruitment officer brought him home. "Come back in a few more years," he told him. "We've not taken to signing on fourteen-year-olds yet."' Rosie laughed, 'The little sod wanted to fly the planes, so he did.'

Crossing the room, Molly sat on the arm of Alfie's chair, her hand in his. 'I'm not surprised at anything he does. When Alfie makes up his mind, there's no stopping him – I know *that*.' She also knew from what Alfie had since told her, that he adored his father and cherished his memory.

'Huh!' Alfie wagged a finger at her. 'I know somebody else who's just as stubborn!'

Rosie made a suggestion. 'Ye can stay a while longer if you like,' she told Molly, 'but you'd best go and tell yer mam where you are first.'

'Amy will know where she is.' As he held his fiancée's hand, Alfie's eyes swam with love as he gazed on her homely features. With her untidy tousle of hair and strong features, Molly could never be described as physically beautiful, yet she was beautiful of nature, with a good heart that found the best in everyone. 'Stay?' he urged. 'I'll go along and tell yer mam you'll not be long.'

Molly's blue eyes softened as she looked down at him, but she shook her head and gave her answer to Rosie. 'Thanks for the offer,' she said gratefully, 'only I'd best get back and help Mam with the kids.' She rolled her eyes. 'You know what Dad's like if they're not abed when he gets home.'

Rosie groaned. 'Huh! We *all* know what your dad's like when he's had a few,' she retorted forthrightly. '"The drink drives out the man and lets the devil in", that's what me mammy used to say.'

Michael chirped in, 'I hope you're not tarring us all with the same brush.' Winking cheekily at Alfie, he said, 'Like any man, I'm fond of a pint. Sure there's no harm in that!'

Rosie glared at him. 'Not for you mebbe, Da, but for some it might as well be poison.' For years now, ever since their children were small, she and Amy had been the best of friends. It angered her to see what the poor woman had to put up with. 'My Bill was fond of a pint an' all,' she reminded them, 'and I have to say, in all the years we were wed, drunk or sober, I never once saw him violent!'

Uncomfortable with the way the conversation was going, Molly said her goodbyes. 'I'll tell Mam you'll be along to see her in the morning,' she told Rosie.

Ashamed that she had let her emotions run away with her, Rosie gave her a hug. 'Don't forget to tell her I've finished that skirt I promised. She'll not be able to wear it yet, but it'll fit her a treat after the babby's born.'

'Thanks, Rosie.' Molly really liked Alfie's mam. 'That'll please her. She's always on about how she's looking forward to getting her figure back.'

'The trouble is, your dad seems to like her better with a big belly.' The taunt was out before Rosie could stop it. 'Sorry, darlin'!'

Molly's bright eyes had shadowed momentarily, then: 'It's all right.' She offered a forgiving smile. 'Mam has a hard life. Nobody knows that better than me.'

Realising she had touched a raw nerve, Rosie added hastily, 'Oh, and tell her I've a lovely cream-coloured blouse she can have with the skirt. It'll fetch out the brown in her eyes.'

Thanking her again, Molly followed Alfie to the front door. 'She didn't mean any harm,' he apologised as they walked up the street to the Tattersalls' home. 'She'd do anything for your mam, you know that.'

'I know. But she was right, and it makes me feel ashamed.'

'You've nothing to be ashamed about.'

'Alfie . . .'

'What's on your mind, sweetheart?'

'It doesn't matter.' Glancing up at this tall, well-built young man with his black hair and midnight-coloured eyes, Molly felt privileged as always. There were any number of girls in this street and elsewhere who would have given anything to have Alfie Craig look their way. But he only wanted her, and that was grand.

He gently nudged her. 'Hey! Don't look at me like that with them soft blue eyes.'

She laughed. 'Why not?'

Bringing her to a halt he put his arms round her shoulders. 'Because you're turning me to jelly, that's why not.' Bending his head to hers, he kissed her tenderly on the mouth, right there in the street. 'I love you, Molly Tattersall,' he murmured.

Maggie Lett's voice sailed through the air. 'Have you no shame, you young 'uns?' Waving her arms, she let fly with a stream of abuse that would have shamed a navvy. 'Gerroff out of it, afore I fetch a bucket o' cold watter!'

Laughing and blushing, they ran on, almost colliding with Amy, who was hurrying down the steps to fetch her daughter. 'I were just coming to get you,' she told Molly. 'Your dad'll be home soon, and you know what he's like. Lottie's playing me up again, and Eddie's messed himself twice . . . I can't think what ails him. One thing's for sure, your dad won't like it, eating his tea with the smell of Eddie's dirty nappies in the air. I've rinsed 'em out and left 'em soaking in a pail of Omo, but your dad will still smell it, he always does.'

In the light of what Rosie had said, Molly's anger was quick to rise. 'Happen you should remind him they're *his* children, too.'

Amy shook her head. 'You know what he's like, lass.'

'I'm sorry, Mam,' she apologised. 'Don't worry, I'm on my way in. When Dad gets home, you can leave the kids to me.' And if he started throwing his weight around, he'd hear a few home truths from her, and no mistake.

Relieved, Amy shifted her attention to Alfie. 'Hello, Alfie, lad. All right, are you?'

'Yes, thank you, Mrs Tattersall.'

'That's good.' With that she went back inside, calling behind her, 'Don't be long, Molly.' The pain in her back was giving her gyp, and there was a strange sensation in the pit of her stomach. 'Drat that Jack. He's unnerved me, that's what it is,' she muttered, pushing the door shut. At the back of her mind, she prayed to God it wasn't the start of an early labour.

Outside, Alfie lowered his voice to a mere whisper. 'You still haven't given me a proper answer.'

'I haven't heard the question yet.'

'Aw, come on, Moll, don't torment me!'

Smiling, she teased him as always. 'Oh, you mean the question you were asking, before your mam got me up dancing?' She had hoped he would ask again, and now that he had she was thrilled enough to keep him suffering a minute or two. It *was* a girl's privilege, after all.

'You're a minx!'

'But you love me?' Her hands reached up to stroke his face. With her gaze holding his, she told him what he wanted to hear. 'You already know what my answer is,' she said. 'To be your wife . . . Mrs Alfred Craig.' She let the words linger on her lips. 'Oh, Alfie. It's all I've ever wanted.'

'Me, too.' Covering her small hands in his, he asked, 'But when?'

'Whenever you like.' Tomorrow, if it was possible, she thought joyfully.

'What about Easter?' he suggested. 'It's only seven months away. By that time we'll have saved enough money for a month's rent on a decent house, with a few quid left over to buy the essentials. We'll not be able to furnish a house top to bottom, straight off,' he warned, 'but as long as we have a bed to lie in and a couple of chairs for sitting, we can eat off our laps and buy whatever else we need as we go along. What do you say, sweetheart?'

She groaned. 'I hope we can start with more than a bed and a couple of chairs!' But, like Alfie, she knew it wouldn't be easy. 'I know the war's over and things are slowly getting back to normal, but there's still a shortage of some items.' Reluctantly, she agreed with him on one thing. 'It's a good idea to wait for another six months or so. I think we should try for a house on Derwent Street; they all have three bedrooms and they've got nice size back yards. Then, I'll want a new lavvy put in. I'm funny about using other folks' lavvies, especially if they haven't been changed since the house was built.'

Alfie laughed out loud. 'You can have a new lavvy for a wedding present – how's that?'

Ignoring him, Molly lovingly described her ideal lavatory. 'I'd like a white one,' she said dreamily, 'with blue flowers, and a china handle, and a seat that fits proper, so when you sit down, it won't tip to one side.' It was something she had set her heart on.

'I see.' There were times when he couldn't fathom this lovely creature. 'All right then, forget the diamond ring and the fur coat. You can have your lavvy with its blue flowers and china handle. What's more, I'll have it wrapped in crimson ribbons with a great big bow. And *nobody* will be allowed to sit on that seat, until you've tried it for size.'

But she was adamant. 'Laugh if you like, but you've never had to use ours – that'd soon wipe the smile off your face.'

'And is that all you want?'

'Well, I'd also like a nice rug in front of the fire, and a full-size stove.' Her eyes sparkled as she looked up at him. 'I've seen one at Barney's second-hand shop. I know he'll keep it for us if we put down a small deposit. Later on, we can change it for a better one, if you want?'

'Anything you say,' he replied, thinking how little she wanted, and how much he would love to be able to give her. 'Promise me one thing?' he asked.

'If I can.'

'When we're married, you won't want more than two children, will you?' He loved kids but only in small numbers.

22

'Four!' Molly had her brood all mapped out.

'Settle for three?' Looking pitiful, he put his hands together as though in prayer.

'Coward!' But Molly understood how he felt; in fact, though she would never tell anyone this, there were times when she swore she would never have any kids at all. Being one of six children in a cramped house with parents who spent their life rowing and fighting was a terrible trial. But when she asked herself if she could go through life without children of her own, she knew how empty that life would be, even with Alfie by her side.

'Is it three then?' he asked hopefully.

'Depends how careful you are,' she answered boldly. 'If you're anything like my dad, we'll likely end up with an army!'

'And what would you think to that?'

Molly's smile disappeared. 'I'd think you were selfish and thoughtless,' she said quietly.

Alfie was equally serious. 'I wouldn't want us to have more children than we could feed and clothe,' he told her softly. 'I know how hard it is for your mother. I don't want that kind of life for you . . . or me, come to that!'

Irrepressible, Molly grinned. 'So if I suddenly said I wanted seven children, what would you do?'

There was only one truthful answer he could give. 'If that was what you *really* wanted, then seven it would have to be.'

'Do you love me that much?'

He grimaced, eyes rolling in horror. 'God! What have I let myself in for?' Snatching her to him, he kissed her hard, but said gently, 'I'll tell you this, Molly Tattersall, I'll never love any woman the way I love you.'

'*Molly!*' Amy's voice startled them.

'All right, Mam. I'm on my way.'

But they held each other for a few more seconds, before Alfie wanted to know, 'What was it you tried to ask me before? Back there?'

Unsure, she hesitated.

'Tell me,' he urged.

'It was just . . . well, I don't like you street-boxing.' Her voice trembled. 'It frightens me.'

Alfie was well aware of her concern about his way of earning a living. 'It's what I do,' he admitted. 'I know you're worried, and I can't deny it's a worrying game. There was a time when it was a clean game and you knew what you were up against, but not any more.'

Walking her to the foot of the steps, he grew thoughtful, lowering his voice as though talking to himself. 'It all seems to be changing, what with the thugs who think they can get in on the act with brute force and ignorance, the money men with their threats and dirty tricks, and managers you thought you could trust.' Shaking his head, he revealed, 'Now all they want is a quick, easy percentage, and to hell with everything else. Then of course, there's the law. Once they get scent of a fight, they won't leave it be.'

When he saw the look on Molly's face he realised with a jolt that he was only making matters worse. Raising his face to the skies, he groaned like a man in pain. 'Me and my big mouth, and here I am, supposed to be reassuring you!'

Molly's worries were now tenfold. 'Is it worth it, Alfie, tell me that?' She didn't want to bully him, nor did she have the right but, as she told him now: 'There are other ways to earn a living.'

'Not for me.' He shrugged. 'Boxing is all I know. Even from a kid I've been able to take care of myself. My grandaddy and his daddy afore him . . . they were the best.' His dark eyes shone with pride. 'That's what *I* want, too,' he said. 'To be the best – just like they were.'

Embarrassed by this rush of emotion, Alfie joked, 'Besides,

I'm no good at anything else. Ask me mam – she'll tell you.'
Mimicking Rosie, he wagged a busy finger. 'Ah, you're useless,
so ye are! Ye can't wash a pot without dropping it, and Gawd
only knows who taught yer to brew the tea.' When he grimaced
he had Rosie off a treat. 'Sure it tastes like bleddy dishwater, so
it does!'

Molly chuckled. 'She's right an' all.'

'There you are then,' he beamed. 'I'd best stick to what I
know best.'

Her smile faded. 'It worries me though.'

'What – scared that I might meet my match, is that it?' Rolling
his eyes, he grabbed her to him. 'Or is it that you don't want me
to lose my handsome looks?'

Playfully thumping him, Molly retorted, 'Can't you be serious
for one minute?'

He didn't want her getting into a state. 'Look, lass, there's no
need for you to be frightened. I can handle anybody they set up
against me.'

Reluctantly, she agreed. 'I'm sure you could!' In spite of her
obvious concern, there was a measure of pride in Molly's chiding.
'Running to Revidge and back every morning, and half your life
spent down at Fred's gymnasium.'

'Ah well, you need to keep fit and sharp if you want to stay
on top.' Loving her so much he would do anything for her, he
said, 'I'll make you a promise.' Tenderly wrapping his two hands
round her face, he smiled into her soft blue eyes. 'The day I meet
my match, I'll give up the fighting. How's that?'

She smiled back at his promise. 'And if you're nabbed by the
law, what then?'

'Same thing. I'll chuck it in.'

'Even if it means you have to work in a factory, six days a
week, hemmed in on all sides by high walls and the windows so
blackened with grime you can't see daylight?' Molly wondered

if she was asking too much of this lovely bloke. Especially when he craved the open air and his whole life had been built round the thrill of boxing.

Alfie hesitated for only the briefest moment. 'Even then,' he promised. 'If it stops you worrying unnecessarily, my beauty, closed in or not, I'll clock in with the rest of 'em.' His eyes betrayed the depth of his feelings for her. 'I'll even sweep the streets if I have to. There's many a decent soul earning a wage from doing the very same.'

Molly answered with a twinkle in her eye. 'And you'd be content with that, would you?'

He reflected on his rash promise. 'Happen,' he teased.

She chuckled. 'Aye, an' happen *not!*'

From the window of the house, Amy saw them, still deep in conversation. 'Poor old Molly,' she sighed. 'I make such demands on her, and she never complains.' Turning away, she busied herself with getting the dinner. 'Lottie, put the plates and things out,' she said. 'This hotpot's almost ready.'

'Where's our Molly?'

'Canoodling,' her mother answered frankly.

'Will I fetch her in?'

'No. We'll give her a minute or two longer. So long as she's here afore your dad gets home, that's all as matters.'

Outside, the lovers were still discussing their wedding arrangements. 'Let's not tell anybody just yet,' Molly pleaded. 'It's a difficult time, what with our mam about to have the bairn and all. I'd rather we waited until after, if that's all right with you.'

'Like I said, sunshine, whatever you want is all right by me. Just as long as you don't change your mind.'

The conversation was suddenly cut short by the arrival of Alfie's wayward twin sister, Sandra. 'Hey! Look at you two, kissing and cuddling in the street,' she cried. 'It's a wonder old

Maggie ain't emptied her chamberpot over you!' Drunk and unsteady on her feet, she came at them with a laugh. 'But never you mind . . . sod old Maggie, eh? Sod 'em all, that's what I say. Ain't that right, Molly me ol' sugar?'

Winking knowingly, she gave her friend a powerful nudge, sending Molly one way and herself the other. 'Well, I never!' she screeched, falling sideways into Alfie's waiting arms. 'I'm blowed if I ain't three sheets to the wind!' She took a fit of the giggles and Molly couldn't help joining in.

Alfie's own sense of humour was stifled by his obvious concern. 'Take a hold of yourself, Sandra! Twice in a week you've come home plastered.' Where his twin sister was concerned, nothing got by him. 'I reckon it's time you and me had a little talk.'

'Aw, stop moithering!' Shrugging him off, she belched and staggered. 'Hark at him,' she complained. 'Bossy boots, ain't he? I wouldn't mind, but he's only five minutes older than me. Tell him, Moll,' she cajoled. 'Tell him I can do whatever takes me fancy. He'll listen to you. Go on . . . tell him!' She gave her friend another little nudge, but this time Molly was ready for her.

'No,' she answered firmly. 'Alfie's right, Sandra. You're getting a bit out of your depth. We're all worried about you.'

'Well, there's no need,' the girl replied good-naturedly. 'I'm having a wonderful time. I've been dancing and singing and everybody clapped and the landlord said I could have a job in his pub any time I wanted . . .' looking sheepish, she went on '. . . if only this cheeky bugger hadn't tried it on and got me in the landlord's bad books!'

'Uh oh.' Alfie could only guess. 'You've been fighting again, is that it?'

Sandra looked appealingly at Molly, who wisely decided not to interfere between brother and sister.

'It weren't *my* fault!' Sandra bunched her fists and waved her arms about as if shadow-boxing. 'It were this randy old bloke who started it, I swear to God!'

Surprisingly light on her feet, she began leaping about. 'Best rough and tumble I've seen in a long time. Ollie Pleasant got a bloody nose, an' Fat Lizzie waded in with her umbrella, till somebody took it off her and jumped on it.' Teetering with laughter, she clamped hold of Molly. 'Whoops – I'll wet meself if I'm not careful. You shoulda come with us, gal, you missed a good night. Still, I expect you had summat better to do, eh?' She winked knowingly.

Molly couldn't help but chuckle. 'You'd best do as Alfie says and get off home,' she said. 'I'll see you in the morning like we planned.' They were off to Blackpool for a paddle with the kids. 'We'll need a bright start if we're to catch that early tram.'

But Sandra was still in full flow. 'You know old Bella as runs the flower stall on Blackburn Market . . . well, you'll never believe it! She wears a *wig*! I'm telling yer, a real, live *wig*! I know, 'cos I saw it clear as I can see you now.' Although truth to tell, with the world swaying before her eyes, nothing was very clear at the minute. 'The landlord grabbed her hair and the whole bloody lot come off in his hand. Give him the fright of his life, it did.'

While Alfie and Molly tried desperately hard to keep a straight face, Sandra had no such qualms. Her roars of laughter echoed up and down the street, bringing Rosie to the door in a rush. 'Is that you, Sandra?' she yelled. 'Drunk again is it, ye little heathen? Get in here with ye!'

'I'm not coming in yet, Mam!' Falling against the wall, she took a dizzy spell. 'Ooh, the wall's moving.'

'Right, that's it.' Taking her by the shoulders, Alfie stood her upright. 'You can tell us all about it tomorrow.' Turning to Molly he winked, making her smile.

'I met this good-looking bloke . . . ooh!' Sandra held out her arms as if embracing some imaginary being. 'He kissed like an angel, he did.' Struggling fiercely, she almost fell, taking Alfie with her. 'Aw, look I'm sorry, don't be mad at me. I'm drunk and I've no excuse, but . . .' She began giggling again. 'I think I'm in love.'

Alfie had heard it all before. 'Come on, sis,' he sighed. 'Let's get you inside before you have the whole street out.'

'You and Molly get off. Leave your sister to me!' Rattled and ready, Rosie came at the trot, rolling up her sleeves.

'Don't get mad, our mam.' Sandra had seen her mother in a temper before and it was not a pretty sight. 'I were already on me way. Ask them, they'll tell you. "I'd best get off inside," that's what I said, and here I am, coming down the street of me own free will.' She burped again.

'You don't say?' Rosie was having no nonsense. Catching hold of Sandra's coat collar, she took her down the street at a march. 'Whatever are ye coming to? Shaming yer mammy like that! You're a disgrace, so ye are, a downright disgrace!'

'I'm sorry, Mam. I'll be off to bed and you'll hear no more from me till morning. Me and Moll's taking the kids to Blackpool, it's all planned.'

'Sure, I don't care if youse are going to the ruddy *moon*. And you'll not be going to your bed in a hurry neither; not until I've turned you upside down in a bucket of cold water.'

'Aw, Mam!'

'Aw, Mam nothing. I'm not having you throwing up all over my clean sheets.'

The two of them could be heard arguing all the way down the street.

'Wait till yer grandaddy gets a sight of ye. He'll tan yer arse, so he will!'

'I don't care.' As always, Sandra gave as good as she got. 'I'm in love, Mam. Honest to God, it's the real thing this time. Wait and see . . . it won't be long afore I'm walking down the aisle. He's asked me to marry him and I've said yes, and there ain't nobody gonna change my mind.'

'Away with yer!' Rosie, too, was familiar with this tale. 'Tell me his name, why don't you? Come on then, let's hear it. This fella who's asked you to wed him . . . tell me his name.' Landing Sandra a clip round the ear, she hurried her on. 'That's if you can remember it at all?'

'Course I can remember it,' the girl cried, indignant.

'Ah well, that's all right then. So you'll not mind telling yer old mammy, will ye?'

Sandra was mortified. Try as she might, she could not recall his name. 'You're not being fair. How am I expected to remember anything with you yelling at me?' she retaliated. 'And besides, I can't think straight when I've had a pint or two!'

At the door, Rosie gave her daughter an almighty shove, sending her into the front passage at a run. 'I should think they're all having a laugh at you back at the pub. Ye silly young article, have you no sense at all? Sure, there was no man, and no proposal, and if you've let him have his wicked way with ye, all I can say is, you'd better pray to Mary Mother of God, that he hasn't made you with child!'

At this point, Sandra began to wail. 'Oh, Mam! I can't remember if we did it or not! What if we did? What if I'm pregnant?'

'Then you'll be sick as a pig of a morning. You'll grow fat and clumsy and waddle down the street like a duck stuffed ready for the oven. And when your time comes you'll go into labour and that's when you'll wish to God you'd never clapped eyes on the fella. Then o' course you'll have the bairn as easy as shelling peas, and afterwards I'll chuck the pair of youse right out the door, so I will.'

'Aw, you wouldn't, would you, Mam?' Sober as a judge by now, Sandra was beginning to panic.

'Ah, will ye stop the whining and get inside now.' Though Rosie's anger was already subsiding, she didn't let on. 'We'll see what your grandaddy has to say about all this.'

With that, the door shut behind them and all was peace again.

Down the street, Alfie tutted. 'It's like thunder and lightning when them two start.'

Molly smiled, then Alfie, and in no time the two of them were laughing aloud.

'I wonder who the fella was?' Alfie said.

Molly had few illusions about her friend. 'Happen there wasn't a fella at all.' All those who knew Sandra were aware of her vivid imagination. 'You know how she likes to fancify.' And yet Sandra had sounded definite enough to cause doubts in Molly's mind. 'On the other hand, maybe she really has met somebody she's taken a liking to.'

Alfie nodded. 'We'll see.' Giving Molly a hug, he said, 'It's time I was off to the gymnasium.'

Glancing at the window, Molly saw her mother looking out. 'Our mam's watching for me. If everything's not shipshape when Dad gets home, there'll be another row, and with Mam the way she is, that's the last thing she needs.'

Reluctantly, they parted company, Alfie to Blackburn town and the gymnasium; Molly indoors to give her mam a helping hand.

She found Amy seated in front of the fire. 'Are you all right, Mam?' Molly thought her mother looked to be in pain. 'The baby hasn't started, has it?' Excitement mingled with terror.

Forcing a smile, Amy shook her head. 'No, lass,' she said. 'I've got a bit of a backache, that's all.' Her weary gaze shifted to the door. 'It's them little buggers upstairs, they wear me out.' Lowering her voice she confided, 'Sometimes I wonder what to make of our Lottie. She allus seems to be looking for trouble.'

'What's she been up to now?' Molly was always wary of her

younger sister. Where Sandra was foolish and vulnerable, Lottie had the makings of a really nasty piece of work.

'She's not been up to anything exactly.' Amy gave a sigh as deep as her boots. 'But she will keep asking questions . . .' Realising she had said enough, Amy clammed up.

'Questions?' Molly detected an odd note in her mother's voice. 'What about?'

'Nothing in particular.' Amy thought it best not to mention Jack's visit. 'Our Lottie's head is too old for her shoulders, that's the trouble.'

'Well, she seems to have worn you out, that's for sure.' Molly had never seen her mam look so tired. 'Get yourself off to bed.' She glanced at the mantelpiece clock. 'It's twenty to ten. I'll get Dad's meal.' Throwing off her coat she hung it on the nail behind the door. 'And don't you be worrying about what he might say. I'll tell him you're feeling a bit worse for wear, and I packed you off to your bed.'

Amy was fearful. 'No, lass. You know what Frank's like. When he walks through that door he expects to see me ready to wait on him hand and foot. He won't like it if I'm not there to put his food in front of him.'

'I'm not worried about what he wants, Mam,' Molly bristled. 'It's *you* I'm concerned about.' She looked searchingly at her mother's face, so grey and troubled. It hurt the girl to see how subservient her mother had become, and all in the name of peace. 'He can rant and rave all he likes,' she said. 'Go on, our mam . . . away upstairs, eh? You look all in.'

Amy shook her head. 'No, lass, I can't go to my bed. I'll just sit here awhile and catch my breath.'

Molly knew better than to argue with her. 'Right then,' she said, rubbing her hands together. 'What's to be done?'

Relieved, Amy told her, 'I've made him a meat pie – it's baked to a turn; there's cabbage and taters keeping warm on the hob, and it'll only take a minute to make the gravy. He likes it fresh and hot, does your dad.' She gave a smile, but it was a sad little thing, never reaching her eyes. 'All it needs now is for me to strain the cabbage water into the meat juices, and stir it together with a pinch of raising flour. Oh, and the table needs setting.'

Before going into the scullery, Molly had more to say. 'Our Lottie really upset you, didn't she, Mam?' There was something about her mother that she couldn't put her finger on. 'Happen I should have a word with her.'

'No, lass, don't do that. It were summat and nowt. It's my fault anyway. I palmed young Eddie off on her, and he's such a handful I'm not surprised she was put out.'

'And is that what all this is about? Because you asked Lottie to keep an eye on Eddie? She didn't want the responsibility, so she threw one of her famous tantrums?'

'Like I said . . . it were summat and nowt.' Ashamed, Amy stared into the fire. Never in her life had she lied to her eldest daughter. In fact, ever since she was twelve years old, Molly had been more of a best friend to her than a daughter. Funny, she thought, Molly was the only child who didn't belong to Frank, and yet she was the only one she really loved. It was a shocking thing to say, but it was true, God forgive her.

Molly rolled up her sleeves. 'You sit there until I've got it all ready to serve up,' she ordered. 'I might as well set the table, too, while I'm at it.'

Too worn out to argue, Amy settled back in the chair. 'You're a good lass,' she said, closing her eyes with a sigh.

Molly's answer was a cheeky wink. 'I'll tell you what though,' she said, bustling into the scullery. 'Before I look to feeding *his* face, I'll make you a brew.' One swift glance caught the strain on Amy's countenance. 'You look as if you need it.'

Chapter Three

Half past ten came and went, and still Frank Tattersall wasn't home. 'I expect he's gone off somewhere with his drinking cronies.' Amy had seen it all before. 'Gone gambling, I dare say. Wasting more money.'

For the next hour, she snoozed in the chair and Molly sat with her. When Amy woke with a start, Molly insisted on her going to bed. 'I'll wait for him,' she promised. 'It'll be all right.' And Amy was too weary to argue.

The next hour passed quickly, with Molly checking the meal and making herself a brew, then going back and forth to the window to watch for him. 'You selfish bastard,' she muttered, dropping the curtains. 'You've no thought for anybody but yourself.'

Molly was half asleep in the chair when she finally heard him fumbling at the door. A quick glance at the mantelpiece clock told her it was almost one o'clock in the morning. 'Shame on him.' Scrambling from her chair she went into the scullery, only to find the dinner steamed to a pulp.

'Amy! I'm home!' Throwing open the front door, Frank stumbled into the passage. 'I'm a bit merry,' he giggled. 'Met an old pal in the boozer . . . we had a drink for old times' sake.' While he shouted, he made numerous attempts to shut the door, without success. 'Bloody thing!' Standing back he gave an almighty kick that sent the door home with a shudder, and himself sideways against the wall. 'Amy!' His voice rose to the rafters. 'AMY!'

Making his way to the parlour, he kept on calling, 'What's your game, eh? Didn't you hear me?' Straddling the doorway he glared into the room. 'What's this then, eh?' He felt oddly uncomfortable with his eldest daughter's gaze on him. 'What the hell are you staring at,' he said rudely, 'like I've got the pox or summat! And where's yer mam?'

'I'm here, Frank. Leave the lass alone.' Behind him, Amy clung sleepily to the banister.

Taking her roughly by the arm, he dragged her inside. 'So! Yer couldn't even wait up for me, eh, you lazy bitch.'

Instinctively afraid, Amy dropped her gaze, but not Molly. As always, she stood her ground. 'You're drunk,' she said in disgust.

'So what! If I'm drunk it's *my* money I'm spending, not yourn.'

Drawing from Molly's strength, Amy looked up. 'You haven't spent *all* your wages, have you, Frank?'

'None of your business.' He blundered into a chair and cursed. 'Bloody women!'

'You've not been gambling, have you, Frank?' Amy said fearfully. She knew from old that gambling would take his every penny, and hers, too.

He glared at her through bleary eyes. 'And what if I have?'

When he saw her face fall he jeered, 'You'll manage. You always do.'

Suddenly he noticed there was no food on the table. 'Hey! Where's me bloody supper, eh?' Banging his fist on the table, he screeched like a madman. 'DID YOU HEAR WHAT I SAID, WOMAN? Move your arse and get some food on this table.' His voice fell to a sinister tone. 'Before I do summat I might regret.' Already he was moving towards her.

'Leave her alone, Dad.' Molly took a step forward. 'She's not feeling too good.'

'I don't give a toss. She'll get my food *now*! Or she'll feel the buckle end o' my belt, an' no mistake.' To make the point he began undoing the wide stiff khaki belt from around his waist.

'Your dinner was kept warm for hours. It's not Mam's fault if it's spoiled,' Molly told him. 'I'll get you summat now. There's eggs and bacon and a couple of sausages left over. Sit yourself down. It'll only take a few minutes to throw it all in the frypan.'

Out of the corner of his eye Frank regarded Molly with contempt. 'It's *her* place to look after me,' he said, tightening the khaki belt round his knuckles. 'You'll stay out of it, if you know what's good for you.'

Undeterred by his bullying, she thrust herself between the two of them. 'I already told you, our mam's not well.'

Sensing trouble, Amy intervened. 'It's all right, lass,' she said. 'Go up and see to the children.' In a softer voice she added, 'I expect they're awake now.' Frightened, too, she imagined.

In great pain, she began to hobble towards the kitchen; not resisting when Molly eased her gently into a chair. 'Stay where you are, Mam,' she insisted. 'I'll get his meal.'

'Like bloody hell you will!' Darting forward, Frank thrust Molly aside, before wrenching Amy from her chair. Surprised when his daughter lunged at him from behind, he lashed out with the strength of an ox, sending his wife careering across the room, and Molly with her.

Steadier now, he strode towards them, his cruel eyes fixed on Amy's terrified face. 'Frightened of me, are you? Well now, that's how it should be an' all.' His soft laugh sent a chill through both women. 'I expect you'll be quick enough to get my dinner now, but you see, Amy lass, I reckon you still ain't learned your lesson. Not by a long chalk.' Raising a clenched fist he steadied himself to administer the punishment.

'No, Dad.' Stepping forward, Molly held out her arms. 'Touch her and you'll have *me* to deal with!' Her blue eyes blazed with anger.

'*You!*' Spitting in her face, he brought his fist down on her temple. The blow seemed to lift her into the air and launch her to the far side of the room, where her head struck the corner of the sideboard, before she slithered, unconscious, to the floor.

When he raised his foot to kick her, Amy cried out, 'No, Frank. Leave her be, or I swear to God, you'll be sorry!'

Something in his wife's frightened eyes stirred a deep-down suspicion in him. '"Sorry"? What does that mean, eh?'

'Nothing.' Unable to look at him any longer in case he saw the truth of what she had in mind, Amy turned away.

Stooping, he grabbed her by the throat, and raising her face to his, asked quietly, 'What's going on?'

'I don't know what you mean.' She felt the colour of guilt crawling up her face and knew he had seen it.

'Summat's been going on,' he persisted. 'Has there been somebody 'ere?'

Fearing for her life, Amy shook her head. 'There's been nobody here, Frank.'

'You're a bloody liar! There's guilt written all over your lying face! Who were it, eh? Some fancy man you intend running off with? Is that what you meant just now when you said I'd be sorry?' With one hand gripping her swollen midriff, he pulled the collar of her blouse until it was like a gallow rope round her neck. 'How do I know this brat is mine?' he demanded. 'You coulda been playing dirty behind my back.' As his voice rose, his spittle spattered her face. 'Happen it weren't me as filled yer belly after all.'

'You're wrong, Frank. This bairn is yours all right.' More's the pity, she thought. 'Besides, how could I have a fancy man? I tell you, there's been nobody here . . . man *nor* woman.' As the words were squeezed from her throat, Amy believed they would be her last.

'Filthy whore!' Drawing her close, he sniffed her, like a dog with a bone. 'There *has* been a man round yer,' he growled. 'I can smell the bastard!' Raising his fist to beat the truth out of her, he was stopped by the sound of Lottie's voice calling from the doorway.

'The man came to take her away,' she said callously. 'They were kissing.'

'*What were that?*' Swinging round, he looked directly at Lottie, making her shrink away. '*What* did you say?'

Suddenly, Amy clutched her side, her face contorted with pain. 'Run, Lottie!' she cried. 'The bairn's started. Fetch Maggie.'

'You stay right where you are, my girl.' Lumbering across the room, Frank uncurled the khaki belt. 'You'd best tell me, you bugger, or I'll flay the hide off yer!' Making a grab for Lottie he swore when she turned and fled back up the stairs. 'Come back 'ere!' he yelled, chasing after her. Then, changing tactics, his voice softened. 'She'll not tell me, but *you* will, won't you, lass?'

Cajoling and smiling, he pursued his daughter to the top of the stairs, where he quickly caught her to him by the hanks of her hair. 'We're the same, you an' me,' he cooed. 'We look out for each other. I won't belt you, lass – not if yer tell me the truth.' When she hesitated, the sound of his belt buckle echoed ominously against the banisters.

Downstairs, Amy was frantic. On her hands and knees, she crawled over to Molly. 'Are you all right, lass?' Holding one arm across her writhing stomach, she gently shook her daughter with the other. 'Wake up, love. For God's sake, wake up!' When the pain seemed to tear her apart, she screamed out, 'Molly! Help me!'

At first it seemed Molly couldn't have heard. But then, with agonising slowness, she opened her eyes. 'Mam?' At the sight of

Amy's desperate face, a stark realisation shot through her. 'Where is he?'

'Lottie told him.'

'Told him what?' Molly was confused.

'Never mind that now.' Later she would have to confide in the girl, but not now. 'Your dad's gone after Lottie, but she can take care of herself. They're two of a kind.' Bending double, Amy gasped, 'Dear God, I never had this sort o' pain with you lot. It's the bairn, lass. The bairn's started and there's summat wrong. I *know* there is.' The pain was so bad she could hardly speak.

Taking a minute to gather her senses, Molly noticed a thick trail of blood where Amy had crawled across the floor. 'Be still, Mam.' Swallowing her fear, she spoke calmly. 'Lie here, be very still, while I fetch Maggie. She'll know what to do.'

From upstairs she could hear Lottie and her dad arguing. 'Out with it, lass! What else did he say?' Frank meant to worm every last truth from her. But her mam was right; Lottie wasn't afraid. Not when she thought there might be something in it for her.

'Don't be frightened, Mam.' Laying Amy down, Molly took her coat from the door and laid it over her. 'I'll away and get help.'

'Hold me!' More terrified than she had ever been in her life, Amy clung to her. 'Don't leave me.'

There was a sudden commotion from upstairs, then a yell and a thud close by. Scrambling to her feet, Molly was horrified to find her father lying face down at the foot of the stairs, and Lottie standing on the last step staring down with big, scared eyes. 'He wouldn't let me go,' she whimpered. 'I pushed him off . . . he was hurting me.'

A swift examination revealed that Frank Tattersall wasn't dead, nor was he injured. 'He's just overcome by the drink if you ask me,' Molly said disgustedly. 'Now then, Lottie.' She forced her voice to remain calm so as not to panic the girl. 'I want you to run and fetch Maggie as quick as you can.' From behind them, Amy's cries grew louder. 'Tell her she's to come straight away because the bairn's on the way and there's summat wrong. Run as fast as you can now.'

With that she tugged her sister from the step and propelled her towards the front door and out into the cold, dark night. 'Tell her what I said. The bairn's on the way, an' Mam says it doesn't feel right!' She called the same instructions time and again, before returning to the parlour.

'It's all right, Mam,' she murmured, stroking Amy's head. 'Maggie's on her way.'

By the time Lottie returned bringing Maggie with her, Amy was in a terrible state.

'She's losing so much blood, Maggie.' Molly was frantic. 'I don't know what to do.' Cross-legged on the floor, she held her mother, who was nearly unconscious, in her arms.

'Let's have a look, shall we?' Still panting from the short run up the street, the old dear dropped to her knees. 'What 'ave yer done to yerself, eh?' she said kindly. 'Been lifting them childer, I expect. You'll not be told, will yer?' Carefully she laid Amy back and began to raise her skirt, at the same time advising Molly, 'This is no place for young 'uns.'

'Lottie, you'd best go back to your bedroom,' Molly instructed. 'You're to stay there till I fetch you, all right?'

As usual, her sister felt cheated. 'It's not fair.'

'Do as you're told!' Molly meant business and the girl knew it.

With a contemptuous glance at her father, who had come to and dragged himself to a chair where he sat quiet as a mouse, she scurried away, going no further than the top of the stairs, where all the children were huddled, frightened by events and not knowing where to turn. 'Get back in your beds,' Lottie ordered.

'And don't give me no lip or you'll feel the back of my hand.'

Her siblings didn't need telling twice. When Lottie was in this mood, it was wise to get out of harm's way.

It didn't take Maggie long to find out what was wrong, but she kept her opinions to herself and, speaking in calm, unhurried tones she told Amy, 'I can't help yer on this one, lass.' Squeezing Amy's hand, she shook her head. 'It's beyond me capabilities.'

Quieter now, Amy looked up at Maggie and read her thoughts. 'Do whatever you have to do,' she gasped. 'I just want it to be over.'

The old woman was adamant. 'I'm sorry, Amy, lass. It's the infirmary for you this time. I'm not teking no chances with yer.'

Amy was equally adamant. 'Well, I'm not going to no infirmary neither.'

Ignoring her, Maggie addressed Molly in urgent tones. 'Send Lottie to fetch my Charlie. Tell him he's to get the wagon and mek sure there's no rubbish or owt in the back. And he's to be quick about it. Yer mam needs the infirmary, whether she likes it or not.'

Laying Amy gently into Maggie's arms, Molly scrambled up. 'Oh, Maggie! She'll be all right, won't she?'

The old woman didn't answer. Instead she asked, 'Where's your da? We'll need some help lifting yer mam into the wagon.'

Molly pointed across the room to her father, who was slouched in the chair, his wide, stark eyes on Amy, and his mouth opening and shutting, as though wanting to say something, but not knowing how. 'Best leave him be,' Molly suggested quietly. 'He's drunk.'

Maggie snorted. 'Like all bloody men! No use at all when yer need 'em.'

Molly was meanwhile having doubts. 'Charlie's old wagon will shake her about too much. Wouldn't it be better to get an ambulance?'

'There's no time for all that. By the time an ambulance gets here, we can have your mam tucked up safe and sound in yon infirmary.' Gesturing to Lottie, who was eavesdropping round the corner, she ordered sharply, 'Off with yer, lass. Get my Charlie to fetch the wagon. Quick as yer can!'

With Lottie gone, she set about making Amy more comfortable. 'Leave yer mam to me,' she told Molly. 'Away upstairs an' mek sure the young 'uns are safe in their beds.' She lowered her voice to a whisper. 'I'll need summat to clean her up . . . a bucket, warm water and a good helping of disinfectant, and don't forget the towels and such.'

Molly was already on her way, more instructions following her as she went. 'After that, you're to fetch Rosie Craig,' Maggie told her. 'She's a good woman with a sensible head on 'er shoulders.' Addressing Amy now, she explained, 'I'm hoping she'll stay with the young 'uns, while me and Molly come with you to the infirmary.'

It took Molly only minutes to reassure the children. 'Mammy's going to the infirmary, but there's nothing for you to worry about,' she promised them. 'Rosie will come and look after you till I get back.' She then collected as many blankets and towels as she could find and ran down the stairs two at a time, the sight of her mother's deathly pallor turning her stomach over. 'That's all I could find,' she said, handing Maggie the pile of rags.

'Warm water, lass,' Maggie reminded her. 'And a bucket.'

'There's boiled water in the pan. I'll get it.' With that Molly fled to the scullery and prepared the bucket for Maggie.

'That's fine, lass.' Without disturbing Amy too much, Maggie washed and dried her. 'The bleeding's stopped for the while,' she confided, 'but yer mustn't move in a rush,' she warned. 'There's enough of us to carry yer to the wagon and lay yer flat in the back. Me and Molly will be with yer, so there's nowt for you to worry about.' Yet she knew from experience that both Amy and her bairn were in real danger.

With the raging pain having subsided for the time being, and the bleeding stemmed to a trickle, Amy felt more comfortable. 'I'm losing the bairn, aren't I?' she asked. She had given birth too often not to know the signs.

Wisely, Maggie would not be drawn. 'We shall have to wait and see.' Wiping Amy's sweating face, she gave a kind, crinkled smile. 'You'll soon be in safe hands now,' she promised. 'Till then, you do what old Maggie says and, God willing, you'll come to no harm.'

In no time at all, Molly and Rosie were at the door and it wasn't much longer before Charlie and Lottie arrived with the wagon. 'I've laid a couple of blankets in the back,' Charlie said. He was a big, rough-looking fella, with a drooping moustache and trousers to match. 'She ought to be going in an ambulance,' he argued. 'That old wagon ain't smooth over the cobbles, you know that.' Like Frank, he was shocked to see Amy all curled into a ball and looking like death warmed over. 'I'll not be responsible if owt happens,' he warned in a trembling voice.

'Don't be so bloody daft, man!' Maggie tutted. 'Just drive like you've a crate o' booze in the back, an' we'll *all* be safe!' Creaking and groaning as she struggled to her feet, she quickly got things underway.

'It's no use asking *him* to help.' Giving Frank a cursory sideways glance, she marshalled the rest of them. 'Lottie . . . fetch a pillow, an' them towels and blankets. Put 'em in the back of the wagon, roll 'em up and make a kind o' bed for yer mam to lie on. Hurry now, there's a good lass.' Time was passing and she was beginning to wonder if she'd done the right thing in not calling an ambulance.

It was a difficult job to get Amy up safely without starting the bleeding again, but they managed it. With Molly at her shoulders and Charlie beside Maggie at her feet, Amy was wrapped in a blanket and taken slowly along the passage and down the front steps. Outside, a few early risers had learned of the emergency. 'God bless yer, lass,' they told Amy as she was placed into the wagon. 'Mind how you go now.'

They watched Molly and Maggie climb in the back, and waved as Charlie drove away at a steady pace. 'Poor lass – she looked bad, didn't she, eh?' As they made their way to the mills, the women muttered of scoundrels like Frank Tattersall. More than that, they thanked their lucky stars their childbearing days were well and truly over.

Behind them, Lottie threatened the children with sudden death if they so much as whispered. 'I'll be listening,' she warned, 'and if I hear them floorboards creak, I'll be up here and tan yer arses, so help me!' Her warning was enough to keep them quiet, for the time being at least.

Downstairs, Frank was coming to his senses. It was six-thirty in the morning, the time he usually got up for work. He recalled what Lottie had begun to tell him about Amy's visitor, and he remembered how, when pressed, she had fought with him at the top of the stairs, sending him all the way to the bottom.

Muttering and mumbling, he paced the floor, punching one fist into the other, occasionally going to the bottom of the stairs and listening for her approach. 'I can wait,' he whispered wickedly. 'You see to the brats, then I'll see to *you*!'

The minute Lottie approached the room he was waiting for her. With a swift, unexpected move he had her by the ears. 'You were telling me about this man who came to see your mam.' Snatching her into the room, he slammed shut the door and pinned her against it. 'You didn't tell me everything though, did you, eh?'

Like all bullies in the face of danger, Lottie was terrified.

'Leave me alone!' Wishing she'd had more sense than to open her mouth in the first place, she began to panic. 'He came to see Mam, and that's all I know.'

'Don't you lie to me, girl!' He tugged her to him, his voice low and sinister. 'You told me how he'd come to take her away. He kissed her, that's what you said. What else did you hear, eh? I know you'd have hid away where they couldn't see you . . . spying like you always do.' Cajoling now, he chucked her under the chin. 'What did they talk about, Lottie? Tell your dad now, there's a good girl.'

'I never heard anything else.' Even now, trembling with fear, Lottie's quick mind could see a way to make herself some money. 'He went away,' she said. 'Our Eddie messed himself and Mam had to send the man away.'

Unsure, Frank shook his head. 'You'd better not be lying to me.'

'Honest to God, Dad, I wouldn't.'

'This man . . . what did he look like?'

'He were kind of old – same as you. He had dark hair, but it were a bit grey in places.'

'What were his name?'

'I'm not sure.'

'His name!' Bringing his fist up he clouted his daughter hard across the head. 'Tell me, or I'll knock the living daylights out of you.'

Reeling from the blow, Lottie looked at him with hatred. 'I think Mam called him Jack,' she answered sullenly.

'Jack!' Stepping back a pace he relaxed his grip. 'Jack who?'

'Just Jack, that's all I heard.'

'About my age, you say?'

Still seething, Lottie nodded.

'My God!' Shocked to his roots, he stared into her face. 'There's only one Jack that I know of, and that's Jack

Mason . . . one of your mam's fancy men from way back.'

Taking hold of her again, he shook the girl hard. 'Did he say where he was going – where he was staying? If he reckons to take her away from me, he can think again. He can't do anything – not with her in the infirmary, he can't. He'll be holed up somewhere, waiting. *Think*, lass. Where can I find him?' Find him and break his bloody neck, Frank thought grimly. Amy was *his* woman, and any man who thought to steal her away would have to come through *him* first.

'Leave me alone!' Twisting from his grip, she sent him stumbling. 'I don't know anything.'

As she ran down the passage and out the front door, his voice sailed after her. 'Come back 'ere, you little bitch!' But Lottie was already halfway down the street.

She had things to do. Money to make, and no time to lose.

Like the other guests staying at the modest Darwen Hotel, Jack Mason was up and about, seated in the bar and partaking of a bacon buttie and a huge mug of tea. 'I'm sorry, lass, you can't come in here.' Having spied her from across the room, the landlord barred Lottie's way. 'What is it you want?'

Pointing to Jack, who was too deep in thought to know what was going on, she answered, 'I've come to see him.'

'Wait there.' Closing the door, he shut her out.

A minute later the door opened and Jack was looking down on her. 'You're one of Amy's young 'uns . . . Lottie, isn't it?' He recalled how she had been the defiant one. A quick glance at the clock told him it was only half past seven. 'What the devil are you doing out so early of a morning? And why are you here?' Hope shone in his eyes. 'Did your mam send you?'

'No.'

'Then what do you want with me?' Hope faded and despair set in.

'I've summat to tell you.'

'I'm listening.' Intrigued, he waited. Either Amy was coming or she wasn't. And if she wasn't, then why was the girl here? All Amy had needed to do was not turn up. That was the loose arrangement, and one which would have told him all he needed to know.

What Lottie said next only increased his curiosity.

'I'm not talking here, where everyone can see.' All eyes were on them, and Lottie was clever enough to know that anything overheard now could land her in trouble later.

'In that case,' he closed the door behind him, 'we'd best take a wander.'

Lottie had an idea. 'You can take me for a toasted teacake and a brew in the Railway Café,' she suggested. 'It's allus open.'

He smiled. 'You've got it all figured out, eh?' As far as he was concerned, it was tantamount to blackmail, but if it was to do with Amy he wasn't about to argue. She was the only reason he was here, and if there was the slightest chance he could take her back with him, he would move heaven and earth. But the choice had to be Amy's. That was the only way.

'Why are you here?' he asked. 'Is your mam all right? If she's come to any harm, I need to know.'

'I'm not talking on the street.' Casting her eyes to right and left, Lottie satisfied herself that they weren't being watched. If she was to tell him where her mam was, and make him pay into the bargain, it wouldn't do for all and sundry to see them together – especially now, when her dad was out for blood.

The walk to the station wasn't far, down towards the boulevard and up along Ainsworth Street, and there it was, a grand building with iron structures and huge arches at the entrance.

The small, homely café was situated inside. With its pretty net curtains, young, friendly waitresses and inviting smells of newly baked bread and hot soups, it was very popular, though for the moment, and much to Lottie's relief, there were few customers about. 'Yes, sir, can I take your order?' With her rosy cheeks and ready smile, the young woman was a breath of fresh air.

Jack gave the order. 'One toasted teacake and a pot of tea for two, please.'

The order was soon delivered, but not quickly enough for Lottie, who wanted the whole thing over and done with. In a soft, intimate voice, she began, 'You want our mam to come away with you, ain't that right?'

He snorted. 'Huh! There's not much you don't know, is there?'

'How much would it be worth if I were to tell you summat?'

He studied her for a moment, wondering how someone so young could be so mercenary. 'Depends on what you have to tell me.'

'Summat that might get our mam to come away with you.'

Slapping his wallet on the table, Jack kept his hand over it. 'There's more than a guinea in there,' he confided quietly. 'If I could persuade your mam to come away with me, there'd be another guinea on top of that.'

Bending forward, she smiled up at him. 'How do I know I can trust you?'

Sitting back in his seat, he took a long, deep breath. 'My God! You're a right little rogue, aren't you, eh?' Moving in closer, he looked her in the eye. 'I don't know what game you're playing, young lady, but I'll warn you now: if you're trying to get one over on Jack Mason, you'd best think again!'

Lottie was adamant. 'I'm telling you . . . summat happened last night, after you'd gone. I'm sure our mam would never have gone with you before. But if you were to ask her now, she'd be of a different mind, I reckon.'

'Don't talk to me in riddles.' Grabbing the girl by the wrist, he held her in a vice-like grip. 'If you've something to say, then *say* it.'

Having faced her manic father, Lottie was unafraid. 'The money first.'

Opening his wallet, Jack took out two ten-shilling notes and a shilling coin. 'Well?'

Reaching out, Lottie took the money. 'There was real trouble after you'd gone. Early this morning, it was. Me dad never came home till one o'clock.'

'What kind of trouble?' Jack felt very uneasy.

Sparkling with excitement and malice, Lottie whispered, 'Our dad found out you'd been to the house. He knows you want to take Mam away.'

'Jesus!' Jerking away, Jack seemed at a loss for words.

'There was a big row and, like I say . . . summat happened.'

Now he was leaning forward again. 'For Chrissake, Lottie!'

'If you go to her now, she'll welcome you with open arms.' Enticing him further, she revealed, 'It's no use going to the house though, 'cos she ain't there no more.'

Jack really believed at this point that he might find pleasure in strangling her. 'What d'you mean, she isn't there? Where the bloody hell is she then?'

'Somewhere you won't be allowed in – not without me, you won't.'

'Take me there. *Now!*'

'Not until I've had the rest of my money.'

Realising he might scare her away, he softened his tone. 'You'll have your money, I promise you. Just as soon as I see your mam.'

'All right. But I still want the money, even if she won't come with you after all.' Lottie had long ago learned how to cover her back.

He nodded. 'As soon as I've made sure she's all right, you'll have your money, whether she comes away with me or not. I promise.'

There was a moment when he feared she might not go along with him, but then she grinned and he knew he was safe. 'All right,' she agreed, 'but if I don't get the rest of my money, I'll tell our dad where you are, and he'll pull your bleedin' head orf!'

Chuckling, Jack had to admire her. 'You remind me of myself when I was your age.' In a more serious tone he warned, 'There are them as you can trust and them as you can't. And there's them as would cut your throat for a shilling. Watch yourself, young 'un. It's a big, bad world out there. Stay alert, and mind you don't get sucked in too deep.'

He knew she would not be taught by others. People like Lottie had to learn from their own experiences. Some survived, some didn't. All he could do for Amy's child was to offer advice. Whether she took it or not was up to her.

Chapter Four

'Get me off this bloody bedpan! Me arse is stuck to it!' The woman's voice echoed round the maternity ward, alerting the young woman next to her.

'What's wrong, Agnes?' she asked. 'What's all the shouting about?'

'Oh, I'm sorry, lass. I don't want to spoil yer breakfast, but I've finished with the bedpan and the nurse is nowhere in sight.' The older woman was in her early forties, but had not missed a year without having a bairn. Misshapen and contented, she was now the proud mother of twelve; it would have been fifteen, but she had lost three in their infancy. 'Only it seems like I've been on this bedpan for ever,' she complained. 'What's more, it's damned cold. I'm in here to have a bairn, not to catch bleedin' pneumonia.'

Looking down the ward, she began yelling again until, red-faced and flustered, the nurse hurried to her bedside. 'Now then, Agnes, what's the matter with you? You know very well we're short-staffed and I'm having to serve breakfast on my own. If you keep yelling and screaming like that I'll have to put you in a side ward, where you can't disturb anybody.'

'It's not my fault if you're short-staffed.' Agnes was not easily intimidated. 'I've been on this bedpan so long, my arse has gone to sleep.'

Expertly slipping the bedpan out, the nurse quietly confided, I've been busy with Mrs Tattersall.'

'What, the emergency, you mean?' Peering up the ward, to where Amy lay pale and seemingly lifeless, Agnes respectfully lowered her voice. 'Is the lass all right?' Riddled with shame, she was made to realise how her own complaint was a trivial thing in comparison to Amy's ordeal.

The nurse was grateful for Agnes's change of mood. 'You know it was panic stations when she was brought in earlier – well, she's lost the bairn, I'm afraid.'

'Oh, I'm really sorry to hear that.' She noticed the young woman sitting beside Amy, so quiet and pretty. 'Is that her daughter?'

The nurse confirmed it. 'Her name's Molly. She wouldn't leave her mam's side, not even for a minute.' Lowering her voice again, she admitted, 'I don't mind telling you, there was a moment or two when I thought we'd lost both mother *and* child.'

Mortified, Agnes slid beneath the sheets. 'I'm sorry to be such a nuisance,' she apologised, 'only me arse is that fat it tends to get wedged if I'm left too long on the pan.' She grinned. 'Never mind, eh? I'm right as ninepence now, so go about your business, dearie, and you'll not hear another peep out of me.'

The nurse nodded. 'Thank the Lord for small mercies,' she murmured, walking away at a rapid pace. She knew from past experience, however, that despite her good intentions, it wouldn't be too long before Agnes was yelling for attention once more.

Emotionally drained, Molly had remained by her mother's side throughout. She had seen it all and was devastated by it. 'I'm sorry, Mam,' she murmured. 'I wish we hadn't lost the little fella.'

Weary and contrite, Amy gazed up at her. 'It's a strange thing, lass,' she replied softly, 'but you see, it's as though . . .' Shrugging, she fell silent, the tears brimming in her eyes but never falling.

Concerned, Molly took hold of her mother's hand. 'What are you trying to say, Mam?'

It seemed an age before Amy answered. 'The bairn . . . me . . . everything.' Looking down, she absent-mindedly twined the bedspread round and round between her fingers. 'Oh, love! Isn't it wicked, the way life plays tricks on us all?' Choking back the tears, she turned away. 'Pay no attention to me,' she urged. 'Go on home now. You look beat.'

'Rosie's looking after the young 'uns. Besides, I'm going nowhere yet,' Molly persisted. 'You started saying something, Mam. If there's summat troubling you, it might help to talk about it.'

'You're probably right. What's more, you're the only one who ever listens.'

'I'm listening now.' Molly had an inkling of what was on her mam's mind, but she daren't even think about it.

Sighing long and deep, Amy opened her heart. 'God forgive me, lass, but the awful truth is . . . I never wanted that little bairn.'

It was what Molly had half expected. Knowing how difficult it must be for her mam to confide such a thing, she waited, giving her time to compose herself.

Amy hesitated. It was a shameful confession she had never wanted to make, especially to Molly.

'I know that sounds terrible,' she murmured, 'and it makes me look like a hard woman, and happen I am, but if I am it's your dad who's made me like that. I'm tired of being as big as a ship from one year's end to another; too heavy to walk, legs like pit props, and so weary at the end of a day I could lay down in the gutter and sleep . . . that's how it's always been with your dad. You see, Molly, right from the start I never wanted all them childer, only what could I do?' Filled with remorse, she let the tears spill over.

Molly understood and told her so. 'What with one thing and another, you've been through a bad experience,' she said tenderly. 'It's bound to take a while but, God willing, you'll be fine, Mam. Just give yourself time.'

'Any other woman would be heartbroken at what's happened,' Amy insisted. 'Only I can't grieve, you see? There was no love in me for the child.' A sob caught in her throat. 'Is that so bad?'

Molly despaired at seeing her mam like this. Normally Amy was strong as a bull elephant; she had always seemed able to cope with anything. Now, seeing her low and vulnerable, Molly's heart went out to her. 'Don't punish yourself, Mam,' she pleaded. 'What's happened can't be undone. None of it was your fault, the doctor told you that.'

Through her tears, Amy gave the tiniest smile. 'I've never turned your father away, but I should have done. I should have had more respect for myself than to keep giving in to his drunken demands. Only, well . . . you must know what he's like. So overpowering – a real bully when he can't get his own way. I've always had to give in, if only for the sake of peace and quiet.'

'Ssh.' Moving closer, Molly drew Amy's head to her breast. 'You don't need to apologise for *anything*,' she said. 'Not to me . . . not to *anybody*!' Anger filled her soul. She knew the way of things, for hadn't she heard her dad time and again, laying down his demands? And hadn't she herself fought down a feeling of nausea and hatred because of it?

Having mustered the courage to confide, Amy had a need to empty her heart to someone, and unlike Lottie, she knew Molly would never betray her. 'Sometimes I feel as if I've never had a life of my own,' she told her eldest daughter. 'It's like I've missed out on everything, and now it's all too late. Your dad will never change, I can see that now.' All her children had been born at home, with Maggie in attendance. Now, one step back from the awful situation with Frank, she had somehow gained a new insight into her miserable life.

Molly did her best to reassure her. 'It's got to be different from now on, Mam,' she said. 'I'll talk to Dad. I'll tell him how we nearly lost you, as well as the bairn. I'll warn him that things have got to change. *He'll* have to change!'

'He can't change, lass. He doesn't know how.' Bowing her head, Amy quietly wept. Her tears had been suppressed over the years, and only now were they released. 'I know you mean well, but it's too late. Like a fool, I've let it go on for too long, until there's nothing I can say or do that will make him change his ways.'

Knowing it to be the truth, Molly felt helpless. 'Do you still love him, Mam?' The thought had never entered her head before but now, somehow, it seemed all-important.

Amy shook her head. 'I stopped loving him a long time ago,' she murmured. 'To be honest, I don't know if I ever *did* love him.' Looking up, she confessed, 'There was someone else, you see.' Her fleeting smile was incredibly beautiful. 'Someone I gave my heart to a long time ago.'

Molly was intrigued but strangely, not shocked. 'I never knew.'

'No one did.'

'Who is he?'

Amy laughed. 'He was as crazy as they come; you never knew from one minute to the next what he was up to. He had these grand plans, you see. But they never came to anything.' Until now, she realised with astonishment, because *now* all his dreams seemed to have come true – except for having her. But then, he had given up that right after he walked away when she needed him most!

'We all have dreams, Mam.' Molly knew this more than most, especially where she and Alfie were concerned.

'He made me laugh, you know. He was a wide boy and a waster, but oh, he did make me laugh.' Remembering, Amy shook her head and tutted. 'You wouldn't believe the things he got involved in. One minute he was rich as a king, and the next as poor as a church mouse.'

Molly had never seen her mam this way before, her voice soft and caressing, her face aglow with joy. It was obvious this former sweetheart was etched deep in Amy's heart. 'How long did you know him?'

'Long enough to know there'd come a day when he would break my heart.' In the end, that was exactly what Jack Mason had done.

The bitterness in her mother's voice was a stark contrast to the happiness that had lit her face only a moment ago. 'And did he?'

Mentally shaking herself, Amy glanced up. 'Did he what?'

'Break your heart?'

Realising she couldn't explain what had happened without Molly learning the truth of her birth, Amy skirted the question.

All the same, fired by the past, and eager to share some of it, she went on, 'We were all friends together . . . me and Frank, and Jack Mason – that was his name. Then there was Bernard and Richard Brindle and the other Brindle brothers – Billy, Joe, Harry, Sonny and Alec . . . three sisters an' all – Anita, Winnie and Mary Jane.' She chuckled warmly. 'By! We did have some fun though. Me and Frank started courting, and as for Jack the Lad, well, he had one sweetheart after another, and none of them lasted more than a fortnight. After a time, he upped sticks and moved on and nobody knew where he'd gone.'

Molly was beginning to see the whole picture. 'You liked him, didn't you, Mam?' she said. 'I mean, *really* liked him.'

'Yes, lass, I did.' Amy's tender smile betrayed her. 'I were that upset when he left. But he did come back a few months later. By that time though, I were promised to Frank.'

'And did you never tell Dad how you loved somebody else?'

'I daren't,' she admitted. 'Frank had such a fiery temper even in them days. I did tell him I wasn't sure whether we should get wed so soon, and happen we were being too hasty.' She recalled the shocking rows. 'Frank were that angry he took off with the fairground for a time. After he'd gone, me and Jack went out a few times, and for a while I thought he loved me, too.' Resentment set in. 'He didn't care about commitment though, or family. He didn't want to be tied down. All he ever wanted was a bloody good time!'

'So what happened?'

'Frank came back and did his best to warn me off Jack. "He's no good," he said. "He'll use you then he'll be off, like always."'

Amy's eyes clouded over. 'He were right, o' course. Jack Mason was a rogue and a charmer, and he'd have the drawers off you before you even knew what was happening . . .' she chuckled at the memory '. . . but I was in love for the first time in my life, and I wasn't about to listen to *anybody*, let alone Frank!'

'But it obviously didn't work out, did it?'

'I always thought it would but no, lass. It all went wrong.'

Molly's curiosity had built with the telling of the tale. 'So, how did you come to be married to Dad, instead of to this Jack?'

'It's a long story,' Amy answered warily. 'All water under the bridge.' Frank had married her without knowing she was carrying Jack's child, and Amy had vowed she would take the secret to the grave. To this day, nobody knew.

Dear God, she thought now. If Molly knew she was Jack's child, what would she say? How would she take it? Happen it was her right to know, and happen it would only turn her whole world upside down if she did.

'Jack went away again, didn't he?' Molly realised. 'And you picked up with Dad?'

Amy's voice grew cold. 'There was a terrible fight. Jack put Frank in the hospital. When he came out he went looking for Jack, but he was long gone. We never saw him again.'

And now he's back, she thought bitterly. Oh, she was not an innocent, but some of the fault for what had happened had to lie with Jack. If only he had taken her with him all those years ago, she would never have given herself to Frank. She might have had a better life. She might have been happy, instead of being treated like the dirt under Frank's shoes.

'I'm sorry, Mam.'

'So am I, lass. I'm sorry about Jack being the way he was, and I'm sorry about the life I've led with your dad. But most of all, I'm sorry about the bairn.' Haunted by guilt, Amy couldn't forgive herself. 'Happen if I'd wanted it enough . . .' She covered her face with her hands. 'It were too much! Another bairn, and Eddie only just two years old, Bertha not yet four . . . then Milly and Georgie. All bairns. All dragging on me, day after day. And at night your dad the same, *dragging* on me, using me for his own selfish ends, the same as he's always done. A belly full o' booze, and me underneath him while he satisfies himself. That's all he's ever cared about, the bastard!'

Concerned, Molly spoke firmly. 'You mustn't get yourself all worked up like this, Mam,' she said. 'I'm on your side, and I'll do all I can to help you.' Wiping the sweat from Amy's face, she pleaded, 'Be strong, Mam, or you'll make yourself really ill.'

'You're right, lass.' The rage began to die down. 'We all have a cross to bear. Besides, it doesn't do to rake up the past.' She settled down into the bed, sighed, 'What's gone is gone.' Yet it wasn't gone, was it, because Jack was here, waiting for her. Not for long though. He'd clear off soon enough.

And with him would go her only chance of escape.

* * *

As Molly prepared to leave, her heart ached for this poor, unhappy woman who was her mother. It was not hard to understand how she felt and, given the same circumstances, Molly wondered how she herself would have coped.

For now though, there was little she could do to ease her mother's heartache. Not least because there were things here she didn't understand. Things that seemed to have taken place long before she was born.

Quieter now, Amy held her daughter's hand, her pretty eyes shining with pride. 'You're the best of them all, Molly. All these years, it's only you who's kept me sane.' Kept her sane and kept her dreams alive, because in Molly, she saw the past, and the past had been her greatest joy.

'I'd best go now, Mam.' Choked with emotion, Molly placed a kiss on Amy's brow then eased herself away. 'Rest now,' she ordered. 'I'll be back later on today, with a clean nightgown and anything else I can think to bring.' Apologising, she explained, 'I can't come straight back. I'll have the young 'uns to see to.'

In the end, Amy wasn't sorry to see her eldest daughter leave. Right now, she needed to be alone with her thoughts. 'Bye, lass.'

'Bye, Mam.' Glancing up the ward Molly saw the nurse approaching with the breakfast trolley. 'Try and eat something,' she said. 'Keep your strength up.'

'Molly?'

She turned. 'Yes, Mam?'

'Thank you, lass.'

Molly smiled down on her. 'It'll be all right, Mam. You'll see.'

In her heart though, she knew that nothing would ever be all right again.

Having learned from Lottie that her mother was in Blackburn Infirmary, Jack lost no time in rushing to be with her.

Anxious for her money, Lottie had followed him. 'I've taken

you right to where she is, and now I want my dues,' she whined. Nothing he could say would shake her off his trail.

'Keep on the way you are,' he said, 'and you may well live to regret it.'

'Oh, and what's that supposed to mean. Gonna murder me, are yer?' She took an involuntary step backwards.

Amazed, Jack laughed out loud. 'Good God! I might be guilty of some shady deals in my time, but murder isn't one of them. All I'm trying to say is this: you seem to have no sense of shame. What you're doing now is tantamount to blackmail but, worse than that, you've betrayed your own two parents. Oh, don't get me wrong, I've no qualms where your dad is concerned, but I think your mother deserves better consideration than you've shown her.'

'Huh! I suppose you think I've sold her out?' In fact, that was exactly what she had done, and she knew it.

'Your words, not mine,' he answered wryly.

Lottie was not easily shamed. 'Give me the money an' I'll be on my way.'

'You're going down a hard road,' he warned sombrely.

His words were wasted. 'What I do is none of your business, mister! As for betraying my dad, he's just rubbish. I don't want advice from you or anybody else. All I want is my money. I've kept my side of the bargain. Now it's your turn!'

Shaking his head, Jack felt in the back pocket of his trousers and drew out a handful of half-crowns. 'That should do it.' Planting the cash into her open palm, he began to walk up the infirmary steps.

Dogmatic as ever, Lottie followed him. 'Hey, mister, you're a liar! You said you didn't have no more money on yer.'

Turning, he smiled. 'Lies,' he answered, 'from one rogue to another. Now clear off. And you'd better not be leading me a dance!'

'I'm not. Me mam's in there all right, just like I told yer.' With that she went off, quietly singing and counting her money.

Taking the steps two at a time, Jack strode into the reception area, where he made straight for the nurse at the desk. 'Amy Tattersall,' he said. 'Can you tell me which ward she's in?'

Regarding him with some surprise, the nurse answered warily, 'She is in the Martha Grant Ward. But it's too early for visiting, I'm afraid. Are you a relative?'

Playing it safe, Jack decided not to answer. 'She was brought in earlier today.' Fearful he might be sent away, his heart sank to his boots. 'I *must* see her. I have to be sure she's all right.'

'Well, I dare say I could turn a blind eye for five minutes, but no more.'

'Thank you, nurse.' He turned to find the ward, but was stopped in his tracks.

'You'll have to wait though, sir,' she said. 'There's already someone with her. Mrs Tattersall has been through a bad ordeal. I'm sorry, but I can't allow more than one person in at a time.'

'I'll wait.' Determined, he informed her: 'I'm certainly not leaving until I've seen her.'

A look of horror spread over her plump features. 'Oh, I'm so sorry. You must be Mr Tattersall . . . the husband?'

Allowing her to assume that he was Amy's husband, he explained, 'I couldn't get here any earlier. I was on a late shift, you see. I've only just been told.'

Mortified, the nurse apologised. 'I understand. But she's still very weak, so I really can't allow more than one visitor.' Seeing how concerned he was, she suggested, 'I'll go in and bring your daughter out, if you like?'

Jack was startled at the news that one of Amy's daughters was with her. Probably Molly, he thought, and graciously declined. 'How long will she be, do you think?'

'Only a minute or two now,' she answered. 'I've already reminded her it's time to leave.'

'Is Amy in any danger?'

The nurse shook her head.

The last thing he wanted was to come face to face with Amy's daughter. 'Then I'll wait.' It was his only option in the circumstances.

Curious as to why he had not asked for more information, the nurse gestured to a nearby chair. 'Take a seat. I'll see if I can organise a cup of tea for you.'

'Thank you.' The nurse seemed nervous, he thought. 'I came straight from work,' he began, but when she looked at his smart clothes with some surprise, he quickly added, 'I was attending a Union meeting. I'm the shop steward, you see. Wherever there's trouble, you'll find me there, looking out for the workers.'

'I see.' Again, he got the distinct impression that she was uncomfortable in his presence.

'Excuse me, nurse?' There was something about her manner that unsettled him. Lottie had told him there had been a terrible row, and that her mam was crippled with pain. 'I was told she might have gone into labour. Did she have the bairn?' Again the nurse began to fidget. 'She *is* all right, isn't she?' he insisted.

'Look, Mr Tattersall, by the time you come out from seeing your wife, the doctor should be free. He'll answer all your questions far better than I can.' Moving away, she told him, 'I'll let him know you'll want to see him before you leave.'

Convinced that something was terribly wrong with Amy, he ran after the nurse. 'No, wait!' Catching up with her, he spun her round by the shoulders. '*You* tell me! You said Amy was all right. Were you lying? Did something go wrong? I want to know!'

Swallowing hard, the woman began, 'Mrs Tattersall is fine, but . . .' she took a deep breath '. . . there were complications with the baby.' Frustration swept through her. 'The doctor will explain. Please, Mr Tattersall, go and sit down. I'll find the doctor and ask him to see you now.' With that, she passed him on to a nearby auxiliary. 'See Mr Tattersall back to the waiting area, will you, please?'

As Jack paced the floor, he was so preoccupied that he didn't notice Molly emerge from the ward until he collided with her.

Apologising profusely, he looked into the young woman's face and was momentarily taken aback; despite the bruises already rising on her temple and cheek, he had the oddest feeling he knew her from somewhere. 'I'm sorry,' he muttered. 'I haven't hurt you, have I?'

Molly smiled, but it was a weary smile. 'No,' she answered. 'Besides, I should have looked where I was going.' Without another word she went on her way, and he, after first glancing about to make sure the nurse was not around, made his way into the ward and up to Amy's bed.

Amy couldn't believe her eyes when she saw him. 'What on earth are *you* doing here?' she hissed. 'Who told you where I was?'

'It doesn't matter who told me,' he whispered, cupping her face in his hands. 'You're all right, just like the nurse said. That's all I needed to know.'

Amy didn't have to guess any further. '*Lottie* told you, didn't she? The little devil . . . listening on the stairs, I might have known it. And I bet she wheedled money out of you, didn't she?'

'She told me there was a row. That Frank was drunk and started throwing his weight about. I was worried about you, my darling.'

'It's a pity you weren't worried years ago, when it mattered.'

Her bitter comment was justified, so he let it go. Noticing the deepening bruise on her wrist, he cradled her hand in both of his. 'If he's harmed you, I swear to God—'

'Stop it!' Snatching her arm away she told him contemptuously, 'Fighting – is that all you men understand?'

'The bastard won't get away with it, I can promise you that.'

'Go away, Jack,' she ordered. 'It's none of your business. I'll not have you interfering, d'you hear me?'

He quietly regarded her; the pale, bruised features and the sadness in her brown eyes, and he felt more in love than ever before. 'I only want *you*,' he murmured. 'Just you, and to hell with everything else.'

'That's what you said then.' And just like then, his gaze swept over her and she was lost. 'I don't want you here, Jack,' she whispered lamely. 'I don't need you.'

Slowly, he leaned forward, his eyes on hers and his hands either side of her face. When his mouth came down on hers she melted into him, and he knew she needed him, too. 'I'll wait for you,' he murmured, drawing away. 'Nothing's changed.'

The sadness intensified. 'I lost the bairn,' she whispered, a solitary tear trickling down her face. 'I didn't want it, and the Lord took it from me, like I deserved.'

Realising why the nurse was so jittery, he held Amy close. 'Don't go back to him,' he pleaded. 'You've given him your best years, and he's thrown them away. Do as I ask, Amy. Whenever you're able, come away with me. *Please!*'

'Can I bring the children?' Still smarting from all that had happened, she asked more out of duty than love.

'You know I don't want that, Amy.'

'Eddie then, and Bertha. They're only bairns.'

'No, Amy. I'm sorry . . . really.'

'I've already lost one bairn, Jack. I don't want to lose them all.' Part of her wanted freedom, yet part of her was afraid.

'The children will survive. They'll have their father. And there's Molly. You said yourself, she's a gem. She'll take care of them. All I want is for you and me to have a life. We've earned it, Amy. Surely you can see that?'

She drew away. 'You're asking the impossible.' Yet, in the light of what Frank had done, what he would continue to do at every given turn, didn't *she* have a right to some kind of happiness before it was too late? Or was it already too late?

Dear God, how she wanted to leave! How she wanted to close that door behind her and never again be afraid. But how could she? What of the children? If she did as Jack asked, what would become of them?

A great tide of guilt swept through her. The truth was, she felt ready now. She was desperate to take what she wanted, and to hell with everything else, as Jack would say. But she wasn't Jack. In all her life she had never shirked her responsibilities, especially where the children were concerned. Whatever had transpired between her and Frank, it was no more the children's fault than it was hers.

'I want you to go now, Jack,' she told him softly.

Undeterred, he told her, 'When you're better, I want you with me. We'll go anywhere you like – America, Paris, London. Just name it and it's yours.'

'I can't.'

'You *can* . . . if you really want to.' He kissed her again, a wonderful, warm kiss, the like of which she had not experienced in a very long time. 'I can wait until you're better. I've a few old pals to look up, and a bit of business to see to. That should fill the time in between.'

'Don't hang around on my account, Jack,' she warned, 'and don't come looking for me again.'

'As you say, sweetheart. But when I leave I want you by my side.'

'Then you'll be disappointed.'

He smiled, a small, hopeful kind of smile. Then he held her

hand, kissed her fleetingly, and left her there.

Her face expressionless, Amy watched him walk down the ward. She watched him open the door without a backward glance, and for one incredible minute she wanted to shout his name; to ask if he would take her away *now*, before she had a chance to change her mind.

Then the door closed and he was gone. 'Goodbye, Jack,' she whispered. 'I'll always love you.'

Chapter Five

'I'm sorry I'm late.' Flushed and anxious, Molly came rushing in. 'I got to finish work early so I could pop in and see Mam, and the bus was late as usual,' she explained breathlessly. 'Honest to God, you'd think they could be on time just for once!'

Rosie took her bag and led her to the armchair. 'Sit yourself down, child,' she ordered firmly. 'You look all in.'

'Where are they?' Molly's first thought was for the children.

'Aw now, don't you worry your head about them,' Rosie answered with a grin. 'They're all fed and watered and won't give you a halfpence worth o' trouble. Eddie's asleep in his pram in the back yard, Bertha's upstairs out to the world, and Milly's in the front parlour drawing pictures to her heart's content.'

'Is Lottie home yet?'

'Home and out again.' Rosie snorted with disgust. 'If you ask me, your sister hasn't been to work at all!'

Groaning, Molly admitted, 'She's beginning to be real trouble. I just don't know how to deal with her any more.' Lottie had always been a bit of a heartache, but ever since their mam had been away, she seemed hellbent on making life difficult.

Rosie agreed. 'Aye well, she's a law unto herself is that one.'

Molly's eyes roved round the room. 'And where's our Georgie?' Although she would never admit it, Georgie was her favourite. With his infectious sense of humour and willingness to help wherever he could, the lad was a tonic in these dark days.

Hesitating momentarily, Rosie said, 'Lottie took him to the fairground.'

'Why?' Letting one of the children tag along was so unlike Lottie. It made Molly suspicious.

'Because he wouldn't let her go without him, that's why. "I want to ride the horses," he said. She tried her heaven's best to shake him off, but he was having none of it.'

Practical as ever, Molly objected, 'But he hasn't got any money.'

'I gave him a bob to spend – though judging by the money I caught her counting, Lottie had enough for both of them.'

'Hmh! Not from working for it, I'll be bound.'

Rosie agreed. 'But there's no use you worrying. Have a talk with her when she gets back home if you've a mind.' Her voice sharpened with anger. 'And while you're at it, ask her why she sent the lad home on his own, in tears.' Shaking her fist as she spoke, she went on, 'I never would have let him go with her if I thought she'd abandon him like that!'

Taking off her jacket, Molly hung it on the doornail. 'Where is he now?'

'In the front parlour. I managed to get some food down him, but he wouldn't talk to me. "I want our Molly," he said, and since then he's been in the parlour, listening to the wireless.'

'Thanks, Rosie. I'll see what I can find out.'

Going along the passage to the front parlour, she opened the door softly, and there was Georgie fast asleep on the rug, the wireless full on and his face still grubby with tears. 'Hello, love,' she said. She knelt beside him. 'Georgie, it's me.'

Opening his eyes, it took a minute for his senses to focus and then he was in her arms, sobbing about how Lottie 'went off with a man, and told me to find my own way home'.

Molly forced a smile. 'It's all right, sweetheart,' she murmured, 'don't upset yourself. Just tell me quietly. What happened?'

The boy sighed, then he wiped his snotty nose on the cuff of his shirt and, just as Molly had instructed, he told her the whole story. 'She gave me threepence and told me to go away. Only, I got on the wrong bus, and had to walk all the way home from King Street.' His lip quivered.

Recounting the incident was too much for him. 'I were scared,' he wept. 'I couldn't find my way, and then this woman asked me if I were lost. She brought me to the end of the street . . .'

'Ssh. That's enough for now.' Reassuring him that all was well now, and he was safely home, Molly made a suggestion that caused his eyes to light up. 'I bet you'd like a big mug of Ovaltine, wouldn't you? All hot and frothy, the way Mam makes it?'

Wiping his tears away, she took him into the kitchen. Rosie must have been listening at the door, for she was already making a mug of Ovaltine, and a jam buttie. 'There ye are, me darlin',' she cooed. 'Your big sister's home now, and everything's all right.' And so it was.

Lowering their voices, Molly and Rosie discussed the day's events while the little boy enjoyed his supper.

'What in God's name possessed her to abandon him like that?' Molly wondered.

'I don't know any more than you do, me darlin',' Rosie sighed, 'but I know this much. If you don't stop fretting, you'll drive yourself crazy!' She felt for the girl. At eighteen, Molly was not much older than Lottie herself. It didn't seem right that she should be landed with such responsibility. 'Look, love, you've just got in, and I can see you've had a long day. The lad's come to no lasting harm, and besides, I dare say that little vixen is having a whale of a time, without a thought for anybody but herself. So, you sit down and put it all out of your mind.' Though she didn't believe for one minute that Molly could do such a thing.

'I'll swing for her, Rosie, I swear I will.'

'Tomorrow,' Rosie joked. 'You can swing for her tomorrow.'

Returning the smile, Molly kicked off her shoes and fell wearily into a chair. 'You're right. Whatever I say to her, she'll take no notice – she never does. But in future she won't take the childer out of this house, I'll make sure of it.'

'You can count on me, too,' Rosie promised, 'especially after what she did to young Georgie. He could have been molested or anything. It doesn't bear thinking about.'

'You're right, but like you say, he's home safe now. That's all that matters.' Drawing in a long breath, Molly gave a sigh that seemed to empty her heart and ease her mind, for the moment at least. 'You're a godsend, Rosie,' she declared gratefully. 'These past few days I don't know what we would have done without you.'

Rosie gave her a hug. 'I'm only too glad to do whatever I can, pet,' she answered. 'You've had a lot on yer plate, so ye have.'

'All the same, Rosie, you've been wonderful. I don't know how I'll ever repay you.'

'Just make my Alfie a good wife, that's all I ask. But then I know that's a foregone conclusion, so the debt's already paid . . . if ever there was one.'

Molly's heart was warmed. 'It won't be difficult to make Alfie a good wife,' she said. 'He's all I've ever wanted.'

In fact lately, Alfie was the one thing that had kept her going. Though she loved them all, the children were a real handful, and now, on top of that, she had just heard news which only increased her worries.

Astute as ever, Rosie saw the cloud come over her. 'What's wrong, love?'

Going to the back window, Molly checked to see that Eddie was still all right. 'What makes you think there's something wrong?' she asked. Eddie was fast asleep, just as Rosie had said.

Wisely, their neighbour didn't push the matter. If Molly wanted to confide in her, she would do so in her own good time. 'Listen, I've the kettle on,' she cajoled, 'and there's some of the apple pie that Maggie Lett brought round. There's corned beef left over from the children's tea, and a piece of barm-cake I made myself. What if I make us a couple of sandwiches and a brew. Then you can tell me how your mam is.' Rosie wisely surmised that, with a little encouragement, one thing could lead to another. Molly trusted her, she knew that.

Molly appreciated the offer. 'Thanks, Rosie. Tea and corned-beef sandwiches sound good to me.' She didn't really need the food and drink, but she *did* need someone she could confide in. Sandra was her best friend, but it was no good talking to her because, ever since she'd met this new fella, she'd gone all dreamy.

When they were seated round the table, the conversation first turned to Amy.

'And how is yer mam coping?' Molly had previously mentioned how quiet and preoccupied Amy was. 'More like her old self, is she? Wanting to get home as soon as she can?'

'To tell you the truth, I wouldn't blame her if she never wanted to set foot inside this house again.'

'I see.' Rosie wouldn't have blamed her either, although she was careful not to say as much. Until these past few days, she had not fully realised the way of things in this house. Now though, after minding the children while Molly went to work and visited her mam, the Irishwoman had glimpsed the life Amy led, and it sickened her.

Like Amy, she was caught up in a situation which gave her no peace, and no time to call her own. With an army of children running round her feet, constant squabbles and tears, noses and bottoms to wipe and mouths to feed, there were times when she didn't know which way to turn. But the worst time of all was when Frank Tattersall came home. Bad-tempered and drunk more often than not, he was a beast of a man.

Glancing discreetly at Molly, Rosie saw that she was lost in thought, no doubt concerned about her mam, and with good reason to be. 'She'll get over this, my pet, you'll see.'

Before answering, Molly sipped her tea. 'I don't know what to make of it. She worries me.' Looking up, she said quietly, 'There's summat playing on her mind, and I don't know what it is.'

'Ah well, it's only to be expected,' the other woman answered gently, 'what with losing the bairn and all.'

'It's not just that.' Molly was sure of it. 'There's summat else. When I tackle her, she tells me I'm imagining things, but I know her, and I know it's not just the bairn.'

'She might be fretting because yer da hasn't been to see her.' God help the poor woman, Rosie thought. I wouldn't want him anywhere near me, and that's a fact!

Molly gave a small, cynical laugh. 'I don't think it's that,' she answered. 'The last thing she says to me when I'm leaving is "Keep your dad away, love. Right now I don't want him within a mile of me!"'

Rosie nodded. 'And who can blame her, eh? Sure, isn't yer da the very reason she's lying there in the infirmary? Look now,' she glanced at the clock, 'half past five and there's not a hide nor hair of him. It wouldn't surprise me to see him come rolling home drunk at midnight.' Shaking her head, she muttered under her breath, 'He's enough to drive a saint to despair, so he is.'

Molly had a confession to make. 'D'you know, Rosie, sometimes I hate him.'

'Don't say that, lass.' Bad though he was, Frank was her

father when all was said and done. 'Hatred's a terrible thing. It can destroy you if yer not careful.'

Even though she knew Rosie was right, Molly gave no reply, for she had spoken the truth. God forgive her, there *were* times when she hated her dad. Lately she had wondered if they wouldn't all be better off without him.

More than anyone, Molly understood how her mam felt. The more responsibility she herself was made to take on, the more she had come to realise what a hell on earth Amy's life had been. 'I promised I'd go back and see her later, if that's all right with you, Rosie.' She had a feeling her mam needed her right now. 'I'll bath the children and get them off to bed.'

Always ready to help, Rosie agreed. 'Is that why yer feeling so down, lass . . . because of yer mam, and everything?'

'No, it's not just that.' Her voice wobbled.

'D'ye feel like talking about it?'

The girl took a deep breath. 'You'll know soon enough,' she answered, 'so I might as well tell you now. The truth is, I've lost my job. I got notice this morning.'

'What? I can't *believe* it!' Rosie was shocked. 'You've been at that cake shop ever since you left school. Mrs Parsons thinks highly of you – she was talking about putting you in charge, our Alfie said. Something about her wanting to spend more time with her family?'

'That's right,' Molly said slowly, 'but you know how it is, Rosie. Just when you think your life's running smoothly, every-thing goes wrong, and that's what happened to Mrs Parsons.'

'How d'you mean?'

'You remember how upset she was last year, when her eldest son left to work in London. Then soon after that, poor Mr Parsons was killed in an accident at work. The moment she started to recover from that, her daughter Lucy got wed and emigrated to Australia.'

Rosie nodded. 'If you ask me, it was a very selfish thing for the girl to do . . . going off and leaving her mam all alone so soon after her husband was killed.'

The very same thought had crossed Molly's mind but, 'Who are we to judge?' she asked softly. 'Happen we all have to cope with grief in our own way.'

'Yes, you're right there,' Rosie conceded. 'Only it seems hard on her poor mother, that's all I'm saying.'

'Harder than anyone realised,' Molly agreed. 'She never stopped missing Lucy, and you're right, she *did* have a mind to put me in charge of it all. "I can trust you", that's what she said. The idea was for her to go off when the fancy took her. That way she could see more of both her children – especially Lucy, who she always doted on.'

'Sure, there's nothing wrong with that. I feel the very same way about our Sandra.' Stretching out her long fingers, Rosie laughed. 'Though I don't mind admitting there are times when I could throttle her with me own bare hands!'

'You and me both,' Molly joked. 'But Sandra is Sandra, and unlike our Lottie, there's no malice in her.'

Wisely changing the subject, Rosie asked, 'What will you do – about your work, I mean?'

Sighing from her boots, Molly took a minute to answer. 'One thing's for sure,' she mused, 'Mrs Parsons won't change her mind. She's had word that Lucy is expecting her first baby. In the letter, Lucy says how she's frightened of being so far away, and she needs her mam. Now Mrs Parsons has a cash buyer for the shop, and he wants to close the deal as soon as possible.'

'Hmh! It's a shame you can't afford to buy it. You'd double the takings in no time with your bright ideas.'

Molly gave a small, whimsical smile. 'We'll never know now.'

'Maybe the new owner will keep you on.' Rosie knew how the customers respected Molly. 'If he has any sense he'll hang on to you for all he's worth.'

'No chance of that, I'm afraid.' Molly had been hoping the same. 'He has a wife and two daughters who'll help him run the shop. On top of that, he has plans to buy the empty premises next door. He reckons to knock down the dividing wall and run a café and cake shop alongside each other.'

'But that was *your* idea, wasn't it? I recall you saying how you'd mentioned it to Mrs Parsons and she went for it like a dog for a bone.'

'All the same, it's a good idea and should do well. I don't know why Mrs Parsons didn't think of it herself.'

'Ah, love! I am sorry.' Rosie knew from experience, it never rained but it poured.

Always an optimist, her future daughter-in-law shrugged. 'It's no good worrying about it. As from four o'clock on Friday, I'm out of a job. Come Monday, I'll be looking for work, and with a bit of luck it won't be long before I'm bringing home a wage again. The way things are, I can't afford not to.'

'You'll not be out of work long if I know you.' Rosie had every faith in her.

'Look, Rosie, I'm not sure when they'll let Mam home so I might need you to help me a while longer – with the children, I mean. Once I'm wage-earning again, I'll pay you.'

'You'll do no such thing!' Rosie was adamant. 'Sure, I'm pleased to be helping out, so I am. And I dare say your mam will be glad of my help, too, for a short time anyway, after she gets home.'

'You're a good friend to her, and me.' Molly was immensely grateful. 'But for her sake as well as mine, I've got to find work, and quickly.'

'Don't you worry, lass. It'll all come right in the end.'

Although, having learned more about the way of things in this house, even Rosie had her doubts.

Molly felt so much better for having talked things over with Rosie. She was such a kind, understanding soul. 'I feel a lot more confident now,' she confessed. 'With any luck, I'll not be out of work more than a day or so, then our mam will be home, and we can look to the future.'

But unfortunately, the future wasn't up to Molly Tattersall. It was up to Amy, her mother.

And she was hopelessly torn between the life she had, and the new life that beckoned.

That evening, after Rosie left to see to her own family, Molly bathed the children one by one, and got them ready for bed. 'When's Mammy coming home?' Bertha was missing Amy badly, more than any of the others.

Towelling her dry, Molly paused to wrap her in a bear hug. 'Soon, sweetheart,' she told her. 'Mammy will be home soon.'

Bertha's dark eyes swam with tears. 'Will she be here when I wake up?'

'No.' There was no use lying. 'But it won't be too long now, I promise.'

Struggling with her nightgown, her older sister Milly had a question. 'Will they give her another bairn to fetch home?'

'They can't do that,' Molly replied gently.

Bertha started crying. 'I want *our* bairn!'

'Well, you can't have it!' Popping her head through the neck of the nightgown, Milly gave what she considered a grown-up sigh. 'God took it back, because it wasn't strong enough to stay here. That's what Molly said, ain't it?'

'That's right, sweetheart.'

Pleased to have got it right, Milly wagged a finger at Eddie, who was splashing about in the tin bath. 'Mammy's feeling a bit sad, so when she comes home, you'll have to behave yourself!'

Wanting to play, Eddie flattened his hand and thumped it hard on the water, sending a spray all over the three girls. 'See!' Milly said indignantly. 'He just *won't* behave, will he?'

Plucking the infant from the bath, Molly wrapped him in the towel. 'When Mam gets home, you'll *all* have to behave.' Asking Milly to help Bertha put on her nightgown, she then dried young Eddie, fastened a terry square round his pink bottom, and pulled the comb through his wispy locks. When he cried, Milly said he was a big baby, but when it came to her having her hair brushed, she fought and struggled until Molly told her how Eddie and Bertha were watching. After that she was incredibly brave; Bertha, too, when it came to her turn.

As always, Georgie needed no telling. At eight years of age he was a little man, able to fend for himself and proud of it. After stripping off his clothes, he washed at the tin bath and got into his pyjamas. He combed his hair and presented himself to Molly. 'Shall I take the others upstairs?' he offered.

She gave him a well-deserved hug. 'I'll come up with you,' she said. It was good to see his little adventure had not marred him.

Like a mother hen, Molly ferried them up to their beds. She tucked them in and gave them each a goodnight kiss, and was choked with emotion when Bertha clung to her. 'I love you,' she said. Just a brief, simple remark, but spoken from the heart.

'I love you, too,' her big sister whispered, and creeping out of the room, she left them to their slumbers.

Leaning against the wall, she stayed on the landing for a time, her heart heavy and the tears very close. 'They miss you so much, Mam,' she murmured. 'Be strong, if only for them.' The truth was, she missed Amy, too. The house didn't seem the same without her.

* * *

77

Some short time later, having washed at the sink, brushed her hair and changed into a clean, white blouse and loose dark trousers, Molly was waiting for Rosie to return when the door opened. 'Now there's a pretty sight!' Handsome and cheeky as ever, Alfie hurried across the room, arms outstretched. 'Any chance of a kiss?' he enquired, then took it without waiting for her answer.

'You're full of yourself, aren't you?' Molly teased, and her joy in him was evident. When all else was going wrong in her life, Alfie was the one element that was right.

Leading her to the sofa, he kept his arm round her, his mood more serious. 'Mam says you had some bad news today?'

She nodded. 'Oh, I'll soon find something, don't worry.'

'I'm sure you will.' He winked. 'Once the word gets out, they'll be queuing up for you.'

'Huh!' Worried though she was, Molly had to laugh. 'I hope you're right.'

'I reckon you deserve a night out. How about you and me going to the flicks? The Odeon is open again at long last.'

'Sounds lovely, but I promised Mam I'd go back this evening. I'm worried about her, Alfie. She seems so strange.'

'What d'you mean, strange?'

'I'm not sure . . . kind of distant.' Molly couldn't put her finger on what was wrong. 'She had a slight infection, but that's all cleared up now, so it can't be that.'

'Have you spoken to the doctor?'

'I'm seeing him when I go back tonight. The nurse says he should tell me when we can bring her home – Sunday, she thinks, but she wouldn't commit herself.'

Hugging her close, he passed on Rosie's assurance. 'Our mam won't let you down, you know that.'

'I know.'

Tilting her face towards him, he kissed her on the mouth,

holding her close, and wondering when he should break his own news to her. It wouldn't be well received, he knew that, but she had to be told, and soon.

When Molly glanced up, she thought he seemed uneasy. Tuned into his every mood, she asked, 'Is everything all right, Alfie?' She had seen the guilt in his eyes.

He smiled, that dark boyish smile that gave her goosebumps. 'I've a confession to make,' he said.

'What kind of confession?' Nervously, she joked, 'You've not fallen for another woman, have you?'

His voice was soft, endearing. 'There's no other woman for me, Molly. Not now. Not ever. You should know that.'

'But there *is* something wrong, isn't there?'

'Well, not wrong exactly, but I don't think you're going to like it.'

Sitting bolt upright, she prepared herself. 'Try me.'

Alfie took a long, invigorating breath. 'I've been offered a wonderful opportunity, and more money than we've ever seen.'

Momentarily speechless, Molly reflected on his words. 'What do you have to do for this money?' she asked. Suspicion crept in. She knew you got nothing for nothing in this life.

'All they want me to do is what I'm good at.'

The pride in his face told her all she needed to know. 'They want you to fight, don't they? They want to put you up against some backstreet killer. Tell them no! Please, Alfie, for my sake, tell them no.' Unlike Alfie, she feared the unscrupulous villains who ran the fight game.

'It's not like that,' he said. 'Yes, they want me to fight, but not in the back streets. Not any more.'

'What are you saying, Alfie? Are you giving up the fighting game?' In a day of upsets, that would be the best news ever.

He dashed her hopes with a shake of his head. 'Please, my love. Just listen.'

Intrigued but apprehensive, she listened while he outlined the plan.

'Unbeknown to me, the manager's had an American scout watching me at every turn. Wherever I've fought, he's been there, taking notes, reporting back to the big-shots in New York.'

'Why?' Molly's fears heightened. 'What do they want with you?'

Clutching her shoulders, he trembled with excitement, his dark eyes afire. 'Oh Molly, it's every fighter's dream! They want me in America. There's a house, money, contacts, training and everything. It's big-time, lass! Big-time!'

Sensing her dismay, he lowered his voice. 'Don't you see? It's a once-in-a-lifetime chance, to ditch the street-boxing and go professional.' He gave a small laugh. 'I can't believe it. The scout said I was the best he'd seen in a long time.'

Overwhelmed by the news, she asked, 'Is it what you really want?'

Joy flooded his eyes. 'You know it is.'

'And what about me . . . *us*?'

Gently shaking her, he chided, 'What do you think, eh? That I'd leave you behind? I've already told them: you're part of the deal. If you don't go, then neither do I.'

His smile was confident now. 'I want you with me, Molly! I want us to get wed as soon as we can, and start a new life in America.' There was no holding him back now. 'An opportunity like this doesn't come twice. I'm twenty-two years old, with my whole future before me. Honest to God, Moll, it's now or never.'

'I don't know.' She didn't share his excitement. 'It's a big step, moving away from our families, from everything we know. What if it all goes wrong?'

'It won't.' Desperate to convince her, he made a promise. 'Look, sweetheart. I'll tell them we'll give it a year. If I'm not set to make it big by then, we'll come home again. I can't promise more than that, so what do you say?'

'He's told you then, has he?' Stern-faced and anxious, Rosie walked through the door. 'I can see you're as shocked as I am.'

She sat down at the table and pointed behind her. 'I found *him* on the doorstep.' Looking out of place in the small doorway, stood a man the size of a mountain, with a broken nose and bristly face, much like the other old ex-boxer types who frequented the gymnasium.

'Tom Grady sent me to fetch you,' he grunted. 'He said to tell you it's important.'

'I'm on my way.' Concerned about Molly, Alfie assured the man that he would follow on shortly.

'I'll come down to the infirmary afterwards,' he promised Molly. 'We'll walk home together . . . give us time to talk it all through, eh?'

Kissing her soundly, he reminded her, 'Think on what I've said, though. I want you with me.' Bolting out of the door, he called cheerio to Rosie. 'Look after her, Mam.' These two women, and his grandad, were everything to him.

After he'd gone, the two women sat together, silent for a time, Molly on the sofa, Rosie at the table. The mantel clock ticked loudly, and it seemed an age before Rosie spoke; just one word, filled with awe. '*America!*' Her soft voice reverberated round the room, then there was silence again.

The clock continued to tick, and still the two women sat, lost in their own thoughts, until once more, Rosie broke the silence. 'You never know what's round the corner, do you? Things go on the same as before and one day's like the next, then suddenly there comes a bolt out of the blue, and things are never the same again.'

Shaking her head, she lapsed into a trance. 'Now it looks like

I'm about to lose the pair of youse.' Whistling through her teeth, she sat up, shaking her head in disbelief. '*America!* It's like the other side o' the world, so it is!'

Molly, too, was deeply shaken. 'It's a lot to take in, Rosie,' she admitted. 'One way or another, it's been a surprising sort of day.'

Rosie came to sit beside her. 'What will ye do, lass?' she asked. 'Will ye go with him?' There was a kind of desperation in her eyes.

Admittedly, Molly didn't fancy the idea of going that far away one bit but, 'I'd follow him to the ends of the earth if I had to,' she told Rosie. Reaching out, she took hold of the woman's hand, squeezing it so hard, Rosie felt a twinge of pain. 'I can't say I'm over the moon, but it's all he's ever wanted. If he turns it down because of me, how can I ever look him in the face again? Whether I want to go to America or not, it seems I don't have much of a choice . . . not if I love him, which I do, with all my heart.'

Aware of the girl's dilemma, Rosie observed, 'I know how much you love him, and I know what you'd sacrifice to be with him, but America!' She shook her head. 'It's not what you really want, is it, lass?'

Molly had to tell the truth. 'America, London, Lancashire – it makes no difference,' she said hopelessly. 'The truth is, I hate what he does. It's a dangerous business, Rosie. What I'd really like is for him to give it up altogether.'

'I've always felt the very same,' Rosie agreed. 'I blame me da for driving the lad on; living out his own past through Alfie. Streetfighting is no way to make a living, and the better you are, the more the vultures come after you. I for one wouldn't be sorry if the law were to sweep it from the streets once and for all!'

Molly was astonished. 'I didn't realise you felt so strongly about it,' she murmured. 'You never said.'

Rosie sat for a moment or two, reflecting on things. 'I didn't want to worry you any more than you already were. But you need to know the truth of it now, afore you give Alfie your answer.'

'What truth, Rosie?'

In a quiet, clear voice trembling with emotion, Rosie spoke from the heart. 'We both know street-fighting is a barbaric sport, but you don't know the half! Over the years I've seen the spilling of young blood and witnessed things I never want to see again. Brave, stupid men made insane by the incessant, merciless blows that rained down on their heads. I've heard tales of able lads crippled for life by the greedy money-men who lay bets and lose out.'

She paused, before going on in a rush of words: 'If he stays here, like as not Alfie could end up hurt or maimed. Even if he goes to America and takes the boxing up professionally, he'll still be risking life and limb. But he'll be off the streets, and that's a blessing, however small.'

Molly knew what she was trying to say. 'You're telling me I should go with him, aren't you?' she asked. 'You think we should go to America . . . let him try for the big-time, and if it doesn't work out, you reckon he'll be done with it?'

'Sure, you must do what yer heart tells ye.' Rosie felt ashamed. 'Aw, I'm sorry, lass. I'm putting the fear o' God in ye, so I am. When all's said and done, it should be your decision, without me poking me nose in.'

Taking hold of the woman's two hands, Molly held them tight. 'No, Rosie, you do right,' she said. 'I'm glad you told me, because if he goes to America, I mean to be with him.'

Relieved, the Irishwoman laughed aloud. 'When he's hit the big-time, and earned his fortune, and you've a dozen childer round yer arse, he'll not want the fighting any more, you'll see. By then, he'll have got it out of his system.'

'Happen.' Just like Rosie, Molly could only hope.

Peering up, her future mother-in-law asked tentatively, 'Did ye mean it, love? You really *will* go with him? Are ye sure?'

'There's only one thing I'm sure about, Rosie, and it's this: I can't let him go without me!'

Throwing her arms round the girl's neck, Rosie screeched for joy. 'I knew it!' she cried. 'One side o' the world or the other, there'll be no keeping youse two apart.'

Just then, Molly caught sight of the clock. 'Oh my God, I'd best get off or me mam will think I'm not coming.'

Wrenching herself away, she grabbed her jacket from behind the door. 'I've switched Dad's dinner off,' she said angrily. 'If he can't get home at a decent time, he doesn't deserve a decent meal. Things have got to change round here and they might as well start now.'

'Don't you worry about him,' Rosie chided. 'Just you leave Frank Tattersall to me. Get away now, and give Amy my love.'

Before rushing out the door, Molly called out, 'If Lottie gets back before I do, tell her she's to stay up. Me and her need to have a talk!' Molly believed there was still time to save her sister from going bad altogether.

It was the third time Lottie had been on the Waltzer. 'So you've money to burn, have you?' The tall, gangly young man collected her payment, at the same time leaning over her shoulder and looking her in the eye. 'Is it the sight of me that thrills you, or is it the thrill of the ride?'

'Huh!' Lottie had achieved what she wanted. At last she had caught his eye. 'Got a high opinion of yerself, ain't yer?' Though the insult was meant, her laughing eyes told another story.

'Cheeky devil!' Brash and confident, he smiled into her face, his hand touching her hair, making her shiver with delight. When Lottie smiled back, his sharp eyes caught sight of the notes protruding from her jacket pocket. 'Where did you get all that money, eh?' Now he was even more interested.

Stuffing the notes out of sight, Lottie gave him a wary glance. 'I earned it, what d'yer think?'

He quickly changed tactics. 'None o' my business,' he slyly apologised, stroking his hand over her shoulder. 'Only you shouldn't be walking about with all that cash on you, especially like that . . .' he flicked her pocket '. . . where any Tom, Dick or Harry can see it. There's some artful buggers round this fairground, and I should know.' 'Cos I'm one of them, he thought, though he wasn't about to tell her that – at least, not until he'd got what he wanted out of the silly bitch.

'I can take care of myself!'

He grinned. 'I'm sure you can.' A thought occurred to him. ''Ere! I'm no cradle-snatcher! How old are you?' It was no matter. He had her in his sights and was not about to let her loose.

'I'm eighteen.'

'Liar.' Snaking out his tongue, he licked her on the neck, making her giggle. 'You're never eighteen!'

'All right, I'm sixteen. Why d'you want to know?' Lies became easier the more you told them.

Tantalisingly, he licked the inside of her ear and said huskily, 'If I'm about to take you to bed, I need to know if you're old enough.'

'What makes you think I want to go to bed with *you*?'

For a brief minute her coy manner had him foxed, then she smiled up at him and he knew he had her. 'Oh, you want me all right,' he whispered. 'I can always tell.'

'I'm not one of your easy girls!' Anger coloured her face.

'Aye aye – looks like I've got a fiery one here. But that's all right – it's more fun.' He laughed, a low, sarcastic sound that should have warned her. Instead, she was excited.

'Nobody's managed to tame me yet,' she boasted.

'*I'll* bring you to heel my girl, given time.'

'Hey, Romeo and Juliet! Do your courting somewhere else.

I'm waiting to start up! Get your arses off my bloody machine!'
As the man yelled out, the Waltzer started up and began to move,
with them still on it.

Returning the banter, the young man shouted, 'Come on, Will,
switch it off.'

Grinning, the other man threw a switch, and the machine
began to gather speed.

'We'd best get off. That's my mate, and he's mad as a hatter.'
Taking her by the arm, he propelled Lottie down the steps and
on to firm ground. 'Right then, let's get a proper look at you.'
Legs astride and arms folded, he regarded her from top to toe.

Lottie was thrilled. 'Like what you see, do you?'

'Depends.'

'On what?'

'On how well we get on.'

Lottie grinned. 'We'll have to see, won't we?'

'I expect we will.' But he did like what he saw, and what he
saw was a good-looking girl with money in her pocket and a
gleam in her eye that promised endless hours of pleasure . . . until
he tired of her, as he had all the others. 'What's your name?'

'Lottie. What's yours?'

'Dave.'

Just then the ride came to an end, and his colleague was
calling him. 'Wait by the wagon over there, see?' He pointed to
a dilapidated vehicle parked some way from the fairground. 'I'll
ask Will to take over the shift. He owes me a favour anyway.'
Tilting her face to his, he kissed her on the mouth. 'You're not
planning to run away, are you?'

Completely besotted, Lottie shook her head. 'I'll wait there,
like you said.'

'Good girl.' His smile enveloped her. 'I'll be back in no time.
Then you and I can get to know each other.'

On his way to join his mate, Dave glanced back and, much to

his delight, she had followed his instruction without question. 'Like a lamb to the slaughter,' he muttered, and went away to claim his 'favour'.

'Catching 'em young these days, ain't yer?' Discreetly giving Lottie the once-over, Will nudged his wayward friend. 'Not bad, though.'

Dave licked his lips. 'She'll do for now.'

'Easy, is she?'

'Dunno, but I'll soon find out.' He winked. 'Best get off, while she's still warm.'

Will watched his mate swagger off. 'What's he up to now?' Having come up quietly behind him, the older man looked angry. 'He's a bad lot, is that one.' His disapproval was evident as he watched Dave lead Lottie into the wagon, his arm round her and his soft laughter drifting over the night air. 'I wish I'd never took that bloke on,' the man said. 'I've a mind to give him his marching orders.'

'He's a good worker though,' Will argued. 'You'll not find better.'

The other man considered this. 'You might be right, but you'd best tell him . . . if he brings trouble down on my head, he'll be up the road on the end of my boot, and no mistake!' And with that he marched off, muttering and cursing, and wondering if he should sell up and retire to a toffee shop in Liverpool.

Left alone, Will increased the speed of the Waltzer, much to the delight of its passengers, whose shrieks of laughter echoed through the night. His envious gaze travelled to the wagon. 'You'd best watch yourself, matey,' he murmured. 'Beating up women is bad enough, but this one's just a kid.'

From the gathering darkness, the woman hidden in the shadows also looked across to the wagon, her fingers stroking the deep scar that ran from her cheek to her mouth. 'Silly young mare,' she snarled. 'If only you knew what he'd done to me.'

Josephine Cox

Hatred shaped her features, then she was smiling, and now she was laughing. 'You've set your cap at the wrong fella. Let's hope you won't live to rue the day.'

Still cackling, she made her way from the fairground to the pub on the corner where, as on every other night, she drank until her senses were numbed, and the memories dimmed.

Chapter Six

As always, Amy was glad to see Molly. She had been moved to a general ward by now, which was a relief as it got her away from all the other mums and babies.

After a brief nap, she was feeling brighter in herself, but not at peace . . . never at peace. 'I thought you might not come back,' she said, holding on to her daughter a minute longer. 'Just now when I opened my eyes I thought it were your dad come to see me.' She gave a small, bitter laugh. 'God knows what made me imagine that. I expect he's down the pub, swilling back the booze like always. He won't give me a second thought, nor the bairn neither.'

Watching while Molly seated herself on the hard chair beside her, she asked curiously, 'He *does* know, doesn't he – about the bairn?'

A moment ago, Molly had caught her mother sleeping, and seen the fleeting fear when she opened her eyes. It only served to fuel the anger she felt towards her dad. 'Yes, Mam,' she answered. 'He knows well enough.'

Amy sighed. 'It doesn't matter anyway. He'll not care one way or the other. Not so long as he's got his drinking cronies, and the floozies behind the bar to wink and giggle with.'

'They're not all floozies, Mam,' Molly said gently. 'If you

recall, Madge Bonnie's daughter works behind the bar at the local. She's a sweet little thing, wouldn't say boo to a goose, and if Dad so much as winked at her, she'd run a mile.'

The idea of it made both women laugh out loud. 'Come to think of it,' Amy added with a chuckle, 'I reckon *anybody* would run a mile if your dad winked at 'em.' And they set off laughing again, much to the annoyance of a bad-tempered patient.

'Some of us are trying to sleep!' she called out, and Amy made a gesture that sent colour into the woman's cheeks.

Thinking her mam had changed her mind after all and wanted Frank to visit, Molly asked cautiously, 'Do you want me to tell Dad you'd like to see him?'

Amy's smile slipped. 'No, I ruddy well don't!'

'Sorry.' The girl felt uncomfortable. 'Only, the way you were talking just now, I thought you might have changed your mind.'

Filled with guilt, Amy gazed at her daughter, love and regret shining in her pained eyes. 'I didn't mean to snap at you,' she apologised. 'But I don't want him near me again, not now – *not ever.*'

For the next half hour they talked of Rosie and the children. When Amy asked where Lottie was, Molly replied, 'She should be home by now, waiting for me to get back.'

But her mother was not fooled. 'She's a right little madam, is that one,' she said. 'You watch her like a hawk, lass, or she'll walk all over you.'

They chatted about Alfie, but Molly kept the news about America to herself. She also made no mention of losing her job. 'You're a good girl,' Amy said, taking hold of her hand. 'You must be worn out, rushing home from work and seeing to the children, then coming here to visit me. You'd best get off now. I'll be fine.'

Before she left, Molly asked impulsively, 'What's troubling

you, Mam? And I'm not talking about the bairn, or Lottie, or being in here.' In an unguarded moment she had seen that same faraway look on her mother's face, and couldn't let it pass. 'There's something else, isn't there?'

Amy forced a smile. 'You're imagining things, love.' It came as a shock to think Molly had noticed. 'There's nothing but what we've already talked about.'

'Are you sure, Mam? Because if there *is* something, and it's playing on your mind, we can talk about it, just you and me.'

'There's nothing to talk about!' Irritation crept into her voice. 'So stop moithering and get off home.' She paused, her brown eyes softening as she looked into the girl's upturned face. 'Go on! Before I have you thrown out of here.'

Realising she had overstayed her welcome, Molly bade her mam goodnight.

On the way out, she had a brief word with the duty sister. 'It's natural for your mother to go through a stage of depression,' she assured the girl. 'Give her time. The main thing is, she's doing very well. In fact, we're expecting to send her home quite soon.'

With that in mind, Molly went off to meet Alfie with a lighter heart. At last she had something positive to tell the children.

Waiting until Molly was out of sight, Frank made his way to the reception desk.

'Can I help you, sir?' Polite as ever, the nurse regarded him with some suspicion. Slightly unsteady on his feet and now leaning over her counter, Frank Tattersall presented an unsavoury picture. His bold eyes roved her young face before lowering to the top button of her blouse and the swelling of her breasts beneath.

'I said, can I help you?' She could smell the booze, and

something else, too – the rank smell of clothes worn too long before being washed.

When he leaned further forward, she instinctively drew back. 'I've come for the wife,' he grunted. 'Amy Tattersall's the name. She came in here with a bairn and now she'll be going home without it, not that I give a hang about that. All I want is to get her back where she belongs, quick smart!'

When the nurse opened her mouth to speak, he raised his voice. 'We've too many kids. Our Molly's worse than bloody useless at looking after 'em! They need their mam, that's who they need.'

Reluctantly, the nurse pointed him in the direction of the general ward. 'Visiting time is over,' she warned, 'but I shall let you have five minutes.'

'So when's she coming home, eh?'

'I've an idea she'll be allowed home any time now, but the best person to ask is the doctor.'

Without replying, Frank ambled down to the ward, muttering, 'Ain't got no time for doctors and 'orspitals. I don't like these places and never have!'

At the top of the ward he was stopped by the duty nurse, who took an instant dislike to him.

'I've come to see my wife,' Frank said belligerently. 'Mrs Tattersall's the name . . . Mrs *Frank* Tattersall.'

As he made his way over to Amy's bed, the nurse thanked her lucky stars he didn't belong to her. 'I'd drown him soon as look at him,' she murmured under her breath, and her pity for Amy was tenfold.

When Amy saw him approaching, her heart sank. 'What do you want?' she said. Her whole body stiffened. 'Visiting time is long over.'

'A man has his rights.' Leaning over, he slobbered a kiss on her cheek. He would have kissed her full on the mouth but she turned away. 'I can see you're not pleased to see me.'

'I'm tired, Frank.' She didn't want trouble, not in here. 'Can't you leave it till tomorrow?'

Grinning inanely, he imparted what the nurse had told him. 'According to her back there, you could well be home in the next few days. What d'yer think to that, eh?' Winking meaningfully, he slid his hand under the bedclothes and fondled her bare thigh. 'I've missed you, lass,' he said in a voice laden with lust. 'Since you've been gone, there's been nobody to keep me warm of a night.' But it wasn't warmth he wanted. It was *her*!

Squirming, Amy tried to free herself. 'Give over, Frank,' she urged. 'Somebody's bound to see!'

Glancing round, he saw the woman in the neighbouring bed sneaking a look at them. In a loud voice he said, 'Let the buggers see. They're only jealous 'cos I've got my hand on *your* arse instead o' theirs.'

Trying desperately to pull him off, Amy only succeeded in exciting him more. Sidling towards her, he grabbed her hand and placed it on his flies so that she could feel the hardness there. 'See that?' he hissed. 'It's desperate I am.' He began kissing her ardently, his hands all over her. 'Oh Amy, I want you that badly,' he moaned. 'If I close the curtains, they'll not know what we're up to, will they, eh?' With that he swung round and began yanking on the curtains.

'No, Frank!'

Incensed, he took her by the hair and yanking her head back, mimicked her to perfection. 'What d'yer mean "No, Frank"! You're my wife an' you'll do as you're bloody well told!'

'No, Mr Tattersall.' The quiet, disciplined voice stopped him in his tracks. 'It's you who will do as you're told.' The night sister had been summoned, and Frank was swiftly escorted to the main doors, yelling and cursing all the way.

'I'll be back tomorrow,' he raved. 'She'd better be dressed and ready for home or I'll raise the bloody roof, so help me!'

For a long time after he'd gone, Amy lay there shuddering, her mind in turmoil. The more she thought of what Frank had done, the more she loathed him.

She thought of the children, and Molly, and the tears ran freely down her face. If only they'd never been born, she thought. If only I'd never met him. But it was done now, and could not be undone, more's the pity.

When the lights went out and everyone else was sleeping, weariness finally engulfed her. She closed her eyes and let oblivion take her away.

It was the sound of the tea trolley that woke her. Rattling its ancient wheels along the shiny floors, it heralded a new day.

'Morning, Mrs Tattersall.' The round-faced, cheery woman poured her a cup of tea. 'Milky, wasn't it, dearie, with half a sugar. I'm glad you don't have a sweet tooth, because Miss Routledge in the end bed insists on four spoonfuls. I could cheat a bit, if only the old bugger didn't keep her eagle eye on me while I shovel it in. Honest, you can stand the spoon up in it, and what with sugar being hard to get in any quantity, I'm having to rob Peter to pay Paul.'

Replacing the teapot, she clattered a teaspoon on to the saucer. 'Goodness only knows how you manage with your brood. Still, we mustn't grumble. We've been through worse times. Besides, I'm sure it won't be long before we can throw away the ration books altogether.'

After placing the teacup on Amy's bedside cabinet, she threw back the curtains and let the morning sun shine in. 'Look at that,' she declared with a smile. 'Another lovely day.'

Sitting up in bed, Amy thanked her and, enjoying her cup of tea, she glanced around the ward. It was filled with all the noises and chatter that came with the morning. The woman who had been peeking at her and Frank last night was full of apologies.

'He's a bit of a handful, that husband of yours,' she declared. 'By! I'm glad I never got wed. I couldn't be doing with all that.'

Amy made excuses for Frank, but in her heart she bitterly regretted the fact that the nasty little scene had been witnessed by others. The woman was a nosy biddy and, according to the gossip she'd heard from the tea-lady, was something of a loner. Yet, in a way, Amy envied her. Misshapen and plain-faced, she had apparently not received one visitor in the three weeks she'd been there. Yet, given a chance, Amy would have swapped places with her there and then.

Feigning tiredness, Amy turned away. In her mind she relived the incident with Frank which, if it hadn't been so disgusting, might have been comical. Last night she had done a lot of thinking. Now, in the cold light of day, she knew what she must do. Her mind was made up. If she was ever to have any life at all, there was only one way for her to go.

And, right or wrong, there would be no turning back.

At half past nine, while breakfast was being served, Amy got out of bed and sat in the chair. 'Nothing for me,' she told the nurse. 'I'm not hungry.'

There followed a brief, though well-intentioned lecture on how breakfast was the best meal of the day, and should not be missed. 'It will take a few days yet for you to feel stronger,' she was told. 'You must take care of yourself.'

Amy kept her there a moment longer. 'My husband said he was told I could be going home any day now – is that right?' Knowing Frank, it could have been sheer wishful thinking.

'Well, yes, as far as I know, the doctor is satisfied with your progress, but I think it will be a day or two yet before he discharges you.' She wagged a warning finger. 'He'll pack you off with a whole list of instructions – and skipping breakfast is not one of them!'

An hour later, the doctor confirmed the nurse's words. 'I think it might be wise to give it another couple of days,' he told Amy. 'That's my advice.' Easing himself on to the edge of the bed, he suggested kindly, 'They tell me you've refused to see the priest. I know it's none of my business, but I do think you should talk with him. A priest can always help in matters of this kind.'

Ignoring this well-meant advice, Amy came straight to the point. 'I'd like to go home now, doctor.'

Regarding her for a moment, he seemed to be turning the idea over in his mind before soundly rejecting it. 'No. I'm sorry, Mrs Tattersall, but I think you need a couple more days at least.' And there was no changing his mind.

Moving away, he spoke privately to the ward sister. 'I'm not satisfied that Mrs Tattersall has fully accepted the loss of her child,' he said. 'I'm thinking of that young woman last year . . . the same kind of thing. *She* wouldn't talk about losing the child either. She was quiet and withdrawn, and she refused to see the priest, just like Mrs Tattersall. We missed all the signs and let her go home. Two days later, if you remember, she hanged herself. We were wrong on that occasion, sister. I don't mean to make the same mistake again.'

'Very well, doctor, as you say.' Though she wouldn't have minded Amy going home sooner. She personally didn't think the woman was suicidal, and there was always need for the bed.

Amy, however, had no intentions of leaving the matter there. Cadging some notepaper, a pen and an envelope from her neighbour, she shut out the world and wrote what was in her heart:

Dearest Molly,
    I know what I'm doing is wrong, and I hope there will come a day when you will find it in your heart to forgive me.
    For too many years, I've been your father's dogsbody.

Not a day has gone by when he hasn't proved how little he cares for me. I'm a convenience to him, and that's all I'll ever be. It's too late for him to change now, and besides, somewhere along the way I've changed. I'm not the young girl he wed. I'm a woman, with a woman's feelings. I've got a right to some respect and consideration. I've borne his children and taken his abuse, and now the only feelings I have for him are anger and disgust.

The thing is, I've been offered a new life with the gentle, caring man I knew in my youth, and who is now back in my life. At first I turned him away, because he didn't want to be burdened with another man's children. But now, being in here and having the time to think, I know I have to go with him. If I don't, I shall regret it for the rest of my life.

I had all but decided I could never leave you and the children, but then I realised, one day, when you all fly the nest, I'll be left alone with only your father for company. The thought fills me with dread.

It was your father who forced the decision when he came to the hospital last night. Drunk and full of himself as usual, he tried to take liberties with me, until someone called the sister, and he was escorted from the premises. As you can imagine, he screamed and cursed all the way out, so everybody could see and hear. Oh, Molly! He makes me so ashamed.

I know my going will put a terrible burden on your head. I pray to God you can forgive me for that. But you're young, Molly, with your whole life in front of you. You can afford to wait a few years, until the children are older. The best part of my life is gone, and I don't know if I could spend another day with your father, let alone years on end.

Please, try to understand. I can't go on the way things are. If I stayed, I believe I would end it all.

We will go a long way away, where no one will ever find us in this world. So it will be of no use for anyone to try to trace us.

Please forgive me, and let me go with your blessing.

I will always love you. Wish me well, lass.

Goodbye then, Molly. Don't hate me.

Your Mammy.

X X X

After writing the letter, Amy folded it into the envelope and addressed it: *For Molly Tattersall (Amy Tattersall's daughter)*, then she sealed it down.

The letter was for Molly's eyes only; not for those who could never understand how a mother could leave her children. They didn't know how it was, how a man like Frank could drive you to despair. In those few moments an endless procession of shocking scenes paraded through her mind. Of how he had spent his wages too often at the pub and the betting shop, leaving her to scrape by on what she could muster. Scenes of him drunk, and violent, and of how he would use her in the bedroom like she was a woman off the streets, and nearby her children listening to every ugly sound.

Frank Tattersall had degraded and humiliated her in every way possible. Now it was *her* turn. The payback was long over-due. The only pain she felt was for her children, but Molly would keep them safe, she knew that.

A few moments later, she took her belongings from the bedside locker, and quietly made her way to the bathroom. No one stopped her. No one saw her.

Inside the bathroom she laid out her clothes – a cotton slip and bra, with white sturdy knickers and brown nylon stockings. These latter were her most treasured possession, since even three years after the war, it still wasn't easy to find them at a price you could afford. She carefully unfolded the plain brown skirt and blue jumper that had seen better days, black shoes with stubby heels and ankle strap, and a grey, button-up jacket which Rosie had given her last year.

Wasting no time, she washed and dressed, combed her brown hair and dabbed on a dusting of rouge to brighten her pale cheekbones. A touch of treasured lipstick, bought for her by Molly, and she was ready to face the world.

Staring at her image in the mirror, she saw a thin, weary woman at the end of her tether. All the same, it was a bad thing she was doing, and she knew it. 'May God forgive me,' she murmured, and quickly made her way to the sister's office. 'I'm signing myself out,' she said, and the sister, looking up from her work, was astonished.

'Why didn't you mention this to the doctor while he was here?' The sister liked orderly routine and everything in its proper place.

'I hadn't altogether made up my mind,' Amy lied. 'But I have now, and I must get home to the children. Eddie's been crying for me, and Bertha's started wetting the bed again. They need their mammy. Besides, I'm sure you would not want a repeat of last night, when my husband caused an uproar in the ward. The trouble is, he's likely to be here again tonight and every other night until I go home.'

The sister hesitated, her mind going back to the doctor's warning. 'I see. You do understand that if you sign yourself out, the hospital cannot be held responsible?'

'I understand.'

'Are you absolutely certain you know what you're doing?'

'I was never more sure.'

'The young woman who was here with you . . .'

'That was Molly. My eldest.'

'Is she prepared to help you with the children?'

'Molly's a good girl: I can always count on her. And I have a wonderful friend and neighbour just a few doors away.'

'Very well.' Heaving a sigh, the sister took out a dog-eared ledger. Consulting this, she wrote out a prescription for Amy to take to the pharmacy. 'Mind you read the instructions and take your medication religiously,' she warned. 'Watch for any signs of bleeding, and should there be anything at all which concerns you, I want you straight back in here. Do you understand all of this?'

'Of course.'

'I'll give you a letter for your own doctor. Take it to him as soon as you can.'

Placing the doctor's letter and the prescription in her bag, Amy thanked her. 'Don't worry about me,' she said, 'I'll be all right.'

'Oh, and there's this.' Sliding a form in front of her, the sister insisted she read it. 'This frees the hospital from any responsibility, and declares that you have signed yourself out, *against* our express wishes.'

When Amy had signed the form, the sister filed it in her drawer. 'One more thing,' she said kindly. 'Won't you please reconsider what the doctor suggested . . . about seeing the priest?'

Amy nodded. 'Maybe.' But what could a priest tell her? Except that she was being selfish, and seeing that the Good Lord had blessed her with so many children, shouldn't she be grateful. Bitterness flooded through her. *What would he know?*

Taking Molly's letter out of her bag, she gave it to the sister. 'My daughter planned to come here straight from work. She'll be worried when she finds I'm gone. This little note will explain.'

'There's no need for that. One of us can tell her you've gone home.'

'Please,' Amy insisted quietly. 'It's better this way.'

'Very well.' Laying the envelope on the desk, the woman promised Amy, 'We'll make sure she gets it.'

After Amy had left, the sister picked up the letter. Turning it over in her hands, she wondered aloud, 'Have I done right in letting her go?' Yet apart from tying Mrs Tattersall to the bed, she had no choice in the matter.

Chapter Seven

Wiping his beer mugs clean, the barman at the Darwen Hotel cast a curious eye over Jack. 'I thought you were leaving us today?' A big, round fellow with a gammy leg, he took delight in studying people. He prided himself on being able to guess a body's business but, to his frustration, Jack was an impossible nut to crack. 'Finished here then, have you?' he asked, thinking there was still time to win him over.

Secretive as ever, Jack shook his head. 'Nope.'

'So it's not gone as well as you expected then . . . the reason for your visit to these parts, I mean?'

'Doesn't seem like it, no.'

Ever optimistic, the barman persisted. 'Er . . . you never did say what kind of business you were in?'

'That's right.' Taking a deep gulp of his shandy, Jack glanced towards the door. 'You say there's been nobody looking for me the whole time I've been out?' He had been sure Amy would be waiting for him when he got back from his errand.

Sniffing, the barman shook his head. 'You'll have to ask at reception, but I've seen nobody,' he answered. 'You weren't gone all that long anyway.'

'I'm off up to my room.' Jack shoved the price of his shandy across the counter and instructed, 'If anybody does ask after me, will you send them straight up?'

'Man or woman?' This bloke obviously never gave up.

'Whoever.' Jack wouldn't give this nosy bugger an inch. Besides, if anybody did come here after him, it would only be Amy, because nobody else knew where he was.

As he went upstairs, it crossed his mind that, somehow, Frank might have learned of his whereabouts. 'If that scum comes after me, I'll be ready for him,' he muttered grimly. 'Happen it might be best to have it out with him once and for all!' But he didn't want Amy caught in the middle. To his mind, she'd suffered enough at Frank's hands.

As she hurried from the tram stop, her legs as weak as water, Amy also had Frank on her mind. 'What if he finds us?' She was talking aloud, oblivious to those who turned to stare at her. 'What if he comes after us? Oh, dear God, he'd kill us both with his bare hands!' For all his violence, she had never really been afraid of Frank. But now, as she imagined the consequences of her and Jack being together, the fear was like a hard fist inside her.

Outside the Darwen Hotel, she paused, glancing up and down, terrified in case she'd been followed. 'Pull yourself together, Amy, lass,' she told herself. 'How could he know?' Even so, she was frantic. Happen it might be best if she turned round and went straight home.

Instinctively, she turned, before his voice called her back. '*Amy!*'

Closing her eyes she gave silent thanks. When he placed his hands on her shoulders and turned her towards him, the tears broke loose and ran unheeded down her face. 'Oh Jack, I didn't know what to do,' she sobbed. 'I just didn't know what to do.'

She fell into his arms and he folded her to him. 'It's all right now,' he said. 'I have you safe.'

Taking her inside, he collected his portmanteau from the barman. 'How much do I owe you?' he asked.

'Four pound ten shilling.'

Counting out the money, Jack noticed the barman staring at Amy. 'Hmh! Don't blame you for waiting for that one,' the man said cheekily. 'She's not a bad-looking sort.' Winking at Jack, he grabbed up the cash and rang it into the till.

Leaning over the bar, Jack caught him by the scruff of his neck. 'You're talking about a lady!' he warned. 'What's more, you never saw her,' he said threateningly. 'Do I make myself clear?'

Finding it difficult to talk with his shirt collar pulled tight round his neck, the barman nodded.

Letting him loose, Jack took another ten-shilling note from his wallet and placed it on the bar. 'If anybody comes looking . . . you never saw her.'

The man looked at Jack's fiery eyes and his clenched fist. 'Anything you say, sir,' he said nervously. 'I didn't see nothing and nobody.'

Jack nodded. 'I know your face, and I know where to find you, should your tongue run away with you. Remember that, and keep your mouth shut!'

Leaving the barman with the impression that Jack Mason was a man to be reckoned with, he took Amy by the arm and together they walked away from the pub and into a café on the corner of Rosamund Street. Here he asked the girl behind the counter for two full English breakfasts.

'I bet you haven't eaten a thing this morning, am I right?' he teased Amy.

She smiled. 'How did you know that?'

'Because I haven't either,' he admitted. 'I've been living on my nerves, not sure whether you'd come or whether you wouldn't.' Placing his two hands round her face, he kissed her tenderly. 'I love you, Amy,' he murmured. 'You do know that, don't you?'

Amy nodded. 'I love you, too,' she said, and held his hands so tight he thought she would never let go.

Still nervous in case they were seen by someone she knew, Amy only pecked at her food. 'Where will we go, Jack?' she wanted to know.

'We're going to my home. I have a place in Bedford, down in the south. I hope you'll like it, Amy.'

'Will Frank be able to track us down there?' Her voice shook, and he knew the terror in her.

'I don't think so,' he replied softly. 'And even if he does, you've no need to be frightened. I can deal with Frank Tattersall. But I'll promise you one thing: he'll never hurt *you* again, not as long as I live!'

Breakfast done with, they climbed into Jack's car and sat holding hands in the front like two young lovers.

'I can't believe I'm going away from Blackburn with you beside me.' Jack had dreamed of this for so long, and now it was reality. He thought himself the luckiest man in the world.

'Jack?' Amy turned her pensive gaze on him.

'What is it, sweetheart?'

'Won't you change your mind . . . about the children?'

Slowly, agonisingly, he shook his head. 'I can't.'

Leaning back in her seat, Amy let her thoughts wander to the children. In her mind's eye she could see little Eddie, running round the parlour, his napkin round his ankles; and Bertha, laughing, always laughing. Then there was Milly and Georgie – and Molly. *Oh Molly, what have I done to you?*

But in spite of her sorrow, she could never go back. Not now she had found the courage to leave.

'Amy?' Seeing her distress, Jack's heart went out to her. 'Look at me, darling.'

When her brown eyes were uplifted to his, he affirmed his

promise, but this time he wisely qualified it with, 'While I have money, I won't see them go without.'

Opening her heart to him, she asked, her voice raw, 'Am I a selfish woman, Jack? Am I so wicked to leave them behind?'

Regarding her now, seeing how thin and pale she was, and how the pain of what Frank had done to her had dulled her pretty eyes and made her so desperate, he could hardly bear it. 'There isn't a selfish, wicked bone in your body,' he said, 'otherwise you'd have left him long since. Think about it, Amy. If you went back now, what would become of you?'

Amy knew already, for hadn't she thought of it time and again, wishing there was an escape, hoping Frank would die and she might make some sort of a life without him.

In a faltering tone, she gave Jack his answer. 'I'd be an old woman before my time. The same life, the same Frank. With my spirit shrinking day after day, until there was nothing left.'

With a shock, she suddenly saw what he was getting at. 'I'd be no use to the children then, would I?' she said. 'That's what you mean, isn't it, Jack?'

His answer was to take her in his arms. Grateful to be in a safe place at last, Amy snuggled up to him. It was so comforting to be in a man's arms, knowing it was love that made him want to hold her. It was good not to dread what might come next and, knowing Jack, never again to be thrashed to within an inch of her life for daring to say 'no'.

Despite her joy, she was engulfed with guilt over the children, and Molly. Especially Molly, because she was left to carry a burden not of her own making.

Jack had said there was not a selfish or wicked bone in her body, but nothing had been said about her being a coward. For that was exactly what she was. Her cowardice had robbed a lovely young woman, of many carefree years, and maybe the chance to be happy in a life of her own.

* * *

As Jack drove down the country roads, getting closer to home with every mile, he felt a deep contentment at Amy's presence by his side.

To his mind he had done the right thing in plucking her from a life of misery with Frank Tattersall. Yes, he regretted the fact that she had left her children behind, but he had been straight with her right from the start. He was not a man to have brats running round his feet. It wasn't that he disliked them, just that he simply couldn't cope with their boisterousness. He made no pretence about that.

All the same, he did feel a rush of guilt about Amy's eldest daughter, Molly, who had been forced to take on the chaos her mother had left behind.

He consoled himself with the fact that she was only eighteen, with time and energy to spare. Then there was the fact that she would not have to endure Frank Tattersall in the same way her mother had.

He told himself that and felt a little easier.

Molly was amazed to learn that her mother had left the hospital, and even more astonished to be given the letter. 'I told her we could let you know she'd gone home,' the sister, who was still on duty, said. 'But she was adamant about leaving you the note.'

Molly thanked her, and in the privacy of the outer hall, she opened the letter and read it. With each word her heart sank inside her. She could not believe what she was reading. Dear God! It was like her mam had lost her mind. Afraid and confused, she folded the letter and slid it into her pocket.

Returning to the sister's office, she said heatedly, 'You had no right to let her out. She's not well enough.'

'This is a hospital, not a prison,' the sister told her patiently. 'We can't force anyone to stay against their will. As long as they put their signature to this form, they're free to leave – although of course we do try to satisfy ourselves they are in no immediate danger.'

'Oh, and how did you do that in my mam's case?' Molly demanded. 'You didn't try to reach *me*, did you?'

'Look, my dear,' the sister said kindly, for the girl before her seemed so distraught, 'your mother wasn't ill in the true sense of the word. Her injuries were mostly flesh wounds and bruises; there was nothing broken. And although it may sound harsh, we have women in here who lose their baby and go home the following day. Then there are others who need two weeks or more to regain their strength. Your mother is an exceptional woman. Moreover, she was perfectly composed when she asked me to give you your letter.'

'She isn't well in her mind. She's been troubled these past days,' Molly said desperately. 'I saw it, why couldn't you? Instead you let her go without even knowing where she was headed!' She choked back a sob.

'Why, your mother has gone straight home, hasn't she? What's more, she seemed well enough to leave hospital. You say she was troubled, but it's quite normal to suffer a measure of grief over a lost baby. You mustn't worry unduly. Mrs Tattersall is a strong, sensible woman.'

Desperate to get away, Molly bade her goodnight.

The sister called her back. 'If you're worried about your mother, perhaps you should contact the authorities.'

'Why would I do that?'

'It was just a suggestion.'

Molly forced a smile. 'I'm sorry if I lost my temper,' she said. 'It was just such a shock to come here and find her gone. I expect you're right . . . I'll get home and there she'll be.' But she knew different. She had read the letter, and it was clear enough: her mam had no intention of going home ever again.

* * *

Molly didn't go straight home either. Instead she made her way to the nearby park, where she sat on a bench and took out the letter once more.

Three times she read it, looking for a clue as to where her mam could have gone with this man. It seemed so final, so cruel to Molly. Would she ever see her mother again? And what of her future with Alfie? She would never be able to go to America now. And – oh God! – how would she break the news to her siblings? *And to Frank?* It didn't bear thinking about.

For the next hour she toured any likely place where she might discover her mother's whereabouts; no one at the bus station could recall seeing anyone of that description, nor could the ticket clerk at the railway station. 'I've been here all day,' he grumbled. 'If there'd been a woman like you mention, I reckon I'd have noticed.'

The man at the local taxi firm, who served the infirmary, told her assuredly, 'Sorry, luv, I can't help you.'

Molly cursed Jack Mason, and cursed her mother, and cried at her going. Through all of it, her heart ached with the worst pain she had ever experienced.

After the tears came the anger. 'I'll never forgive you for what you've done, Mam,' she muttered. *'Not as long as I live!'*

Hardening her heart, she thrust the letter into her coat pocket, and made her way back to Victoria Street. Tomorrow, when she'd had more time to think, she would decide what to do.

Chapter Eight

After putting the children to bed, Molly dozed in a chair, the letter lying open in her lap. She had read it over and over.

The truth was, she found it hard to believe that her mam could just run away and leave her children. She had so wanted to confide in Rosie, but when she got home, that dear soul was in a rush to get back to her own home and cook the men's dinner, and so there was no opportunity.

Alfie had been round, and they'd talked once more of his plans, and their future, and Molly found she didn't have the heart or courage to show him the letter. Instead, she smiled and chatted while inside, her heart was broken.

As usual, her dad hadn't come home from work, and in the silence of the little parlour, Molly cried many tears. Which way to turn? What to do? She couldn't think straight any more.

In the small hours she woke with a fright. 'Who's there?' she gasped. Sitting bolt upright in the chair, she gathered her senses and glanced through bleary eyes towards the doorway, relaxing when she saw that it was Frank, come home at long last. Villain or not, at least he was a familiar face and one which she was surprisingly pleased to see. 'Oh, it's you, Dad!'

Her relief at seeing him didn't last long though, not when she saw what he'd brought home.

'What the devil are *you* doing up this time o' the morning?' Unsteady on his feet and with a woman curled in his arm, Frank Tattersall staggered across the room. 'Get yerself off to bed!'

Ignoring him, Molly's glance went to the woman; tall and skinny, with bleached hair and made-up eyes, she had seen better days.

'Did you go in to see our mam?' Molly asked him straight out. She wondered if he already knew that his wife had run off with her fancy man!

He answered with a snarl. 'Been to see *'er*? Have I heck as like. Right now, yer mam's neither use nor bloody ornament to me. Had me thrown out of that 'orspital like I were a bloody criminal, she did.'

He turned to fondle the woman's breasts. 'Besides, why would I want to see yer mam, when I've got the pick of any woman on the streets?' He began undoing her blouse, at the same time telling Molly, 'You clear off . . . unless you've a mind to stay and watch.'

The two of them began to giggle. Just then, a tousled little Bertha appeared at the doorway, rubbing her eyes and crying, 'I want my mammy!'

Horrified she might see, Molly swept the little girl into her arms. Closing the door, she hurried up to the bedroom. 'It's all right,' she told the sobbing child. 'Molly's here.' And the way things were, here she must stay.

Exhausted, she cradled the bairn, and fell asleep beside her.

In the morning, the woman was gone, and Frank Tattersall lay slumped across the sofa, snoring loudly. Shaking him until he opened his eyes, Molly told him, 'It's half past six. You'd best clean up and look sharp, or you'll be late for work.' Disgust trembled in her voice. 'You stink of beer!' Throwing open the windows, she let in a blast of cold air that woke him in a minute.

'Shut that sodding winder, you silly cow!' Clutching his shirt about him, Frank struggled from the sofa and hobbled across the room, where he took it on himself to slam the window shut again. 'This is *my* bloody 'ouse, and *I'll* say when the winders are to be opened.'

There followed a heated argument, during which Molly warned him, 'Bertha almost saw you and that tart last night. What in God's name were you thinking of?'

Without warning, he swung round and slapped her hard on the face. 'Don't tell me what I can and can't do,' he yelled. 'I'm my own boss, and don't you forget it. I don't answer to nobody, least of all a snotty-nosed little bugger like you. And yer mam's not 'ere, is she, eh? Oh no! She's lying in that 'orspital, being waited on hand and foot, and not giving a sod about what *I* need!'

Her face burning from the slap, Molly straightened herself to her full height, swung her arm back and hit her father with all her might, almost falling over with the impact. Then, as he stared at her with disbelieving eyes, she warned him in a trembling voice, 'Don't you ever raise your hand to me again. I'm not our mam, and I won't be knocked about, not by you or anybody.'

With that she turned and strode into the scullery. She filled the kettle from the cold tap, and was about to turn towards the stove when she felt herself being grabbed by the shoulders and flung across the room.

Running at her like a madman, Frank pinned her to the wall by her throat, his hand gripping so tight she fought for breath. '*I'm* the man of this 'ouse,' he growled in her face. '*Nobody* tells me what to do. An' if that doesn't suit yer, then get out an' stay out. There's plenty o' women as'll keep 'ouse for me while yer mam's pampering herself in that place.'

Leaving her shaken and gasping for air, he grabbed up his belongings and slammed out of the house.

For what seemed an age, Molly leaned against the wall, her

hands to her throat, her eyes closed. She imagined her mam away with her fella, laughing and free, not caring about the chaos she had left behind. Suddenly, rage boiled up inside her. Giving a cry of pain, she lunged at the shelves, and with one sweep of her arm sent the entire contents to the floor; cups went crashing, jars of jam splattered open across the scullery floor, and when there was nothing left on the shelves, she thumped them with her bare fists until the skin split open and the blood ran down her arms.

'*Whatever's going on here, child?*' Rosie's shocked voice cut through Molly's insanity, instantly calming her.

'Oh Rosie, if only you knew!' She at once began clearing up the mess. 'Look what I've done! Oh dear God, Rosie, what's to become of us?'

Leading the trembling girl away from the scullery, Rosie took her into the parlour, where she eased her on to the sofa. 'I think we'd best bathe your arms first,' she suggested. 'After that, you might want to tell me all about it, eh?'

Rosie quickly cleared up in the scullery, and after a few minutes came back into the parlour, where Molly had composed herself and was now mortified by what she'd done. 'Thank God the young 'uns are still fast asleep,' she told Rosie. 'I'd never have forgiven myself if they'd seen all that.'

Setting a bowl of water at her side, the older woman chuckled comfortably. 'Kids'll sleep through all hell let loose. Whereas me, I wake at the drop of a hat, so I do.' She had her eyes on Molly's face and could see the pain there. 'Whatever made yer do it, lass?' she asked, serious now. 'I've never seen you like that afore.'

Jumping to the wrong conclusion, she said suddenly, 'It's Lottie, isn't it? She's gone and got herself pregnant.'

Molly shook her head. 'No, but I wouldn't be surprised if she had. She hasn't been in all night. Honest to God, Rosie, I'm at my wits' end. Later, when I've got the older children off to school, would you mind watching the bairns while I go and look for her?' Troubles never come singly, she thought cynically.

Rosie agreed without hesitation. 'If it weren't Lottie who upset you, it must have been your da,' she concluded. 'I saw him go striding down the street, a face like thunder. He left the door ajar. That's how I got in – I hope you don't mind?'

'Course not.' Dipping her hands into the luke-warm water, Molly washed her arms and dabbed at the wounds with the flannel. When she winced, Rosie explained, 'I've put a measure o' salt in there. It stings like the very devil, but it'll heal the skin in no time at all.'

When Molly lapsed into a troubled silence, Rosie wouldn't let go. 'What's happened between you and your da?' she asked gently. 'What made you go off the rails like that?'

Molly looked up at her, the enormity of what her mam had done only now beginning to sink in. 'There's a letter in my coat pocket,' she said, 'hanging up behind the door.'

Going across the room, Rosie reached into the coat pocket and drew out the letter. She then brought it back to Molly and laid it on the arm of the sofa. 'Is this the one?'

Drying her arms on the towel Rosie had brought, Molly told her, 'I want you to read it.'

While Rosie sat down to read the letter, Molly carried the bowl into the scullery. She tipped the water down the sink, rinsed the bowl out, then picked up a few small pieces of broken glass that were still lying on the flagstones. That done, she took the mop and bucket from the corner and gave the floor a quick wash over.

When she returned to the parlour, Rosie was sitting, the letter opened on her lap and a look of horror on her face. 'I can't believe it!' she kept saying. 'I never would have thought she could do a thing like that – leave your da, yes, maybe – but never the children!' Shaking her head, she looked up at Molly. 'Do you know who this fella is?'

'Someone she knew years ago and now he's back, like it says in the letter.'

'Any idea where she's gone?'

'No.'

'If we were to track her down somehow, do you think we could persuade her to come home?'

'You've read the letter, Rosie. What do you reckon?'

'She must have thought long and hard about it,' the Irishwoman imagined. 'No, I don't think a team of wild horses would fetch her back.'

'Or half a dozen children!' Molly's voice hardened. 'I would have done anything for our mam, you know that. I've seen what *he's* put her through and there have been times when I wanted to kill him myself. But she left the bairns. How could she bring herself to do that?'

'Happen she thought there was no other way.' Rosie tried to put herself in Amy's shoes. 'After all, it's hard for a woman who's got four young childer and no man to provide. Folks tend to turn the other way.'

'*I* wouldn't have turned the other way, and neither would you. I would have helped her . . . found her a place to rent, given over part of my wages. And Lottie's out to work now, too. We'd have managed, if she'd left my dad. She should have done it years ago.' Molly felt like weeping.

'I don't think it would have worked, lass.'

'Maybe not. But we might have worked summat out, only she never gave us the chance.' Now, in the light of day, and after the initial shock, there were other, more pressing things to consider. 'However am I to tell the children, Rosie? And what about me and Alfie?' Coming to sit on the sofa, she looked at the other woman, and for a while, neither of them dared voice their thoughts.

Finally, Rosie spoke the obvious. 'He'll never go to America,' she said. 'Not without you.'

'But he *has* to,' Molly fretted. 'One way or another, he must go.' Already she had the makings of a plan in her mind, but she daren't mention it to Alfie's mother, not yet. 'Will you do something for me?' she asked.

'What's that?'

'Don't mention the letter to them at home, or say anything about our mam having run off. I need time to think it all out.'

'I'll not say a word, but what will yer do now? You'll have to tell your da. If he should turn up at the infirmary, there'd be blue murder!'

'I know.'

'And what about you?' Rosie felt for Molly; she saw how Amy's selfish action had devastated the girl, and yet her anger at Amy was tempered by the fact that life under Frank Tattersall's rule must have affected her more than anybody realised. 'You'll not be able to work, will you. You'll have to take on your mam's role. Hard though it is, you'll need to be a proper mother to them kids.'

'That goes without saying,' Molly said quietly. 'They've got nobody else.'

'I'll help you all I can, you know that.'

'You've always been a good friend to Mam and me, Rosie. Thank you for that.'

Just then the front door slammed, the shock of it waking Eddie, who began yelling upstairs at the top of his lungs. Leaping up from the sofa, Molly hurried to the door. 'Lottie!' She found her sister leaning against the wall, giggling to herself. 'What in God's name are you playing at?'

Rushing up the passage she took hold of the girl and marched her into the parlour. 'I waited up for you last night. Where the devil were you? What mischief have you been up to now?' When Lottie went into a sulk, Molly shook her hard. 'Answer me! I want to know, and you're not going up those stairs until I do.'

'Who says so?' Staring up defiantly, Lottie couldn't take her eyes off the vivid red mark across Molly's cheek. Reaching out, she poked her in the face, making her cry out. 'Been scrapping with your Alfie, 'ave yer?' she sneered. 'Yer want to watch out, or he'll end up like our dad . . . knocking you from one end o' the house to the other.'

'Hey! You mind your tongue, young lady!' In spite of her decision not to interfere, Rosie took offence at Lottie's remark.

The girl gave her a hostile look. 'What's *she* doing here?'

'Rosie's a friend, that's what she's doing here,' Molly replied angrily. 'Now you tell me where you've been all night, and who you've been with. NOW!'

'Get off me!' Fighting and kicking, Lottie was impossible to contain. 'I don't need to tell you nothing! Wait till Mam gets back – I'll tell her what you're like. I'll tell her how you bully me at every turn. She'll have summat to say about it, and then you'll be sorry!'

Already drained by the news of her mother leaving, and then the fight with her dad, Molly was exhausted. Releasing Lottie, she said flatly, 'I'm only looking out for you, can't you understand that?'

Scrambling up, Lottie glared at her sister, her face hard as brass. 'I don't *want* you looking out for me,' she retorted, 'I can look out for myself. And if you must know where I was last night, I was with a girl from Argyle Street . . . we went to the fair and I stayed the night at her house, so there you are. That's all there is to it!'

Molly breathed a sigh of relief. 'That's all I needed to know,' she answered. 'All the same, you should have got word to me somehow, and then I wouldn't be thinking the worst.'

But Lottie had won the day and she knew it. 'That's the trouble,' she snapped. 'You *allus* think the worst!' She flounced off upstairs, secretly smiling and promising herself that the wonderful night she'd spent with the lad from the fairground would not be the last. Not if she had her way.

Rosie wondered how much more Molly could take. 'She's a shocker,' she remarked, her gaze going to the doorway. 'If she were mine I'd tan 'er backside till it were black and blue, so I would.'

'What am I going to do with her?' Molly felt drained. 'She defied Mam, and she'll defy me.'

'Aye – and she'll rue the day, you mark my words.'

Molly glanced at the mantelpiece clock; it was already half past seven. 'I'd best get the children up and fed.'

'And I'd best get that lazy Sandra out of her bed, or she'll be late for work.' Rosie chuckled. 'Mind you, it won't be the first time and I dare say it won't be the last. But there's a few minutes spare for me to give you a hand with the young 'uns before I go.'

'No, thank you, Rosie. You've done more than enough.'

Rosie suddenly remembered: 'What with all the goings on, I forgot to tell you. Alfie gave me a message afore he went to work. He said to tell you he'll see you tonight, and you're to put on your glad rags. He plans to take you to the flicks.'

Molly wasn't sure. 'I don't know if I could sit through a picture with him, knowing what I have to tell him.'

Rosie wagged a finger. 'You go, lass,' she urged. 'I'll watch the childer. It'll do ye good, so it will, and you don't need to tell him anything. Not yet, anyways. Tomorrow will do. Tonight, you're to get out and put some colour in that pretty face of yours.' Softly pinching Molly's cheek, she told her, 'You're as pale as a winter's day, so ye are.'

'Happen you're right.' Walking with her to the door, Molly paused by the dresser. 'Wait, Rosie,' she said. Opening the dresser drawer she took out a soft blue neckerchief. 'I told Sandra she could borrow this.'

'Are you sure ye know what you're doing?' Rosie chuckled. 'Knowing her, you'll not get it back.'

'That's all right.'

These past few days, Molly had learned that there were more important things to worry about than an old neckerchief.

'I'll be back as soon as I can,' Rosie promised. 'I can take Georgie and Milly to school, or I can mind the bairns at home. Whatever suits you.'

'I'd be glad if you'd watch the bairns,' Molly decided. 'I'd best take the children as usual. There's no point changing routine now.'

As she was leaving, Rosie touched her on the shoulder. 'Later on, we'll sit and work out what's to be done. What d'yer say, lass?'

'That would be good.' Right now she needed company more than anything.

'See you in a while then.' Giving Molly a bear hug, she whispered in her ear, 'Chin up, me darlin', we'll work something out.'

And then she was gone, and Molly was left standing at the door, more alone than she could ever remember.

At her own front door, Rosie glanced back to see Molly looking wistfully up at the skies. With a sorry heart, she shook her head and loudly tutted, 'Amy Tattersall, you've done a terrible thing to that lovely girl of yours. May God forgive you, because nobody else will. Shame on you, Amy. Shame on you!'

Behind Molly, Milly's excited voice rang down the passage. 'Look, Molly!' she called. 'Eddie's coming down the stairs all by himself.'

From the front step, Molly swung round, horrified to see the little chap coming down the stairs, his arms open as if to leap all the way to the bottom. Every time Milly went to get him, he screeched with laughter and wobbled dangerously. 'No, Eddie!' Rushing to the stairs, Molly plucked him into her arms. 'You little monkey, that's enough of that.' Later, now he'd found his courage, she would have to teach him how to come down backwards.

'Milly, run back and tell the others it's time to get up.' Taking the bairn into the parlour, she added, 'Tell them breakfast is ready. That'll shift them.'

Putting Eddie on the floor so he could toddle about, she laughed when he scurried straight for the stairs. 'Oh no you don't,' she said and much to his frustration, shut the parlour door.

Giving him an old cardboard box to play with, she set about getting the toast under the grill. She then put a slab of butter in the dish; rather shame-facedly got out a new pot of jam from the store cupboard and put them both on the table, together with two knives. She half-filled the cups with milk and carried them through. Next, she put a kettle of water on to boil, ready to wash their hands and faces, and while that was singing, she laid out their clean clothes all in a row on the settee.

'Come on, you lot!' With Eddie tucked under her arm, she yelled up the stairs. 'Down here now, or you won't have time for breakfast before school.'

A small face appeared at the top of the stairs. '*I'm* not going to school till after Christmas.' It was Bertha, big-eyed and with her dark hair a-tumble.

Molly smiled. 'I know you're not, sweetheart,' she said, 'but I need to get you all washed and dressed, so come down now, there's a good girl, and fetch the others with you.'

Milly was next, then Georgie. 'I can wash myself,' he protested when Molly dabbed a wet flannel at his face. 'I'm already eight. Wash Milly, she's only six, and she's a *girl*!'

Sighing, Molly left him to it and brought another flannel,

which she first scrubbed with soap and then gently dipped into the warm water. With Milly squirming and grumbling, she washed and dressed her, then sat her at the table. Hot on her tail was Bertha, who stood still as an angel while Molly got her washed and ready. 'You're a good girl,' she told her, sending her up to the table.

'So am I.' Milly was indignant, until her big sister kissed her soundly. 'Yes, love, you're a good girl, too,' she said, and her heart ached for the little ones.

It didn't take long to wash Eddie and change his nappy. 'Right!' Sitting him on her lap, Molly gave them each two chunks of bread. 'You can help yourself to butter and jam,' she told Georgie, 'and try not to drop anything on the tablecloth.'

Then she buttered the girls' bread and, spreading a generous helping of jam on top, she told them, 'Eat up, you lot. We've only got fifteen minutes before we need to be on our way.' God only knew how it had got so late.

When breakfast was over, Rosie showed her face round the door. 'Just in time, am I?' she said, and all the children cheered to see her there. 'I got my own breakfast,' Georgie proudly told her. ''Cos I'm eight, and I'm a *boy*.'

'Yes, and you spilt a dollop o' jam on the table, when our Molly told you not to.' Milly always had to have the last say.

'Hey! Stop arguing, you two.' Coming into the room, Rosie lifted the bairn from Molly's arms. 'I'll see to the two young 'uns,' she offered. 'You'd best get off, lass, or you'll never catch that tram.' She gave a shudder. 'I'll tell ye summat else an' all. October's in the air. You'll need your coats, it's bitter outside.'

A few minutes later, Molly had the two children ready; dressed in their heavy coats and scarves, they were prepared for Siberia.

'Right!' Ushering them out the door, she hurried them down the street and up to Cicely Bridge. As luck would have it, the tram was ten minutes late and they had plenty of time, though the wind was keen, just as Rosie had said. 'I don't like being late for school,' Milly whined. 'Everybody looks at you when you go in.'

Georgie had the answer. 'Put your tongue out at them.'

'That's no way to behave,' Molly scolded. 'I'm surprised at you, Georgie.' He was always such a little gentleman.

Subdued by her reprimand, Georgie was quiet on the journey to school. 'I didn't mean it,' he said sheepishly as they got off the tram, and his smile readily returned when his big sister gave him a hug. Then it was Milly's turn. 'Hurry in, and don't forget to tell them the tram was late.'

She watched them through the gate and into the building, and waved as they went through the door.

A few minutes later she was back on the tram and on her way home. Inevitably, her thoughts turned to Amy. 'Oh, Mam! What am I supposed to say when they start asking after you?' Rage had turned to despair. Her own life must take second place. With her mam gone, her job now was to hold the family together.

It was a daunting prospect.

By the time Molly got back, Rosie had the table cleared and the tea made. Bertha was seated cross-legged on the rug, playing with her doll, while Eddie was content in his pram with a bottle of warm milk.

While they were quiet, the two women had time to talk about the future.

When Rosie took herself off to the scullery to pour the tea, Molly struck a match to the kindling wood in the firegrate. With a few knobs of coal from the scuttle close by, there was soon a cheery fire underway. 'You're right about it being cold outside,' she told Rosie. 'There's a real sharp nip in the air.'

Setting the tea on the fender, Rosie eased herself into the armchair opposite. 'Have ye been able to think things through at all?'

'What . . . you mean about Alfie?' Reaching down, Molly collected her tea and took a sip. She had thought about nothing else all morning.

'Not just Alfie,' Rosie answered. 'I mean *everything*.'

'Course I have, but there's not a lot I can do,' Molly told her. 'I'll not be able to work because of the children, so my dad will have to start tipping up his wage on a Friday. If he doesn't, there'll be no money at all coming in. At least our mam had my board and lodgings, and a bit over the top whenever I could manage it. I don't know if I'll get anything out of Lottie.'

'Do you really think he'll start tipping up his wages?' Rosie couldn't see it, somehow.

'Hmh!' Molly was under no illusions either. 'I'm sure he'll kick up holy hell, but like it or not, he'll have to start facing up to his responsibilities.'

'You'll have your work cut out,' Rosie sighed. She saw Frank for what he was, a womaniser and a waster. 'The trouble is, he's got away with it for too long and now he's set in his ways. Once he finds out your mam's gone off with some fella, he'll run riot.' She gave a low whistle. 'Sure, I'm glad I'm not the one that has to tell him!'

Molly didn't look forward to that task either, but it would need to be done. 'I'll tell him tonight,' she decided. 'I daren't leave it any longer.'

'Aye, I can see that.'

The girl gave a sad little smile. 'D'you know, Rosie, I really thought she'd come home. Last night, I was so sure she would just turn up and be full of apologies, but she didn't – and now I know she never will. I don't even know if any of us will ever see her again.'

Choking back the lump in her throat, she went on, 'I've been thinking about earning some money from home – you know, so I can be with the children. Mrs Pearson down the street, she earns from home, doing other folks' washing. Happen there's summat I could do like that.'

'I'm sorry, lass.' Rosie felt guilty. 'You know I'd have the childer while you went out to work, but I can't leave Dad all on his own, and I can't take the childer there because, however much he puts on a brave front, he's not a well man. An hour at a time is about all he could stand of little ones round his feet. That's not to say he doesn't think the world of them, because you know he does.'

'Thanks all the same, Rosie, but I'll manage somehow, don't you worry.'

'If you don't mind me saying, it's not nice doing other folks' washing. Sure, there must be something else ye can turn your hand to?'

Molly had been considering it long and hard. 'There are three things that come to mind – the washing and ironing, dressmaking, but I'm not that good with a needle and thread, and there was one other thing . . .'

'Go on?' Intrigued, Rosie leaned forward in her chair.

'I couldn't really do it on my own though,' the girl admitted. 'Not with the children.'

'I'm listening.' Rosie wanted to help in any way she could.

Taking the last swig of her tea, Molly put the empty cup in the hearth, and outlined her plan. 'Have you ever seen them old folk down the market – they buy their potatoes and such, and then can hardly walk upright, 'cos their bags are so weighed down.'

Rosie laughed. 'I know what ye mean, lass,' she said. 'I struggled home with vegetables and fruit the other day, and it took me all the time to climb on to the tram, the bag was that heavy.'

'What if you didn't have to go down the market, or the greengrocer's, or the bakery at the top of Cicely Bridge?' Molly grew excited. 'What if it were all brought to your front door?

Would it be worth the price of your tram ticket, and sixpence beside?'

'Well, I never!' Rosie clapped her hands together. 'Is that what you're planning to do?'

'I thought I could do all the shopping, and deliver it to their doors. Do you think it might work? Will folk pay for the service?'

'Sure, *I* would, and that's a fact.' Rosie was impressed, but realistic. 'But why would folks come to you, when there are already delivery vans going up and down the street?'

'There'll be a difference, Rosie. You see, I won't just turn up at the doorstep with my goods. I'll ask them first what they need, and I'll go and fetch it for them. That way they'll get exactly what they want, and not have to take what's left by the time the delivery van gets to their door.'

'A glorified errand girl, you mean. Well, me darlin', I think it might just work, especially since some of these delivery men sneak yesterday's left-overs in, and you can never get what ye want 'cos they've already sold it along the way. But how will you do it?'

'I'll buy a second-hand barrow. Old Tom Connor's got a few standing outside his pawnshop on Ainsworth Street. Happen I could do a deal with him. And I've got a few bob put by.' She paused, her voice falling quiet. 'I were saving for me and Alfie's wedding. I've got a few little bits that I bought an' all – pillow slips and that kind of thing. Happen I won't be needing them now.'

'Oh, it can't be altogether lost, surely to God!' Torn between her fondness for Molly and the love of a mother, Rosie didn't know what to say.

Molly sensed her dilemma. 'I do love him, Rosie.'

'I know you do, but that only makes it worse.'

'I want you to help me.'

'In what way?'

'When Alfie finds out what's happened, he might think it his duty to take me and the children on.'

'It's likely.' Rosie knew her son. 'Sure, he loves you enough to do something like that.'

Molly was sad, but adamant. 'It wouldn't work, Rosie. It wouldn't be fair on him, and in the end, it might come between us, and that would break my heart. Besides, knowing our dad, he would probably forbid me to take the children, and fetch in one of his tarts to look after them. I couldn't stand by and watch that happen.'

'So, what's on your mind then?'

Molly hesitated. What she had planned would split her and Alfie apart, maybe for ever. But what choice did she have? What choice had her mam left her? With a heavy heart, she outlined her plan. 'I have to make Alfie believe I don't love him enough to get wed, or to go to America with him.'

'That's a bit drastic.'

'It's the only way.' Molly was thinking of Alfie and his dreams. 'You want him to go to America, don't you, Rosie?'

'You know I do.'

'You said yourself, if he keeps on with the street-fighting, he could be maimed, or even killed. I don't want that and neither do you. If his only chance of getting off the streets is to take up the offer of America, I don't have the right to stand in his way, you must see that.'

'Yes, I see that, but it's not fair on you. What you're saying is, let him think there's no hope of you and him ever getting wed, and he'll go to America without you. Only he'll be devastated.' Rosie knew it was a terrible sacrifice for Molly to make. 'I can't let you do it,' she said. 'Not to him and not to yourself.'

Molly was desperate. 'So you want him to be lumbered with four children that don't belong to him, plus Lottie, taking on another man's responsibility, and street-fighting until he's crippled or worse? Because that's what it will come to in the end.' Molly had to convince her or Alfie was lost, and his dreams with him.

Rosie couldn't deny it. 'Oh lass, I'm so afraid for him.'

'Then help me. Please, Rosie . . . help me!'

Lost for words, Rosie dropped her head to her hands, and for the first time in years, she cried shamelessly, partly through guilt, partly relief. 'It's a wicked thing your mam's done, so it is.' Sniffling and dabbing at her eyes with a hankie handed to her by Molly, she said fondly, 'You're a special person, dear, to put my lad before yourself, especially when you could have him taking care of you and the children both.'

'I can't let him do it, and you wouldn't want me to. He's too young to be burdened like that. Besides, it's not for him to make the sacrifice. What's happened in this house is nothing to do with him. Alfie has his dreams and he has a right to see them come true.'

'Yes – but will he want it without you? I don't think so.'

Taking hold of Rosie's hands, Molly told her firmly, 'That's why you have to help me. You can convince him, I know it. Forget about me and think of him. He's your son. Do it for *him*.'

'And what about you?'

'I'll be all right. At least I'll know he's off the street and building a future for himself. It's what he wants, Rosie, and it's what I want. But I can't do it without you. You *have* to help me!'

Rosie was badly shaken. 'I didn't think it would come to this.'

Scrambling out of her chair, Molly got to her knees in front of the older woman. 'It'll be all right,' she murmured. 'He'll get over me.'

But she would never get over Alfie. Not till the day she died.

Chapter Nine

When Rosie was gone, Molly set about her work. With the children happily occupied, she immersed herself in the housework; anything to stop her dwelling on the situation in which she found herself. Besides, the house needed a good clean.

Since learning of her mam's hurried departure from these parts, Molly had been able to think of nothing else. Now though, she deliberately set her mind to other things.

Turning the wireless on, she let the music invade her senses, even humming the tunes on the Home Service as she washed the breakfast things and put them away. She then took out a small galvanised bucket from under the pot sink; filled with rags and small shoe-brushes, it held all the tools with which to clean and blacklead the fire-range.

Setting the bucket down beside the hearth, she removed every ornament from the mantelpiece . . . her mam's sewing box, the pretty brass candlesticks given to her by Rosie last Christmas, a sprig of lucky heather palmed on to Amy down the market by some toothless old Romany. Hanging underneath the mantelpiece was one of Frank's old socks; tucked into this was a box of matches and two penny candles. When Molly came home from work one day to wonder at the sock hanging from under the mantel-cloth, Amy told her, 'If the gas goes, we won't all be in the dark.' The gas had gone many times since then, and Amy had saved them all with her funny little idea.

Taking down the sock, Molly felt her tears rising and quickly put it with the other artefacts. But when she came to take down the small cameo frame holding a photograph, the tears finally fell, and with them went the last vestige of her self-control.

The photograph was of her mam and dad on their wedding day, and behind them, standing proud and stiff, were their respective parents. There was Grandad Henry, with his long droopy moustache and balding head; his wife, small and pretty, wearing a black hat with a feather; and her mam's parents, Granny Mary and Grandad John, both wonderful people. All gone now these past ten years and more.

Molly looked at the face of her mother and was struck, as always, at how pretty she had been, the fresh young skin and smiling, bright eyes, and the joy in her face as she held on to the arm of her new husband. Stroking the tip of her finger along her mother's face, Molly murmured, 'I don't suppose you thought he would ever turn out the way he did.' For a moment she felt a surge of empathy with her mam, but the sound of laughter caused her to cast her gaze down at the two children, and her heart was filled with bitterness. Laying the photograph on the table, she told her mam, 'You *both* turned out bad!'

Tearing into the work, she took down the mantel-cloth, a beautiful green velvet thing, with long tassels that danced in the heat from the fire. With great care, she took it out to the back yard where she gave it a gentle shaking; as the dust flew upwards and away, Molly wished she could go with it.

Taking the mantel-cloth back indoors, she folded it and laid it over the back of a chair, then set to washing the mantelpiece. That done, she put back the cloth and all the ornaments. Next, the hearth rug was taken outside and hung over the line. After giving it a good beating, Molly left it to freshen in the breeze, while she swept the carpet and dusted the furniture.

The next job, and one she hated, was black-leading the fire-range. Taking the old socks out of the galvanised bucket, she drew them over her arms, then got out the cloth and black-lead and rubbed a generous measure into the ironwork, working it round and round like her mam did, until the whole thing was covered. Next, she took off the surplus, then finished the job with the soft brush, polishing and polishing, until the range positively glowed. Stepping back to study her handiwork, she gave a sigh of satisfaction. 'That should do for a month at least,' she muttered.

Her mam used to black-lead it once a fortnight, but though she had no intention of neglecting the wonderful old range, Molly had other plans for her spare time.

After all the work was done and the parlour was neat and tidy, Molly discovered that Eddie had a dirty napkin. 'We'll have to get you used to the potty,' she said, changing his nappy and making him laugh when she tickled his belly. Amy had already started with his potty habits, but Molly hadn't yet had the chance to get herself properly organised. Tomorrow though, she would make it a priority.

Bertha was hungry and wanted elevenses – a jam butty. Molly sat with her at the table while Eddie played on her lap. 'Do you want to come out with me while I wash the windows?' she asked Bertha, and the answer was a whoop of joy.

Securing Eddie in his pram, Molly took him outside. Manoeuvring him so she would be able to see him, she put on the brake and went back inside. 'I want to go out *now*.' Bertha was being impatient.

'Come and help me first,' Molly said. The child followed her into the scullery, where Molly got ready the bucket and cloth for the windows, and the hard stone for the front step. Taking one of Frank's billycans from the cupboard she half-filled it with warm water and gave it to Bertha to carry. 'Steady now,' she warned. 'We don't want it all over the floor.'

Before going out, Molly rummaged about in the wash-tub and found a bolster case. Taking a baggy old jumper from the pile of dirty washing, and a smaller one for Bertha from the cupboard, she pulled the big one over her own head and carried the other to where she found Bertha poking a finger into the bucket. 'Hey! Hands off,' she laughed. 'That's *my* bucket.' It took only a minute to slip the woolly on to Bertha, roll up the sleeves, and they were all ready.

'Right. Let's go.' Taking Bertha in one hand and the bucket in the other, she made her way outside.

'Eddie's gone to sleep,' Bertha observed, and Molly was glad of it. 'Don't you go to sleep on me, will you,' she teased. 'At least not until you've white-stoned the front step.'

Tying the bolster-case round Bertha's waist, she set her to work. 'I'll draw the lines down either side,' she explained, 'then you dip the stone in the water and rub it over the step until it comes up white. And don't dip too far into the water or you'll get your arms all wet. Then you'll be cold and I'll have to take you back inside.'

Molly was up the ladder, washing the windows, when Sandra rocked the ladder from below. 'I can see right up your drawers,' she laughed crudely. 'Shame on yer, Moll Tattersall!'

Concentrating on her work, Molly was taken by surprise. Clinging on for all she was worth, she yelled back, 'Give over, you daft devil! You'll have me off!'

'You'd best come down then, hadn't yer?'

When Molly was safely on the ground, Sandra teased her mercilessly. 'You've a good pair o' legs on you, gal,' she chuckled. 'If the old knocker-upper had seen your bare arse wiggling about up there, he'd have had nightmares for weeks.'

Molly burst out laughing. 'You're daft as a brush, Sandra,'

she said. 'Anyway, my posterior certainly was *not* bare.'

Sandra made a face. Mocking Molly, she teased, 'Posterior, eh? Does that mean the same as arse? Anyway, you're wearing them French knickers off the market, aren't you? They don't leave much to the imagination, I can tell yer that!'

Ignoring her, Molly asked, 'Why aren't you at work?'

'I've got a right bad cough.' And to prove it she began coughing and spluttering like a good 'un. 'Ready for the knackers-yard I am,' she said pitifully.

'Liar!' Molly knew her only too well. 'You've no more got a cough than I have.'

'Hey! Don't tell our mam that. It took me *ages* to convince her I were at death's door.'

'So where are you off to now?'

Sandra lowered her voice. 'Me mam thinks I'm off to the quack's, but I've a date with a fella and it won't wait.'

'What – the one you picked up with the other night?'

'The very one.' She winked cheekily. 'He's – how shall I put it? – *well-built* and, I'm happy to say, very generous with it.'

'I see.' With Sandra grinning wickedly like that, her meaning couldn't be clearer. 'And is that his only merit?'

'It's enough to be going on with.'

'Honestly, Sandra, you want to be careful who you pick up in pubs and clubs. You don't know this fella from Adam.'

'Give it time, gal. Give it time.'

'Does he have a name?'

'His name's Dave.'

'Dave who?'

'Never asked. All I know is, he thinks the world of me.'

'Does he work?'

'Bleedin' hell, gal, you want to know a lot!'

'So would you if it was the other way round.'

'All right then. Yes, he *does* work, and bloody hard, I'll have you know.' Leaning forward she confided, 'He's got an old lorry that he lives in . . . honest to God, Moll, you should see it. It's got a little cooker and a table with stools, all screwed to the floor, for when he travels about. There are curtains, and rugs on the floor, and little cupboards on the wall for his bits and bobs.' Rolling her eyes she declared with amazement, 'Oh, it's like home from home.'

Giggling like a naughty schoolgirl, she added softly, 'There's even a double bed. It makes a lot o' noise when you bounce about a bit, but that don't bother us.'

Molly was worried. 'Be careful, Sandra,' she advised. 'He's probably married with a dozen kids.'

'Nah. He ain't married.' But she looked uncertain.

'How d'you know he's not?'

''Cos he would have said!' Irritated, Sandra prepared to leave. 'Jesus, Moll, I aint telling you no more, and I don't want you telling Mam neither.'

Molly knew that whatever she said, Sandra would go her own sweet way. 'Just don't let him use you, that's all.' In spite of the anguish she caused from time to time, Sandra was a good friend.

In her usual boisterous way, Alfie's twin threw her arms round Molly, almost knocking her over. 'He can "take me in" any time he likes,' she joked filthily. 'Now you get back to cleaning yer winders. Hey!' She suddenly remembered. 'You never said why *you* weren't at work? Skiving, are you, like me?'

'Not exactly. I've lost my job.'

'*Never!*' Sandra's eyes were like saucers. 'What will you do now?'

'I've got a few ideas.'

'Oh, you'll do all right, gal. Somebody's bound to snap you up.'

'I hope so.'

'Mind you, I expect you and our Alfie will be tying the knot any day now, then there'll be hundreds o' kids and you'll have more than enough to keep you on your toes.'

Molly didn't answer. It was obvious Sandra hadn't stood still long enough to catch up with what was happening.

'How's yer mam?'

Carefully phrasing her answer, Molly told her, 'As well as can be expected. Isn't that what they say?'

'Well, that's all right then. Hey, Molly, can I use your parlour?'

'What for?' What was Sandra up to now?

'Look.' Holding out her bag, she explained, 'I need to change. I daren't let Mam see me go out all dolled up.'

'Oh, go on then.' You couldn't argue with Sandra. She always got her own way in the end. 'But I won't lie for you if she asks!'

'Fair enough.'

When Sandra went inside, Molly got back up the ladder. 'Daft as a brush,' she muttered, but the girl's antics brought a smile to her face all the same.

In no time at all, her friend was back, anxiously peeping from the doorway. 'Me mam's not about, is she?'

When Molly shook her head, Sandra ventured out. Dressed in a tight skirt and an equally tight-fitting top, she teetered down the step on high-heeled shoes. 'Do I look nice?'

Molly gave her the once-over. Sandra had plastered her face with make-up, and her hair was piled up and secured in a pretty comb on top. 'You look . . . different.'

Sandra was delighted. 'Thanks, gal,' she said, and gave the ladder another shake. 'Cross your legs if anybody passes,' she laughed. 'You don't want to give 'em a fright, do yer?' With that she went away down the street at a clumsy run.

'Sandra!'

Screeching to a halt, the girl yelled back, 'Now what?'

'Happen you should take off some of that make-up.'

Indignant, Sandra dismissed the idea with a two-fingered gesture. 'Like hell I will,' she retorted. 'It took me long enough to put the bugger on.'

Molly could advise her no more, except to call out, 'Mind how you go then. We'll talk tomorrow.' She watched her friend skip down the street like a two-year-old, and couldn't help but be concerned. This new fella sounded like a fly devil to her.

In the pit of her stomach, she had a feeling it would all end in tears.

When the windows were sparkling all over the front of the house, Molly packed away her equipment and took the children inside. The bairn was still asleep in his pram, and Bertha was already yawning. 'Tired, are you, sweetheart?' Molly asked, and no sooner had she finished speaking than Bertha climbed on to the sofa and was away in the Land of Nod.

'Well, I never!' Molly was amazed, but pleased. 'I'd best get on with that washing while I've a chance.'

Taking off the woolly jumper, she laid it over the little girl. Then she placed a few knobs of coal on the fire, and taking herself into the scullery, she drew all the dirty linen from the wash-tub and separated it into different piles; coloureds in one, whites in another. Flicking the switch beneath the dolly-tub, she then filled it with water, and throwing in a handful of soap flakes, began putting the whites in one by one.

When the clothes were dancing in the hot water, she took the washboard down from the nail on the wall and slid it into the tub. Grabbing one item at a time, she drew it over the board and, scrubbing it up and down on the ridged surface, pummelled the dirt out of it.

When both lots of clothes were washed and dumped in the basket, she switched off the tub and fed the garments through the mangle, to squeeze out the surplus water. That done, she took the basket outside and hung the clothes on the line; there was nothing Molly liked better than to see the washing blowing in the fresh breeze.

Returning to the scullery, she emptied the dolly-tub and tidied up.

'By! That's a good morning's work,' she sighed, and made herself a cup of tea, even treating herself to a slice of the bread pudding that Rosie had brought round the day before.

Like Molly, Rosie had been busy doing the washing. When it was finished, she made her way up to the Tattersalls' house and let herself inside; as usual, the door was on the sneck.

Pushing open the parlour door, she smiled at the scene before her. The bairn sleeping in his pram by the back window, the child lying on the sofa, fast asleep, and there beside her was Molly.

With one arm round her little sister, and the other hand clutching a half-eaten portion of bread pudding, Molly, too, was dead to the world.

For a long, emotional moment, Rosie looked down on Molly's sleeping face. 'Had a hard day, have you, lass?' she murmured, and gently eased the bread pudding from her hand. She placed it on the saucer and took it quietly into the scullery, where she replaced it in the larder.

A quick glance at the bairn to make sure he was all right, then another at Molly and the child, and she departed, closing the door behind her.

As she went down the street, Rosie held the picture in her mind. 'Poor wee girl!' she muttered. 'She must have been exhausted.'

Shaking her head in despair, she quickened her steps. 'I wouldn't want that lass's life for a gold clock. There's Lottie, who causes more trouble than she's worth, a dad who likes booze and women and doesn't give a tinker's cuss for anybody but himself, and a mother who's turned her back on her own flesh and blood.' She took a breath. 'Five childer not of her own, and no money coming in. It doesn't do thinking about!'

Glancing up at the skies, she saw the storm clouds brewing – in more ways than one. Climbing the steps to her own front door, she glanced back at the Tattersalls' house. 'It's a big cross for a young 'un to carry,' she whispered. 'And this is only the beginning.'

Chapter Ten

Molly was at the end of her tether. 'I'm not having you lying in bed when there's work to be done,' she told Lottie. 'You turn up here after being out all night, then take yourself off to your bed and refuse to get up. You know that Dad will be in any minute. Are you deliberately trying to cause trouble, or what?'

Drawing the bedclothes up over herself, Lottie screamed abuse. 'Leave me alone and stop your nagging. You're not my mam!'

'No, but I'm the one who has to put up with you.'

'Only until our mam gets back, and then we'll see.' Turning away, she ended the heated conversation.

Knowing she couldn't leave it there, Molly sat beside her on the bed. 'Lottie, I've summat to tell you,' she began. It was time for her to know that Amy wasn't coming home.

'I don't want you to tell me *nuthin'*!' Lashing out, Lottie caught Molly hard on the face. 'Get away from me.'

Realising there was nothing to be gained by trying to tell her now, Molly backed off. 'I'll leave you,' she agreed, 'but I want you out of that bed and dressed before Dad gets home.'

'Sez you!'

'If you don't, I'll have to tell him you stayed out all night.' She wouldn't tell him, but Lottie couldn't know that.

'You cow!' Glaring at her sister from beneath the blanket, Lottie snapped, 'You would an' all, wouldn't you?'

'Not if you promise to be out of that bed and dressed before he gets home.'

'I'll get out when I hear him come through the front door.'

'I need your help downstairs, Lottie. There's the dinner on the boil, the table to be set, and the children to be seen to.'

Lottie would have none of it. Turning away she growled, 'I'm no bloody nursemaid! I'll get out when I hear him come in, and that's it.'

Apart from dragging her out of bed and forcing her downstairs, Molly could only bide her time. 'You and I had better have a long, hard talk,' she warned. 'You can't go on as you are, Lottie. Right now, none of us can afford to be selfish.'

With Lottie remaining sullen, Molly decided the best thing was to leave her be, for now. There would be time later to pull her up by the bootstraps. 'Just think on what I've said,' she urged. 'We have to talk, and soon.'

'*Go away!*'

'I mean it, Lottie. There are things you have to know, and rules to be kept to . . . whether you like it or not.'

Leaving the room, Molly deliberately left the door open. She wasn't surprised when, even before she'd reached the bottom of the stairs, Lottie had scrambled out of bed and slammed it shut against her. 'I'll have to get tough with her, or she'll run rings round me,' Molly decided.

But it was a hard thing, because Lottie was a law unto herself and, judging by her attitude now, always would be.

When she got downstairs, Bertha and Eddie were playing tents with Molly's winter coat. The sound of their laughter echoed through the house. 'Come and see, Molly!' Bertha peeped out from beneath the tail-end. 'Me an' Eddie are gonna live in here all the time.'

Getting down on all fours, she crawled in with them. 'Cor!' Feigning astonishment, she told them, 'It's as big as a house.'

Bertha rolled over, laughing. 'No it's not,' she said, and told Eddie, 'Molly's pretending.' Whereby she tickled their tummies and got them both helpless with laughter. 'You found me out,' she chuckled as she crawled out again.

'You keep an eye on Eddie,' she told Bertha. 'I'd best get the washing in before the rain comes.' Like Rosie, she had seen the storm clouds closing in fast.

She was coming up the yard steps when Rosie herself appeared. 'Here, let me give you a hand.' Taking a heap of washing from over Molly's shoulder, she told her, 'You'd best get yourself off down the street and on that tram afore the heavens open.'

Molly took her advice and was soon ready. 'I'm sorry, you two,' she told the youngsters, 'but I need my coat.' When Bertha looked at her with big cow eyes, she took her dad's old khaki coat from behind the scullery door and threw it over them. 'It's better than mine,' she said. 'It's bigger.' And they were happy enough.

'Eddie will need his napkin changed,' she told Rosie. 'I meant to do it myself, but I thought it best to fetch the washing in first . . . I didn't realise what the time was.'

'Away with ye!' Rosie ushered her out the door. 'Have ye got your purse now?'

'I have.' And to prove it, Molly waved it in the air.

'And something in case you get caught out in the rain?'

Molly showed her the umbrella she'd collected from the front parlour. 'Now will you stop fussing?' But it was so good to have somebody fussing over her, and Rosie was such a sweetheart.

'Right then. Leave me to the young 'uns and get away down the street, will ye? Get a move on, for goodness' sake. You'll miss the tram, so ye will!'

Molly ran all the way. Even so, the tram was already in. With one last spurt of energy she hopped on board.

'Another minute an' we'd have been gone.' The conductor was a familiar face; with little clumps of ginger hair sprouting out like carrot-tops all over the top of his balding head, and a cheery word for everyone, he always brought a smile to Molly's face.

'Morning, Horace,' she answered. 'How are you today?' Falling into the nearest seat, she fished threepence from her purse and handed it to him.

He clipped her ticket and laid it in her open palm. 'Not as bad as yesterday,' he answered with a grin. 'But better than I'll be tomorrow, I expect.'

'Why's that?' Fidgeting about, she made herself comfortable.

''Cos tomorrow I've to see the dentist and have two teeth pulled.' He grimaced. 'I'm not looking forward to it, I can tell you.'

'I don't blame you.' Molly shivered; she hated the dentist. 'I only go when I really have to.'

'Hey!' Wagging a finger, he laughed. 'You're supposed to cheer me up, not frighten me even more.'

'Sorry.'

'But then you've got beautiful teeth.' He saw that every day in her lovely smile. 'Mine are falling apart,' he moaned. 'Rotten inside, crumbling outside.'

'It's that tobacco you keep chewing.'

'Aye, an' I'll keep *on* chewing it an' all,' he declared defiantly. 'Teeth or no teeth, it's the only pleasure I've got.' Winking, he gave Molly a naughty nudge. 'Except when the wife's in a good mood,' he chipped, 'which is not often enough these days.' That said, he went away, whistling merrily. Hoping his luck might be in tonight, Molly thought with a silent chuckle.

Settling herself down for the ten minute journey, she glanced out of window at the darkening skies. Rosie was right about the rain, because even while she watched, it began pattering on the window pane, its frantic rhythm growing faster by the minute.

Getting off the tram at the first stop, she ran all the way to the school, dodging the raindrops as she did so. The children were waiting inside as usual. Giving them both a hug, she decided, 'We'll hang on a bit for the rain to let off.' Rosie was with the little ones now, so there was no need to panic.

'I did a drawing for you,' Milly told her, and held up a mangled piece of paper. On it was a pencil sketch of what looked like a scarecrow. 'It's *you*,' she said proudly, and Molly had to stifle her laughter.

'It's beautiful!' she gasped. 'Thank you.' And she gave Milly another hug.

Georgie tutted. 'It looks like a scarecrow to me.'

Out of the mouths of babes, Molly thought, and raised her eyebrows warningly at Georgie. 'And what have *you* been doing today?'

'It isn't a scarecrow!' Milly's face began to crumple. 'It's our Molly!'

Shaking her head meaningfully, Molly looked at Georgie. 'You didn't really mean that, did you?' she pleaded, and peace was restored when he told Milly, 'I can *see* it's our Molly.' Looking at the picture, he fibbed, 'I were only joking before.' He smiled all over when Molly gave him a grateful wink.

A moment later, the rain began to ease off. 'Look, Moll, it's Mrs Bolton, our teacher!' Filled with awe, Milly tugged at her sister's hand. 'She gave Paul Martin the cane . . . right on his little arse. He cried for ages and ages.'

Molly was horrified. 'Where did you hear that word?'

Milly was mystified. 'What word?'

Georgie obliged. 'Arse.'

Milly grinned. 'Well, Paul's mam had a fight with Mrs Bolton, and *she* said it . . . "You'd better not lay a cane on my Paul's arse ever again", that's what she said.'

By this time Molly was beside herself, holding back the laughter and praying to God she wouldn't let it loose in front of

Mrs Bolton. 'Right, well, we'd better go,' she spluttered, and began pushing the children forward.

But just as she had feared, Molly was stopped in her tracks. 'Ah, let me see now . . . *Molly*, isn't it?'

Full of apprehension, Molly turned. 'Good afternoon, Mrs Bolton.' She felt ten years old, and more afraid of Mrs Bolton than either Milly or Georgie were. And with every right.

For Mrs Bolton was a formidable sight. A huge mound of a woman, with tiny spectacles and a round red face, she looked terrifying when she smiled, as she did now at Molly. 'Tell your mother the children are a credit to her,' she purred, her body filling up the little porch. 'They know their manners, and that's more than I can say for some of the little horrors!'

'Are they doing all right with their work?' Molly was new at talking to teachers, and she felt uncomfortable.

'Well, Georgie has trouble with his reading, but he's good at sums, and Milly has trouble with her arithmetic, but she's better at reading.' Giving a hearty laugh, the woman suggested, 'They should share it out better, don't you think?'

Molly didn't know quite what to say, so she smiled politely instead. 'Thank you,' she mumbled, and immediately felt silly.

'Good!' Clumsily throwing open her umbrella, Mrs Bolton almost poked Molly in the eye. 'Tell your mother if she ever wants to see me, I'm available for ten minutes at the end of each day.' With that she pushed her way through and marched regally out into the rain like a real hero.

'She's fat!' Milly didn't mince her words.

'It's not her fault,' Georgie retorted. 'Her mam gave her too many sausages when she was a baby.'

Molly laughed out loud. 'Who told you that?'

'Mrs Bolton. She told it to Dicky Donley when he called her fat in the playground. Then she gave him a hundred lines saying, *Mrs Bolton is not fat, Mrs Bolton is not fat, Mrs Bo—*'

'That's enough!'

Grabbing hold of the children, Molly made a run for it. She was still chuckling when they got on the tram, five minutes later.

It was time for Rosie to pop back home. 'I'll get the men's dinner then I'll be back,' she promised. 'Don't forget I'm minding the bairns while you and Alfie go out tonight.'

Walking to the door with her, Molly said sombrely, 'I'll have to tell him tonight, Rosie – about America, and everything.' But first she had to be sure. 'You will back me up, won't you?'

For a moment the woman looked into the girl's troubled blue eyes. 'I can't see any other way.' Like Molly, she was desolate. 'I'll do all I can,' she promised. 'And may God help the pair of us!'

The first thing Molly did when Rosie was gone was to go up to Lottie and remind her, 'I want you out of that bed before Dad gets home, or there'll be hell to pay.'

Lottie turned over and didn't answer, but her sister knew she'd heard, so she left it at that.

Downstairs, she busied herself. Getting out the big bowl and rolling pin, she set to making a meat and potato pie. The leftover potatoes were sliced in half and put in a tray of lard to bake in the oven. Together with the carrots and gravy, it would make a tasty meal.

While that was cooking, she washed and bathed all four children and got them into their nightgowns. 'Later on, I'll be leaving you with Rosie while me and Alfie go out,' she told them.

'Will Dad be here?' Milly wanted to know.

'He might be, or he might decide to go out, I don't know, sweetheart.' She added wryly, 'Your dad doesn't tell *me* his plans.' Any more than he used to tell our mam, she thought angrily.

'I don't want him to be here.' Georgie was honest to a fault.

'And I don't!' Bertha started to cry.

'Hey!' Grabbing them all to her, Molly promised, 'I won't be gone long. Rosie will be here, and Dad will probably be going back out once he's had his dinner.'

Little Eddie's bottom lip began to tremble. 'Want my mammy!' he cried, and flung his arms round Molly's neck.

'No tears,' she said, wiping them away. 'You're a big brave boy, aren't you?' She dreaded the moment she must tell them the truth.

Singing a song, she began clapping her hands, and soon they were all clapping. 'Let's do "Ring-a-Ring-a-Roses",' Bertha cried excitedly, so they all joined hands and went round and round, until Milly felt sick and they had to stop.

'Can we stay up late?' Georgie asked.

'We'll see.' She made no promises. If their dad was in a bad mood when he got home, she'd rather they were in bed out of his way, but if he went straight out again, or didn't come home at all, happen Rosie would let them stay down an extra hour.

By the time they had finished their meal – though Bertha only picked at hers as usual – Rosie was at the door. 'Alfie's washing,' she told Molly. 'He'll not be too long.'

While the children played on the rug, the two women talked, and when the clock chimed seven Rosie commented, 'Your dad's late again.'

Molly glanced anxiously at the children. 'I expect he's gone down the pub for a jar,' she said, and wished in her heart that Frank Tattersall would never set foot in this house again.

In a hushed voice she told Rosie what the children had said about not wanting him there. 'I'm not surprised,' Rosie answered. 'They're not blind and they're not deaf. They know what goes on.'

Molly opened her heart. 'If I had the means, I'd take them as far away from here as I could.'

Rosie shook her head. 'Sure, you'd not be happy,' she replied. 'It's not wise to move too far out of your roots, and besides, I'd miss you all, so I would.'

'Do you think Mam will regret it?'

'What's that, lass?'

'Moving out of her roots?'

'Only time will tell.' Rosie was philosophical about these things. 'We shall just have to wait and see.'

When Molly began clearing away the dinner things, Rosie took the dishcloth out of her hand. 'I'll do that. You away and get ready.' And she wouldn't take no for an answer.

Giving her the privacy she deserved, Rosie told Molly to close the scullery door while she washed.

While Molly strip-washed at the pot sink, Rosie scraped all the leftovers on to one plate. Piling the plates one atop the other, she placed them on the corner of the dresser. She then scooped any bits of food into the centre of the tablecloth and folded it like a huge dolly bag so the scraps stayed put. This, too, she placed on the dresser, then taking the duster from the drawer, she wiped the polished table clean and replaced the potted plant in the centre. 'Good as new,' she said, and was proud of herself.

By that time, Molly was washed and dried. Slipping the towel round her shoulders, she thanked Rosie and quickly made her way upstairs.

Once in her room, she rummaged in the wardrobe, choosing a plain black skirt and a pink twin set. She groaned when she unrolled her stockings to discover that one had the tiniest hole in the knee. 'Never mind,' she muttered and put them on anyway, hoping the hem of her skirt would cover the offending hole; much to her relief, it did.

Sitting before the oval dressing-table mirror, she brushed her brown hair until it shone; next came the face cream, and then the rouge . . . just a dab on each cheek. A touch of mascara, and a smudge of lipstick and she was ready.

'Shoes!' Hunting for her brown ankle-straps, she found them under the bed next to the jeremiah. Slipping them on, she went to Lottie's room, and finding her still asleep, gave her a good shaking. 'I'm going out now,' she warned. 'If Dad comes in and finds you still abed, I wouldn't like to be in your shoes!'

When Lottie merely drew the bedclothes back over her head, Molly was hard-pressed not to fling them back again and yank her sister out of there. Instead, she left her to it. Her patience had been tried too far. She was finished with arguing and cajoling. In light of what had happened, starting tomorrow, Lottie would have to pull her weight in this house.

Five minutes later, Alfie arrived, looking incredibly handsome in a roll-neck sweater and dark jacket, with the green cord trousers Molly had bought him last birthday.

'I've changed my mind,' she teased him with a serious face. 'I don't fancy going to the pictures, so me and Sandra have decided to go out on the town . . . girls' stuff and all that.' When he stared at her in disbelief, she added with a cheeky grin, 'If we're lucky we might even pick up a couple of good-looking blokes.'

'You little devil!' Diving at her, he snatched her into his arms and swung her round. 'I've a good mind to tan your backside.'

Rosie laughed. 'Not in front of the children, you won't!' she chided. 'And not in front of *me* neither.'

'Right then, we'd best be off, or we'll miss the start.' Taking Molly's coat from the back of the door, Alfie arranged it over her shoulders. 'It's a good ten minutes' walk.'

Molly kissed the children one after the other. 'Do as Rosie says and be good,' she told them, and they promised they would.

Leaving Alfie to stroll up the passage before her, Molly took

Rosie aside. 'If Dad comes home the worse for drink, take them straight up to their beds,' she urged. 'And please . . . see if you can get that lazy sister of mine down. If he comes in and finds her still in bed, he'll tan the arse off her.'

'Aye, an' it'd serve her right, so it would.'

'All the same, I wouldn't like her to get on the wrong side of him. You know what he's like.' When her dad got going there was no stopping him.

Rosie sighed. 'All right, pet, I'll do my best.' Given half a chance she wouldn't mind tanning Lottie's backside herself. 'And don't you worry about the little 'uns. I'll take care of them, you know I will.'

Taking a deep breath, Molly squeezed her hand. 'When it comes to it, I don't know if I'll have the courage to tell Alfie . . . about him going to America without me, and me not wanting to get wed.' She loathed the idea of deceiving him. 'I've thought and thought about it,' she confessed, 'and I know I'm doing right. Oh Rosie, what else can I do?' She paused to compose herself. 'I love him too much to take away his future.'

Seeing the girl's eyes fill with tears, Rosie was lost for words. She merely smiled and nodded, before, with a fleeting kiss on the cheek, she propelled her gently out the door.

With the cool breeze on her face and Alfie's arm round her, Molly hurried along, her mind on what had to be done before the night was over.

'Penny for them?'

Startled, she glanced up at him. 'Sorry, Alfie, I was miles away.'

'I know – I've been talking to myself for the past few minutes.'

'It's just . . . I've got a few things on my mind, that's all.'

'If you're worried about finding work, you shouldn't be. The minute your mam's back on her feet you'll be fixed up in no time.' He planted a kiss on her head. 'Besides, it won't be all that long before we're off to America.' He chuckled. 'Oh, love, you don't know how much it means to me!'

When she didn't answer, he went on talking, about America – the land of opportunity – and his plans for the two of them there. 'It's not as if we're on the moon,' he reminded her. 'We can come back and visit. At first we'll have to rent something small and reasonable, but when we've got a bigger place of our own, and money in the bank, we could fetch the whole family over, wouldn't that be great?'

At the cinema kiosk he asked for, 'Two one and nines, please.' When the tickets were bought, the slim, uniformed usherette showed them to their places with her torchlight. 'The big picture's already started,' she whispered. As they shuffled down the row, Alfie glanced at the big screen and tripped over somebody's feet. 'Sorry mate,' he apologised, and quickly moved on.

The film was a jungle adventure, with animals roaring and natives throwing spears. 'It's supposed to be good,' Alfie had told her along the way. 'If it's not, we'll come out and go dancing at the Palais. There's a good band on tonight.'

For now though, it was all they could do to get to their seats. 'They would have to be right in the middle, wouldn't they?' he groaned, squeezing past people's knees and constantly apologising when they cursed and complained. 'Miserable blighters!' he whispered, as they thankfully found their seats and made themselves comfortable.

Engrossed in the film, Alfie watched the hero fighting for his life, and it brought home to him the events of the recent war. He thought of how it might have been. 'Sometimes I wish I'd been old enough to go in the Army during the war,' he told Molly. 'In a way, I'm sorry I wasn't there to do my bit, but then you wonder about the ones that never came home, and you thank God for the chances you've been given.'

Taking hold of her hand, he held it tight between his large, strong fists. 'We're two of the lucky ones, you and me,' he said. 'We mustn't waste a single minute, d'you understand what I mean, love?'

She told him she did, but her heart sank when she thought how close she was to shattering his contentment.

Excited and on edge, he couldn't seem to settle. Every now and then he would whisper something in Molly's ear and she would look up and smile. Then he'd kiss her, and they'd chuckle at some funny thing he might say, until suddenly Alfie was reeling from a clap round the head.

'Young man, will you *please* be quiet!' The woman behind was a sour-faced old biddy who was already wishing she had stayed home and put her feet up by the fire. 'And keep your head still, or I'll call the manager!'

Like a pair of naughty children, Molly and Alfie didn't dare move after that. Instead, they sat very still and became very quiet, stifling their laughter until the interval, when the ice-cream and popcorn came round. Fishing in his pocket for change, Alfie asked Molly what she wanted.

'Anything but popcorn.' Molly discreetly gestured to the woman behind. 'She'd be bound to find fault with that, especially when we started crunching and rattling the bag about.'

'I'm not letting *her* tell us what we can and can't have.' And off he went, hackles up. 'If I want popcorn, I'll damn well have popcorn, and that's that!'

Curious, Molly watched as he walked down the aisle to join the queue; the ice-cream attendant looked like a little soldier, with her newly pressed uniform and tray of goodies slung round her neck. 'Oh, dear!' Molly held her breath as the woman seated behind them suddenly went rushing down the aisle to position herself directly beside Alfie. 'He won't like that,' she chuckled. 'One word out of line and she'll have him!'

Alfie was the first to return, carrying two lolly ices. 'I thought you weren't going to let her dictate to you about what you should have.' Molly had a twinkle in her eye. 'What happened? Scare you off, did she?'

'Not a bit of it,' he lied. 'If you must know, I thought the popcorn looked a bit off.' All the same, he, too, had a twinkle in his eye. 'She's even worse, face on,' he confessed. 'Gave me the willies, she did, creeping up on me like that.' And before she came rushing back again, ice-cream tub in hand, they had a good chuckle about it.

Behind them, the woman settled down and opened her tub, spooning out the vanilla ice-cream with a little wooden scoop. She slapped her lips, sucking and licking and, according to Alfie, making more noise than a pig at the trough.

Before the picture started up again, she made a great fuss of getting out of her seat. In fact, she trod on so many toes, she left a trail of devastation behind her.

Unfortunately for Molly and Alfie, she paused behind them and issued a stern warning. 'Holding hands and canoodling, indeed! Goodness only knows why they let hooligans like you into the pictures at all . . . spoiling it for other, respectable folk!' With that she gave Alfie another hearty clip round the ear. 'I shall report the pair of you to the manager on my way out, you see if I don't!' And off she stomped to cause more mischief at the desk.

A few minutes later, the manager came down to the end of their row. 'I shall have to ask you to leave,' he said as quietly as he could. 'There's been a complaint.'

Alfie was immediately up in arms. 'What complaint?' The light quickly dawned. 'Oh, no! Not that old biddy. Surely to God you're not taking any notice of her, are you?'

The manager was outraged. 'Mrs Baker is a valued client,' he retorted in a normal voice. 'She's been most offended by your behaviour.'

People were beginning to listen, distracted from the film by all this carry-on.

'And we've been offended by hers, so I suggest you ban her from the picture-house, because if you ask me, she's a born trouble-maker!'

'Are you telling me how to run my premises, young man?'

'Well, *somebody* ought to tell you. Throwing innocent people out, who've paid good money, and all on the word of a cranky old woman.'

The manager squared his narrow shoulders. 'That's enough. I want you out NOW!' Raising his voice as loud as he dare while the picture was rolling, he threatened, 'If you refuse, I'll have to call a Bobby.'

Things were getting out of hand. Molly swiftly intervened. 'We'll leave quietly,' she said. 'But my boyfriend's right. The woman *is* a trouble-maker.'

'Nonsense. She's a poor old thing.'

Unbeknown to them, Alfie and Molly had not been the only ones to feel the length of that 'poor old thing's' tongue. 'Miserable old faggot. Good shuts to her,' said the man who had sat next to her during the film. 'She's done nothing but fart and groan and cram snuff up her nose. What's more, she stinks to high heaven . . . hasn't had a bath in a month of Sundays, if you ask me.'

By this time, the picture-house was in uproar. 'Shut up, back there!' . . . 'If you want to argue, get outside and let decent folks watch the film!' There were others present who knew Mrs Baker personally. 'She's an old hag, and should be put down,' one man declared, and another agreed. 'She's an artful old bugger. The young fella's right – she *should* be banned.'

Realising he'd got it all wrong, the manager sheepishly offered his apologies and told Molly and Alfie they could stay and watch the film twice over if they'd a mind.

Alfie thanked him but refused. 'What I'd like is my money back,' he said crossly, and was astonished when the manager didn't argue.

Once outside, the pair collapsed with laughter. 'That was more entertaining than the picture,' Alfie chortled, and Molly agreed. For those few precious minutes she had forgotten her troubles and her heart felt lighter.

Rattling the coins in his hand, he asked her, 'Right then, me beauty, what's it to be? The pub or the Palais?'

Molly didn't feel like dancing. 'The pub.' It would be quieter there. It could be her opportunity to talk matters over with him.

The nearest public house was only a short walk away, but it wasn't quiet as she had hoped. It seemed as if the whole of Blackburn had a thirst on tonight; swilling ale and smoking, the patrons filled the place with the fog of tobacco and the stench of booze.

Alfie asked if she'd changed her mind and would rather go to the Palais after all. She said no, and so he sat her at a corner table and brought their drinks . . . a lemon and lime for Molly, and for himself a pint of the best.

It took Alfie longer than usual to make his way back to the table. 'Good lad!' The calls came from all over. 'You won me a bob or two the other night.' 'Let me pay for them drinks, lad.' One man had heard a whisper. 'If it's true what they say about you moving to America, they'll need to look hard for someone to take yer place. When you're stripped for action you're a joy to watch.'

'Hey! I wouldn't mind seeing you stripped for action.' The toothless old hag was harmless enough; her name was Aggie, and she had long ago won every man's heart. 'Ask *me*, Aggie,' the landlord teased. 'Say the word an' I'll strip for you here and now.'

'Like hell yer will!' When she laughed, her mouth was dark

and cavernous. 'I want summat nice to look at, not one to gimme bloomin' nightmares!'

Soon, the punters were crowding round Molly and Alfie. 'Is it right, Alfie, lad?' they wanted to know. 'Are you really thinking of leaving for America?'

'I reckon so,' he answered. 'Me and Molly here are getting wed and thinking of going out there, just for a year at first. If all goes well, we'll probably settle down over there.' Reaching out, he took hold of her hand. 'Ain't that right, sweetheart?' Molly nodded and smiled, while inside she was falling apart.

During the few brief minutes they'd been on their own, she had put on a brave face. She'd talked of anything and everything and had responded to Alfie's jokes as always. Now she listened to his plans for their future together in America, and wished to God the others would all go away so she could stop him before he went any further. Instead of which they were full of the news about Alfie, and constantly coming over and asking for more.

When at last the questions and the folk drifted away, Alfie gave her a meaningful wink. 'Hey.'

She knew he was about to say something suggestive, but playfully feigned ignorance. 'What?'

'You know what.'

'No, I don't.'

He sighed and winked again. 'Would *you* like to see me stripped for action?'

'I'm sure I don't know what you mean,' she said, pretending to be offended.

Leaning closer, he whispered, 'You and me . . . later?'

Molly simply grinned. Oh, how she loved him. 'You're a bad 'un,' she said, and took a sip of her drink. After a moment she felt his eyes on her. 'What now?'

He hunched his shoulders. 'Nothing.'

'Are you ready to leave?'

'Not yet.'

'Well, *what* then?'

'Are you all right, sweetheart?'

'Yes, why?' But she wasn't all right. Far from it.

'It's just that, well . . . I've never known you so quiet. What's wrong? Is it your mam? I've been thinking, I'd like to come with you to the hospital tomorrow night after work. I know she hasn't wanted any visitors, and I can understand that, but now that you say she's out of the woods . . .'

Molly gave a wry little smile. Oh yes, her mam was out of the woods all right . . . out of the woods and out of their lives. 'It's not that,' she sighed.

'So, what is it?'

For one frantic moment, it was on the tip of Molly's tongue to tell him the truth about her mam and everything else that went with it. But this wasn't the place or the time. Her courage failed. A moment later, when he asked her if she was ready for off, she nodded gratefully.

It was half past ten when they left the pub. Outside, the weather had taken a turn for the worst, with the breeze blowing up to a cutting wind, and the skies full of rain clouds. 'Looks like the summer's well and truly over,' Alfie said, turning up the collar of his jacket.

How right he was, Molly thought. The summer was definitely over – in more ways than one.

Strolling back to Victoria Street, he drew her close to keep her warm; the touch of her body against his sent a thrill right through him. 'You're doing things to me,' he whispered, and guided her into a darkened doorway. 'You drive a man crazy.'

Pressing her to the wall, he murmured passionately, 'I love you, Molly, more than you'll ever know.' For a long, wonderful moment he looked into her eyes, those pretty blue eyes that seemed so deep and mysterious tonight.

'Kiss me,' she whispered, raising her face to his. She needed him to kiss her – a long, melting kiss that lifted her soul and filled her with joy.

When the kiss was over, Molly held on to him for what seemed an age. She had a feeling she would want to keep that kiss in her heart for ever and a day.

In that dark, quiet corner, he wanted more, his arms tight about her, and his breathing ragged. 'Nobody will see us,' he murmured, and she knew it was true. 'We've done it before, and got away with it.' That was also true. But not tonight. There were other things on her mind tonight.

She pushed him gently away. 'Let's go home, Alfie.'

Yet again, he sensed there was something not quite right with her tonight. 'Okay, if that's what you want, that's what we'll do.' With one protective arm about her, he led her to the pavement and down the street towards home.

With Molly fearing the minute when she must tell him, and Alfie sensing trouble, there was not a word spoken the whole way.

Rosie was anxious to see them. One look at Molly's face and the shake of her head, told the older woman she hadn't yet found the right moment.

'I'll be off,' she said quickly. 'Leave youse two to yourselves.' Lifting her coat from the back of the chair where she'd thrown it, she gave a hurried account of her evening. 'Lottie's gone out. She got up a few minutes after you left and took herself off to God knows where.'

Molly had expected it. 'She'll find her way back,' she said flatly. 'She always does, and anyway it's bitter cold out there tonight.'

'The childer are sleeping like little angels. Bertha had a nightmare but she's all right now.'

'Did Dad come home?'

Rosie shook her head. 'I haven't seen hide nor hair of him.'

'Thanks then, Rosie.'

'Right! I'll see you the morrow.' Widening her eyes, she sent Molly a message. 'Mind how you go, darlin'.' It was a warning to impart her news carefully, gently. 'See ye later, son.' Then she was gone before he could even open his mouth.

Alfie was bemused. 'What the devil's wrong with her?'

'What d'you mean?'

'You saw her! She couldn't get away quick enough.' No one was behaving normally tonight.

Molly took off her coat and hung it on the nail behind the door. 'I expect she's tired.'

But he knew it was more than that. 'Women!' he smiled. 'What would we do without 'em, eh?' Taking Molly into his arms, he kissed her again, on the neck, down in the hollow of her throat, and on her mouth – every kiss a memory. 'We're home now,' he whispered passionately, and she knew what he meant.

Molly had never needed him more than she did right now. When he laid her tenderly on the floor, she closed her eyes and savoured the moment. His hands were all over her, gently caressing, exciting her senses until she forgot everything else. They were taking a chance, for either Lottie or Frank could have come home suddenly and burst in on them, but Molly wanted Alfie so badly, she threw caution and care to the wind.

She felt her jumper being pushed up and his long, strong fingers reaching to cup her breast. With the tip of his tongue he teased her nipples.

She did not resist when he took off her stockings, then her panties, and now he was on her, naked from the waist down, hard against her thigh. A few moments and then he was inside her. Warm and thrilling, he moved her body with his.

At the height of their passion Molly looked into his eyes, and her love for him was all-consuming.

* * *

Afterwards, when passion was spent and cold reality took hold, Molly was swamped with guilt. Silently, she dressed herself, unable to look her lover in the face, knowing what she must do. And now it was a thousand times worse.

Going to the dresser, she took out a jar of elderberry wine, bought from some old gypsy and never opened. 'Want some?' Holding up the jar, she took two glasses from the cupboard.

Alfie quietly regarded her for a moment. 'No, thanks.' Pulling on his trousers, he thought how tense she seemed tonight. It worried him.

When a moment later she came to sit beside the fire, glass in hand, he sat astride the chair-arm and looked down on her with troubled eyes. Voicing the question that was playing on his mind, he asked softly, 'Is there something you want to tell me?'

Raising her drink, she gulped it down, gasping aloud when the fiery liquid scalded her throat. She had hoped it might give her the courage she needed, but it only left her empty.

In another minute her whole life would change for ever. If only her mam would miraculously walk in through that door, everything would be all right. She even glanced up at the door, as though to greet her.

Convinced there really was someone there, Alfie spun round. He was bewildered by her behaviour.

'What's wrong with you?' he asked. 'You've been strange all night, and now I ask you a question and you can't even give me a straightforward answer.'

The tears burned behind her eyes but she mustn't let him see. 'I'm sorry.' It sounded so inadequate.

Alfie grew afraid. He could see the tears in her eyes and the slight tremble of her hand as she brought her glass up again. 'No more, Molly!' Taking the wine from her, he placed it on the table.

'Not until you tell me what's going on, and I'm not leaving here until you do.'

Folding her hands one into the other, she stared at the fire. 'You're right,' she answered, 'I *have* got something to tell you. The trouble is, I don't know how to start.'

'At the beginning is usually a good place.' The anger spilled over into his voice.

Taking a deep breath, she got out of the chair and began pacing the floor. 'It's about you and me,' she began hesitantly. 'I can't wed you, Alfie. It's all got to be cancelled – the wedding plans, me going to America with you. I can't be part of it, not any more.'

'What!' Alfie was shocked to his roots. 'I don't understand.'

'Just let me explain,' she pleaded. 'Something's happened. It's changed everything. I've been wanting to tell you . . .'

One minute he was shaking his head slowly from side to side, as if trying to shrug off what was going through his mind. The next minute he had leaped from the chair. Grabbing her by the arms, he shook her. 'My God! Now I understand. There's someone else, isn't there? That's what you've been trying to tell me!'

'NO!' Molly was shocked he could even think such a thing.

His voice breaking with emotion, he pleaded, 'Don't lie to me. Don't take me for a fool.' Thrusting her away he kept his distance, his face contorted with disgust. 'But then, I must be a bloody fool, or I would have seen it. Lately you've been acting strange.' Throwing back his head, he groaned. 'You've met somebody else, and you want rid of me, that's it, isn't it?'

Grabbing her again, he held her still, his face looking down on hers, the pain in his eyes awful to see. 'For God's sake, Molly, be honest with me.'

She opened her mouth to explain how he couldn't be more wrong, when like a bolt out of the blue, it came to her how it could all be settled quickly, though not painlessly. Never painlessly. Unwittingly, Alfie had given her a way out.

'All right!' Feigning anger, she broke away from him. 'I *have* met somebody else, only I didn't know how to tell you.' Her voice softened. 'I didn't mean for any of this to happen,' she said truthfully. 'You have to believe that.' She wondered how she could sound so calm, when inside she was in such turmoil.

Grey-faced, he pulled away from her. 'Who is he?'

When she shook her head, as if refusing to tell, he gave a small, cynical laugh. 'I see.'

'I'm sorry, Alfie.' In the circumstances, there was nothing more she could say.

He turned to collect his jacket, and when he looked back she was standing there, head bowed, her heart like a lead weight inside her. When she felt his gaze on her, she almost ran to him and told him it was all a lie, all a trick to make him turn against her so he could follow his dream without a conscience.

For what seemed an age neither of them spoke. Eventually, when he walked to the front door, she watched from the parlour doorway.

At the door he paused, his head low, his voice accusing. 'We made love,' he murmured. 'How could you bring yourself to do that, when you knew all along?' A moment later and he was gone, out of the house. *Out of her life.*

The sound of the door clicking shut echoed in her brain. Closing her eyes, she leaned back against the wall and sobbed shamelessly.

'Don't cry, Molly. Please don't cry.' Bertha was at the top of the stairs, unsure of what was happening, and scared by the sound of her big sister crying.

Molly ran upstairs and folded the child to her. 'It's all right,' she murmured, kissing the rosy cheek and carrying Bertha back to bed. But it *wasn't* all right.

How could it be?

Chapter Eleven

It was midnight when Lottie came home, arrogant as ever, and looking for a fight. 'Don't go up yet.' Molly had waited for her and now she stood by the parlour door, barring the younger girl's way.

'What are you playing at?' Lottie had never seen Molly so serious. 'I'm going upstairs, so you'd better clear off out of my way.'

'Sit down. I've got something important to tell you.'

'What's so bloody important it can't wait till tomorrow?'

'Sit down. *Please!*'

'Not if it means another damned lecture, I won't!' Pushing hard against Molly she tried forcing her way through, and was surprised when the other girl stood her ground. 'All right, but be quick,' she snapped, backing off. 'I need my sleep.'

When Lottie was sitting down, Molly came and sat beside her. This time there was no hesitation. 'Mam's gone.' The words were like a slap in the face to Lottie.

Springing out of the chair, she regarded Molly with suspicion. 'What d'yer mean, "Mam's gone"? Gone where?'

Molly asked her to sit down again, and when Lottie fell into the chair opposite, she confessed, 'I don't know where she's gone.' Reaching into her pocket she handed Lottie the note. 'She left this.'

While Lottie read the letter, Molly paced the floor. Telling her sister had not been easy. Telling her father would be even harder.

'Oh God! How could she do this?' Dropping the letter to the floor, Lottie scrambled out of the chair and ran to the door. Flinging it open, she went up the stairs two at a time and into her room.

Placing the letter on the table, Molly followed more slowly. She knew how her sister was feeling, for hadn't she felt exactly the same herself? Besides, bad as she was, Lottie was still only a kid. Her mam leaving them for good was a lot to take in.

Molly found her looking out the window at the night sky, her face drained and streaked with tears. 'Come back downstairs,' she suggested kindly. 'It's not good to be up here on your own.'

Lottie's face hardened. 'Leave me alone!' Folding her arms, she deliberately turned her back.

Recalling how she herself had wanted to be on her own when she first read that damnable letter, Molly understood. 'All right, love. I'll be downstairs if you need me.'

She was out on the landing, about to close the door behind her, when a muffled voice called her back. 'Moll. Wait!'

Molly turned and went back in.

'She might come back . . . mightn't she?' Lottie's voice trembled.

Molly shook her head sadly. 'I don't think so, love. You've read the letter. It seems final enough to me.'

'Was it because of me?' Lottie's face twitched nervously. 'Tell me the truth, Molly. Did *I* drive her away?'

'She's got herself another man – another life. That's what she said in the letter.' Molly hated the pain she was causing and tried her best to lessen it. 'No, Lottie. Of course it wasn't because of you.'

Suddenly, the girl was in Molly's arms, sobbing as if her heart would break. 'I don't want her to run away. I want her to come back. Please, Molly, make her come back. I'll behave myself, I promise I will!' Then she couldn't talk any more, and Molly held her close, her own tears rolling down her face.

Life was so cruel.

The mantelpiece clock was striking two o'clock when Frank Tattersall finally came home. It was a wonder he managed to get up at six of a morning, Molly often thought, with the hours he kept.

Her heart in her mouth, she had waited up for him after Lottie had cried herself to sleep. If she didn't tell him tonight, he would find out another way, and life wouldn't be worth living.

Red-faced and merry, he came through the parlour door, visibly taken aback to see Molly there. 'Time you were in bed, my girl,' he grumbled.

Having dozed intermittently, Molly stared at him through bleary eyes. 'I've been waiting up for you.'

'Oh, have you now?' Turning aside, he beckoned, and a scrawny redhead appeared. Gesturing at his daughter, he told the woman, 'This silly little bitch thinks I'm some snotty-nosed kid to be told off when I'm home late.'

He swaggered into the room. 'Well, I'm home *now*,' he hissed, 'so you can sod off to bed, and be quick about it.' With his arm round the woman he said, 'Can't you see I've got company?' And the two of them started giggling.

Calm and collected, Molly got out of her chair. Perhaps it would be easier with a stranger present. 'I have a letter for you,' she said, and taking it from the table, she held it out to him.

Frank stared up at her, his face creased in a frown. 'What the devil do I want with a letter! Have you gone mad, girl?'

'It's from Mam.' She thrust it closer to him, her eyes never leaving his. 'I think you'd better read it.'

Seeing she would not leave until he took the letter, Frank

snatched it from her. 'She must have gone off her head!' he sneered. 'What's the idea anyway? Bleedin' letters. I thought she were due out any day now, and about time, too, the lazy whore.'

Squashing the letter under the cushion, he said, 'I'll read it later. I've more pressing business for the minute.' Winking at the woman he added slyly, 'It can wait till me company's gone.'

Molly was adamant. 'I think you should read it now.'

'I don't give a toss what you think,' he growled. 'Are you bloody deaf or what?' Making a move towards her he threatened, 'I thought I told you to get upstairs!'

'Please yourself,' Molly retorted. 'I just thought you'd like to know about it before the whole street starts gossiping. I didn't want to find out that way, but if you're not bothered about folks knowing your business before you do, that's fine. Tear it up. Burn it. What do I care?' With that she departed the room, and left him to his giggling company.

Just as she had suspected, the minute she had gone, he picked up the letter and began reading it, his jaw dropping in disbelief as he took in the words.

Molly was halfway up the stairs when she heard him yelling, 'Get out of 'ere, you old hag! Get back to the bloody streets where yer belong!'

Pausing, Molly looked down to see her father manhandling the redhead out the front door. When he saw Molly on the stair, he ordered, 'You! Get back down 'ere this minute.'

Taking her time, she returned to the parlour.

Wild-eyed and furious, Frank flung the offending letter across the table. 'What's all this bloody nonsense then? What game does she think she's playing?'

'It's no game.'

Appearing not to have heard, he gave a nervous little laugh. 'Happen she's heard rumours about them streetwomen who keep following me home.' Pacing up and down, he was like a man demented. 'Well, I'll soon put paid to that, 'cos I'm off to the 'orspital right now, and just let the buggers try and throw me out this time!'

'It's no good you going there.' Molly thought it amazing how the shock of that letter seemed to have sobered him up. 'If you read the letter properly, you'll know she's not there.'

'She's bloody there all right, but not for long, 'cos I'm fetching her back 'ere, where she belongs.'

'You're not listening to me, are you?' Molly had expected him to go berserk and turn the place upside down. Instead, it seemed like all the stuffing had been knocked out of him.

Looking at Molly, he cocked his head to one side, his eyes too bright, his voice beginning to crack. 'Aye, that's what I'll do. Yer mam's had time enough now.' Running his hands frantically through his thinning hair, he said, 'No wonder she's writing silly stuff like that. She'll be going out of her mind in that place. Oh, aye. Once our Amy's home, this damned house might get back to normal.'

When he grabbed up his coat from the sofa Molly cried out to him, 'It's no use you going to the infirmary. *She's not there!*'

He paused in the doorway, coat in hand, head bowed and his back to her. 'Don't go fooling yourself,' she told him harshly, hating him. 'Mam's gone, thanks to you, and judging by that letter, she's never coming back.'

For what seemed a lifetime, the silence in the little parlour was unbearable.

Frank remained quite still, head hanging low, coat in hand; neither he nor Molly made a move. In the background the clock ticked and from somewhere upstairs came the creaking of a floorboard.

'No.' One solitary word, spoken by a man who had been deserted, and who knew, deep down, that he *was* the cause of his wife leaving.

In all her life Molly had never felt so alone. 'Come back inside, Dad.' Wearily going to him, she put her hand on his shoulder.

Shrugging her off, he kept his back to her and, leaning against the door like an old man, he appeared to sag into himself; one arm hanging loose to let the coat slip to the floor, and his head buried deep into his neck.

To her amazement, Molly thought she heard him crying. Then his shoulders began heaving and the sound of his sobbing filled the room.

Shaken to her soul, Molly felt she had to get out of the house. She went into the scullery and opened the back door, then sat on the steps in the dark, breathing in the fresh night air, steeped in thought.

After a while the sights and sounds of the night invaded her senses: a man's voice, whistling a merry tune as he wended his way home; rats scurrying about in the cellar; the shadow of a solitary cat gliding over the wall. Overhead the stars winked at her, seeming to say, 'Take heart, Molly. Take heart.' And her heart did grow quieter.

Suddenly, without warning, the quietness was shattered and all hell let loose.

From inside the house she could hear Lottie and her father screaming at each other. Scrambling up, she rushed inside. 'Stop it!' she cried. Taking Lottie by the arms, she held her off and pleaded, 'The children, Lottie. Think of the children!'

But with so much pent-up hatred and fear spilling out, Lottie was unstoppable. 'You've got to tell him, Molly,' she roared, struggling like a wild thing. 'It's his fault as well as mine!' she cried, her face contorted with loathing. 'He was a pig to her, a vicious, violent pig – and it's no wonder she's gone! I hate you, Dad!' Breaking away from Molly, she fled back up the stairs, sobbing as if her heart would break.

'Little cow!' Frank muttered, pacing the floor. 'Our Amy's never gone,' he said obstinately. 'She *can't* have gone. She wouldn't do that to me.'

Within minutes, Lottie was down again, all her belongings crammed into a bag. Keeping her distance, she yelled from the doorway, 'You're no good. You're allus drunk . . . eyeing other women when me mam's stuck at home with your bairns. You spend your wages soon as you get 'em, leaving her to do the best she can with what's left. She said you were neither use nor ornament, and she were bloody right!'

With a deep-throated growl, he lunged at her from across the room. Throwing Molly aside, he took his younger daughter by the throat. 'One more word outta you, and I'll do for you, see if I don't!' He grinned when she began fighting for breath. 'No good, am I?' A spray of his spittle showered her face. 'I'll show you what's no good.' The more she struggled, the tighter he squeezed.

Dazed and cut where he had knocked her down, Molly saw what he was doing and was horrified. 'GET OFF HER!' she screamed. Any second now, Lottie would stop breathing. Thrusting herself between them, she tried to separate one from the other, but his grip on Lottie was like iron. 'Dad, you're killing her. For God's sake, let go, or I'll fetch the police.'

Some of her words must have got through, because with an almighty shudder, he threw Lottie aside. In that moment, when he was spent of energy and Molly was bent double trying to catch her breath, Lottie grabbed her bag from the floor where it had fallen. Stumbling down the passage, she made for the door before he could have her again. 'You're mad!' she screamed, her throat aflame from his mauling. 'Mam hates the sight of you, and so do I!'

'Come back here!' Incensed, Frank went after her again, only this time Molly had the strength to hold on to him, until Lottie was safely away.

When the front door slammed, he went wild. Screaming like a banshee, he clenched his fist and ran straight at the parlour door, sending his fist through the panel, his arm split open by the exploding splinters. 'Jesus!' With the blood dripping down his arm, he took hold of Molly by the shoulders. 'I'll swing for that girl!' His eyes stood out like cold bright marbles. 'If she ever sets foot in this house again, I swear to God, I'll do for her.'

Meeting his gaze defiantly, Molly told him, 'Let go of me.'

At first it seemed he might hit out at her, but then he lowered his hands and turned away. 'It weren't my fault,' he muttered. 'Yer mam didn't go because of me.' Watching Molly out of the corner of his eye, he asked, 'How will I find her, lass? How will I know where she's gone?'

Molly's voice was cold and unforgiving. 'You won't.'

He nodded heavily, his eyes bloodshot. 'Happen it's just as well.'

Because in that moment, he had murder in mind.

Just as she was, without coat or thought for herself, Molly ran out of the house and into the night. She *had* to find Lottie.

Calling her name from every corner, she found her way to the old recreation ground where the fair was set out, ghostly and silent, and there, seated on the steps round the Waltzer, was her sister. Dropping down beside her, she draped an arm round her shoulders. 'What did you want to rile him like that for, eh?'

'He's a bad 'un, Molly . . . worse than me.'

'Who says you're a bad 'un?'

'They all do – me dad, Rosie, and most of the folks down the street.'

'Take no notice,' Molly consoled her. 'Anyway, none of it matters now. All I'm concerned about is you.'

'Well, yer shouldn't be.'

'Come home, love. He'll have calmed down by now.'

Lottie gave a funny kind of laugh. 'It's too late,' she answered dully. 'I've left home now. The fair leaves here first thing in the morning, and when it does, I'll be with it.'

Molly glanced about, at the big, awesome machines. 'You can't mean that,' she protested. 'What, travelling from place to place, out in all weathers, no proper home of your own? What kind of life is that?'

'The *best*.' It was another voice that answered. The young man who spoke was obviously part of the fairground; tall and lanky, he had an easy, arrogant look about him, and straightaway Molly could see how women might be attracted to him, especially one as young and impressionable as her sister.

Lottie's face lit up. 'This is Dave,' she said proudly. 'He's my fella.'

For some reason she couldn't explain, Molly wasn't all that surprised. After all, Lottie had stayed out a couple of times lately, and had been more restless than usual.

But Molly was angry and fearful. Her voice shaking with emotion she told the young man, 'I don't know you, and I don't want to. But I'll tell you this: my sister is going *nowhere* with you! You should be locked up. Have you any idea how—' She had been about to remind him of Lottie's age, when her sister quickly intervened.

'Leave him out of this, our Molly.' Before Molly could answer, Lottie addressed the young man. 'Go away, Dave. *Please*. Go back to your wagon and go to bed. I'll see you later.'

He studied Molly, then Lottie, and then he was smiling, silently congratulating himself. Once he took a woman, they stayed until he told them to go. Lottie was no different. When he left here tomorrow, she would be with him, no matter what her sister wanted.

'Be seeing you,' he said, giving Molly an insolent smile, and returned to his wagon.

When he was far enough out of earshot, Lottie took her sister to task. 'You were gonna tell him how old I am, weren't you?'

Molly was shocked. 'Are you saying he doesn't already know?'

'He won't neither, not if I have owt to do with it.'

Molly tried again. 'Come home, love, that's all I want.'

Lottie looked around her, recalling the fair in working hours, when the air was filled with merry music, and the delighted screams of people on the rides echoed through the night. Lost in a world of fantasy, lovers walked arm-in-arm with eyes for only each other, and everywhere myriads of folk strolled about laughing and chatting. 'I *am* home,' she said, and to Molly's amazement, there was a sense of peace and contentment in her sister's voice. 'I belong here.'

Strangely humbled, Molly looked into Lottie's young eyes and saw something there she had not reckoned for; Lottie was no longer a young girl but a woman, grown up and ready for the world. And yet she was still only fifteen, too young to leave home. 'I'm sorry,' she said painfully, 'I can't let you go like this.'

Tossing her head defiantly, Lottie retorted, 'How will you stop me? Will you drag me home by the hair of my head? Maybe you'll tell Dave my real age and hope he throws me out as well. Or one day, when he comes home drunk and looking for a fight, Dad might really kill me.' A look of desperation hardened her face. 'If you take me back there, I might even kill myself. Is that what you want, Molly? To bury me in the churchyard? Because that's where I might as well be, without Mam and my Dave.'

'Don't talk like that, Lottie,' Molly said in a choked voice. 'It won't happen. I won't let it.'

But Lottie had a warning of her own. 'You can't be there *all* the time, can you, Molly?'

Molly knew it was the truth. She also knew Lottie well enough to believe she would carry out her threat. 'But you're so young, Lottie. Too young to be all alone in the world.'

In a rare moment of tenderness, Lottie took hold of her sister's hand. 'I won't be alone,' she answered. 'I've got Dave. And besides, I'm not all that young. I'll be sixteen next birthday. Noreen Taylor got wed when she were sixteen and now she's only eighteen and already got three kids.'

Seeing her argument crumble before her, Molly was moment-arily lost for words.

'I'll be all right, honest I will. I can take care of myself.' The younger girl smiled. 'Besides, if you make me come home, I'll only run away, and I'll keep on running, until one day I'll be so far out of your life you'll never, ever find me. You wouldn't like that, would you?'

Molly's answer was to fold her arms round Lottie's neck and draw her close. 'You know I wouldn't.'

'I do love you, Molly. I want you to know that.' Her voice broke and, like Molly, she could not stop the tears.

'I'll keep in touch,' she promised. 'Wherever I am, I'll let you know.'

In the background, she saw Dave waiting on the steps of his wagon. 'Come and meet my sister properly.' Lottie was confident Molly would not now disclose her age.

Arrogant as ever, Dave remained where he was.

Realising he had no intention of making the first move, Lottie made excuses for him. 'He's a bit wary of folk,' she told Molly. 'His mam were a bit of a pig and he's been on the run for a long time. He's learned not to trust folk, but he's a good sort, Molly. You mustn't worry.'

Unconvinced, Molly walked up the steps to where he sat. Looking up at him, she saw the defiance in his eyes, and it struck her how alike these two were.

For his part, Dave observed how she was not as pretty as

Lottie, and decided he'd got the best bargain. Admiring her boldness in coming to him when he wouldn't go to her, he held out his hand. Taking her small fist in his, he said, 'I'm Dave. Nice to meet you.'

Molly nodded. 'I'm sure you know that I don't want her to go with you?'

'So I understand.'

'Do you think I'm being unreasonable?' She needed to dig beneath that hard exterior and find out what he was really thinking.

He smiled. 'No. If it were my kid sister, I'd want the same.'

'Will you help me?'

Again he shook his head. 'Sorry. It's not up to me.'

'She might listen to you.'

'It's not my fight. I've made it a rule never to get involved in family matters.' With that he thrust his hands deep into his pockets and, looking beyond her to Lottie, he made an impatient, beckoning gesture with his head.

Running up the steps, Lottie urged, 'Go home, Molly. Look at yer, you ain't even got a coat and it's bloody freezing. I'll be all right, you know I will.'

'How will you manage?'

'I'll work here, on the fairground. They're allus looking for young, strong hands.'

'And where will you live?'

Dave's voice cut the air. 'She'll live with me, in my wagon. It's warm and cosy and she'll not go hungry.' Neither will I, he thought slyly. Only his hunger was of a different kind.

There was something about the young man Molly couldn't take to, but then, Lottie was obviously fond of him, so he couldn't be all that bad. Besides, Lottie had always been able to hold her own, even against their dad at his worst.

Suddenly, Molly looked from one to the other, and realised

that here was an alliance meant to run its course. She feared for Lottie, yet feared more what would happen if she forced her to come back to Victoria Street.

'Please, Molly.' Lottie's voice shattered her thoughts. 'I've made up my mind: I'm going with Dave. Let me go with your blessing.'

Molly raised her eyes to Lottie's, and for a time they looked at each other, their faces wet with tears, their hearts aching. They remembered how it had been before, and how it was now, and came to realise that nothing stayed the same. Everything moved on, and now Lottie, too, was moving on. 'Keep in touch?' Molly asked, and Lottie promised she would. 'Wherever I am.'

They fell into each other's arms and the old childhood love flowed between them; that same love which had been momentarily smothered by circumstance, adolescent selfishness and the unhappiness of others.

After a time, they drew apart and Lottie said, 'Tell Dad I don't really hate him.'

Swallowing hard, Molly nodded. 'I suppose I will.'

'And give the kids a hug for me.'

Taking a deep breath, Molly placed both hands on her sister's shoulders. 'Looks like I have no option but to let you go.'

'You won't send the authorities after me, will you?' It was the frightened little girl speaking. 'They'll put me away.'

'I might,' Molly threatened with a wag of the finger. 'If I don't hear from you regularly.'

Relieved, Lottie smiled. 'I've already said, haven't I?'

Looking to Dave, Molly conceded, 'Seems as though I have to trust you, whether I want to or not.'

He gave no answer. Instead he merely nodded, but for Molly it was all she could ask and no more.

Another tense moment followed, before Lottie went up the steps and stood beside her fella; when Molly went away, her heart felt like lead in her chest. She didn't look back, though she knew they watched until she was out of sight.

Head bent to the cold wind, she made her way home. 'Take care of yourself, Lottie,' she murmured. 'And may God keep you safe.'

The following night, after her dad had gone out to drown his sorrows, Molly opened the door to Rosie. 'Kids in bed, are they?' Rosie asked.

'This past hour,' Molly answered, leading the way into the parlour.

'So, ye managed to tell your da, then?'

'He took it bad, Rosie.'

'So he should.' Rosie had little sympathy. 'Where is he now?'

'One of his old cronies called and took him down to the pub.'

'I see. And what about Lottie . . . did ye tell her?'

'Lottie took it even worse.' Molly shivered. 'She and Dad had a terrible fight, each blaming the other.'

Rosie then noticed the bruises and scratches on Molly's face and neck. 'And you got caught up in the middle as usual, is that it?'

The girl smiled wistfully. 'If I tell you summat, will you promise not to breathe a word to a soul, not even Sandra . . . *especially* not your Sandra? You know how the drink loosens her tongue.'

Rosie agreed. 'Go on, love. I'm listening.'

As briefly as she could, Molly explained what had happened and where Lottie had gone. 'I had no choice,' she told Rosie. 'Dad had already threatened to swing for her if she came back, and then she threatened to take her own life if I forced her to. So what could I do, Rosie . . . what else could I do but let her go?'

'Nothing, other than what you did. Ye told her you'd come looking for her if she didn't keep in touch, and ye told the young fella he was to take care of her. No matter what ye did or didn't do, she would have gone anyway, if not to this bloke then to another.'

'D'you really think so?' It was small consolation, but consolation all the same.

'I'm sure of it! She's a wild little thing and has to learn from her own mistakes. Sure, when it all boils down to it, lass, ye did exactly what I would have done in the circumstances. You two made friends, and she knows you love her all the same. She went away happy, didn't she? Ye must allus keep that in mind.'

'She was so afraid I'd send the authorities after her. "They'll put me away," she said.'

'Aye, an' they would an' all. But you're not to worry, pet. I won't say a word to a soul – not even to our Sandra.' She chuckled. 'If anyone should ask me, I'll tell them she's gone to her Auntie Mabel's in Northampton.'

'We haven't got an Auntie Mabel in Northampton.'

'Sure, *I* know that,' Rosie laughed. 'But nobody else does, do they now?'

And Molly felt reassured. It was a weight off her mind just to have told somebody.

Now Rosie felt it was time to speak her mind. 'With Lottie off on her own adventure, there'll be less fireworks in this house and no mistake.' Making her way into the scullery, she came back with a tray of tea and barmcakes. 'Ye look like a ghost, so ye do,' she told Molly. 'Get this down ye, afore ye fade away altogether.'

When the two of them were settled, Molly voiced the question uppermost in her mind. 'Is Alfie all right?'

Rosie swallowed the chunk of barmcake, her sorry gaze on the young girl's face as she answered. 'He's done nothing but talk about it, lass. "Did she mean it, Mam?" . . . "How can she end it just like that?" . . . "She's seeing another fella, and now she wants no part of me".'

'Oh, Rosie. I never wanted to hurt him.' Molly's lips were trembling. 'I only want what's right for him, you know that.'

'Aye, an' there'll come a day when Alfie will know it, too.'

'Will he go to America?'

'Yes, it's all planned. His grandaddy is taking him to Ireland for a short while, to visit his kith and kin. He says it's so the lad can have a few days' quiet afore the long journey, but if ye ask me, he's taking him there to show him off, so he is. The Irish half of the family will be sending Alfie straight to America from there.'

'When does he leave for Ireland?'

'First thing in the morning, lass. We've hurried it up a bit, in the circumstances, and it seems best all round.'

Molly smiled, but the tears shone through. 'That's good,' she murmured. 'He'll do well.' Biting back the tears, she lapsed into a deep, thoughtful silence.

Rosie ate her barmcake and drank her tea. Never once did she take her eyes off Molly.

Anger surged through her. She loved the girl like her own. And from now on, if anybody was to hurt that lass, she would kill them with her own bare hands, so she would!

Part Two

CHRISTMAS 1948

THE PRICE OF LOVE

Chapter Twelve

Jack proposed a toast. 'Happy Birthday, Amy.' He chinked his glass with hers, took a sip of his wine and, leaning over, kissed her tenderly on the mouth. 'You're looking lovelier than ever tonight.'

He was right. Amy did look lovely. The pretty cream dress from a shop in Bedford town seemed to lift the brown of her eyes. Her dark brown hair was coiled into the nape of her neck and her skin shone like pearls in the candlelight.

For Jack, although the little restaurant was crowded, there was no one else in that room. All he could see was Amy, and his love for her shone in his face. 'How did I ever live without you?' he whispered.

Amy blushed at his compliments. 'Ssh! Somebody will hear you.'

He smiled. 'Let them. I want everyone to know how much I love you.'

Reaching into his pocket he took out a small velvet box. 'It's been burning a hole in my pocket all night,' he said, handing it to her. 'I saw it in a shop window last week and I knew you would just love it.'

Curious, Amy opened the box, and for a moment she was mesmerised. In all her life she had never been given a gift such as this. The ring was the most beautiful thing she had ever seen; fashioned from gold and silver, its dainty shoulders were enmeshed with tiny diamonds, and the slim, open claws held the prettiest, darkest ruby. 'It's wonderful!' she gasped. 'Oh, Jack, thank you – and you're right, I do love it. I'll cherish it for ever.'

'Are you happy, Amy?' That was his constant worry, that she might grow unhappy away from her children, and he would lose her.

Amy read his thoughts. 'I do miss them,' she murmured, 'Molly and the others. I can't help but wonder what they think of me, running away and leaving them all like that.'

'They knew what your life was like,' he reminded her. 'I'm sure they understand.'

'I hope *he* isn't making their lives as much of a misery as he made mine.'

'Why would he? None of it is their fault, any more than it was yours.'

'I hope you're right, Jack. I hope he sees it that way, too.'

'I haven't changed my mind, love.' He thought to put that straight right now. 'It would cripple me to have the children. I'm not the father type. I wish I was, but I'm not, and I never could be.'

Amy had seen that, and accepted it. 'I know,' she laughed. 'I've seen for myself how you cringe when a child comes near you.'

'That's what comes of being brought up in a children's home,' he said. 'You never have space enough for yourself. They're everywhere. You can't escape them day or night . . . children of all ages, some so young they cried for their mammies every waking minute, and others, the bigger ones, who bullied us all without mercy.'

As he spoke, she could see the tension in his face. 'We were squashed into these awful dormitories – even had to share a bed if there were none going spare. Three in a bathtub, and sometimes eighteen or twenty round the table, always crowding . . . noise and fighting every day.'

He visibly shuddered: the awful memories of his parents dying, and the trauma of growing up in the children's home still affected him badly. Taking a gulp of his drink, he told her truthfully, 'I'm sorry, Amy. If I could change I would, but I can't . . . not even if it means losing you.'

'It's all right, Jack. I understand, really I do.' She had witnessed his nightmares and seen the pain in his eyes whenever he talked of 'that place', and she knew him now, better than she had ever done. She had come to understand how he grew to be a tearaway, and how hard it must have been for him to make a success of his life the way he had. Jack was a good man; Frank was not. 'You won't lose me,' she said passionately. *'Never!'*

He looked at her then, and no man had ever loved a woman more. 'You're the only light in my life,' he whispered. 'I've always loved you, Amy. Ever since I first saw you.'

'And you're the only man I've ever loved,' she confessed. 'I've never known such joy and contentment before.' But there was a price, and whatever others might believe, she would pay it every time she saw a child on the streets; every time she woke with a start, haunted by the faces of the innocents she had left behind.

Frank had been the biggest mistake of her life. The consequences of that were hard to live with, yet she saw no way out of it, not if she wanted to stay with Jack. And she wanted that with all her heart and soul.

His voice broke through her thoughts. 'Are you ready for home, Amy?'

'Yes,' she answered with a smile. 'Whenever you are.'

* * *

Home for Amy was now a big, grand house down by the River Ouse in a beautiful suburb of Bedford. Built in Edwardian times, it had spacious rooms and huge windows that overlooked the park at the back and the river at the front. The sturdy furniture had been bought with the place, and from the moment Amy walked in the door, she had felt at home.

She had the same feeling now, as they parked the black saloon and walked up the garden path. Shoving the key in the lock, Jack flung open the door and waited for her to pass inside. 'Fancy a nightcap before we go to bed?'

Amy shook her head. 'Not tonight.' Too many memories seemed to have crept in on this, her fortieth birthday. Normally, Molly would come home with flowers for her, and the children would sit round the table after dinner and make something very special; a card, or a picture for her to stick up on the scullery wall.

If she had to choose again, to be with Frank and the children, or to be with Jack, she would still make the same choice. But it was hard not to have the children with her; harder than even Jack realised.

As she undressed in the bedroom, Jack watched from the doorway. He saw her roll the stockings off her slim legs, and take down her panties. He smiled when she folded them with the same meticulous care she took with all the beautiful underwear he had bought for her. Now, when she raised her arms and slid out of her clothes, he caught his breath at her beauty.

As she went to slip the pretty pink nightgown over her head, he hurried across the room to stop her. 'Don't,' he murmured, and the passion was alight in his eyes. 'Let me look at you first.'

Amy laughed. 'You say the same thing every night.'

Taking her in his arms, he kissed her on the neck. 'What man could blame me for that,' he murmured, and held her away from him, his gaze admiring her every curve. 'All those children,' he said, 'and you still have the figure of a young girl.'

'I have not!' Turning to look at herself in the mirror, she saw what he obviously didn't – the sag of her stomach muscles and the way her breasts had begun to droop; she knew this because where once the nipples had been upright and pert, they were now not so prominent. 'I'm forty today,' she said. 'And it shows.'

'Not to me,' he answered, and bending his head, he teased her nipples with the tip of his tongue. When he felt her responding, he slid his hands round her waist and drew her to him.

A moment later, naked and wanting each other, they made love, right there on the rug, without shame or guilt. In their hearts, they were innocents, snatching at life with both hands. And, for whatever reason, at that moment in time, life was good to them.

They didn't mind what tomorrow brought, or whether their contentment would go on for ever. They accepted the gift of each other and, for as long as it lasted, they enjoyed the moment.

Because, more than most, these two lonely souls knew how fleeting a moment could be.

Chapter Thirteen

It had snowed all day yesterday, all through the night, and now, at six in the morning, it was still coming down. 'When in God's name will it stop?'

Molly's gaze followed the constant flurry of snowflakes as they rained down on the windowsill. She thought how beautiful it all was; the solitary tree at the top of the street was hanging low, its branches silvered by the snow, its long arms outstretched like a woman about to cradle her child. The lamp post had a collar of snow round its lumpy neck, and where the snow had settled in between the cobbles, a curious criss-cross pattern was beginning to emerge.

Every house had a white roof, the chimney-pots like little people swathed against the cold. Snow had settled on the window-sills, thick and whipped by the wind, like froth on milk. Some way down, old Jimmy Tuppence, wrapped up in long coat, flat cap and a scarf, was shovelling the snow from his path.

Molly chuckled. 'You might be going on eighty,' she muttered, pressing her nose to the window, 'but you could show the young 'uns a thing or two – eh, Jimmy boy?'

Suddenly, a small hand stole into hers. 'Can we make a snowman?'

Having crept out of bed and down the stairs like a ghost so as not to wake anyone, Molly was surprised to see Bertha standing beside her, shivering in her nightgown. 'Well, well, what have we here?' Lifting the bairn into her arms, she said, 'When I looked in on you just now, you were fast asleep. What woke you, sweetheart?'

Bertha put her arms round her big sister's neck. 'I saw the snow come tumbling down.' And she wiggled her fingers to demonstrate.

Molly showed her the snow on the ground outside the window. 'Only three days to Christmas,' she told the child. 'If it snows on Christmas Day it's supposed to be *magical*. What do you think?'

'I think Father Christmas throws it out of his sleigh, so he can land easy.'

Molly laughed at that. 'Well then, it really *is* magical.'

'Can we make a snowman?' Bertha asked again.

'We'll see. Maybe when you've had your breakfast.'

'Georgie said he once made a snowman, and its head fell off.'

Molly remembered. 'He's right, it did.'

She recalled the very morning; it was the end of November, some three years since. The snow had come early. The children had gone out into the yard and scooped all the snow into the centre. Everyone had helped make the biggest snowman ever . . . Mam and Lottie, and Molly, and Georgie with Milly and wee Bertha. Eddie hadn't been born then.

There had been a lot of screeching and laughing, and afterwards their mam had made hot soup and they sat round the table like a real family.

'I wouldn't like it if my snowman's head fell off.'

'Georgie didn't like it either.'

'What did it look like?'

'Well, it was big and fat.' Molly blew out her cheeks and stuck out her belly. 'And it smiled all the time. Georgie made its head by rolling the snow round and round in the yard. Milly found two buttons for the eyes and I made the mouth out of Dad's old bootlace.' She chuckled. 'The snowman stood in the yard for two whole days, then the weather changed and its head began to shrink, until it fell sideways and dropped to the ground with a splosh. Georgie was so upset he ran to his room and didn't come out till teatime.'

Bertha listened to the story with wide eyes. 'Did he cry?'

Molly winked. 'Just a bit.'

'No, I didn't!' Georgie was at the parlour door, his pride dented. 'It were our Milly who cried, not me.'

Molly pretended to have made a mistake. 'Was it? Oh yes, I think you're right.' Then she quickly changed the subject and told them to go and wash, while she got the breakfast ready.

'I want two boiled eggs.' Georgie licked his lips in anticipation. 'With soldiers to dip in.'

'I want porridge, with jam and sugar and everything.' That was Milly's favourite.

'I'm sorry. No soldiers and no porridge. You had the last of it yesterday, so now you'll have what you're given,' Molly told them kindly.

Her announcement was greeted with a melody of groans.

Bertha was all right. She never worried too much about what was put in front of her; she just ate it. And Eddie was happy with his biscuits and bottle of milk. But the others were grown up enough to know what they wanted, and kept on at Molly. 'Why can't we have what we want for breakfast?' Milly insisted. 'All the other girls at school get to choose, so why can't I?'

'Because this is not a canteen, and besides, I haven't been to the shops yet.' The reason being that lately she had to count her pennies more than ever.

These days, she had to budget very carefully. It was dog's work getting anything out of her dad, although she had managed to squeeze a few pounds to keep them going. But, all in all, times were hard, and getting harder by the day.

Looking at the disappointed faces now, she felt a failure. 'I'll see what I can do tomorrow,' she promised.

Knowing that if their big sister made a promise she would do her best to keep it, they turned their attention to other matters. 'Where's Dad?' Nervous, they all glanced towards the parlour door.

'He's still in bed,' Molly answered. 'You know he always has a lie-in on a Sunday.'

'When's Mammy coming home?' That was Bertha, still hoping after all this time. 'Will she be home for Christmas?'

Molly had already begun to ease them away from the idea that their mother would be coming home sooner rather than later. 'Do you remember how I said that Mammy had not been very well since the bairn, and that she would not be coming home for ages and ages?'

'It's *been* ages and ages. I want her to come home *now*!' That was Bertha again.

Molly took a deep breath. 'When you've all had your breakfast,' she said, 'there's something very important you have to know.'

Thinking it was something good, Bertha shouted, 'Tell us now, Molly, tell us *now*!'

Molly shook her head. 'Breakfast first.'

If she were to tell them now, none of them would feel like food, and besides, she had to decide how best to let them know that their mammy wasn't still in the infirmary, but had gone away.

From the scullery, she could hear Bertha and Georgie talking to each other about what they would make Amy for Christmas. It brought a lump to her throat.

Setting about their breakfasts, she lit the stove, half filled the pan with milk and put it on to heat. Once that was underway, she took out three dishes and broke some bread into each one. Then she added a sprinkle of sugar and now the milk, which by now was just at the right temperature.

Next, she dished out two rusks for Eddie, and put his bottle of warm milk beside them.

Taking a clean bib for him, and three spoons for the others, she placed everything on the tray and carried it to the parlour, where the children were waiting patiently.

'Oh, no!' Milly was the first to moan. 'Not *pobbies* again!'

'Don't start!' Molly had to keep a firm hand. 'I've already told you I'll see what I can do tomorrow. Besides, pobbies are good for you.' Leaning towards her, she whispered so Georgie couldn't hear, 'They make your hair curl.'

That seemed to do the trick. In any event all three of them tucked in and appeared to enjoy their breakfast, though after a time, Milly began toying with her food and only managed to eat half. 'I can do you some toast if you like?' That much at least, she could offer. But Milly shook her head and Molly didn't press the point.

She waited for the others to finish, then: 'I want you all to listen carefully to what I have to say,' Molly began quietly. But before she could go on, Milly scrambled out of her chair and, leaning across the table, yelled at the top of her voice, 'Mam's run away, and she's never coming back! Lottie's gone for ever, too. I heard Dad fighting with her.'

For a moment time was suspended. All eyes turned to Milly, and when she began to cry, so did the others, all except Georgie. 'I don't care if they never come back!' White-faced and shocked, he fled from the room and ran up the stairs.

Before Molly could go after him, she had to deal with the others. Bertha was inconsolable. 'Why isn't she coming back? Doesn't she love us any more?'

Milly went into a sulk and Molly couldn't get through to her. Eddie was crying simply because the others were upset, and she had to juggle her time between them all.

After a while, Milly came out of her sulk. 'I don't want her to come back now,' she said coldly. 'I don't like her any more.' And to Molly, that was worse than if she'd sobbed her heart out.

Bertha was teased out of her misery by the promise of a snowman. 'You go out and make a start, and I'll come out in a minute,' Molly said, and the two girls went off, covered against the cold in woolly hats, thick stockings and winter coats. Muffled up and warm, Eddie went out, too.

Molly stole a minute to watch them from the top of the yard steps. When she was satisfied they seemed to have accepted what she'd told them, she went upstairs to Georgie.

Like all big boys, he kept his tears for when he was alone, and now she found him crying into his pillow.

Sitting on the bed, she made no move towards him. Instead, she assured him, 'Your mammy does still love you all, but she had to go away. I'm so sorry, Georgie, but you know I'm still here for you. I'll be your mammy for as long as you want.'

Lifting his face from the pillow, he crept along the bed to where she was sitting. For the briefest second he looked at her, the tears swimming down his face, and his eyes red raw. Then his mouth began to tremble and he was in her arms. '*You* won't leave us, will you, Molly?' he pleaded. 'Don't go away like Mammy did, will you, Molly? Don't leave me.'

Her voice breaking with emotion, Molly told him she would never leave them. 'Not for as long as I live.'

If she had any regrets about sending Alfie away, they melted in that little boy's arms. 'You're my lad now,' she whispered, 'and I wouldn't hurt you for the world.'

But she *had* hurt Alfie – and for that she would never forgive herself.

* * *

When Rosie came round with news of Alfie an hour later, she found Molly and the children laughing and playing in the yard. 'You're like a big kid, so ye are!' she called down. 'Now, Molly, I've something to tell ye, so I have.'

Leaving the children making the snowman, Molly made her way up to the scullery. 'By! It's freezing!' Rubbing her cold hands together she took off her coat and scarf and draped them over the sink. 'Now then, what's all the excitement?'

Having dumped her coat and hat in the passageway, Rosie set about making tea, chattering away as she worked. 'I've had another letter from Alfie. He's in for his first big fight next week. They're putting him up against a fella called Arnie Wild.' Laughing, she quipped, 'We've only to hope he's not as wild as he sounds, eh? Oh, but what good news, lass. His grandaddy can't sit still. Ever since we got the letter he's been like a cat on hot bricks, and now he's off down the Working Man's Club to tell the others.' She rolled her eyes to the ceiling.

'Oh Molly, at long last Alfie's doing what he really wants. And not on the streets neither, but in the ring, inside, where he should have been all along. Isn't it wonderful news, lass – our Alfie up against the big American fighter, proper money and no running when the police come round the corner. And all under the eye of a professional trainer, too.'

Molly agreed, though she was pleased and sorry at the same time. She thought of all Alfie's sacrifices, and hers, too. At least they hadn't all been for nothing.

Handing Molly her tea, Rosie was surprised when it was refused. 'Oh, come on, lass, ye must be froze. The tea will warm ye up, so it will.'

Apologising, Molly took the tea. 'Sorry, Rosie, and you're right – I *am* froze.' Sitting down at the table with her friend, she asked quietly, 'What else does he say?'

Now, seeing the look on the girl's face, Rosie was mortified. 'Oh, may God forgive me!' she cried. 'I clean forgot, so I did!' Clasping the small hand in both of hers, she shook it gently. 'Here's me, blabbing on about how he's up for a fight, and there's you, wondering how he is, and missing him like nothing on earth.' Fishing the letter out of her pinafore pocket, she gave it over to Molly. 'It's a bit long, but then he always has a lot to say.'

With trembling fingers, Molly unfolded the letter, her eyes misting over as she read:

Hello Mam,

How are things at home?

I'm sorry it's been an age since I've written, but I've not had a minute to call my own. I've been working hard at the gym. I've got a new trainer, Gus Baines, and by God, he's a real slave-driver! I'm up at four and in bed by nine, with nothing but training in between. But I've never been so fit in all my life.

I've had a couple of low-key fights, and won them both, but they were nothing to get excited about. They were just practice for the big one, and now the date's set I can't wait. The big day is 2nd January.

It's so different from the street-fighting. It's real big business, Mam. Everything is so professional. It's all worked out right down to the last detail; the venue, the timing, who'll be there and who won't. I'm not kidding you, Mam, thousands of pounds change hands every minute. If I win this fight, it'll be money in the bank, enough for you and Grandaddy to come out for a long holiday, and plenty more left to buy me a place of my own.

The trainer says, with this one under my belt, I can name my own price. They'll be lining up to meet me, and, if all goes well, I'll be in the big-time before you know it.

Here, the mood of his letter seemed to change:

I've been missing you and Grandaddy. I never thought I'd get used to being so far away from home, but I'm settling down now.

I hope you're both well. Have you seen Molly lately? I hope she is happy with her new bloke. She's a lovely person, and deserves a good man to take care of her; someone with a regular job, who can give her the things she should have.

I imagine her mam is out of hospital and doing well?

Give them both my regards when you next see them, and give the kids a hug for me.

Lots of love. Take care of yourself,

Alfie.

'He sounds so excited.' Caressing the letter, Molly was loath to let it go. 'I'm glad for him.' She smiled, but the smile never touched her heart.

'He asked after you,' Rosie pointed out. 'He still thinks of you, darlin'.'

Handing back the letter, Molly nodded. 'I know.' But it didn't seem as if he still loved her; not in the way she loved him. 'He seems to have got over me,' she said. 'I'm glad about that, for his sake.'

'We'll see.' Rosie was not so sure he *had* got over Molly. And she knew for certain that Molly was not over him.

Molly's mind flew to where he was. Would she ever see him again? she wondered. Would she ever feel his arms round her and hear him whisper in her ear?

It didn't seem likely. She had sent him away, and now she had no rights to him.

She could not blame Alfie for that.

'Molly?' Rosie called her name for the second time.

The girl had been so deep in thought she hadn't heard. 'Oh Rosie, I'm sorry.' She pushed Alfie from her mind. 'I was miles away.'

'Aye.' Rosie's heart went out to her. 'As far away as America, with our Alfie.'

Molly smiled sadly. '*Did* I do right?' she asked. 'Sending him away like that?'

Rosie gave it some thought. 'It was right for *him*, lass. Wrong for you. But, in the circumstances, I don't see what else you could have done. If you'd kept him here, he would have insisted on taking care of you, and that would have meant either leaving the children with your da, or Alfie taking them on as his own. He'd have had to get a job in the cotton mills and hated every minute of it, but he would have done it for you and the kids.'

'And grown to hate me for it.'

'No, Molly, he would never do that.'

'But his soul would be destroyed and it would have been me who did that to him.'

'You just asked if you'd done right in sending him away,' Rosie pointed out. 'I think you've answered your own question, lass.'

'Thank you.' It was what Molly needed, to be reassured that she *had* made the right decision, for Alfie, if not for herself.

A moment later, Molly went out to the back yard. 'I think it's time you came in now,' she told the children. 'You've been out long enough in the cold.'

Her suggestion was met with a wall of protest. 'Not yet, *please*.' Georgie spoke for all of them. 'We've got to make another snowman, for Eddie.'

Eddie was in his pram, clapping his hands and laughing as they rolled the snowman's belly up, bigger and bigger. His nose was red and his eyes were watering, but he was happy enough.

A quick check of his little hands and face and Molly thought a few more minutes would not hurt. She wiped his nose and gave him a hug, and warned the others, 'Ten minutes and you're all inside, whether you like it or not. Right?'

They all shouted together, 'RIGHT!' Smiling to herself, Molly left them to it.

'I told them for sure this morning that their mammy was not coming home,' Molly said to Rosie as the two of them went back inside. 'They were really upset . . . tears and tantrums, and Georgie took it 'specially bad. Seeing them now, laughing and having fun, I haven't got the heart to bring them in.'

They glanced at the children through the window. 'They're such good kids,' Molly said softly, her love for them evident.

Rosie agreed. 'I'd rather have your little 'uns than our Sandra,' she confided. 'She's more trouble than all them put together.'

'What's she been up to now?' It was ages since she'd seen her friend properly. Molly hoped Sandra didn't blame her for the split with Alfie. As she talked, Molly returned to the parlour and stoked up the fire. If the room was cold when her da came down, there'd be hell to pay.

Rosie followed her through. 'I'm at my wits' end,' she grumbled. 'It's all to do with some bloke she's going with. One minute she's all lovey dovey about him, and the next he's telling her he means to end it, and she wants to kill him. One night she came home with a black eye. I swear, love, if it goes on like this, I'll away and see this fella wherever he is, and lay down the law, so I will!'

Clambering up from the hearth, Molly was horrified. 'A black eye! This bloke hit Sandra and she still wants to go out with him? By! She must be mad.'

'That's exactly what I told her, but will she listen? No, she will not!'

'D'you want me to have a word?'

'Sure, I don't know as it would help. You know what she's like, but yes, I'd be grateful if you could give it a try.'

'Is she still in bed?'

Rosie nodded. 'Out to the world, and it's not surprising, seeing as she didn't get home till the early hours. From what I could get out of her, she couldn't find this bloke so she went on to some pub or other and got herself pie-eyed.' Rosie was at the end of her tether. 'How she got home on her own two legs, I will never know. Anyway, I put her to bed, and there she is, sleeping like the innocent.'

Molly could see how upset Rosie was. 'Dad'll be up and out by twelve,' she calculated. 'If you come and keep an eye on the young 'uns, I'll pop over and have a word with her.' Remembering how upset Alfie's grandaddy was when he heard the news of her and Alfie splitting up, she asked warily, 'Will Mr Noonan be in?'

'Don't worry, lass. Like your da, my da will be off down the pub soon as ever they open.' She knew why Molly was wary and reassured her. 'In any case, he'll not say nothing to you, lass. Course, he was led to believe you left Alfie for another fella – I haven't told him otherwise. He was upset as you know, but he seems to be over that now, so don't worry.'

'I don't blame him for thinking I'm a right little tart.'

'He was just disappointed. He always thought you and Alfie belonged together. It was a bit of a shock, that's all. Then, when he found out your mam had gone, I have an idea he's put two and two together. But he'll not say anything – I can promise you that.'

Molly thanked her. 'Michael's a good man,' she said. 'The last thing I want is to fall out with him.'

'Oh, sure he'll not fall out with ye, lass.' She knew how Molly was already hurting from one thing after another. 'I was meaning to ask: have you heard from Lottie lately?'

'She writes every week. That was the deal when I let her go.'

'And how's she doing?'

'Well, in the last letter she tells me she's got a job with the woman on the coconut shy. She gets paid regular, whether the stall is busy or not, and they've made real good friends.' Molly was glad about that. 'It's what Lottie needs . . . an older person to keep her in line.'

'What about this fella of hers? Are they still getting on all right? Is he taking care of her like he said?'

'She seems happy enough. Her letters are full of him.'

'Where is she now?'

'Yarmouth. But they're moving on again the day after tomorrow.'

'Seeing the world, eh?'

'Looks like it, Rosie. As long as she's happy and writes me every week, I'll not go looking for her.'

'Well, she's turned sixteen now, lass.'

But Molly's thoughts had already moved on. 'Rosie, do you remember that little idea we talked about before?'

'What . . . being errand girls, you mean?' Rosie had a wonderfully simple way of putting things.

'That's the one.'

'What about it?'

'I thought we might start up sooner rather than later.'

Rosie nodded knowingly. 'I see. Money getting a bit tight, is it?'

'You could say that.' Molly had few secrets from Rosie. 'Getting money out of Dad is like squeezing blood from a stone, and what with me not earning now, it's difficult. I did have some money saved from my last job, but it's nearly all gone. I'm already having to lie to the children when they ask for their favourite little treats.'

'I can see no reason why we couldn't give it a try.' Rosie was all for a gamble.

'Good!' Settling herself more comfortably in the chair, Molly talked it through. 'We need a barrow, but we can't spend good money on buying one straight off in case the idea isn't such a good one after all. We really need to know if it pays before spending what we haven't earned.'

'That makes sense, so what do we do? We can't hump great bags of stuff from the market, and besides . . . what if we have more than one customer? It's no good turning them down, because that'll finish it before we've even started.'

Molly chuckled. 'I have an idea.'

Leaning forward, Rosie gave a half wink. 'Go on then, let's hear it.'

'We can use Eddie's pram.'

'What, with him in it?'

'Course! Where else would he be?'

'What, in his pram? With bags of spuds and carrots and the dear Lord knows what else?'

'Why not?'

'Poor little mite!'

Molly laughed out loud. 'It won't be so bad,' she said. 'The groceries and such will be up one end of the pram, and Eddie up the other. We won't suffocate him if that's what you're worried about.'

'I should ruddy well hope not.' Seeing the funny side of it, Rosie couldn't help but smile.

'So – what d'you reckon?'

'It's worth thinking about.'

'But will it work until we make a bit of money and can get a barrow?'

Rosie thought for a minute. 'Well, it might, if the good Lord wills it.' She laughed out loud. 'Mebbe we should ask the lad what *he* thinks, eh? He might not like the idea o' sharing his pram with a pound o' smelly fish.'

'Happen we'll offer him a share of the profit. He's a sensible fella. He knows a good thing when he sees one.'

The conversation ended in laughter. 'I'd better go,' Rosie said, 'before I'm as daft as you!'

'See you later then.'

'I'll be back soon after twelve. She'll be out of that bed even if I have to drag her out by the scruff of the neck.' With that Rosie marched off, leaving Molly glad it wasn't her who was about to be 'dragged out by the scruff of her neck'.

After Rosie had gone, Molly ushered the children in and gave them a hot drink. 'It's the last of the cocoa till I get to the shops,' she warned, 'so make the most of it.' Sitting Eddie in his high-chair, she fastened a bib round his neck. 'When you've finished that, you can all sit down by the fireside and warm yerselves.'

'Aw!' As usual, Milly had something to say. 'We wanted to go out and play in the snow again.'

'You can want on,' her big sister answered firmly. 'Snow or no snow, you're not going out any more today.'

'Let's play hide and seek!' Bertha cried. 'Go on! I'll count to ten. Go on! Go and hide!'

Taking Eddie with them, they ran from one room to another, upstairs and down, one minute screeching and the next silent as church mice. 'Take care not to hurt your little brother,' Molly told them, and smiled when she saw his little legs running to keep up, his hand in Georgie's and a big smile on his dear little face.

Grateful for a few minutes to herself, Molly went into the scullery and prepared the Sunday dinner: mashed potatoes, rabbit pie and cabbage. There was jam tart for afters and custard to go with it.

With the vegetables ready to cook on the stove, and the pie in the oven, Molly turned her mind to the ironing.

Washing her hands, she took the flat-iron and a block of wood from the cupboard, then returned to the parlour. Positioning the wood block on the table, she placed the iron cradle on top and took the iron to the fire, wedging it firmly between the coals. That done, she fetched the ironing basket from the stairs cupboard; the clothes were piled so high she could hardly see over the top. 'God! It'll take me weeks to catch up with this lot.' Somehow the work had piled up, and yet she never seemed to stop.

Setting the basket down by the table, she turned on the wireless and sat by the fire. In between the children's excited screams, she listened to the news. There was talk of a first military round-the-world flight, and an outline of the weather for the next few days. There was going to be a thaw: 'Brighter, drier weather expected,' it said, 'but a smattering of snow for Christmas.' Molly thought that would put a smile on the children's faces.

Lulled by the fire and fond thoughts of Alfie, Molly soon found herself drifting off to sleep.

She woke with a jolt when Milly yelled out, 'Got you! Now it's my turn!' Georgie let out a blood-curdling cry as she grabbed him.

Quickly coming to her senses, Molly checked the iron. 'A few more minutes yet,' she decided. 'Best give Dad a shout.'

Switching off the wireless, she went to the bottom of the stairs and called, 'Dad, you'd best get up. It's gone eleven!'

Back came the shout, 'Piss off, you! Let a man sleep, why don't yer?'

When Molly turned round, all four children were looking up at her with scared faces. 'He's not coming down, is he?' That was Bertha again, speaking for everyone.

Molly smiled. 'Doesn't seem like it,' she said and, whooping and hollering, they ran off again, this time with Eddie hanging on to Milly's hand.

Wrapping the tea-towel round her fist, Molly took the iron out of the fire and spat on it; the spittle lay there, unmoving. 'Still not

199

ready,' she decided, and turned her attention to the ironing basket. Taking the scorched blanket from the top, she folded it before laying it across the table, a little pile of ironing alongside.

She tried the iron again, and this time the spittle sizzled and danced. It was ready. Laying it in the cradle, she called her dad again. 'Dad, are you getting up or what!'

'Thought I told yer to piss off!'

So she did. 'Stay there till Kingdom Come for all I care,' she muttered.

She was halfway through the ironing when Rosie returned, right in the middle of a silent 'hiding' session. 'Where's all the childer?' she asked. 'Sure, you've not let the wee mites out in the cold again?' She almost leaped out of her skin when they all jumped out on her. 'That got you, didn't it, Rosie?' Georgie couldn't stop laughing.

'Ye little varmints, I almost had a heart attack, so I did!'

While they ran off in fits of laughter, she told Molly, 'Well, I managed to get Sandra out of bed. Dad's off down the pub, so the road's clear if you want to go and talk with her now.'

Molly began packing away the ironing. 'No, don't do that, lass,' Rosie protested. 'Sure, *I* can carry on with it till yer get back.'

'Dad's still abed. If you managed to get Sandra out, happen you'll try the same technique on him?'

'I don't think so.' Rosie actually blushed. 'I threw the clothes off her and smacked her arse, so I did. I can't see me doing that to your father, can you?'

Molly saw what she meant. 'Better not,' she giggled. 'Just keep yelling at the bottom of the stairs. He'll get fed up with it in time.'

'Our Sandra's the same. It's like drawing teeth to get her outta bed, so it is.'

'I've the dinner cooking, Rosie. Can you take a peep at it every now and then? The veg will need to go on soon.'

'I'll ask the same of you, lass. I've a hotpot in the oven, and given half a chance our Sandra would let it burn to a cinder.'

Before she left, Molly changed Eddie's nappy and put him in his pram. 'The way he's been running round, he'll be asleep in minutes,' she predicted.

As she went out the door, she heard Rosie saying, 'You *were* tired an' all, weren't ye, lad, eh?' From that, Molly assumed Eddie had already dropped off to sleep. After all, he was only a bairn, bless his heart.

Chapter Fourteen

Walking down the street, Molly saw the car out of the corner of her eye; a big, posh car, nosing its way along the street. From inside, a small-faced man with dark, swept-back hair appeared to be peering out the window to examine the house numbers.

Molly thought both the car and the man looked out of place. 'You'll find none of your kind down Victoria Street,' she mused.

Knocking on Rosie's door, she stamped her feet in an effort to keep warm. 'Come on, Sandra, where the devil are you?'

A minute or two passed and there was still no answer, so she knocked again, muttering, 'If she's gone back to bed, her mam'll have her guts for garters.'

Just then, Sandra flung open the door, looking fed up and hung-over. 'Talking to yerself now, is it?' she grumbled. 'They lock you away for less than that.'

Molly pointed to the car. 'I reckon that bloke's lost.'

Sandra shrugged her shoulders. 'So what?'

'Happen I should see if I can help?'

'Don't be bloody daft, it's freezing. Get yerself in 'ere.' Stepping aside to let her friend in, Sandra poked her head out to yell at the driver, 'Piss off, you . . . afore some common old dog cocks its leg up your car!'

Horrified, Molly pushed her way through. 'Honest to God,

Sandra, you'd get anybody hanged.'

'Well, what's he doing down here? Posh sod, let him get back where he belongs.'

Going straight to the fire, Molly rubbed her hands to get the circulation back.

'What d'yer want anyway?' Throwing herself into the arm-chair, Sandra gave a long yawn. 'Yer as bad as my mam. I told her an' all . . . it's too bloody cold to be running up and down the street.'

Molly glanced at her miserable, dishevelled friend, and she had to smile. 'Well, good morning, Moll,' she teased. 'How the bloody 'ell are yer?'

Surprised, Sandra looked up, the whisper of a smile fleeting across her face. 'The kettle's boiled if you want a drink.'

'No, thanks all the same.' Sitting down in the chair opposite Sandra's, Molly confessed, 'I've come for a little talk.'

'I'm not in the mood for talking.'

'Well, if it's all right with you, I shall sit here till you are.'

Sandra gave a cynical little laugh. 'I don't need to ask who sent you, do I?'

'She's worried about you, Sandra,' Molly told her. 'And can you blame her, when you're coming in at all hours. She doesn't know where you've been or who you've been with. You turn up with a black eye and tell her you still want the bloke who did it.'

'If you've come here just to lecture me, you can bugger off. I get enough o' that from me mam!' Tucking her legs under her, the girl sat, arms folded against the world.

Shaking her head, Molly pointed out, 'We both love you, Sandra, but how can we help if you won't let us near?'

'I don't need any help, thanks very much. I wish everyone would mind their own business.'

Molly had never seen her friend like this. 'You know I'm not here to pry,' she said. 'With us being long-time friends, and having shared all our secrets . . . I just thought you might talk to me where you won't talk to yer mam. But if you want me to go, I'll go.'

For a moment Sandra remained sullen. Then, as Molly rose to leave, she tugged at her skirt. 'Sit down, yer silly cow. Course I don't want you to go.'

When Molly hesitated, Sandra sat up in the chair. 'Please, Moll. I didn't mean to be so grumpy. It's just that I've got a lot on my mind at the minute.'

'Do you want to talk about it?'

Breathing a sigh, Sandra nodded.

Relieved, Molly sat down again. 'What's wrong?'

'Everything!'

'Such as?'

For what seemed an age, Sandra looked at her. Then, in a small, anguished voice, she said, 'I'm pregnant.'

Molly's mouth fell open in astonishment. She recalled the many conversations in which Sandra had sworn to God above that she would *never* have kids. In fact, she was adamant about it.

Sandra read her thoughts. 'I know what you're thinking,' she said, 'and I ain't changed me mind. I still don't want kids. It were an accident, but if it keeps him with me, I'll put up with the brat.'

Having got over the initial shock, Molly asked, 'What does he think?'

'He doesn't know, not yet.'

'And what d'you think he'll say?'

Sandra grinned sadly. 'He'll say I'm a silly cow for letting it happen. Then again, he might try and get out of it by saying it don't belong to him.'

'And how will you convince him it *does* belong to him?'

'Oh, he knows right enough. If he tries to send me on my way, he'll soon find out I'm not that easy to be rid of.' She looked up at Molly with cow eyes. 'I love him, gal. I've never loved anybody like I love him.'

'I can see that,' her friend replied softly. 'When will you tell him . . . about the baby?'

Untucking her legs, Sandra gave a groan. 'When I can find him! The bugger's gone off, and nobody seems to know where.'

Molly laughed. 'If I know you, you won't give up till you find him.'

'You can bet on it, gal.'

The mood grew serious again. 'You haven't told your mam, have you?'

'No, and I'm not going to – yet. Once she meets Dave, she'll love him, the baby, too. You know what she's like with kids.'

Molly saw how the other girl's mood had completely changed. 'I'm glad you told me,' she said warmly. 'It's a big thing to keep to yourself.'

Leaping out of the chair, Sandra clasped her arms round Molly's neck. 'I'm glad I told you, too,' she admitted. 'I feel better already.'

Just then a knock came on the door. 'Who the bleedin' hell's that?'

Molly had no idea. 'You'd best go and see.'

When the knocking grew more insistent, Sandra ran down the passageway, yelling as she went, 'All right, all right! Keep yer hair on, yer noisy bugger!'

From the parlour, Molly caught snippets of the conversation. '*Who?* . . . Yes, she is. Wait here.'

A moment later, looking puzzled, Sandra appeared at the parlour door. 'It's for you, gal.' Lowering her voice she offered, 'I'll send the bloke away if yer want?'

But Molly didn't want. Instead, confused and a little afraid, she told Sandra, 'I'd best go and see.'

With Sandra immediately behind her, she walked up the

passage and was startled to see that the man waiting on the step was the same one who'd been riding up and down the street in the fancy car. 'Are you sure it's me you want?' she asked nervously.

'Are you Molly Tattersall?'

'That's right.'

'I called at the house and a lady sent me here.'

Sandra's voice crept over Molly's shoulder. 'That must 'ave been our mam.' Prodding Molly in the back, she urged, 'Go on, gal. Ask him what he's after.'

Before Molly could say anything, she was handed a long brown envelope. 'I'm to give you this.'

'What is it?'

'It's not my place to know. I've been asked to deliver it, and that's what I'm doing.'

Hesitantly, Molly took the envelope. When the man turned to leave, she told him, 'No, wait. It might not be for me after all.'

'As you will, miss.'

Prodding her again, Sandra hissed, 'Open the bloody thing, then!' Like Molly, she was curious.

Slightly apprehensively, Molly tore open the envelope. Drawing out its contents, she could hardly believe her eyes. 'What in God's name . . . !'

Peeping over her shoulder, Sandra caught a glimpse of the money she held; a wad of notes so fat, Molly's small hand could hardly contain it.

'Jesus, Mary and Joseph, you've come into a fortune!' Winking at the man, she asked cheekily, 'Are you *sure* it's not me you're looking for?'

'"Molly Tattersall", that's what Mr Mason said . . .' And as soon as he let slip the name he clapped his hand over his mouth. 'I'd best be off. Good day to you, ladies.'

Jack Mason's instructions had been clear enough. 'Make sure

it's Molly Tattersall herself you hand the money to, and don't say anything. Just give her the envelope and leave.' They were his instructions and the messenger had already gone against them by mentioning his boss's name. Now he couldn't get away quick enough.

But it was too late.

Molly had heard the name before and recognised it as that of her mam's fancy fella. '*Jack Mason!*' Waving the wad of notes at him, she demanded, 'Are you saying *he* sent this money?'

'Like I said, I'd best be off.' Before I lose my job, he thought worriedly.

As he scurried down the steps, Molly quickly scanned the brief note which was secured to the wad of money by an elastic band:

Dear Molly,

I send this by hand, because to reveal where me and your mam are living might cause problems. She's not been happy about her decision to leave all of you, though the roses have come back to her cheeks and her eyes are as bright as they were when she was a young girl.

Your dad was slowly destroying her. I saw it and took her away. So, if you need to blame anybody, blame me. I asked her to start a new life with me, and I refused to take no for an answer.

She does miss you all, but gradually she's finding happiness with me. You don't know who I am, and it's better that way for all concerned. All you need to know is that I will take care of her and, from a distance, I'll take care of her children. From time to time, you'll receive a similar amount of money.

From what your mam tells me, I know you will spend it wisely.

Please don't ever forget your mam for the mother she was to you all. She never wanted to leave you, but your dad and, I'm ashamed to say, myself, gave her no choice.

Don't hate her. If you can, please try and be happy for her now.

I wish you well,

Your benefactor.

Sandra read the note over Molly's shoulder. 'Well, I never! Seems to me like you and the kids are set for life, gal!' Giving Molly a congratulatory slap on the back, she was astonished to see her run down the steps to where the man was trying desperately to start his car.

Flinging open the door, Molly dropped the envelope and its contents on his lap. 'Take it back where it came from,' she told him fiercely. 'And you can tell Jack Mason this while you're at it: I don't want his money! I don't want to hear from him or my mother ever again, and if I see you down this street, I'll set the dogs on you. Do you hear what I'm saying? DO YOU?'

The man looked at Molly's tear-stained face, and his heart went out to her. He had a daughter much the same age. 'I'm sorry,' he said sympathetically, and, calmer now, he was able to start the car and drive away. Yet all the way up the street his eyes looked through the rearview mirror at Molly standing there, a small forlorn figure in the snow; head bent and shoulders bowed, she seemed like a lost soul. For the first time in his life, he hated himself. 'Next time Mason wants a dirty job doing, he can do it his bloody self because, work or no work, I'll hand in my notice before I'll do this again.'

Seeing Molly like that was too much for Sandra. Running the few steps in her bare feet, she took her friend by the shoulders. 'Come away, love,' she urged. 'Yer don't want the nosy neighbours to see you out here like this, do yer, eh?'

She led Molly back to the warmth of the Craigs' parlour. 'Sit yer arse down there while I make you a brew,' she said, in her own inimitable way. 'It'll not take a minute or two.'

Sure enough she was soon back with two steaming mugs of tea. 'Get that down yer, gal.' Handing her one of the mugs, Sandra sat beside Molly. 'I didn't mean to be so unfeeling. You know – saying you were set up for life an' all that,' she apologised. 'I just opened me big, stupid gob and out it came.'

But Molly had said her piece to the man and felt better for it. 'I didn't think you knew about Mam having run off,' she commented. 'I wasn't sure if Rosie had told you, and I don't see enough of you these days to tell you anything myself.' She took a sip of her tea. 'How did you find out?'

'Down the pub.' She didn't want to hurt Molly any more but, 'The whole town's talking about it. You know what they're like, gal . . . dogs after a bone.'

Molly smiled sadly at that. 'I can't blame them. It's only natural.'

'S'pose so.'

Molly's thoughts drifted, her voice incredulous as she spoke, almost to herself. 'How could she do that? What made them think money could put it all right again?' Anger reared its ugly head. 'Doesn't she know the kids want her back! Instead, their mammy and her fancy man send a wad of blood-money to ease their consciences. They deserve each other, damn them both.'

'Hey!' Sandra was shocked at the vehemence in her normally gentle friend's voice. 'Don't get yerself all worked up like that. They're not worth it, gal.'

Turning to Sandra, her eyes swimming with unshed tears, Molly said quietly, 'In that note he asked me not to hate her, and with Dad being the way he is, I've tried so hard not to. But now, I don't know *how* to feel towards her. If she really thinks we can be bought off, she's not the mother I've known all my life. She's a stranger to me, Sandra . . . a stranger.'

Her friend was mortified. 'Surely you can't shut her out of your life altogether?'

'I haven't,' Molly replied sadly. 'She's done that herself.'

'Happen yer mam's just trying to help the best way she can. After all, she must know you can't earn a wage, the way things are.'

'I'll manage all right. What's more, I'll do it *without* her help. In fact, me and your mam are already talking about starting a little business, soon as the children get back to school.'

'You and Mam!' Sandra couldn't imagine her mam helping to run a business, but with Molly's help, it might not be so impossible. 'What kind o' business?'

Molly chuckled. 'Glorified errand boys, I think you'd call us. We mean to run errands for folks as can't get out, or don't want the nuisance of fetching their own groceries and such.'

'Hmh! I'd rather you than me.' The other girl laughed. 'But then, I'm a lazy bugger an' you're not.'

Molly felt confident. 'So you see, Sandra, that's how I'll manage, and without any handouts from them two.'

'Yer a proud bugger.'

Molly shook her head. 'Not proud, love,' she replied quietly. 'And not a sponger neither.'

'Aye, well, yer different to me an' that's for sure, 'cos I'd have tekken that money and gone out on the town with it. But you! By! *You* turned it down like it had the pox.'

Molly took a deep breath. 'I couldn't do anything else and live with myself afterwards.'

'I understand. Really I do.' But she didn't, and she never would. To Sandra's mind, money was money, no matter where it came from.

The faintest of smiles crept over Molly's tragic features. 'That poor man though,' she said, giggling. 'I've an idea he won't dare show his face round these parts again.'

Sandra sniggered. 'I'm bloody sure he won't! Not after you threatened to set the dogs on the poor sod.'

They looked at each other and took a fit of the giggles. In fact, to laugh at themselves was what they both needed. These past weeks they had seemed to lose the thread of their friendship, but now they were as close as ever, and it was wonderful.

'What will you do?' Molly asked, when once they were quiet again. 'About the bairn, and everything?'

Sandra sat for a moment, stiff and upright in the chair, her face hard, her hands twisting round and round each other. 'I heard he had a new woman,' she said, so quietly Molly could scarcely hear her.

'You shouldn't listen to gossip.'

'Ah, but this wasn't gossip,' Sandra revealed. 'I got it from somebody who should know.'

'And who was that?'

'The landlord at the pub where he used to drink. I went there to see if he knew where Dave had gone.'

'And did he?'

'No, but I'll find him. It's just a matter of time.'

'Then what?'

'He'll be made to face up to his responsibilities. New woman or not, I'm having his kid, and it's his place to look out for us.' Shaking her fist in the air, she declared, 'He can kick this other woman out for starters!'

'And if he refuses?'

A terrible look came into Sandra's eyes. 'I'll cut out his heart,' she promised.

And Molly was filled with dread.

Suddenly, her mood changed and Sandra was concerned about Molly. 'That's why you sent Alfie away, weren't it, gal?' she said. 'Because yer mam ran off and left you with the kids. You knew yer dad weren't up to much, so you sent Alfie away, so's he'd have some sort of a life. You didn't want him lumbered with your lot – not when he'd just been given the opportunity of a lifetime.'

'Seems you've got it all worked out.'

'So, am I right?'

Molly nodded. 'What else could I do?'

'By! I don't know if I'd make such a sacrifice. You must really love him.'

'I do. I always will.'

'Mam kept it all to herself, did you know that?'

'I asked her to.'

'She didn't even tell Grandaddy.'

'If she had have done, he might have gone straight off and told Alfie.'

'I don't know about that. You know how mad Grandaddy is about boxing an' all? Even though he thinks the world of you, I'm not sure he'd have told Alfie, knowing he would have insisted on staying here, with you.'

'Nobody must tell Alfie.'

'Nobody will.'

'He's got a big fight coming up, did you know that?'

Sandra looked at her sheepishly. 'I've been out of it a bit,' she confessed. 'Me and me mam have been at loggerheads over this bloke of mine, especially when I came home with a black eye. She went off her bleedin' rocker! That's why I daren't tell her about the bairn. Hey!' A look of horror came into her eyes. '*You* won't tell her, will yer?'

'You know I won't,' Molly assured her, 'but I think you should talk it over with her all the same. Your mam's a good woman. However angry she might be, she'll be on your side.'

'Aye, well, I'm not so sure. That's why I'm saying nothing,

at least not until I've got its daddy well and truly where I want him. If I can fetch him home and let me mam see he's not such a monster, she might come round to our way of thinking. That's when I'll tell her she's about to become a grandma.'

'This bloke of yours, Sandra . . .'

'What about him?'

'Is he worth all the aggravation? He sounds like a womaniser to me, and violent into the bargain. What makes you think you can change him?'

'Because I will.' She laughed. 'Or I'll die in the trying.'

'Be careful, Sandra. Be sure you know what you're doing.'

'Aw, stop worrying, gal. I'm not as daft as yer think.' She joked, 'Not daft enough to throw a fat wad of money away, at any rate!'

The conversation ended with Molly having to confirm her promise not to say anything to Rosie about the bairn, and Sandra promising in return not to do anything stupid if and when she found her fella. 'But if he *has* got another woman, I'll cut his balls off an' no mistake!'

Before Molly left, she quickly checked the Craig family's hotpot, giving it a good stir as she had promised Rosie, and then walked home, thinking about Sandra, and about Lottie, realising suddenly how alike they were. 'A law unto themselves,' she muttered. 'Wilful and hot-headed, the pair of 'em.'

And a constant worry to both herself and Rosie.

Amy had been on edge all day. 'What time will he be back?' She glanced at the grandfather clock. 'It's already half past six. What time did he say he'd be back?'

'Another hour or so. It's a long way, my love, and what with the snow and everything, it's bound to slow him up.'

'I'm sorry, Jack, but I can't help worrying.'

Coming away from the big, open fire, she crossed the room

and stood in the bay window, her sorry gaze stretching down the drive to the road beyond. 'What if he didn't find her? She could have been out, and he had to come away without giving her the money.'

'If that's the case, he'll make another trip.' Getting out of his comfortable leather chair, Jack came to stand beside her. 'Amy! Will you stop your worrying?' He kissed her on the neck. 'You'll wear yourself out.' He made a suggestion. 'Look, why don't you go and get yourself dolled up and we'll go to the club in Bedford town. It'll do you good. In fact, it'll do us *both* good.'

'Not tonight, Jack.'

'Fair enough, but like I say, stop fretting. He'll be here shortly, you'll see. Molly will have got the money, and all will be well. It should be enough to keep them going for ages – until the next payment.'

Turning to him, Amy looked up with adoring eyes. 'Thank you, Jack. Thank you for being so thoughtful and generous when you don't have to be.' Kissing him on the mouth, she told him softly, 'I don't know what I've done to deserve such a good man as you.'

'Oh, I'm not so good.' Holding her tight, he smiled fondly. 'I've told you before, and I'll tell you again . . . you've made me the happiest man on God's earth.'

Another kiss, and this time a smile to go with it. 'I'm glad,' she said, and meant it.

It was nine o'clock when the long black saloon came up the drive. 'He's here!' Like a cat on hot bricks, Amy leaped out of her seat by the window. 'Oh Jack, he's here!'

She would have run out, but Jack told her to stay where she was. 'I'll see to him. There's no need for you to come out in the cold.'

Amy watched the two men, deep in conversation. She saw

Jack lean into the car and she saw him glance up towards her. When he smiled, she beckoned excitedly, and he began his way back.

Breathing heavily from the cold, he took off his long coat and hung it on the hallway dresser. 'Apparently he had a terrible drive home,' he told Amy. 'There was a bad accident on the A5. It seems the traffic was held up for some time.'

'What did he say?' Amy could hardly contain herself. 'Was Molly there? Did he give her the money? Was she pleased? Oh Jack . . . it will do so much for her and the children.'

Seeing her bright anxious face he didn't have the heart to tell her the truth. 'Everything's all right,' he lied. 'He took the money and Molly was in. So now you can stop worrying.'

'Did she send me a message?'

He shook his head. 'No message.'

Amy's face fell, then she was smiling again. 'But she did get the money? That's what he said, isn't it? Molly was in, and she got the money.'

Not wanting to lie again, he merely nodded.

Like a child, Amy clapped her hands. 'Oh Jack, that's all I want to know. I didn't expect a message, not really.' But it would have been wonderful to know Molly had forgiven her.

'Now, will you get ready and we'll go to the club for an hour?'

She glanced at the clock. 'It's a bit late for that, don't you think?'

'Maybe you're right.' He slid his arms round her. 'Let's have a quiet drink here, just the two of us, and afterwards, an early night?' He winked. 'What d'you say?'

'I say yes.'

'And no hanky panky.' He smiled down on her. 'I've a string of business meetings in London tomorrow.'

'I wouldn't dream of it!' she said in mock horror.

Later, when they walked across the hallway, he noticed the

envelope jutting from his coat pocket on the dresser. 'You go on up,' he suggested. 'I'm not sure whether I locked the back door.'

'Don't be long,' she warned with a twinkle in her eye. 'Or I might get fed up waiting.'

He patted her backside. 'I'll be quick as a wink.'

As she turned the corner at the top of the stairs, he hurried back to his coat and took out the envelope. Peering inside, he saw that not a penny had been accepted by Molly. 'Yer a proud little sod, Molly Tattersall!' he sighed. Then he took the envelope into the front room, where he tucked it neatly into his briefcase.

Lying to Amy had not come easy. But he knew if he had told her the truth, she would never have had a minute's peace. 'It's better she doesn't know,' he told himself. 'I've tried, and done my best. That's all any man can do.'

Chapter Fifteen

It was Christmas Eve. The thaw had been and gone, and the fall of snow promised for Christmas had not materialised. 'I can't say as I'm sorry.' Mr Bruce, the owner of the corner shop, would complain whether the sun was shining or the heavens had opened. 'Damned weather, it's never what you'd call comfortable. Always either too hot or too cold, or raining so bloomin' hard you can't see a hand in front of you.'

Granny Arkwright shook her head and tutted. 'Yer a miserable old git,' she told him, whistling through the gap in her false teeth. 'You ain't never satisfied about nuthin'!'

Even at the back of the queue, Molly and Bertha heard it all. 'Why is that lady whistling?' Bertha wanted to know, and Granny Arkwright laughed out loud. ''Cos me teeth are falling apart, lass – that's why. They're old and bent, just like me.'

'Right then!' Having weighed her potatoes in his scale, Mr Bruce told her to hold up her shopping bag. Sliding them into her bag, he asked, 'Is there owt else?'

Red in the face from holding the bag up, the old woman put it to the ground. 'I'll have a cabbage, and not a big one neither. I'm not paying good money to throw 'alf of it in the midden. There's only me to eat it, as well you know.'

Grumbling under his breath, Mr Bruce sorted out a small round one. 'How's that?'

The old woman examined it up and down, then sideways and back to front. 'Is that the best you've got?'

'It is.'

'Hmh! Well, I've seen better, but it'll do.' She wagged a bony finger. 'And don't go pushing your hand down on them scales when you weigh it.' Screwing up one eye, she peered at him through the other. ''Cos I've got my beady eye on yer.'

With the cabbage safely stowed in her bag, she nagged at him some more. 'I'll 'ave a box o' snuff . . . oh, and two apples,' she concluded. 'Not hard ones neither. They're no good to me when I can't chew the blessed things.'

A few minutes and two arguments later, she toddled out the shop. 'The old Scrooge!' Mr Bruce was well and truly riled. 'Two and bloody ninepence, that's all she ever spends. It's a mystery to me how she manages to keep it within a farthing every time – unless she does summat to them scales when me back's turned. That wouldn't surprise me one bit.' Granny Arkwright was a thorn in his side. 'She counts them pennies like they're never gonna make any more, while everybody knows she's rolling in money since her husband died.'

'Aye, an' he earned it, too!' said Bert Turner, now at the back of the queue. 'I miss that shop. I allus used to get me baccy there, and everything.'

Molly's turn came and it didn't take her long to spend her few coins. 'A loaf of bread, a pot of your strawberry jam and some margarine, please.' Knowing the circumstances, Mr Bruce threw a couple of big taters in as well. 'You can make some good chips with them,' he told her with a wink.

Outside, she found Granny Arkwright bent double, her bag lying on the ground beside her, while she fought off a stray dog with her walking stick. 'Mangy thing! I dropped me bag and now it's after me apples.'

Picking up the bag, Molly helped the old woman home. It

wasn't far. 'Number two, Duckworth Street, dear,' she told Molly. 'Every day the journey to the shops gets longer, and my legs seem to get shorter.'

She laughed at Bertha, who had not stopped staring solemnly at her. 'I'm a comical old bugger, ain't I?' she cackled. 'But you'll be old one day, my beauty. Everybody gets old, or dead, and I'd rather be old.' After that she held tight to Molly's arm and muttered to herself all the way home.

Helping her as far as the door, Molly was told, 'That's far enough, lass. I don't ever let anybody into my house – not that yer might rob me or owt, but I have to be careful, what with being on my own.'

She smiled on them both. 'But you've been very kind and I want to thank you.' Reaching into her purse, she took out a florin. 'That's for your trouble,' she said.

Molly graciously refused, but it was pressed into her palm. 'You take it for the children,' the old woman insisted. 'Tomorrow's Christmas Day. I don't suppose you've got a tree nor trimmings neither, so go on, lass. You've earned it. You carried an old lady's bag all the way . . .' She laughed until she began coughing and could hardly breathe. 'You very nearly carried me an' all.'

Molly wasn't satisfied until the old lady had the door open and her bag inside the passage.

'Will you do it again for me, lass?'

For a minute, Molly wasn't sure what she meant. 'Do what?'

'Well, carry me bag, o' course!' the old lady tutted. 'I'm too old to be carting heavy bags about. What's more, that Mr Bruce wears me out with his arguing and moaning. I'm asking you to do me shopping, lass. I'll pay you a florin a week. That's for a trip to the butcher's in town, and a trip to Mr Bruce's corner shop. What do you say? Will you help me out?'

Molly didn't need to think twice. 'It's a deal.' They worked out which days she would come and at what time, then shook hands on it.

Molly ran Bertha all the way home. Bursting into Rosie's front room, she grabbed her by the waist and danced her round. 'We've got a job!' she cried. 'Granny Arkwright's took me on to do her shopping – a florin a week!'

When she was let loose, Rosie fell into the nearest chair. 'Oh, that's grand news. When do we start?'

'Not tomorrow 'cos that's Christmas Day, but we'll walk the streets on Boxing Day and knock on every door in Blackburn.' Lifting Bertha into her arms, Molly swung her round in turn, making her scream with delight. 'We're on our way!' she cried. 'We're on our way!'

Rosie smiled. 'God bless yer, lass,' she murmured. 'It's only what ye deserve, so it is.'

Christmas Day was one of the best ever, despite Amy Tattersall's absence.

Thanks to Granny Arkwright, there was a small tree and some trimmings. With some of her savings, Molly had bought and hidden a scarf each for Rosie, Sandra, Michael and her father, together with a little present for each of the children; all bought from the market and all very much appreciated.

There were two rag dolls, one for Bertha and one for Milly, though Molly wisely bought one with red hair and one with brown, so the girls could tell them apart.

Georgie had a wooden engine that screeched when you blew into its tail end. Eddie had a little duck that quacked when pulled along, and everybody opened their presents amid much laughter and fun.

Molly received a knitted jumper from Rosie and a matching bobble hat from Sandra; Michael Noonan, Rosie's father, gave her two bob to, 'Get yesel' a nice treat, me darlin'.'

Sandra rather unkindly told him that Molly wouldn't be able to buy much with two bob, but her friend thanked him graciously and said she had seen a pair of gloves that would match her jumper and scarf. 'And I'll still have a penny change.' She was fibbing to save his pride, but it got her a thank you and a kiss.

From the children she received the best present of all. 'It's really special,' Milly said, and so it was.

'It's beautiful!' Molly exclaimed. The children had made a large pencil drawing of her, complete with big droopy eyes and flyaway hair, one arm longer than the other and a skirt up to her backside. Her odd-sized feet were like clogs and there was a smile on her face that would frighten the dead.

Really, it was a comical thing, but it brought a lump to her throat as she hung it on the wall with pride.

Rosie looked at it from all angles. 'It looks like the scarecrow in Ted Bateman's allotment,' she spluttered into Molly's ear. But Molly didn't care if it looked like the bogey man himself. The children had spent time drawing it with her in mind, and that was wonderful.

There was nothing for Amy and no mention of her from the children. To Molly, that was a sad, sad thing.

When the day was over and Rosie gone, with her dad and Sandra, too, Molly put the weary children to bed and sat by the fire, thinking of her mam and the way she had sent money to the door. 'I won't need your money now, Mam,' she said bitterly. 'Not while I've got health and strength and two good arms to work with.'

After a while, her thoughts turned yearningly to Alfie.

Going to the dresser she took out the bottle of elderberry wine, bought by Rosie and half-emptied by Alfie's grandaddy. Pouring herself a drop, Molly raised the cup with the greeting, 'Happy Christmas, Alfie, wherever you are.' She took one sip and placed the cup in the hearth.

Then she softly cried. For all the loved ones here, and all those now gone.

At ten minutes past midnight, Frank came home and found her curled up in the chair. 'You needn't have waited up,' he told her and, to Molly's surprise, for once he didn't seem drunk.

'Happy Christmas, Dad,' she said.

'Aye, lass.' He seemed oddly embarrassed. 'You, too.'

When, a short time later, she went to bed, he sat on the sofa, his head bent into his hands. 'Goodnight, God bless,' she murmured. When he seemed not to have heard her, she went on up the stairs.

It occurred to Molly how lonely her father must be.

Moreover, Frank Tattersall had some thinking to do. And not before time either.

Chapter Sixteen

New York was a mad, exciting place.

Since coming here, Alfie had worked harder than he had ever worked in his life. He was up with the birds and on his feet from dawn to dusk. He put his every ounce of energy into his work, and heeded the trainer's every word. The days sped by; he trained, he fought, he earned a formidable reputation. *But still his heart wasn't in it.*

Now, just two days from the biggest fight of his career, he tried hard to push Molly from his mind. 'Keep sharp!' his trainer Gus Baines warned. 'You ain't going up against small fry this time, Alfie boy! This one's a real killer. An' he ain't looking to lose – you can be sure of that.'

Taking a swig of water, Alfie got ready for his run.

A few minutes later, with Gus Baines cycling alongside, he ran several miles around Central Park, met at every turn by fanatics who knew that, on 2 January, in two days' time, this young Englishman would be up against one of the all-American best. 'He'll make mincemeat of you,' they taunted. 'After one round, you'll wish you'd never been born!'

There were others, more encouraging, but Alfie turned a deaf ear to all. One thing he had learned: it was fatal to leave yourself open to doubt before a fight, big or otherwise.

When the run was over, they headed back to the gym. Here, Alfie showered and changed.

'I'll see you in the morning,' he told Gus, and before the trainer could say it, Alfie said it for him, in his best New York accent. '"No boozing, broads or partying. I want you here, four o'clock sharp . . . looking like you mean it."'

Gus grinned. 'You got it in one,' he said, wagging a finger at him. 'But look, I got something to ask you.'

'Oh?' He hoped Gus wouldn't keep him too long. He had a letter to write.

Gus beckoned him closer. 'I think you should tell me what's on your mind, son.'

'I don't know what you mean.'

'Don't gimme that shit!' Gus had a reputation for being a bastard when needs must. 'Something's got you by the balls, and I want to know what it is. There's a lotta money at stake here, Alfie.'

Alfie's hackles rose. 'Nothing's bothering me, Gus.'

Chewing his gum, the trainer looked him in the eye. 'You ain't afraid, I know that.'

'I've never been afraid in my life,' Alfie retorted. 'I wouldn't know *how* to be afraid.' Yet he was afraid; not of the imminent fight, but of never again having the chance to tell Molly how much he loved her.

Gus saw the look in his eye. 'Jesus! I figured as much.'

'What?'

The ex-boxer's battered old face broke into a grin. 'If it ain't the fight, it must be a woman. If that's the case, I'm telling you now, son,' the grin turned into a scowl, 'forget her! Keep it on ice, until this is over. You already know the rules. No dancing, no boozing and NO BROADS! There's too many people got too much money riding on you.' He slapped Alfie on the shoulder. 'D'you hear what I'm saying, son?'

Alfie nodded. 'Don't worry, Gus. You can count on me.'

'I hope so, son. I sure as hell hope so!'

As Alfie walked away, an old boxer by the name of Buster Tyrell came up behind the trainer. 'What's the verdict on this new British boy then?'

Gus took a deep breath, then nodded his head and gave his verdict. 'He's got the makings of a champion,' he said proudly. 'He's young and strong, and he has the heart of a lion . . . talented, too. He has a natural right hook that could floor the best of them.'

'But?'

'But nothing! He'll win on the second. I ain't got no doubt about that.'

'You're worried about something though, I can tell.'

Gus gave an almighty sigh. 'Dames!' he muttered. 'That's what I'm worried about. They sure as hell complicate things.'

Alone in his apartment, Alfie lay on the bed, arms crossed under his head and eyes closed, his mind back in Blackburn, with Molly.

Plagued by all manner of misery and suspicion, he wondered aloud, 'Where are you now, Moll? Who is he? How could you let me go on believing we had a future, when all the time you were seeing somebody else?' The questions never went away.

In his mind's eye he saw her face, laughing at him the way she used to; looking serious whenever he took her in his arms. And those pretty blue eyes, seeming so sincere, when all the time they were lying to him . . . cheating.

These past weeks he had told himself the same thing over and over, and he still couldn't bring himself to believe it of her.

He couldn't sleep. All he could think of was Molly. She was in his blood, in his every nerve-ending. *In his heart for all time.*

He got up and paced the floor. Then he lay down again. Restless. Angry. Wanting to shake her until she told him the truth; needing to hold and protect her. It was impossible.

After a while he forced himself to lie still. He closed his eyes and pushed all thoughts of Molly away. 'The fight,' he reminded himself. 'The fight is all you have to keep in mind. Nothing else.' He parroted Gus. 'January second . . . Arnie Wild. The big fight. Got it, son?'

After all, wasn't that the reason he was here?

'Stay with it, Alfie,' he told himself. 'If you don't win this one, you might as well give up now!'

The big day dawned and Alfie was ready.

In the stadium, the atmosphere was tense and exciting.

Now, as Alfie walked into the arena, he kept his eyes straight ahead. He felt the thumps of encouragement on his back as he made his way through the crowds, and the buzz as he climbed into the ring. Suddenly, the spotlight fell on him, cheers and boos rang out and the crowd went wild.

The bell sounded and there was no one else in that ring but him and his opponent, a mountain of a man, black as coal and mean as they come. 'Go on, son,' Gus's voice echoed in his ears. 'He ain't as dangerous as he'd have you believe.'

The fight was on. The crowd roared with every punch, and twice Alfie went down. 'GET UP, DAMN YOU!' Gus kept him on his toes.

Round one was easy-paced, with each man assessing the other's strength.

Round two was fast and furious.

In round three, Arnie Wild took a hard blow to the jaw and stayed down for the count of four. Seconds later, it was Alfie's turn, only he was back on his feet in two.

After round four, they returned to their corners, where Gus

had some advice. 'Keep low,' he suggested. 'Go *up* to him, son. The jaw . . . go for the jaw! It's his weakest point.'

At the end of round five, both men came off bloodied and bone-tired, the sweat pouring down their bodies. 'You've got him on the run!' Gus was sure of it. 'Keep at him. Don't let him crowd you.'

But Arnie did crowd him. For a time in round six, it looked as though the black boxer had the fight in the palm of his hand. Clever and quick on his feet, he sensed victory. Then he made a mistake.

Just when he thought the fight was in the bag, Alfie swung a right hook and caught his opponent on the jaw. He went down – hard.

With the crowd baying for blood, Arnie stayed down for the count, and then the whole stadium was on its feet, the noise deafening.

Alfie was declared the winner, and it was all over. 'You did it, son!' Gus was trembling with excitement. 'I knew you were a champion the minute I set eyes on you.'

In the dressing room, they treated Alfie's cut eye and people crowded in to congratulate him. 'You'll go far,' they said, and drank to his health. When the chips were down, they wanted a winner and they got one.

After the furore abated, Alfie was ready to leave. His first port of call was to see Arnie Wild. 'You almost took the fight in three,' Alfie said. 'You're a formidable opponent.' They shook hands. 'I'm sure we'll meet up again.'

The other man laughed, his perfect teeth like pearls against his black skin. 'You won fair and square, man,' he said softly. 'But like you say . . . there *will* be a next time. I look forward to it.'

The two men parted without animosity.

The night's excitement over, Gus called a cab and accompanied

Alfie back to his apartment. When the young man got out, his trainer stayed inside. 'You did well,' he said. 'Take some time out. You've earned it.'

Alfie watched him go before turning not to his door, but into the night and the awful loneliness. Head down and shoulders hunched, he walked the length of the block before coming to a bar. There was only one man there and he took little notice of Alfie. 'A Scotch,' he told the barman.

When it came, he didn't touch it. Instead, he stared at it for what seemed an age, then pushed it away and went out, back into the night. He circled the block and walked the busy streets of Manhattan. When he came to the gates of Central Park, where he had run his heart out day after day, he began to wonder what it was really all about.

'Hey!' A man with his sweetheart stared Alfie in the face. 'Ain't you the fighter?'

Shaking his head, Alfie walked away. He needed to think. He needed to get away from the bright, busy streets into the quietness of the park, where he could lose himself.

Tonight he had won his biggest fight so far. He had made a name for himself here in New York, and now they were toasting his health and future.

It was his dream come true. A wonderful victory, long in the making. But it was an empty victory. Without Molly, the joy had gone from his life.

He had a choice. He could either go back to England and see if there was a chance for the two of them after all. Or he could stay here in America and work his way right to the top. His father would have been proud. His grandaddy would be over the moon when the news of his win reached him.

Time and again, Alfie turned all this over in his mind, and always he came to the same conclusion.

He wanted Molly.

More than anything else in the world, he needed her. But what to do? Which way to turn? If she was happy with another man, what right had he to try and come between them?

Torturing himself, he walked until he was too weary to walk any more, then he hailed a cab and made his way back to the apartment.

But still he didn't sleep. Instead, he looked out of the window and let his thoughts drift to England and Molly, asking, always asking, 'Where are you, Moll? *Who is he?*' And then the agonising question, 'What should I do?'

There were no easy answers.

Chapter Seventeen

News of Alfie's win spread rapidly, and the whole of Blackburn town was out celebrating. 'Sure, I knew he could do it, so I did!' Michael Noonan was so proud, he was fit to burst.

Slapping a note on the counter of his favourite public house, he told the landlord, 'A pint for everybody, and I'll have a drop of the hard stuff for meself.' He winked at the man and got a whiskey in return.

When the second one was ordered, the landlord shook his head. 'Take it easy, old fella,' he said. 'You're not used to spirits.'

'He won!' Michael was so excited he couldn't keep still. 'My grandson Alfie went to America and beat the Yankee, so he did!' And everyone raised their glasses to Alfie. 'Our lad!' they chorused.

Three days later, Michael was still in bed, recovering from the after-effects of his celebrations.

'Honest to God, Molly, wouldn't ye think the silly old sod would have more sense than to be off boozing all the night long!' Rosie was up in arms. 'Sure, anybody would think he was in his twenties, instead of his late seventies.'

Strapping Eddie into his pram, Molly looked up apologetically. 'I'm sorry, Rosie, I wasn't listening.'

Something in the girl's eyes made Rosie pause. 'No, darlin'. It's me that should be sorry.'

'What for?' Straightening up, Molly put on her coat and tied a scarf round her head.

'For going on and on like a fool, about me da coming home paralytic the other night, when all the time you've not heard a word I've said.'

'Is he no better this morning, Rosie?'

'Huh! If ye ask me, the old bugger's still drunk as a skunk. He's got a head as thick as a plank, and his hands can't be still long enough to hold a cup, never mind the amount o' whiskey he musta swallowed. An' on top of all that, he's up and down to the lavvy all the night long, so's I can't get a wink o' sleep.'

Throwing her hands up in frustration, she groaned, 'Honest to God, I'll throw him out the window if he doesn't stop, so I will.'

Molly laughed. 'Don't be too hard on him,' she pleaded. 'He's so proud of what Alfie's done.' She hesitated. 'And so am I.'

'Aw, sure don't I know you're proud like the rest of us, but in your case, it might be better if the boxing was out of his blood altogether.'

Putting on her own coat and scarf, she followed Molly along the passage to the front door. Here she helped her lift the pram down the steps. 'Ah, will ye look at that!' she cooed, peering into the pram. 'The wee soul's fallen asleep, so he has.'

'That's because he was awake half the night with an upset tummy,' Molly explained. 'But he seems to have settled down now, thank goodness.' Turning the key in the lock, she came down the steps to take charge of the pram. 'Bertha played me up this morning an' all,' she said. 'Before you came round, she was throwing tantrums and upsetting Milly. And even as far as the classroom door, she was giving me grief.'

Rosie was surprised. 'That's not like her. Mind you, when I

think about it, I could see she was in a mood straight off. You, too, if ye don't mind me saying.'

Molly didn't mind at all. 'I didn't mean to be grumpy,' she apologised, 'but I'd had a bad night myself. When them two started on each other it put me out of my stride, that's all.'

'What gave you a bad night then?'

Molly shrugged her shoulders. 'Something and nothing.'

'Don't give me that, lass.'

Molly knew there was no use trying to keep anything from Rosie. 'All right. I couldn't go to sleep for thinking of Alfie. God only knows what he must be feeling like, out there all on his own, thinking I cheated on him with another fella.' She dropped her gaze to the bairn. 'When nothing could be further from the truth.'

Rosie agreed. 'If it weren't for the boxing, you and Alfie would still be together. *Married* even.'

Pushing the pram across the street, Molly thought about what Rosie had said. 'No, we wouldn't,' she answered. 'First of all, it wasn't the boxing that took him away. It was me mam, and her fancy fella. The reason Alfie went away alone was because I *made* him do so.'

She touched Rosie on the hand in a gesture of friendship. 'You helped me to convince him, and I'll be forever grateful for that. If he'd stayed, we'd have got wed like you said. Alfie would have been lumbered with all the kids and spent his life working to support us.' She shook her head. 'Much as I love and miss him, Rosie, I couldn't let that happen, and *that's* why he had to go away.'

'Aye.' Rosie had seen it all. 'But it seems a sad thing all the same . . . you here and him in America, and the pair of youse head over heels in love. It's a cruel old world, so it is.'

Thrusting thoughts of Alfie out of her mind, Molly urged, 'Come on, Rosie, get a move on or we'll have Granny Arkwright and the others out getting their own shopping. And we don't want that now, do we?'

'No, we certainly don't!' And Rosie put on a spurt that had Molly almost running with the pram.

It was a busy day, with two customers down Penny Street, one down Bent Street and an old fella from Back Lane. 'Mind you tell the butcher to skin the chicken leg for me,' he croaked. 'I don't want choking.'

Granny Arkwright wanted meat from the butcher, so Rosie and Molly combined the two errands. 'You're an enterprising pair, that you are,' the butcher said in admiration. 'Keep the customers coming, that's all I ask.' And he swung his cleaver with such force it had Rosie ducking.

Outside, Rosie asked, 'What's enterprising mean?'

Molly wondered how best to explain. 'It means you go out and do things,' she said. 'You know . . . to make a better life.'

Rosie's chest swelled three inches with pride. 'He's right,' she said grandly. 'That's what we are – "enterprising".'

The last port of call was Mrs Panter from Duckworth Street. 'Two barmcakes and a small Hovis,' she told Molly. 'And I don't want a burnt one neither.' She was adamant. 'Me teeth get stuck in a hard crust an' I can't get 'em out.'

The two women were hard put not to chuckle at this.

'I'll tell you what,' Rosie said, as she and Molly made their way to Ainsworth Street, 'she's an ugly old sod as it is. I wouldn't like to see her *without* her teeth, that's for sure!'

Despite her fondness for the old woman, Molly giggled all the way to the shops.

Come three o'clock and it was time to fetch the children from school. 'Eddie's slept right through,' Molly said. 'I hope he's all right.'

Rosie felt his face. 'He's fine,' she said. 'Cool as a cucumber, so he is. I'll make my way back with him now. By the time you get home with the children, I'll have him fed and changed and ready to fight the world.'

Molly thanked her. 'We've had a good day,' she declared, taking out the bag of money. 'By my reckoning, we've earned six and eightpence.'

'But that's three and fourpence each, and it's only the first day!'

Sitting on the bench at the tram stop, Molly spilled the coins into Rosie's palm. Counting them out she told her, 'There! You'll be able to buy yourself a packet of snuff on the way home.'

Rosie was horrified. 'Hush your mouth!' She glanced anxiously up and down the street. 'Sure, you and me are the only ones who know I take snuff.'

'Singleton's is the best,' a voice intervened. 'I've tried 'em all, but I allus come back to Singleton's.'

A red-faced woman popped her head round the corner of the shelter. 'Mark my words, once you've had a pinch o' Singleton's, you'll not want no other.' To prove it, she opened a small silver tin, and taking a pinch of brown powder between finger and thumb, she stuffed it first up her right nostril then up her left, each of them stained brown from years of taking the stuff.

'By! That's grand!' she exclaimed, giving a little cough and a sigh. Then she went off down the street like a young 'un, leaving Molly and Rosie open-mouthed.

'Did ye see the cut of her nose?' Rosie wanted to know.

'All brown and gooey, you mean?' Molly was trying desperately not to laugh out loud. 'Yes, I did. Why?'

'*Why?*' Rosie stared at the girl as if she'd gone mad. 'Because it's put me right off, that's why!'

'What? D'you reckon *your* nose might end up like that?' After a fine day's work, Molly felt mischievous.

'No, it bloody won't!' Rosie retorted. ''Cos I'll not give it a chance.' With that she dipped into her pocket and, taking out her little snuff-tin, she marched to the waste-paper bin and disposed of it. 'That's the end o' that!' she declared, though she did take a peep to see where it had landed.

'What about the spare tin you keep in the drawer at home?'

Rosie hummed and hawed. 'Aye well, you never want to burn *all* yer bridges,' she argued, and would say no more on the subject.

Chapter Eighteen

Sandra threw open the door and bounced in. 'I think I know where to find him,' she told Molly excitedly, not stopping to say hello. 'There were a bloke in the pub, and he said I should look for my Dave in Skegness.'

With the children round her feet, Molly had been peeling potatoes for dinner. Now she ushered them into the front room to get on with their drawings. 'I'll call you when dinner's ready,' she promised.

Returning to the scullery, she washed her hands and left the potatoes to soak in the bowl. 'You'd best sit down,' she told Sandra, 'and calm yerself. You're all red in the face.'

Sandra threw herself into a chair. 'That's 'cos I'm excited. I've been searching for the bastard these past weeks, and now I've found him, I can't believe it.' She grinned. 'I'll tell yer summat else an' all. I can't wait to see his face when I walk up to him.' She laughed out loud. 'Gawd knows what he'll do when I tell him he's gonna be a daddy!'

'Have you told your mam yet?' Molly thought that was just as important, maybe more so.

Sandra's face dropped a mile. 'Have I heckerslike, and you mustn't neither.'

'I've already promised I won't say a word. Though I think it's a big mistake, and very selfish of you not to let Rosie know what's going on.'

'It's best she don't know, at least till I've got him to admit it, and made him face up to his responsibilities.'

'And when are you thinking of doing that?'

'Tomorrow morning, first thing. I'm taking a day or two off.'

'If you do, you'll lose your job for sure this time.' Molly had lost count of the number of days Sandra had taken off work. 'If you're pregnant *and* without wages, it'll only make things harder, and I should know.'

'What d'you mean?' Her eyes nearly popped out of her head. 'Jesus, Mary and Joseph! You're *not*, are you? Our Alfie didn't leave you with a bairn on the way, did he?'

Molly dispelled Sandra's excitement with a wave of her hand. 'No, he didn't.' More's the pity, she thought. 'I meant with that little lot in there . . .' She pointed to the door.

'But you're doing all right, aren't you? Now that you've got the errand thingy working well?'

'That's not what I'm saying.'

'I know what yer saying, Moll, and it doesn't bother me one bit. I'm going after him if it's the last thing I do, and I'm going in the morning, job or no job!'

'It's up to you.'

'That's right. It is.'

'It seems to me he's not worth running after. Do you really think he'll accept responsibility on your say so?'

Angry that her friend should be so dead set against her going, Sandra demanded, 'What the devil's wrong with you, you miserable cow? *Course* he'll accept responsibility. He's the bleedin' father, ain't he?'

Molly was loath to hurt her feelings, but she was afraid for Sandra. 'I don't mean to make you feel bad,' she apologised. 'I just worry about you.'

'Huh! You coulda fooled me!'

'I've heard your side, and I've heard your mam's side, and it seems to me this bloke is a real bad lot. He's got you pregnant. He's knocked you about. And now he's buggered off and you've had to root him out the best way you can.' She shook her head in disbelief. 'Happen you'd do well to let him go his own way, Sandra. Tell your mam about the bairn. She'll do everything to help, I know she will.'

'You don't know her then. She's a funny old biddy about these sort o' things. Like as not, she'll kick my arse out the door and never talk to me again. Besides, I *want* to find him. I *want* him to accept me and the bairn. Because, God help me, I love him, Molly. I want to be with him.'

Molly saw how desperate she was. 'Then there's nothing me or your mam can say to make you change your mind, is there?'

'Not a lot, no.' Getting out of the chair, she told Molly she would see her when she got back.

'Take care then,' Molly said anxiously. 'If he gets nasty, come away.'

'Why should he get nasty?'

'Any man who can do what he's done to you is capable of anything.'

For a long, emotional moment, Sandra gazed at Molly, her eyes bright with tears, and the strangest smile on her face. 'I love him so much,' she murmured. 'I'd do anything for him . . . just like you with Alfie.'

After she'd gone, Molly wondered at the sincerity in Sandra's voice. It wasn't like her friend to be that serious about any man. 'Love 'em and leave 'em' – that was her motto up to now. And for some inexplicable reason, Molly couldn't help but feel there was something very wrong with this one.

What kind of man would have an intimate relationship with a girl, then for no reason just take off, not leaving an address, or any clue as to where she might be able to find him?

As she set about her work again, Molly expressed her inner-most fears. 'I wish you didn't have to chase after him, Sandra,' she whispered. 'In fact, it's a pity you ever met him in the first place.'

The fat lady from the coconut shy had taken a liking to Lottie. 'It's nice having a pretty young thing like you about the place,' she told her one cold, bright morning. 'Though why you should want to throw in your lot with a bad 'un like Dave, I will never know!'

Lottie finished putting the coconuts atop the stands. 'Because I love him,' she answered. 'That's why.'

'He's had women before, and they've never lasted more than a few days. In fact, there was a woman worked right here on the fairground. Her and that Dave o' yourn had something going, but there was a big fight and he marked her for life.' Slicing her thumb down her face she drew the picture well.

'Gossip, that's all it is,' Lottie said stalwartly, though her heart was dismayed. 'I've heard other things about him that aren't true. I don't believe any of it.'

'Aye, well, as you please, dearie, but he don't keep his women long, that's what I'm saying. Yet here you are . . . weeks later, and he *still* ain't thrown you out the window.' She gave a mis-chievous wink. 'Keep him happy, do you, gal? Is that why he's hanging on to you?'

After working with Lily from her first day, Lottie knew her well enough not to take offence. 'It's *him* that keeps *me* happy,' she declared simply. 'I tell you now, if Dave were to ask me to wed him tomorrow, I'd jump at the chance.'

'Huh! More fool you then.' Taking out a half-toothless comb, Lily ran it through her hair. Having done that and made little or no difference at all to her wild mass of red hair, she then bunched

239

it all together with her podgy fist and tied it up on top of her head, not realising or caring that she resembled one of the coconuts.

Lottie was still on the defensive. 'He's all right, is Dave.'

'For a time, aye, he's all right. But then he goes a bit crazy and smashes the place up.' Tutting, she warned Lottie, 'I've lost count of the times he's tekken a hammer to that lorry of his. I've seen it in tatters from one end to the other. That's why it's so pretty now . . . 'cos he's not long put it right after one of his mad red rages.'

As always, Lottie gave as good as she got. 'Come on, Lily, leave him alone, why don't you? Dave's not as bad as folk make out.' She wouldn't hear one bad word about him, not even from Lily, who'd been like a mother to her.

'You're right, gal,' Lily answered darkly. 'He ain't as bad as they make out . . . he's a bloody sight *worse!*' When she laughed, as she did now, her jaw wobbled – as Dave said, 'Like the arse-cheeks of a rhino on the run'.

'I've heard *you've* thrown a few out the window in your time.' Lottie could say that and not be afraid.

'Who told you that?' Now Lily was on the defensive.

'The big man who mends the rides.'

'Big man, eh?' Erupting in a fit of laughter, Lily frightened away a young couple who were about to have a go on the shy. 'He ain't so big with his trousers down, let me tell you! And I should know, 'cos I've thrown *him* outta my trailer more than once an' all. He's all right mending rides, but he ain't much of a performer, if you know what I mean.' She gave a naughty wink.

Laughing with her, Lottie watched the young couple scurrying off. 'You're frightening the customers away.'

Lily wasn't put out. 'They'll come back,' she said.

A few minutes later, they did, swiftly followed by another three couples, all trying their luck and nobody winning. 'You've got them ruddy coconuts glued to the stands, that's why we can't knock 'em off!' one irate man complained.

He soon made himself scarce when Lily sucked in her breath and confronted him with a bosom huge enough to suffocate him.

After setting up the coconuts for the fourth time, Lottie came back to continue the conversation. 'You were telling me,' she said 'about the big man.'

Lily seemed to blush. 'Never you mind,' she chided. 'You're too young.' Regarding Lottie for a moment, she envied the high cheekbones and the striking hazel eyes; yet, for all her backchat and boldness, she seemed younger than her years. 'By the way, young 'un, how old *are* you? You never did tell me.'

'Seventeen an' more.' Lies came easy to Lottie.

'Never! Are you sure?'

'Course I'm sure. I ought to know my own age!'

'Hmh! You don't look fourteen, never mind seventeen.'

'Well, it just goes to show then, don't it?'

After that, Lottie was well and truly on her guard. If Dave was to find out how old she was, he'd throw her out for sure, and that was the last thing she wanted.

'Hey!' Lily pointed over the river to the sky above. 'There's an old saying: "Red sky in the morning, shepherd's warning".'

Lottie laughed. '*Now* what are you talking about?'

'Look at the sky, gal. It's all red. I ain't never seen that before in January.'

'So?'

'So, like I were saying, "Red sky in the morning, shepherd's warning". Happen there's a storm brewing.'

'I've never heard that saying before.' Lottie learned something new every day. 'I bet you're making it up.'

'All right, have it your way, but I'm telling you what I know. "Red sky at night, shepherd's delight. Red sky in the morning, shepherd's warning".'

Pointing to the river, she smiled serenely. 'Lovely though, ain't it, gal? The river and the ducks and everything. I'm glad we changed direction from Skegness to come here. I've always liked the West Country, and West Bay is so pretty.'

'Why *did* we come here, Lily?' She'd already asked Dave but he hadn't really given an answer. 'I were looking forward to Skeggie.'

'We changed direction because the boss got word that his brother was already there with his own amusement fair. They're arch enemies, them two. If they'd tried to serve the same patch, there'd have been murders, I'm telling you.'

As always, from two o'clock to four, there was a lull in trade. 'It's always the same,' Lily said. 'They feed theirselves and have a pint or two, then they sleep it off and come back with a vengeance early evening.

'You get off and snatch some sleep an' all,' she suggested, when Lottie started yawning. 'You've been up since five this morning. I can see you ain't used to it yet.'

Asleep on her feet, Lottie didn't argue.

'Don't forget to set your clock, and be back here for five,' Lily advised. 'Else you'll get no wages on Friday.' She gave her booming laugh.

Half an hour later, Lottie was in a deep sleep when she felt a hand sliding up her skirt. 'Hey!' Scrambling up, she pressed herself against the wall, relaxing only when she saw it was Dave who had crept up on her. 'Don't ever do that again,' she screamed. 'You frightened the bloody life out of me!' For one split second, she wished she was back home, with her mam and the family.

'Don't gimme the wide-eyed innocent!' he sneered. 'You can't tell me I'm the first to have his hand in your knickers.'

Ignoring his spiteful remark, she got out of bed and went to the stove. 'D'you want a brew?'

'Why not?' He rolled into the warm spot she'd left behind.

'How come you're not working?'

'You first.'

'There's nothing doing at the stall. Lily sent me back to get some sleep.'

'It's always like that mid-afternoon.'

'Is that why you've come back?'

'No, and stop being so bloody nosy!'

'So, why aren't you working?'

He sniggered. 'You're a defiant little bugger.' But he liked it that way. 'We've shut the Waltzer for an hour or two,' he explained. 'There's a grinding noise coming from the motors. It's already gone haywire once this morning. Tom's taking a look at it now.'

'What if he can't fix it?'

Stretching his long legs over the bed, he saw her bending to the stove, and wanted her there and then. 'Tom's good with motors,' he said. 'He'll have it right in time for the rush tonight.'

Handing him his mug of tea, she was not surprised when he set it on the floor and grabbed her by the wrist. 'I'm lonely.'

'So?' She knew what he wanted, and it made her feel good.

'So, put your tea down and get on this bed.'

Lottie climbed on the bed and one thing led to another. The wagon rocked and rolled, and those who knew Dave knew what that meant. 'He's at it again!' they laughed. 'Randy bugger.'

Afterwards, they sat and drank their tea and talked. 'I don't know what to make of you,' Dave told her. 'I've had women before, and I've never let them get to me. It wouldn't matter to me if they walked out the door and I never saw them again. In fact, I've chucked the buggers out the door quick enough and been glad of it.'

Lottie recalled what Lily had said. 'Would you chuck *me* out the door?'

'I might.'

'You'd miss me if you did.'

'Maybe.'

'You'd *have* to chuck me out,' she confessed. ''Cos I would never leave of my own free will.'

He gazed at her lovely face and the cut of her shapely figure, and he knew he would never throw this one out. 'There's summat about you,' he admitted. 'You make me laugh.'

'Is that all?'

'It's enough for now.'

'Do you love me, Dave?'

His mood instantly changed. 'Hey! Don't start talking any claptrap about love and families and all that rubbish. I've been there, remember?'

'Sorry.'

Swilling his tea into the sink, he picked her up by the shoulders and, looking her straight in the eye, warned, 'Don't kid yourself you've got it made, lady. I could be rid of you tomorrow if I had a mind. Don't forget that.'

Lottie cursed herself for having got it wrong. 'I won't,' she murmured. 'And don't *you* forget, I could be gone from here when you get back. *Then* how would you feel?'

The smile began at the corners of his mouth, then he was grinning. 'That's what I like about you,' he admitted. 'You've always got summat to say for yourself.'

He kissed her soundly on the mouth, then thrust her away. 'We're one short on the Waltzer,' he said. 'Julie's gone down with the flu, so we need somebody to take the money. It's a hard, demanding job, with no time to catch your breath.' He was testing her. 'D'you think you could handle it?'

Lottie was thrilled. 'I can handle anything, me.'

'Right.' He glanced at Lottie's shoes; pretty things with ankle straps and medium high heels. 'You can't wear them fancy things,' he warned her. 'Not when you're jumping on and off the Waltzer at speed. Get summat sensible on your feet. I'll see you over there in an hour, and be sharp about it.'

'I'll have to ask Lily if it's all right.'

'Forget Fatso – I'll see to her. You just turn up at the Waltzer quick as you can. All right?'

Lottie was looking forward to it. 'It's harder work than the coconut shy, so I'll want double wages.'

He chuckled. 'That's what I mean,' he said. 'You make me laugh.'

He was still laughing as he closed the door behind him.

Sandra had been on the move for two days.

Having followed Dave's trail, she was weary and spent, and aching to see him. 'At last!' Standing on the footbridge over the river, she looked across the field to the fairground; against the night sky the lights twinkled and shone, and the cool air was filled with music.

Peering into the semi-darkness, she read the name written across the entrance in blazing lights: MULLIGAN'S PARK. Len Mulligan owned the fair. His brother owned a bigger one. When Sandra had arrived in Skegness, and sobbed with disappointment to find out she had followed the wrong fair, Len's brother himself had taken pity on her and directed her here.

Sandra smiled. 'This is it, Dave. You'll not get away from me again, I can promise you that.'

Filled with delight at having finally found him, the tiredness of her long journey seemed to fall away. At a run, she followed the path up the hill, past the caravan site and into the field, her eyes searching for the familiar wagon.

She knew it like the back of her own hand . . . dark blue, with a green door and window-frames, and the picture of a nude woman stuck to the windscreen.

And there it was – tucked away behind the generator, only it wasn't tacky like when she last saw it. 'Been smashing it up again, have yer?' she laughed. 'Had to give it a new coat o' paint, did yer?'

Her gaze went to the windscreen. 'An' where's yer precious pin-up gone, eh?' For a minute she was puzzled. She had once tried to tear down that picture, and got a hiding for her pains. 'You don't touch what belongs to me,' he had said. 'This is my home and these are my belongings. Don't forget that, bitch!'

She had been upset, but later they had made up in bed, and she forgave him. But never again did she touch any of his belongings.

Going to the wagon, she turned the knob and tried to push open the door, but it wouldn't budge. That's strange, she thought. He's never locked it before. She looked about. There was no one in the immediate vicinity that she could ask.

She went round the back and banged on the window, thinking he might be lazing in his bed like he used to. She peered through the windscreen and called his name. There were no lights on inside, and not a sound.

After a while she turned away, disappointed. 'He must have had his break already and gone back to work,' she told herself. Recalling that he used to work on both the Waltzer and the Caterpillar in turn, she saw the Caterpillar was nearest, so made her way there.

The place was thronging with people, mostly young, mostly screaming on the rides, or strolling arm-in-arm, or pressed up against some stationary object, frantically fumbling each other.

The fairground did that to people . . . sucked them into a fantasy world and made them abandon their usual inhibitions.

She soon realised he wasn't on the Caterpillar. 'Have you seen Dave?' she called to the operator, but he just shrugged his shoulders. 'Sorry. Don't know anybody called Steve.' The roar of the machines was deafening. 'I've only just started. You might ask Lily, on the coconut shy. She seems to know everybody.'

'Thanks.' There seemed no point in trying to hold a conversation with him over this racket.

She glanced across at Lily, who was busy replacing the coconuts on their stands. 'Lily the fat lady. Still 'ere then, you old bag?' she muttered. A wicked little smile fluttered across Sandra's tired face. 'I don't suppose you'd be pleased to see me. Never did like me, did yer?' She spat on the ground. 'But then I never liked you neither, so we're quits.'

Before Lily could look up and see her, she was off to the Waltzer to find Dave. To tell him he would soon be a daddy and that, whether he wanted a family or not, he'd got one in the making so he'd better get used to it.

The Waltzer was the most popular ride on the fair. Great from buckets of colour and speed were packed from side to side with old and young alike, each bucket whizzing round on its own track, round and round, up and down, faster and faster, its occupants screaming and laughing through the wild music, and, on occasion, being sick over their own feet.

Sandra loved the fair; she loved the rides and the music, and all the noise. Any other time she might have paid her money and climbed aboard. But not tonight. Tonight, she had more important things to do. She had to find Dave.

And suddenly, there he was!

Thrilled at the sight of him, she ran, waving her arms and shouting at the top of her voice, *'Dave! Dave, it's me . . . Sandra!'*

The music was so loud he couldn't hear her. Head down and

eyes intent on the riders, he hopped from one bucket to the next, collecting the money and dropping it into the pouch round his waist. Now the Waltzer was gaining speed and he had no time to look up.

'*Dave!*' Jumping up and down on the edge of the ride, Sandra kept on waving and shouting, desperate for him to see her. Soon, realising she wouldn't be able to attract his attention, she lowered her arms and leaned against the pillar. 'I can wait,' she smiled happily. 'Now that I've found you, what do a few more minutes matter?'

She recognised Tom, the mechanic; he was in the eye of the storm, the centre of the ride, where he operated the machine and smoked his old roll-ups which, according to Lily, 'stank like 'osses' droppings'.

There was somebody else there, too. A girl.

From where Sandra stood, and with the ride going full pelt, people waving their arms and being thrown about, and the buckets swinging noisily past, she couldn't get a good look at her. All she could see was her long, fair hair and her slim figure, and the way she was waving at Dave, who by now was standing on the far edge of the ride.

As Sandra watched, Dave waved back and then began to wend his way skilfully across, avoiding the whirring buckets.

Mesmerised, Sandra followed his progress.

She saw him leap down, into the eye of the storm. She saw him slide both arms round the girl, and when he bent his head to kiss her, a long and passionate kiss, she felt her heart turn upside down. '*Dave!*' His name rang out in a sob from her lips, but he still didn't hear. He was too engrossed with the girl.

Without thought for her own safety, Sandra climbed up. Holding on to a pillar with one arm, she waved, yelling his name again and again, but the buckets shot past and her voice was carried away in the rush of air.

It was when she saw him sliding his hand up the girl's skirt that her senses exploded. With a cry of 'No . . . NO!' she ran forward, dodging the buckets as they came at her.

For a while she seemed to be doing all right. But the buckets were fast and, unlike Dave, she had never learned to dodge them properly. One after the other they came at her, these great iron monsters, swinging round, riding the tracks up and down like fiends from hell. People were shouting at her; others on the outside gesturing frantically, confusing her until she couldn't concentrate. Now, all she could see was Dave. *And the girl.*

Suddenly, alerted by all the commotion, Dave finally swung round and saw her, and his eyes widened like saucers. She could read his mouth, saw the word 'JESUS!' Leaping on to the ride, he yelled something to Tom, who was desperately trying to stop the machine, but once you let the beast loose, it was hard to call it to heel. 'For God's sake, stand still!' She knew what he was saying. 'Hold on to the pillar!' Now the girl had turned and was looking at Sandra, her eyes filled with horror.

Sandra knew her then, and was devastated. 'My God! It's Lottie Tattersall!' The realisation threw her off-balance, leaving her momentarily vulnerable.

When the bucket hit her, she was thrown like a rag doll. As she fell, she saw them both; Dave running at her, hopping from one bucket to the other like he was born to it, and Tom, frantically weighing down on the lever to bring the monster to a halt. And Lottie, her hands to her face, a look of sheer terror in her eyes.

After the first, swift blow, Sandra felt nothing. Crunched between the tracks, she was helpless. The iron chairs swung at her time and again, pinning her there, defenceless against the crippling blows. And though there were those who risked their own safety to get her out, there was nothing they could do.

By the time they got to her, she was showered in her own blood, her poor body twisted and broken. 'God Almighty!'

Falling to his knees beside her, Dave took her tenderly into his arms. 'Sandra, *Sandra*! What in God's name were you thinking of?' He could feel the life ebbing out of her.

She smiled up at him, her eyes swimming with tears. *Dave was holding her.* That was why she had come here; the only reason. '*For you,*' she murmured, her voice so soft he could hardly hear it.

He shook his head and pressed her to him. 'You fool.' His voice broke with emotion. 'You bloody fool!'

Safe in his arms, she looked up and saw Lottie. She didn't mind. Not now. Not when she was the one carrying his child. And so she smiled on Lottie, and felt his mouth close gently over hers. *And nothing mattered any more.*

After the furore came the silence. A hushed, awe-filled silence, and a sense of horror that something so terrible could have happened right before their eyes.

The ride limped to a halt and people milled round. Some were rooted to the spot, unable to speak, others screamed and then quietly sobbed. One old man had gone for help, but it came too late. The police, the ambulance – all were too late.

It was an accident, they said. She ran on to the ride and lost her footing. Shocked and humbled, the people began to drift away.

Dave remained for a long time, holding the dead girl close, talking to her. *Unaware that she was carrying his child.*

The policeman was gentle. 'Come away, son,' he urged. 'Let the officers do their work.'

Shaking in his every limb, Dave left Sandra's body, but he did not go far. Instead, he watched them lift her out from between the tracks, and he covered his face, unable to take in the horror.

Shaking uncontrollably, Lottie was out of her mind. 'It was Sandra!' she kept saying. 'Sandra Craig.' Between the sobs, she

250

grew hysterical. 'She was Molly's best friend.' And try as they might, they could not console her.

When Lily arrived on the scene, Lottie fell into her arms, her screams swelling louder and louder as she realised the enormity of what had happened.

'Stop it!' Raising her hand, Lily smacked the girl hard across the face. At first Lottie was stunned into silence, her shocked eyes uplifted to Lily's face. After a minute, the tears came again, this time quieter, rolling down her face as she stared up at Lily in disbelief. 'It was Sandra,' she sobbed. 'She's dead, Lily . . . Sandra's *dead*!'

'I know, sweetheart, I know.' Holding her tight, the fat woman rocked her back and forth, until Dave came to take her away.

'Ssh, Lottie,' he murmured. 'I've got you now. Ssh!'

As he walked her back to the wagon, he felt a terrible grief, an emotion he had never experienced before. Sandra had come to find him. Now she was gone – *and he was the one to blame*.

Knowledge like that was a heavy cross to bear.

Part Three

JANUARY 1949

A SECRET KEPT

Chapter Nineteen

When they laid Sandra to rest in the garden of St Mary's Church, the priest made a mention of the bright sunshine.

'Sometimes, in the middle of a grey winter's day, a ray of sunshine breaks through to lift our hearts, and give us hope. Sandra Craig was like that; a little tempest one moment, a ray of sunshine the next. Exasperating, infuriating, immensely funny, and never still.'

He smiled at the recollection. 'Many was the time I had to reprimand her for one thing or another . . . as did her mother, Rosie, I know.' He winked comfortingly at Rosie, whose eyes were bright with tears. 'There were days when Sandra could make it feel like winter, then there were other days when her humour made you smile and lifted your heart. She taught us never to take her for granted. She was young and vibrant, and lived her life to the full. Today, we thank the Lord for letting us know her, albeit for such a short time.'

In that churchyard, in the sunshine, he made his blessing and it was done.

Quietly, sadly, they turned away; all but Molly, who lingered there, her sorry eyes downcast to the hole in the ground where her friend lay. Her thoughts went back to the happy times, and the times she had tried so hard to make Sandra see sense.

'You never would listen, would you?' Blinking away the tears, she gave a half smile. 'D'you remember the day when you said you could see the cheeks of my bum up the ladder? I knew you were lying, you little blighter, but after that, I was always wary going up the ladder.'

In her mind she went over the last time she and Sandra had been together, when she had warned her about chasing after this fella of hers. Molly would never forget how Sandra had smiled then, in that serene, assured way, so unlike her. 'I love him,' she said. '*Like you love Alfie.*'

Remembering was too painful; it was too soon. Her tears rising, she gave up a prayer for her friend. 'Look after her, Lord. Sometimes she was mischievous, and maybe she was too easily led. But she had a good heart, and she never hurt anyone. I'll miss you, Sandra,' she whispered. 'I'll miss your endless chatter and your teasing, and the way—'

Her voice broke. '*Why* didn't you listen? Why did you have to go after him? Oh Sandra, if only . . .'

When she could no longer bear to think about it, she turned and ran from the churchyard, through the gate and down the path. *Straight into Alfie's arms.*

He was as startled as Molly. 'Are you all right?' When he put his hands on her shoulders, she felt the warmth trembling through her.

Too choked to speak, she merely nodded, her heart pumping thirteen to the dozen. Rosie had said Alfie would be here, but Molly hadn't seen him in the church.

Even without her asking, he explained, 'I missed my connecting train. It made me late.' His troubled gaze went over her shoulder to the churchyard. 'I didn't miss the service though.' His face twitched into a sad little smile. 'The vicar described her so beautifully, don't you think?'

Molly glanced back, following his gaze and knowing how

devastated he must feel. Still hurting, she didn't know how to console him. Instead, she reached up with both hands and laid them over his. For a wonderful, heartbreaking moment they remained like that, he loving her so much he couldn't tell her, and Molly, wanting to go, wanting to stay.

The moment passed and she nodded her head and went quickly down the path. When she paused at the bottom to look back, he was on his knees to Sandra, his head bowed and hands clasped.

Never had Molly seen him so vulnerable. Except, of course, for that other awful moment, when she had told him she didn't want to wed him any more.

Outside the church, neighbours and strangers alike said what a lovely service it was and how sorry they were about Sandra. 'A bonny lass,' said one. 'Her own worst enemy,' said another, ruefully, 'but the street won't be the same without her, poor lass.'

Afterwards, the little party made their way back to Victoria Street; Michael and Rosie in front, then came Molly, everyone lost in their own private thoughts.

Alfie was standing by the lychgate, watching them leave, but not yet ready to go. He had come a long way and was wearied by it.

The loss of his twin sister had been a terrible blow. It was almost impossible for him to come to terms with what had happened: it was too great a shock. There were other things plaguing him, too. Things that had to be resolved one way or the other. And very soon, or he would go out of his mind.

Walking with Rosie and her father to their doorstep, Molly was concerned about Michael; the old fella was pale and wobbly on his feet. It seemed the tragic loss of Sandra, and the way it had happened, had aged him and taken its toll.

After she and Rosie had helped Michael inside, Rosie came

back to the door with her. 'Will ye mind if I pop down later on?' she asked. 'There's something I want to tell ye.'

'Come down whenever you're ready,' Molly replied, giving her a peck on the cheek. 'I'll be there.'

The noise greeted Molly the minute she opened the door. When Bertha spotted her, and ran screeching all the way down the passage, the others were not far behind.

'Thank God you're back!' Not wanting to face the ordeal of church, especially with the eyes of Father Maguire on him, Frank had reluctantly agreed to watch the children until Molly returned. Now he was cursing himself for having been so reckless. 'It's been a bloody nightmare!' he exclaimed, grabbing his coat and making for the door. 'The little devils won't behave. They fight and carry on like lunatics, an' they mek so much noise a man can't hear himself think straight.' He didn't ask her about the funeral; didn't spare a thought for her feelings. Selfish through and through, was Frank Tattersall.

Before Molly could answer, he was out the door and away to the nearest pub, where he tried to gather his sanity and reflect on what had happened in his own life and in the life of the Craig family. He had been badly shaken by the end of that poor young lass. A bonny thing she was, he recalled. Many was the time she would come in and out of the house, leaving Molly either laughing or pulling her hair out.

Life was a puzzling old thing, and lately he was beginning to realise it couldn't be sorted out from the bottom end of a pint glass.

Molly had never seen her father move so swiftly. 'What *have* you been doing to your dad?' Leading the four youngsters into the parlour, she wagged a finger. 'I hope you haven't been playing him up?'

'We didn't do nothing!' Milly was quite indignant. 'We only played hide and seek like always, and Eddie cried because he was hungry, and Daddy couldn't find his bottle.'

'I *told* him where it was.' Molly had gone to great pains to make sure everything had been left as it should be. 'It was soaking in the saucepan of water. I told your dad I'd already scalded it, and all it needed was a good rinse.

Bertha giggled. 'Georgie told him that, but when he went to the scullery he dropped the pan, and the bottle rolled under the sink and he had to scald it all over again. He wasn't going to though, until Georgie said he'd tell you if he didn't.'

'It weren't *our* fault if Eddie kept on screaming an' screaming,' Georgie declared with a grown-up sigh.

Molly glanced at Eddie, who by now was fast asleep in his pram. She gave a chuckle. It was wonderful, she thought, how children could make you smile through your tears.

Bertha made her laugh out loud, though. 'Why did he run off like that?'

'Because he's a man,' Molly replied with a smile. 'And because you lot frightened the pants off him.'

Satisfied, they ran off to resume their game of hide and seek, the yelling and screaming getting so loud that Molly had to reprimand them. 'Ssh, not so noisy. You'll wake the bairn!'

She could see why her dad couldn't wait to get out, especially if Eddie had been screaming for his bottle an' all. 'Poor man!' The image of him running out the door made her laugh again.

Then another, stronger image came to mind: the haunting memory of Sandra, sitting in that very chair, telling her how much she loved Dave, and how she was carrying his child. Now Molly was consumed with guilt. 'Oh, lass. How was I to know the fella you were trying to track down was the same one our Lottie had settled for?'

Going to the sideboard, she took down the letter received from Lottie only the day before:

I'm sorry, Molly. Me and Dave want to say our goodbyes to Sandra, but we can't face coming to St Mary's.

We'll go into the church in Bridport and light a candle. I'm so sorry, and Dave is, too. Later on, we'll come and see you. But not yet. It's too soon.

Please tell Rosie how sorry we are. She's a good woman, and a good friend to you . . . a better friend than I've been.

I do love you both,

Lottie

XXX

Molly replaced the letter in its envelope. 'Funny how things turn out,' she murmured. 'Sandra and Lottie . . . both loving the same fella.'

It had all come as a big shock. 'Did you tell him, Sandra?' she murmured. 'Did you tell him about the bairn?'

As for herself, she had told no one. Not even Rosie, though during this past week there had been times when she had come close to it. But each time, the thought of her promise to Sandra had kept her silent.

When Rosie came round some half an hour later, it was to talk about Sandra. 'I've a confession to make.' Settling herself into the chair, she refused when Molly offered her a brew. 'No, lass. I've something to tell you, and I'd better do it quick or sure I might not tell ye at all.'

Molly's heart skipped a beat. 'Whatever is it?' In that brief, unguarded second, when Rosie looked at her with such distress, Molly was convinced it had something to do with Alfie.

Her fears were unfounded. 'It's Sandra.' Rosie sat on the edge of the chair, fiddling with her fingers and wondering how to begin. 'You know I had to go and see the coroner and all that dreadful business?'

Molly nodded her acknowledgement.

'The coroner . . . he . . .' Catching her breath she went on, 'He told me that our Sandra was with child.'

Suddenly she was crying, and Molly had to comfort her. 'Can you imagine that? She was having a bairn and she never told me . . . her own mam, who loved her in spite of all her goings-on.' Taking a shuddering breath, she tried to compose herself. 'Why didn't she tell me, Molly? *Why?*'

With Rosie's tear-filled eyes on her, Molly didn't know how best to respond. If she were to admit that Sandra had confided in *her*, while keeping it from her own mother, it might cause a terrible rift between them. Yet if she kept quiet and acted as if she knew nothing at all about it, wouldn't that be a betrayal of Rosie?

She was in a terrible dilemma.

In the end, she knew what she had to do. 'Good God, Rosie. How could she keep such a thing to herself?' It wasn't exactly a lie, but it was the right response, for her and Rosie both.

Rosie regarded her with wide, confused eyes. 'Sure, I don't know,' she answered. 'I've thought about it over and over, and I can't understand it. Was she afraid of me? Oh, I might have stormed about and given her a lecture. I might even have given her a slap in the heat of anger. But she should have known I would have helped her all the way. I loved her, Molly. Surely to God she never doubted that?'

Molly was quick to reassure her. 'I'm convinced Sandra would have told you in the fullness of time,' she said. 'One thing I do know, she never doubted your love for her, and her love for you was just as strong. She adored you, Rosie, but I don't need to tell *you* that, do I?'

'No.' Although Rosie had already half-convinced herself of it, the girl's kindly reassurance was all she needed. A smile lifted her sorrow. 'Think of it,' she murmured. 'I would have been a grandmother. It's something I've wanted for a long time, so it is.'

Drifting deep into thought, she went on softly, 'I had hoped you and Alfie . . .' Pulling herself up sharp, she looked at Molly with horror. 'Oh, lass. Whatever am I saying?'

'Nothing I haven't thought myself, time and again,' Molly replied, and quickly changing the subject she asked, 'Do you intend telling Dave about the bairn?'

Rosie considered her answer. 'At first, I didn't know he wasn't already aware of it. But then I realised if he had been, something would surely have been said. I thought Sandra would have wanted him to know, seeing as she'd gone there obviously to find him. I wanted him to bear the blame . . . to know he had fathered a child and my Sandra had died because of it.'

Pausing, she gathered her thoughts. 'But then I asked myself, what would it achieve? Sandra's gone, and nothing can bring her back. Not revenge, not guilt, and not using a poor unborn child to make him feel shame.'

Molly said nothing. There was nothing more she could say that hadn't already been said.

'Then there's Lottie. She obviously knew nothing of his past relationship with Sandra, and it seems she thinks the world of him. From what you told me, before we either of us knew who he was, Lottie is happier than she's ever been.'

'I'm sorry, Rosie. So deeply sorry that it all turned out like this.'

'Ah, sure, you've nothing to be sorry about, lass. We were none of us to know what lay in store, and maybe it's just as well. All I'm saying is, I can't believe it will do anybody any good if I were to tell that young man how Sandra was carrying his bairn.' Looking Molly in the eye, she asked pointedly, 'Am I right, now?'

Molly felt a profound sense of relief. 'Right or wrong, I would have made exactly the same decision,' she answered honestly.

Taking a deep breath, Rosie visibly relaxed. 'That's good, lass. Sure, it's what I hoped you'd say.'

So, it was settled. Dave would never know the truth, and Lottie would not be made to feel guilty. Sandra's secret would be safe with Rosie and Molly. The two of them had talked it through and nothing further would be said.

But Rosie had another confession. 'I've had this a few days now,' she told Molly. 'I wasn't sure whether to show it you or not.' Taking a folded card out of her pocket, she handed it to Molly.

The first two words, *Dearest Rosie*, brought a gasp of astonishment from Molly. At once, she had recognised her own mother's handwriting. 'It's from Mam!'

Rosie settled back in her chair. 'I don't mind telling you, it was a shock for me an' all.'

Not wanting to read it, but unable to help herself, Molly read the letter aloud:

Dearest Rosie,

I know I'm probably the last person in the world you expected to hear from, and I hope this letter doesn't add to your distress.

I saw the newspaper the other day, and was shocked to learn about your Sandra. I can't imagine how you must be feeling. All I know is how I would feel if it was my Molly, or one of the others.

I know I did a bad thing in leaving them, but it doesn't mean to say I don't love them, because I do.

My heart goes out to you, Rosie. We've been good friends over the years, and I'm thinking of you in your loss. I want you to know you are never far from my mind. I miss you, and I miss my children.

I've enclosed some money. Please, if it's not too painful,

will you buy some flowers and take them to Sandra, with my love.

God bless you, Rosie.

All my love,

Amy.

Her face stiff and unforgiving, Molly folded the card and handed it back to Rosie. 'I'm glad she at least had the decency to write to you.'

Rosie understood Molly's hardness, but it made her sad all the same. 'Is that all you have to say?'

'What else should I say?'

'I mean . . . it sounds to me as if she might be regretting her decision to run off and leave you all.'

'It didn't sound like that to me.'

'Will you never forgive her?'

Molly's heart ached with love for her mam yet, deep down inside, she could not find it in her to forgive. 'She didn't talk it over with me. I'm sure we could have worked something out, if only she'd told me what was going on.' Anger hardened her heart. 'She didn't trust me enough.'

'She must have been so unhappy, love.'

'I think about that a lot, but it still doesn't excuse what she did. Leaving a note like that was such a cowardly thing to do.'

'I don't think your mam is really a coward, do you?'

Fighting back her emotions, it was an age before Molly answered. 'Maybe not. Putting up with Dad, having the last babies one after the other, couldn't have been easy, especially if she was still in love with this other fella after all these years.' Molly recalled the evening at the infirmary when Amy had spoken to her about Jack Mason. 'When she told me about him she seemed years younger, as if she was a young girl again, but I never dreamed she'd run off with him like that, leaving the bairns behind an' all.' Regret engulfed her. 'Oh Rosie, I *do* want to forgive her, but how can I?'

Rosie had no answer to that. Instead she asked, 'Do ye think your dad has tried to find her?'

'Maybe he has, maybe he hasn't. We don't talk about it.'

'Is he still giving you grief over money?'

Molly rolled her eyes to heaven. 'It's hard work getting any housekeeping from him.'

'Have you noticed a change in him lately?'

'He doesn't come home drunk so often, if that's what you mean.' She chuckled. 'He hasn't brought any streetwomen home neither, not since your Sandra . . .'

Her voice faltered and she couldn't go on, and for a time they were silent, lost in fond memories of Sandra.

Presently, Molly had a question. 'When is Alfie going back?'

'I wish to God he wasn't, but he's planning to leave tomorrow, about three o'clock. His trainer has him on a tight schedule.'

'Is he happy, Rosie?'

'No more than you are, lass.'

'Life's a mess, isn't it?' Bitterness crept back. 'That's what I mean, about Mam running off like that. She had no thought for me, or the bairns.'

Her arms opened wide as she glanced round the room. 'Look at me, Rosie! I'm nineteen years old, and I've had to take her place. I can't do what I want, go where I want, or have the man I love. And though I adore the children, they're not mine, are they? All I wanted was my Alfie, and bairns of my own.' Her voice shook with emotion. 'And now it's all gone. Our mam took it with her when she ran off.'

'I know, lass.' Rosie had seen Molly torn apart, and she had seen the same with Alfie. She had almost blurted out the truth to him today, about Molly and Amy, and everything. But common sense prevailed, and she let it go. To tell him now would be to undo everything she and Molly had planned between them.

Molly seemed to have read her thoughts. 'You must never tell him,' she urged. 'Let him go back knowing nothing.'

Rosie nodded. 'Ah, sure, I'll not tell him, don't worry.' Getting out of her chair, she said wearily, 'I'd best get back, lass. Dad'll be wondering where I am. Mustn't leave him alone too long.'

'How *is* Michael?'

Rosie's face clouded over. 'Not good, love. Not good at all. He's up one minute and down the next. This past week has really knocked the stuffing out of him.'

'Give him my love, and tell him I'll come and see him when Alfie's gone back.' She couldn't risk bumping into him again, or she might spill out the truth and that would never do. It had gone too far for that.

Rosie said she understood. 'You look tired, lass. What say I come round and give ye a hand with the bairns tonight?' She gave a little chuckle. 'You wash and I'll wipe, eh? Then we'll get them into their beds and have a good old chinwag over a brew. What d'ye say?'

'Sounds good to me, Rosie. Thanks.'

'See ye later then.' And off she went, with a heavy heart, back to her sorrowful home and menfolk. All the light had gone out of their household, for the time being at least.

By the time Rosie made a reappearance, Molly had fed the children, baked a meat and potato pie for her dad, changed the beds, black-leaded the range, and done the washing. Right now, keeping busy was the only way she could cope.

Assailed by the delicious aroma of newly baked meat pie, Rosie looked at the shining range and the pile of freshly washed bedclothes and was astounded. 'You've been busy, haven't ye?' she exclaimed.

'Got to keep on top of it all,' Molly replied. 'With our new job taking up hours in the day, the housework has a funny way of creeping up on you when you're not looking.'

Not for the first time, Rosie took a discreet look at Molly and was more worried than ever; the girl was thinner, peaky-looking, and just now with the sweat glistening on her face, she looked positively worn out.

'Stop a minute, love.' Molly was turning the vegetables on the stove top. 'You look beat, so ye do.'

Leaning against the door jamb, she addressed Molly in a motherly voice. 'Nobody knows more than I do what you've had to endure, what with your mam shifting her own burden to your young shoulders, then your da giving you grief whenever you ask him for money. The children, our Sandra, and now Alfie going back tomorrow . . .' She sighed. 'Don't punish yourself, darlin'. You've nothing to blame yourself for.'

Turning round, Molly smiled at her. 'Our mam was right. You *are* a good friend.'

Rolling up her sleeves, Rosie asked, 'Are the children fed?'

'Half an hour since.'

'So that's your da's dinner you're cooking now?'

'Hmh! Though judging by the way he ran out of here like a scalded cat, like as not he won't be home till midnight. Which means this lovely pie will spoil in the waiting, an' I'll have wasted my time as usual.'

'Right! The children are fed, so all it needs now is to get them washed and off to bed. Am I right?'

'Eddie's already washed and in his cot. The others are in the front room, but they're too quiet for my liking. I was just about to go and check on them when I'd finished this.'

Rosie made a suggestion. 'While you're seeing to your da's dinner, I'll get the children ready for their wash. We'll have them in bed in no time at all, then you can relax afore Frank comes home.'

'Thanks, Rosie.' Though she chuckled when she heard Rosie making efforts to marshal the children for their wash, and the children protesting, 'It's not fair. We have to wash every single night *and* morning as well!'

Rosie told them that if they didn't, the muck would stick to them, and pretty soon they'd be growing potatoes all over their skin. That did the trick!

By quarter past nine, the young 'uns were not only in their beds, but sleeping like little angels. 'You wore them out with all that soap and scrubbing,' Molly joked.

'Aye, an' it's good to see you relaxing for a change,' Rosie retorted. 'I'm keeping a watchful eye on you from now on, my girl, so I am.' With Sandra gone and Alfie all set to go back to America, Molly was all she had left; apart from Michael, and he was in a world of his own at the minute.

After they'd finished their cocoa, they talked for a while about Sandra, and while Rosie took the cups back to the scullery, Molly fell asleep, curled in the chair. 'That's it, lass.' Rosie covered her over with a coat from behind the door. 'Sleep while ye can,' she murmured. 'I dare say ye haven't slept soundly for many a night.'

For a time she just sat there, warming herself in front of the fire, watching Molly and wondering.

'Should I tell him?' she whispered. 'I love you both. I'm doing what you asked, and Alfie is following his dream, but what about *you*? I know how hard it is for you, me darlin', but I don't know if I should go against you and tell Alfie the truth of it, or leave things to sort themselves out.'

In her heart she wanted these two together. Yet Molly had extracted a promise that she would not tell Alfie, and now she was duty bound by it. *And yet* . . .

Her eyes went to the sideboard, to a picture of her beloved twins, with Molly in the centre. Going quietly across the room, she picked up the photograph and carrying it back to the chair, looked at it for a long, long time. She saw the joy in Molly's face, and Alfie smiling, with his arm round her. Then Sandra, brash and bold as ever, lifting her skirt hem and showing off her legs, a wide grin on her face. 'You were a right little devil, so you were!'

Rosie chuckled at her daughter's antics. Then the chuckles became tears and she softly sobbed, the picture pressed close to her heart, and her heart so crippled with pain she could hardly bear it.

Slightly inebriated, yet sober enough to have come in without waking the children, Frank found her sitting at the foot of the stairs bent over the picture and sobbing uncontrollably. 'Hey!' He went over to her. 'Come on, Rosie. What's all this, eh?'

Ashamed to have been found like that, especially by Frank, she stood up. 'I'll go now,' she murmured. 'Molly's asleep. The children, too.' Looking up at him now, seeing the compassion in his dark eyes, she realised how, by hurting Amy he had hurt Molly and the rest of his children. He had indirectly separated Alfie and Molly, driven Lottie away, and now, when it was all too late, he had begun to mend his ways.

Suddenly, to Frank's astonishment, she was beating at him with her fists, not shouting or accusing, but still sobbing wildly. Grabbing her by the wrists, he drew her to him. 'Ssh now!' He wiped her tears and looked down into her stricken face, and something happened between them; a feeling, a certain loneliness, connected them. Whatever it was, it had them holding each other, unable to let go.

When the kiss came, it began nervously, and then a flood of emotion overwhelmed them and they were kissing with a passion that neither of them had ever felt before.

Shocked and uncertain, Rosie pushed him away. 'NO!' Her face was stark white. She shook her head and fled down the passage. At the front door, she glanced back to see Frank staring at her, his dark eyes frowning, hands at his sides and a look of confusion on his face.

Molly's voice broke the spell. 'Rosie?' The parlour door opened and she popped her head out. 'Dad!' She hadn't realised. 'Where's Rosie?'

'She's gone,' he said flatly, and began to make his way up the stairs.

'Your dinner's in the oven,' Molly called after him.

But he wasn't listening. He had suddenly realised that the slight attraction he'd always felt for Rosie Craig was not just a fancy. Holding her close to him just then, lost in that wonderful kiss, had confirmed it.

At his age, when he had made a mess of his marriage and let his kids down, he had fallen in love. 'Bloody ridiculous!' he muttered. 'A bloke like me doesn't fall in love.'

Rosie was experiencing the same disturbing feelings. Her late husband had been her one and only love. In all this time she had never wanted any other man, not in a serious way. And certainly not a man with the reputation of Frank Tattersall!

Now though, she had been swept into his arms, and to a place she had never thought to be. The truth was, in that wonderful, intimate moment, she had realised something quite shocking.

Somewhere in her heart, she had opened a door. Frank Tattersall had made his way in, and now she couldn't seem to get him out.

'Jaysus, Mary and Joseph!' Her mind and senses were in turmoil. 'What have I done?'

Chapter Twenty

Molly didn't sleep a wink. At six o'clock she was downstairs, pacing the floor. Alfie was leaving today, and she could think of nothing else.

Like a cat on hot bricks she watched the hands of the clock go round, until it was six-thirty, then quarter to seven, and now seven o'clock. Rosie had said he'd be leaving about half past seven, she recalled, and her heart sank.

She lit a fire, then got her dad's breakfast going. He was on a slightly later shift at the factory today. She made herself a brew and sat by the fire. Then she was up again, peering out the front window, hoping to catch a glimpse of Alfie.

At this time of the morning, the street was coming alive with people; some on bicycles making their way down to the mills, others hurrying to the tram stops, and still others pushing through the chill wind on foot, the men with their caps pulled down, women with headscarves wrapped round their heads, all of them bent to the wind, their faces set hard.

Alfie was nowhere to be seen.

Hearing her dad come down the stairs, she returned to the scullery where his breakfast was keeping warm. Dishing up two eggs, a rasher of bacon and a plump pork sausage, she placed it on the table. 'I'll get your tea.'

When, a minute later, she returned with his mug, she found him standing at the back window, deep in thought, and not seeming to care whether he went to work or not. 'Have you seen the time?' she asked. 'If you don't get a move on, you'll be late for work.'

Without a word, he walked across the room and, when he was settled at the table, she reminded him, 'I'll need ten shillings.'

Before he could begin his usual inquisition as to what she needed it for, Molly began her list. 'I owe four shillings to the grocer. Eddie needs a pair of trousers, and Georgie's shoes . . .'

Before she could finish, he fished a ten-shilling note out of his wallet and laid it in front of her.

Molly was dumbfounded. Normally she had to ask him time and again before he came across with the money; and she had no intention of telling him how much she earned from the deliveries, because then it would be even harder to get him to part with a single penny.

To add to her confusion, he put a half-crown alongside. 'I noticed one of Georgie's shoes had a hole in it,' he remarked. 'That should get new soles on the pair of 'em, and a new set of laces too.'

While Molly was left wondering if he'd finally lost his mind, Frank went into the scullery to swill his hands and face at the sink.

Seeing Molly go into the passage, he leaned against the wall and thought about the incident between himself and Rosie. 'She's a fine figure of a woman,' he murmured. 'A *good* woman, too.'

He had always thought of himself as a man of the world. But to his amazement he was still shaken by the press of her body against his, and yet it wasn't only that. It was something much deeper.

Something he had never really felt with Amy.

* * *

It was time for Alfie to leave. 'I'm all packed,' he told his mother. 'Grandad's still asleep. I'll give him another half hour, then I'll go up and say my goodbyes. After that I'll have to make tracks or I'll miss that aeroplane tonight.'

Rosie saw the hollows under his eyes. 'You didn't sleep much last night, did you, son?'

'Not really.' He shrugged his shoulders. 'Thinking about Sandra and . . . everything.'

'Are you keen to be going back?'

Throwing himself into the chair, he pondered on that for a minute. 'I had hoped there might be a future with me and Molly, but I was wrong. She preferred some other bloke to me, and there's not much I can do about that.' But it still hurt so badly. It wasn't so much the rejection, but the losing of Molly. She meant the world to him, and always would.

'Mam?' He hesitated, having tried to broach the subject several times since coming home, and each time drawing away from it.

'Yes, son?'

'Oh, it's all right. Best let it be,' he decided. 'Old coals and all that.'

'I think I can hear your grandad moving about up there.' Rosie knew what Alfie wanted to ask, and she was glad of the intervention. 'If you're going up to him, tell him I'll have his tray along in a few minutes.'

When he was gone, she chided herself. 'When it came right down to it, you just couldn't bring yourself to tell him, could you?' Giving a great heaving sigh, she blew it out noisily. 'Mebbe he's right,' she wondered. 'Mebbe it is all best left alone . . . old coals, just like he said.'

Alfie loved his old grandad. 'Get yourself better and you can come and watch my next fight,' he told Michael. 'I'll send the ticket money for you and Mam both.'

Michael was frail these days, but he had the same cheeky grin and the same sense of humour. 'Knock 'em cold, son,' he wheezed. 'If I were younger I'd soon show ye, so I would!'

Alfie laughed. 'I don't doubt that for one minute!'

He was concerned though, about the old fella's health. 'Look after yourself,' he said. 'Remember what I told you. Get yourself better and I'll send for you. Unless you're frightened of going up in an aeroplane?' he teased.

The old man bristled. 'Huh! You'll never see the day when Michael Noonan's frightened of *anything*!'

'That's the kind of fighting talk I like.' He stood up, tall and strong, and the sight of him brought a tear of pride to the old man's eye.

'You'll need *three* tickets,' he told Alfie. 'I'm not coming without young Molly. She'll be company for yer mam while you and me tend to the boxing.'

Alfie hadn't realised. 'Didn't Mam tell you?' he said gently. He knew how fond the old man was of Molly.

'Tell me what?'

'Me and Molly are finished. She's got herself another fella.'

'Don't talk bloody daft! Oh, I heard 'em talking . . . her and yer mam.' He laughed. 'Got herself another fella? Wake up, boy! Herself worships the ground you walk on. She'd no more get herself another fella than pigs might fly.'

Alfie was puzzled, and excited. His heart began to pound. 'What are you talking about, Grandad? What do you mean . . . you heard them talking?'

'Your mother and Molly. It were just after Amy Tattersall ran off with some bloke or another. Talk to yer mam. Make her tell you the truth.'

Easing himself on to the edge of the bed, Alfie spoke firmly, but kindly. 'Now then, Grandad, I want *you* to tell me what *you* heard. What exactly did Moll and Mam say to each other?'

* * *

Molly was on her way upstairs to wake the children when she was startled by a frantic thumping on the door. 'Molly! Open this door!'

Recognising Alfie's voice, she feared something had happened to Michael. Running down the passage, she let him in. 'What's wrong?'

'*You tell me!*' Pushing his way in, Alfie took her by the shoulders, almost lifting her off her feet. 'You and Mam! Cooking up a story to send me off to America, when all the time it was supposed to be for my benefit. Have you no idea what you've done to me? Don't you know how much I love you, Molly Tattersall?'

Molly didn't have time to wonder who had told him. All she wanted was to convince him it had all been for the best. 'Mam ran off and I was left to look after the children.'

'What's wrong with your da looking after them?'

'Oh Alfie, you know what he's like. He can't look after *himself*, never mind the children.'

'So, what's wrong with *me*? I love them kids as much as anyone, and well you know it. Or didn't you think I'd be man enough?'

'Don't say that! There's nothing I would have liked better than to keep you here with me and the children,' Molly confessed. 'But it wasn't fair to ask. Besides, you'd just got that offer to fight in America. It was something you'd always dreamed of. If I'd taken that away from you, you might never have forgiven me . . . oh, not straight off maybe. But later, when you were older and all your chances were gone, you might have resented what I'd done. I couldn't live with that, Alfie. I love you too much!'

'Oh? And you didn't think I loved *you* enough, is that it? You didn't think I would work my fingers to the bone and look after you and the kids?'

'No! That's exactly why I had to make you believe there was somebody else . . . because I knew you would do just that! I couldn't risk it, Alfie.'

Pausing, she took a shuddering breath. Looking up at him, the tears coursing down her face, she wept, 'I would have lost you. Somewhere along the way, I would have lost you for good.'

He shook his head. 'Never.' His own eyes moist with emotion, he took her to him, his arms wound tightly about her, so she would never get away from him again. 'Oh Molly, I thought I would never hold you again like this.'

Molly knew what he meant, because hadn't she suffered the same agony? But, 'In the end, we found each other,' she whispered.

With the anger and confusion out of the way, they held on to each other, their love all the stronger for having been tested.

In the parlour, Frank had been pulling on his work boots when Molly let Alfie in. He had listened to what Molly had to say, and he was mortally ashamed. 'What kind of man are you, Frank Tattersall?' he asked himself. And back came the ugly truth.

He had been the worst kind of bastard, and because of him, Amy had gone, his children had lost their mother, and these two good people had had their worlds turned upside down. He finished tying his bootlaces, put on his jacket, and sneaked out the back way.

There was something he had to do. Someone he had to see. And the sooner the better.

Part Four

FEBRUARY 1949

SILVER LININGS

Chapter Twenty-one

'No, Amy. Don't come to the door, you'll catch your death of cold.' Holding her inside the hallway, Jack kissed her goodbye. 'I've two meetings today,' he said, 'then it's on to Kent for a look at that derelict house. If what Matey says is true, it might be a good investment.'

Amy smiled. 'Always on the lookout for a good investment, that's my Jack.'

'That's right, my girl, and *you're* the best investment I've ever made.' Kissing her again, he whispered in her ear, 'You look so gorgeous, I could eat you. Come to think of it, get yourself all dolled up and I'll take you out to dinner tonight. Deal?'

She nodded. 'Deal.' Standing at the window she waved him goodbye.

When he was gone from sight, she went to the dresser and took out a small envelope. Inside was a letter from Rosie:

Dear Amy,

Thank you for your letter, and for the money to buy flowers for Sandra. I took them up today, and they look lovely.

I was really surprised to hear from you. I showed your

letter to Molly, but I did not tell her your address. The way things are, I thought it best not to.

I'm sorry about you and Frank, and though I did see it coming, I have to say that I never dreamed you would leave the children like you did. It wasn't fair to them, and more to the point, it wasn't fair on Molly. I'm afraid she's very bitter towards you, Amy.

The other reason I'm writing is to tell you that Molly and Alfie have set the date for their wedding. It's Saturday, 16 March, at St Peter's.

I don't know if you'll come, and in the circumstances, I wouldn't blame you if you thought it better not to.

The thing is, Amy, there's something I need to speak with you about. So, if you'd rather not come, let me know, and I'll travel to you. If that's all right?

Mind how you go then,

From Rosie.

Having read the letter twice over, Amy went into Jack's office, where she found pen and paper, and sat down to write her reply:

Dear Rosie,

I've got your letter. Thank you.

I can't say whether I'll be at the wedding or not, or even if I'd be wanted there; I think not, though it goes without saying that I'm thrilled for Alfie and Molly; I always knew the day would come.

I know I was selfish in what I did, but I was at the end of my tether and could see no other way.

I need to turn a few things over in my mind before I'm sure of myself.

I'll write to you as soon as I can.

Take care of yourself, Rosie, and please don't show this

letter to Molly. With the wedding looming, and her being so bitter towards me, it would cast a shadow over her special day, and as we both know, I've done her enough harm already.

Thanks again, Rosie. It's so good to have contact.

Love from Amy.

Tucking the letter into the envelope, she sealed it then licked a stamp and pressed it on. 'I'm sorry it's such a short letter, Rosie, lass,' she muttered. 'Only I have an appointment in half an hour, and to tell you the truth, I'm dreading the outcome.' She had been in a daze these past two weeks, and now, with the appointment so near, she was all at sixes and sevens.

It took her ten minutes to wash and dress, five to walk down to the tram-stop, and the journey to the doctor's surgery took another ten.

Looking smart in her brown dress and winter coat, and a cheeky little beret pulled over her hair, Amy was at the desk with one minute to spare. 'Take a seat, Mrs Tattersall.' The receptionist thought Amy was very pretty.

No sooner had she sat down than she was called into the surgery.

Dr Edmonds was a kind old gentleman, but his news was devastating all the same. 'From what you tell me, I calculate the date to be September the fourth.' He went on at great length about her care and well-being, 'Especially as you are not as young as you once were.'

Amy hardly remembered the tram journey home. All she could think of was Jack's fear of children. Once inside the confines of the house, she quickly packed her portmanteau, taking only a few of the beautiful things Jack had bought her.

When that was done, she wrote him a note:

Dearest Jack,

I went to see the doctor today. He told me what I had already suspected. I'm having your bairn.

Because of what you told me, I knew you would be filled with horror at the idea of a child in the house. I don't want to wait until you tell me to go, so I'm leaving right away.

You might think I would go back to Frank, but nothing is further from my mind. My life in Blackburn is finished. Too much water has passed under the bridge. Too much bitterness and blame.

I'll go where I've never been, where I won't have fingers pointed at me. I'll make a new life, with our bairn, and may God forgive me.

Thank you for everything, Jack. I have the money you kindly put away in an account for me. The bairn isn't due until September, so I'll be able to work and save a little more for when it's here. I will manage very well, thanks to your generosity,

I wish you even more success in your business, though I know you won't need it. You always were a born business-man.

I love you, Jack, and I'm so sorry it had to end like this.
   Amy.

At the door she took one last look around. 'Goodbye, Jack. God bless.' Wiping away a tear, she quickly left that beautiful house where she had been so happy.

Walking down the street with her portmanteau, she looked a lonely, solitary figure. 'It's a punishment,' she murmured. 'For what I did.'

Chapter Twenty-two

Three days before the wedding, Rosie had a visitor.

When she opened the door it was to see a broken, haggard man with haunted eyes. 'You're Rosie, aren't you?' he said. 'Amy's friend?'

'Yes, and who the divil are you at this time of the morning?' It was not yet seven o'clock.

'I'm Jack Mason,' he answered. 'Amy and I . . .' Glancing up and down the street, he wondered if he'd done right in coming here. The last thing he wished to do was stir up trouble. He wanted Amy, that was all he had ever wanted. 'Look, Rosie, don't you think it might be better if we talked inside?'

It had taken Rosie a minute to put two and two together, and now she understood. 'I'll give ye one minute, then you're to be on your way as quick as you can.' She glanced at the fancy car parked down the street. 'At least ye had the good sense to keep that from the door. There's a wedding due any day now, and I'll not have you upsetting that lovely lass, d'ye hear what I'm saying?'

He nodded. 'Just let me in, Rosie. We need to talk.'

Once inside the parlour, he explained the situation. 'I've searched high and low, but she's nowhere to be seen. She said in her note she wouldn't come back here, but I had to try. I've nowhere else to look.'

'Why d'ye want to find her?'

'Because I love her, Rosie. She ran off because she's having a bairn, and she knows I get really nervous with children about me. It goes back to the orphanage . . . bad experiences and all that. Look, Rosie, I *have* to find her! I'm going crazy. I can't work, I can't think. Everything's wrong without her.'

'And what about the bairn?'

'I've thought about that, and I think it'll be different. It's *my* bairn . . . part of me. I want it, Rosie, and I want its mammy. Please, for God's sake, if you know where she is, *tell me*!'

Rosie took a moment to regard this man who had caused such havoc in their lives. What she saw was a man going out of his mind for the love of a woman. She saw how Amy might have chosen to throw in her lot with him, and she felt compassion for them both. 'Wait.'

Going to the sideboard, she took out an envelope. 'This came only yesterday,' she said, handing it to him. 'It's from Amy. She's no more happy than you are. I reckon you'd best go and get her, don't you?'

Tearing open the envelope, he removed the letter with trembling fingers. He spoke the address out loud . . . 'Fourteen, Albert Street, Lytham Saint Anne's.' When he looked up, tears were dancing in his eyes. 'How can I thank you?' he said brokenly. 'What can I do?'

Rosie clasped his hand in hers. She had a particular reason for wanting these two to get back together again, though she prayed Molly would never know her part in all of this. 'Go and fetch her,' she whispered. 'She's waiting for ye, so she is.'

After he'd gone, she watched through the window. She saw him wipe his face, then draw away in the car, and she muttered under her breath, 'Be happy.'

Then, going to the chair, she gathered the wedding dress in her arms and took it with her down the street to Molly's house.

As arranged, Molly was up and about, so excited she couldn't keep still. 'They're all asleep,' she told Rosie, and there were stars in her pretty eyes.

'Try it on, darlin'.' Rosie handed her the dress. 'I've taken the waist in. It should fit a treat now.'

'We'd best go in the front room, just in case they wake up and come down,' Molly told her. 'I don't want anyone to see it till the day.'

While Molly ran to the front parlour with her precious dress, Rosie went to the scullery. 'There's nothing like a fresh brew to gather your wits, especially when there's a wedding in the making.'

She winked in the mirror. 'Or mebbe *two*!'

Chapter Twenty-three

Molly came out of the house to a crowd of onlookers. The gown had them gawping with admiration; a slim shift of white linen, with sewn-on roses at the shoulders and a neck that showed her small shoulders to perfection, it clung to Molly's every dainty curve.

'Look at that!' one woman cried. 'I'd give owt to have had a frock like that when I were wed! Instead o' which I were big as a bleedin' ship with me first, and wearing a smock like the farmer in Pleasington.'

Everyone laughed, including Molly herself. Rosie glowed with pride, for the dress was the result of her painstaking handiwork. But it was Molly's loveliness that really had them gasping.

Unlike her mother when she was young, Molly had never been a raving beauty, but she looked like a real princess today. In that beautiful dress, with her hair swept back to take the silken headpiece, and the short, bouncy veil around her pretty face, she was every man's dream bride, and every woman's inspiration.

As she waved and smiled, her eyes shone like diamonds, and her heart sang with joy. 'Yer look lovely, lass!' Maggie had waited for an hour to see her come out. Others shouted their good luck, and told her, 'God bless yer, lass. You deserve the best.' And Molly knew that, in Alfie, she had the *very* best.

Outside the church, the long black car drew up and the crowd surged forward. The car had cost Frank Tattersall half a week's wages; it was his wedding present to the couple.

Her dad got out first. 'You look grand, lass,' he said, flushing with embarrassment.

When they walked down the aisle, Frank took Molly by the arm, and the pride on his face was there for all to see. Behind them came Milly and Bertha in their little pink frocks, and Georgie, bringing up the rear in a grey suit made by Rosie; he looked uncomfortable with all eyes on him as he passed by. Lottie and Dave stood watching from a pew on the bride's side of the church.

In his smart dark suit, Alfie was handsome as ever. When he turned to see his bride coming towards him, his heart somersaulted at the sight of her.

They smiled at each other, and he held her hand throughout the service, and when it was over they walked out into the spring sunshine and he kissed her for the camera. Then he kissed her for himself, and everybody clapped and laughed. Suddenly they were showered in rice and confetti, and they ran to the car.

The reception was held in the best upstairs room at Frank's favourite pub. 'I don't see much of you these days,' the landlord told him.

'Aye, well, I've other things to occupy me now,' Frank replied with a wink. And the landlord thought, Hey up! He's at his old tricks with the ladies again. But he could not have been more wrong.

The accordion man played, and the fiddler tapped out his music; the children played under the tables, and everyone said what a lovely couple Alfie and Molly were. Everyone danced with everyone else, and no one noticed how Frank and Rosie never changed partners.

They danced too close and spoke in whispers, and still no one noticed. Except Molly. 'Look at them,' she said to Alfie, and Alfie said he was glad they'd made friends, for her sake.

When Molly grew quiet, her eyes glazed over with memories, he held her close. 'You wish your mam was here, don't you, sweetheart?'

She smiled up at him. 'As long as I have you,' she said, chiding herself for letting him see how, in that one careless minute, she had let her mam overshadow her happiness, 'I don't mind. I love you so much, Alfie.'

Outside, Amy wasn't sure whether to make herself known. 'I gave away my rights to this family when I turned my back on them,' she told Jack. But oh how she ached to see Molly on this, her special day.

Jack believed that she should go in. 'If you don't make your peace now, you never will,' he said, and she knew he was right.

'Will you come in with me?'

He shook his head. 'Better not.'

Nervously, she walked towards the doors; twice she started back. 'Go on!' Jack knew it meant so much to her. He also knew that if forgiveness was in the offing, this was the day when it would be given.

Rosie was the first to see her.

While dancing in Frank's arms, her gaze was drawn to the door, and there stood Amy, small and nervous in a dark suit with a brown beret over her glossy hair.

Frank saw her, too. 'Jesus Christ, it's Amy!' Frozen to the spot, he could only stare in disbelief.

Then the others saw and the voices grew louder. 'Shame on yer!' . . . 'What right have you to ruin the lass's day!' . . . 'Haven't yer caused her enough heartache?' All neighbours, all knowing the circumstances.

Amy's gaze went to Molly, and a sob rose in her throat. 'I'm sorry,' she mouthed, and ran out, blinded by her tears.

Seeing her distress, Jack leaped out of the car and ran towards her.

'Mam!' Molly's voice calmed everyone. Quietly, with great dignity, she walked over to her mother.

Amy turned and looked at her daughter, and her heartache was tenfold. She couldn't speak. Like everyone there, she could only wait for the reprimand she deserved.

For a breathtaking moment, the two looked at each other, and then Molly opened her arms. With a cry, Amy went to her. 'I'm sorry,' she cried. 'Oh, lass, I'm so sorry.'

For what seemed an age they clung to each other, and as the wedding guests looked on, many an eye was brimming with tears.

The children watched from a distance, and when Molly called them they crept over, unsure and afraid, too young to understand. 'We don't want to come with you,' they told Amy. 'We're staying here.' And Amy cradled them in her arms. 'I'm not here to take you away,' she promised, and saw the relief in their faces.

From where he stood, Jack looked across at Frank, and Frank nodded, and at long last, everything was all right.

Suddenly, Michael Noonan's voice called out querulously, 'What's going on 'ere? I'm away outside to the lavvy, and when I come back the whole place is deserted!' He looked at Molly and Amy holding each other, and understood. With a grin, he told them, 'Hey! There's booze and food going to waste in 'ere. Get yer arses back inside, the lot of youse!'

When they were all back inside again, Rosie and Frank had an announcement to make. 'We're getting wed as soon as we can,' Frank told them. 'Unless anyone has any objections?' His gaze went to Amy, and then to Jack, and when Jack winked, Frank put his arm round Rosie. 'She's taking on me and my kids, and who knows, we might have another half dozen into the bargain!'

To which Rosie gave him a sound clip round the ear. 'Like bloody hell we will, Frank Tattersall. You're too old and withered for a start!' she said, and the uproar almost lifted the roof.

The music struck up again and everyone got dancing; Rosie and Frank, Jack and Amy, Lottie and Dave, and the younger children in amongst them.

Dancing in Alfie's arms, Molly looked back at all her family, reunited at last, and her heart was light. 'I'm so glad it all came right in the end,' she said.

Alfie smiled down on her. 'So am I, for your sake more than the others.'

'Do you love me?' Even now she could hardly believe it.

'How could I not love you?' he whispered. 'You're the loveliest, kindest person in the world.'

She placed her finger over his lips. 'No,' she contradicted him. 'I'm the *luckiest*.'

She buried her face in his shoulder, and he took her gently round the floor, safe in his arms. *Safe in his heart.*

Later, the whole family went to the churchyard to lay the wedding flowers on Sandra's grave.

Molly lingered for a while. 'I wished for you to be there on my special day,' she murmured. 'And somehow, I think you were.' She laid her bouquet alongside the others. 'I'll never forget you,' she said.

Then Alfie came and took her away.

And all was well.

JOSEPHINE COX

The Woman Who Left

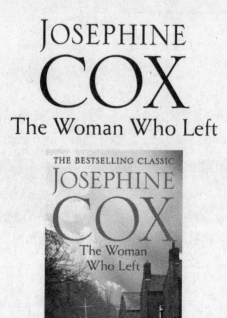

Louise and Ben Hunter's loving marriage is marred only by their unfulfilled longing for a child. Living and working with Ben's father, Ronnie, they are quietly contented. But when Ronnie dies, their whole world changes. Ben's lazy brother, Jacob, returns, convinced he stands to inherit Ronnie's small fortune. And he means to have his brother's wife; though just as she did years before, Louise warns him off. Jacob, however, is not so easily dismissed. When he realises Ben will inherit everything, Jacob is beside himself with rage, and commits a terrible deed, one that threatens to destroy everything his brother and Louise hold dear . . .

HEADLINE